SKINNERS

BOOK 2

Howling Legion

MARCUS PELEGRIMAS

An Imprint of HarperCollinsPublishers

This is a work of fiction. Names, characters, places, and incidents are products of the author's imagination or are used fictitiously and are not to be construed as real. Any resemblance to actual events, locales, organizations, or persons, living or dead, is entirely coincidental.

EOS
An Imprint of HarperCollins*Publishers*
10 East 53rd Street
New York, New York 10022-5299

Copyright © 2009 by Marcus Pelegrimas
Excerpt from *Skinners: Teeth of Beasts* copyright © 2010 by Marcus Pelegrimas
Cover art by Larry Rostant
ISBN 978-0-06-146306-8
www.eosbooks.com

First Eos paperback printing: November 2009

Printed in the U.S.A.

10 9 8 7 6 5 4 3 2 1

Resounding praise for the first book in
MARCUS PELEGRIMAS's
shattering saga of man against the monster tide,
SKINNERS
BLOOD BLADE

"*Blood Blade* peels you right down to the nerve. A must-read for vampire hunter fans."

—E. E. Knight, author of the Vampire Earth series

"With a scalpel-sharp eye for detail, Pelegrimas slices open an entirely new kind of street-smart vampire. . . . A talented storyteller."

—Michael Largo, winner of the Bram Stoker Award

"An action-packed, blood-soaked ripsnorter of a monster-hunter series, *Skinners* will appease any bloodsucker fan's appetite. Pelegrimas weaves a seductive and eerie atmosphere that you'll want to indulge in again and again."

—Tom Piccirilli, Thriller Award-winning author of *The Midnight Road*

"Action packed. . . . Plenty of cinematic gore and wisecracks will keep readers coming back for future installments."

—*Publishers Weekly*

"A hell of a lot of fun. Newcomer Marcus Pelegrimas hits one out of the park. . . . The action is nonstop. Fans of Jim Butcher and Laurell K. Hamilton will definitely want a bite of this!"

—Jonathan Maberry, Bram Stoker Award-winning author of *Patient Zero*

"Exciting . . . creative. . . . So fantastic readers will finish it in one sitting."

—SFRevu.com

By Marcus Pelegrimas

Skinners
BLOOD BLADE
HOWLING LEGION

Forthcoming

Skinners
TEETH OF BEASTS

*As always, I'd like to dedicate this to my wife, Megan,
for tolerating my ups and downs.*

Acknowledgments

Belated thanks to my editor, Peter, for taking a chance and seeing it through. Finally, my thanks to everyone at Nevermore Paranormal for answering my questions, telling me real ghost stories and proudly representing MEG Branch 18.

SHINNERS

Howling Legion

Prologue

Thirty miles east of Kansas City, Missouri

Interstate 70 cut across Missouri like a belt that was hitched just a bit too high upon the state's hips. The drive from St. Louis shouldn't have taken more than three or four hours, but thanks to miles upon miles of orange cones, closed lanes, and detours, it took that long for Bob Rothbard to see any open road. Then again, nobody native to that area would have expected anything else during the middle of summer. There was even an old joke that the four seasons in Missouri were winter, autumn, spring, and construction. Unfortunately, construction was also hot.

Unrelentingly sticky heat seeped in through the cracks of Bob's overly accessorized SUV like tendrils invading his air-conditioned sanctum. It crept through the vents and pulled beads of sweat down his wide, rounded face. Dark circles spread out from his armpits and dotted his light blue dress shirt. Tugging at the buttons running down his chest, he flapped his shirt to work up something of a breeze beneath the starched cotton.

Just as he was about to reach for the radio, Bob remembered the new remote controls he'd recently added to his steering wheel. Considering how much he paid to install the added convenience, he'd be damned if he would go back to doing things the old way. He ran his stumpy fingers over the little buttons that operated the cruise control, headlights, and garage door before finding the miniaturized controls dangling just low enough to scrape his right knee whenever he made a sharp turn. Grunting as he tried to push a button without hitting the one beside it, he finally unleashed some Creedence Clearwater Revival that was loud enough to put a smirk onto his face.

Bouncing his knee and slapping the steering wheel as close to the beat as his chromosomes would allow, Bob gazed at the road he'd all but neglected during his tussle with the radio. Not that there was much to miss. Missouri was scenic in parts, but his view for most of the day had been marred by cement dividers and flashing signs warning him about the next set of dividers. One sign told him to slow down to 50 mph, but he ignored it. No cops were in sight. There were no workers to be found. Creedence was playing. He wasn't about to stop for anyone.

Bob sang in the wrong key, injecting lyrics he'd misinterpreted since the first time he'd ever heard the song. Getting into his performance even more, he slapped the wheel hard enough for his left pinky to knock against the button that had been installed for easier access to his headlights. When his lights flicked off, he cursed and tried to find the switch again.

He accidentally pressed the garage door opener.

The side of his hand hit the radio control.

His left knee crushed the cell phone attached to the dash by a wire bracket.

Bob finally got his lights back on just in time to swerve away from the shoulder and back onto the road. His heart raced as he overcompensated for his lapse. His hands wrapped tightly around the only two clear spots on the steering wheel and his eyes soaked up everything in front of his SUV. The skies had darkened enough for the newly paved highway to blend in with the flat ground on either side of it. Because the vehicle raised him comfortably above the common folks in their little cars, and his lights had been accidentally flipped to high beam, he could see all the way to the next green mile marker on the side of the road.

A car in the oncoming lane flashed its brights and honked in a polite little beep, so Bob lowered his window and flipped the guy off. Fully satisfied with himself, he raised the window, turned up Creedence and slammed into a mountain of black fur that took up his entire lane.

Bob's air bag exploded from his steering wheel and hit him in the face like a prizefighter wearing a canvas pillow around his fist. The SUV's front end groaned as the back end lifted up off its tires, hung there for a second, and dropped back down again. He pulled in a breath, but immediately regretted it. His back and neck hurt like hell and he thought he might have broken his nose. The bitter, coppery taste of his own blood trickled down his throat.

Bob pushed the air bag away from his face. The more pain he felt, the more he flailed to clear his line of sight.

"What the hell?" he grumbled. "Did I hit something?"

As soon as the air bag was out of his way, he looked through his cracked windshield. A glow appeared upon the pavement and grew as it brought along the roar of an approaching engine behind him. The roar was quickly joined by the blaring of a horn and the squeal of tires.

Realizing his window was up, he tried to lower it, but could only get it down halfway. That was enough for him to stick his chin to the opening and scream, "Go around me, asshole!"

His engine was still running but sounded rough. The moment Bob touched the gas pedal, the SUV shuddered and lurched forward. He steered for the side of the road while mentally calculating how badly he'd be screwed by the local mechanics.

"I swear to Christ," he growled as he slammed the SUV into Park and pulled the door handle, "if this is because of some damned deer or an idiot drunk, there's gonna be hell to pay."

It took some work, but Bob managed to get the door open. After wrestling to get free of his seat belt, he got out to survey the damage. He winced at the pain in his legs, gingerly touched his blood-smeared nose, and grunted, "Could've been worse."

A few more cars sped past, all of which made sure to give him plenty of space as they continued along their way. Bob knew well enough that he would never have stopped if the situation were reversed, but swore under his breath at the fact that nobody stopped for him. He swore even louder when he saw the mangled fender, broken headlight, and cracked grille on the front of his beloved SUV. Wisps of smoke curled from the engine and something under the hood rattled. Even though he didn't know a lot about cars, he knew sounds like that were always expensive.

Now that he was looking at the front end of the SUV, he could see long, wiry strands of black hair snagged upon the mangled grille.

"Damn animal," Bob grunted. "I knew it. At least I killed the son of a bitch."

Looking around to verify that statement, he realized there was no carcass on the pavement. He squinted toward the shoulder of the highway but could only see a shadowy outline of some trees and a few buildings much farther along the road. About a hundred yards away a billboard from the Missouri Department of Transportation promised SMOOTH ROADS AHEAD in friendly, illuminated letters.

Another car whipped by, splashing its headlights upon mile marker twenty-six. The flash caused Bob to shade his eyes and shift his focus back to his vehicle. As he walked around to get a look at the passenger side of the SUV, he skidded on the unpaved shoulder.

Something moved a bit farther off the road. Seconds later a pair of crystalline eyes caught a faint glimmer from the starry sky. By the time Bob realized the creature behind those eyes was running toward him, there was nothing he could do about it.

The beast's torso had the mass of a bear, but was shorter in length and wider around the chest. Its front legs were just over half as long as its hind legs, and all four paws were capped by claws that dug trenches into the gritty Missouri dirt. Its eyes flashed in the light of another approaching car, and before Bob could cry out to that fellow motorist, the beast had knocked him flat onto the ground.

His entire body ached from the crash and his head was spinning. The sky and ground tumbled as if wrestling with each other. When his back hit something solid, he got a real close look at one of his brand new radial tires. The paw that hit the ground beside him seemed almost as big as the tire itself. Its fur stank of hot motor oil and antifreeze.

Bob tried to sit up, but was roughly pushed down again. Claws the length of his hand punctured his chest, holding him in place as wide, unnaturally clear eyes glared down at him. The beast's pointed ears, long snout, and wet nose had a vaguely canine appearance and were covered in black fur. A wide mouth filled with rows of dagger-sized teeth stretched all the way back to the base of its skull. Whenever Bob squirmed, the black creature leaned down to mash its paw a little harder against his chest. Flecks of chrome from the SUV's bumper were snagged within the beast's fur along with chunks of colored plastic from the headlight and turn signal.

"Get away from me," Bob snapped in the gruffest tone he could manage. "Go on! Scat!"

The creature curled its lips and studied him carefully. If he hadn't known any better, Bob would have sworn it was grinning at him.

Another car whipped past the SUV. When the creature turned its head toward the highway, Bob slapped at the paw on his chest and attempted to slide out from under it. His plan was to get away from whatever the hell the thing was and climb into his SUV. Even if there was a lot of damage done to the vehicle, he should be able to get to a gas station or something. He might have ripped apart the engine or every other piece of machinery under the SUV's hood, but at least he could get away from the wolf-thing.

It was a good plan.

Unfortunately, it came up short when his fist pounded against the creature's front paw without putting a dent into its thick, wiry fur. In response to the pathetic attempt, the creature snapped its head forward to sink its upper teeth into the meat of Bob's shoulder and the lower set into the flabby layers of his left breast. Bob's eyes were wide-open, but his vision was clouded by a pulsing field of dark colors. The creature's teeth drilled down far enough to hit bone, turning Bob's pain into a solid thing that rose up in the back of his throat to choke him into silence. As the wolf-thing dragged him away from the SUV, Bob scraped and kicked the gravelly earth. Every time he moved, the creature's fangs tore his flesh a little more.

Bob tried to grab the creature's face or claw at its eyes, but he only had the strength for a couple fumbling slaps before clenching his eyes shut tight enough for tears to burn out of him like kidney stones. Even when the dragging stopped, the black creature's teeth were still in him. Straining to look up, he could see one of the beast's crystalline eyes staring right back down at him. It wasn't the eye of a wild animal. In fact, the thing didn't even seem hungry. It wasn't mauling him or tearing away pieces of meat. It simply watched.

Whenever Bob tried to squirm, the creature subtly shifted its weight or adjusted the angle of its head to keep him in place. After a few moments it lifted its paw to place it gently upon the ground next to Bob's leg. Its lips curled up as if to let Bob know there were several more inches of fangs that could be driven into his chest if the need arose.

As the cold, clammy certainty of death seeped through him, Bob lifted a hand to grab at the creature's eye. His hand was less than a quarter of the way there before a growl churned from within the creature that Bob could feel all the way to his fingertips. Along with that sound there came the subtle squish of hellishly long teeth being carefully eased from the pits they had dug into his flesh. The creature then twisted its head about half a degree to one side and sank its fangs in while scraping against a shoulder blade and pushing against a rib.

The wave of pain that followed was enough to take all the fight from Bob Rothbard. He slumped against the ground and let his eyes settle into a comfortable spot. A few cars roared past, but they were too far away to do him any good. Bob could no longer even see the glow of headlights. Pain had become a numb chill, which trickled into his core where it became a burning knot. His guts clenched to kick up a load of bile that rose to the back of his throat before receding.

The creature watched him carefully. When Bob went completely limp, it opened its mouth to pull the long, stalactite fangs straight out of him.

A wet sucking sound filled Bob's ears. He couldn't move. Blood pooled inside each wound before leaking out and spilling onto the ground.

Bob Rothbard was dying.

The creature with the black fur reared up onto hind legs that creaked like old lumber, to become longer than they'd been a few moments ago. After a few bones cracked into place, the creature was able to stand upright. Its gaping smile shrank down a bit and some of its teeth retracted into bloody gums. As its head stretched into this new form, a patch of white fur on its nose thinned out just enough to reveal a jagged scar. The creature stood like a terrible sentinel watching over its meal. All the lights from the highway or the heavens were barely strong enough to cast a glow upon its coal-black fur. When the sound of a passing truck receded, the beast knelt down to enclose both of Bob's feet within one elongated hand.

"Wh-Why?" Bob groaned.

Although it had started dragging Bob by the legs, the creature stopped and hunkered down as if mimicking the four-legged thing it had been a few moments ago. Tall enough to lean toward Bob's face without compromising its grip upon his feet, it lowered its round, wet nose to Bob's wounds.

Gazing up at the creature in the same confused reverence he would give to a tornado, Bob moaned, "Why . . . me?"

What flashed across the creature's face began as anger but quickly shifted into disgust.

Bob was dragged even farther away from his SUV before being set aside. From there, the creature started to scoop out handfuls of earth and toss them into the darkness. Suddenly, it stopped digging. When it found Bob curled into a sobbing ball, it became even more enraged. Thick, meaty fingers wrapped around Bob's torso, lifted him up and slammed him down.

Bob hit the ground as if he'd been dropped from a hundred feet in the air. When the beast spoke, it was in a growl that was colored by a rough cockney accent. "Your whole filthy, noisy species are only good at two things." The creature lifted Bob up over its head. "Breeding," it snarled as it cracked Bob's spine against a rock. "And whining!"

Holding onto Bob's crushed body, the creature lifted him up so he could stare directly into the human's glazed eyes. "Strutting and boasting when you get your way, but listen to you blubber when things take a turn you don't like. 'Why me?'"

When Bob Rothbard hit the rock again, his entire body conformed to its shape as if he'd been pasted onto the uneven surface.

"Why *not* you?"

Death came to Bob like a long-belated gift.

The creature glared at him, kicked Bob's ample gut, and spat out a single, snuffing breath. "Now I'll have to get another one."

Chapter 1

The baton in Paige's hand had been carved from about a foot and a half of wood, but carried the wallop of a lead pipe. Cole was all too familiar with that fact since he'd been on the receiving end of far too many wallops. He had spent the last few months training in several different aspects of hand-to-hand combat, which was basically an excuse for Paige to kick his ass once or twice after breakfast and possibly again before dinner. Although the workouts trimmed a good deal of the fat he'd collected over his last thirty-some-odd years, he collected an ever-changing pattern of bruises on his body and face.

The weapon in Cole's hands was a short spear carved from a bowed piece of wood. One end was sharpened down to a point and the other was split into two smaller points that resembled a forked tongue. Although the weapon was only slightly thicker than a broomstick, a varnish made from shapeshifter blood, vampire saliva, and God knows what else kept it from breaking or even chipping no matter how many times it was struck. Not only did the varnish petrify the wood, it also bonded the weapon to the person who wielded it. The connection between Skinners and their weapon was made by thorns crafted into the weapon's grip, which were treated with another paste that healed the wounds they made. They still hurt like hell.

Cole was told he'd get used to the pain. So far, no such luck.

Paige's baton cracked against the side of his leg. Before he could reposition his spear to one of the defensive stances he'd been taught, Cole was struck on his other knee by a second baton. Pain raced up and down through his lower body. He almost fell over, but managed to keep his balance. The short brunette wielding the batons wasn't impressed.

Usually, Paige wore sweats or some other, fairly standard workout clothes. Today her hair was pulled back as always, but he could see that the heat in their converted practice space must have been getting to her because she wore tight runner shorts and a baggy T-shirt over a sports bra. "You need to focus, Cole," she warned.

The moment he lifted his eyes from her sweaty curves, he caught a baton squarely upon the tenderized nerve running down the side of his leg. "Mother—"

Paige snapped her baton straight forward to deliver a quick, stabbing blow to his midsection. Not only did it cut one profanity short, but it took away the breath required to put together another one.

"We're going to that Blood Parlor uptown tonight," she said as she circled him. "You need to get your shit together."

"I'm trying, but you keep *hitting me*."

"You let your guard down."

Gritting his teeth in a vain attempt to keep from looking like a complete pansy, Cole replied, "You pulled out the advanced moves. I haven't seen that one yet."

"It's called thinking on your feet. Most anyone or anything you fight won't follow a script, you know."

"I know, Paige, but I—"

He was cut short by another crack from the baton. The simple weapon spun around Paige's hand like a propeller, switched direction at the last second, and then knocked against the back of his left hand. Both of her weapons also had thorns protruding from the handles, but the easy smile on her face didn't register the first sign of any discomfort.

"Damn it, I've got to use that hand!" Cole whined.

"That's what I'm trying to get you to do."

"I mean I've got to type with it, not use it as a freaking pin cushion!"

"A pin cushion, huh?" she scoffed. "You'd have to be better at sewing than fighting, so maybe you could knit a nice set of fang cozies for the next Nymar that steps out of line."

Cole tightened his grip around the middle of his spear and circled to the left. They were in the cellar of an old restaurant that must have served a hell of a lot of ham. The smell of it filled the windowless space so much that the cinder blocks in the walls could have been sliced up to make a passable sandwich. He and Paige had plenty of room to maneuver as long as neither of them tried to jump. His skull sported more than a few bumps after knocking against the low ceiling, which paled in comparison to the damage done to his ego when he'd gotten the forked end of his spear wedged in a beam while attempting an overhand swing.

Paige flipped her baton upward to connect with the lower edge of Cole's weapon. Just as the forked spear started to come away from his hands, she brought the baton around in a tight semicircle to crack on top of it. Cole snarled as the thorns in the weapon's handle came out of his palm a bit and were savagely driven back in again.

"Didn't like that, did you?" she mused. "Tighten your grip and keep your guard up."

"It *was* up!"

"Then you should have blocked that."

No matter how cute she looked, he still wanted to smack the shit out of her sometimes. Staring at her intently, Cole struggled to come up with something to say. The blood was flowing too quickly through his entire body for him to arrive at anything better than a few nasty standbys. Since he was hurting enough already, he kept them to himself.

He took a breath and tightened his grip until the thorns dug into his palms. When Paige swung her baton toward his head, he moved to block but didn't commit to the parry until it got to him. Sure enough, she pulled back at the last second to try and convert her attack into a chopping blow aimed at his lower body. He was able to drop his guard and deflect the baton with a definitive crack.

"Good," she said.

Cole smiled and nodded. "Good? Freaking excellent is what that was."

Smiling as she only did while in the middle of a fight, Paige twirled both weapons before feinting with one and swinging the other at his ribs. Although she managed to land one glancing blow, the other was knocked away by Cole's spear. After that, she had to use both batons to defend against a flurry of incoming attacks. Paige blocked one after another before backing off. Although Cole hadn't come close to besting her in their sparring session, the gleam of sweat on her skin told him he was at least making her work for a change. In his first few weeks of training, he'd only dreamed of getting her to work up a sweat. He actually still dreamed of it.

A lot.

As if sensing the mildly pornographic thoughts drifting through his mind, she narrowed her brown eyes and shifted into a sideways stance. That was supposed to present a smaller target to an opponent, but it also brought Paige's taut yet shapely curves to Cole's attention. "Now that," she said with a little smile, "was freaking excellent."

"Thanks."

"Don't sound so surprised. You've been making a lot of progress."

Cole spun his spear in a few quick circles that sliced through the air while passing on either side of his body before ending up in the exact spot where it started. The flashy move was one of the few he'd actually practiced outside of their sparring sessions, and his palms were so slick with blood that he forgot about the thorns for a moment.

Paige let her eyes wander up and down along Cole's body before nodding approvingly. "Don't try to distract me. We need to finish up. I'm about to bake in this cellar, though." With that, she set her batons down and pulled her T-shirt over her head. Once the sweaty garment was off, she tossed it aside and rolled her head around to work the kinks from her neck.

Every line of Paige's upper body was accentuated by the sweat glistening upon her skin. Her shorts clung to her hips and backside in just the right way, and her sports bra didn't leave much to the imagination.

"You ready?" she asked.

"Oh yeah."

Paige bent at the waist to pick up her batons, and Cole took full advantage of the moment to watch how her tight body shifted through the motions. Every movement caused the muscles in her legs or stomach to tense and relax.

Her first few swings were almost playful. She smirked when he batted them away and even looked impressed when he came close to landing an answering blow of his own. Then the batons flew at him a little faster. Cole ducked under some of the swings and blocked one or two, but caught a couple taps along the shoulders and sides.

"Sorry," she said. "Did that hurt?"

He tried to ignore the throbbing in the same two ribs that she insisted on hitting every damn time and replied, "Nah."

"Good. Here comes some more."

Now, Paige hopped from side to side while shifting from vertical chopping strikes to a horizontal swing that used both batons like a giant pair of wooden scissors. Cole impressed himself by wedging his spear in between her weapons to stop them before they hit him on either side of his head.

"God, you're really getting good at that," she sighed.

The tone in her voice was something he'd been dying to hear. A bead of sweat rolled along the side of her neck and slipped between her breasts. When she caught him glancing down to follow the shimmering trail, Paige parted her lips just enough to lick them. "How about we bump it up a notch?"

"That would be just fine by me."

She circled him in slow, sauntering steps. It was a specific movement that Cole had always cherished for the way it got her hips and shoulders moving in perfect synchronic-

ity. She didn't walk like that very often and it never seemed
like something she was doing on purpose. Now, those movements were accentuated to dangerous levels and, for one of
the few times he could remember, she was sauntering toward
him rather than away.

As Paige raised her right arm, she twirled her baton
in a slow circle that quickly picked up speed. She took a
quick swing at him, which he blocked fairly easily. The
swing didn't end after striking Cole's spear. Instead, Paige's
weapon bounced off his spear and immediately rapped him
on the side of the neck.

"Hey, that hur—"

Before Cole could air his full complaint, he was put on the
defensive again. She came at him quickly and landed a quick
flurry of tapping hits against his ribs on both sides. He swatted away the flying batons before attempting to respond in
kind. He landed a pretty good shot on Paige's left side, only
to have his spear trapped when she dropped that arm down
and locked it in place.

Paige cocked back her right arm like a scorpion getting
ready to sting, so Cole ripped his spear out of her grasp and
held it so the forked end was aimed at her throat.

Paige abruptly dropped her playful smile and looked at
Cole in a way that hit him like a cold slap in the face. For the
first time since he'd met her, he saw fear in her eyes.

"Are you really trying to hurt me?" she whispered. "I
thought we'd just have some fun before . . . you know."

"Really?" Cole lowered his spear and reached out to
stroke her cheek. "I would never—"

As Paige snapped her wrist, she tightened her grip upon
her baton to crack it against Cole's forearm. Before the pain
could work its way up to his shoulder, the baton let out a
creaking sound as it shifted to form a sharpened stake at one
end and a thin, curved blade at the other. She slid her other
arm along the bottom of his to lock it in place by cranking
his elbow in the wrong direction.

Cole's upper body stretched back and a pained yelp
wedged in his throat as she lifted her newly sharpened baton
over his chest. Blood dripped from where that weapon's

thorns dug into her palm and, using a technique that Cole hadn't quite perfected, she willed the treated wood to stretch out just enough to touch his throat.

"If . . . this is because I stepped out of line . . . " Cole wheezed.

"This," Paige snapped, "is because you were thinking with the short stick."

"Ouch."

"When you get into a fight, all you need to think about is winning. I've seen you hold back every now and then while we're sparring. I've also seen you hold back when we're dealing with some creature out in the world that happens to be a female with a properly rounded ass."

Cole tried to look offended but couldn't really pull it off.

"You want to get sweaty the fun way?" Paige asked. "Do a search for cheerleaders on your computer. You want to get stabbed, shot, sliced open, or ripped apart? Drop your guard because some girlie girl batted her eyelashes and politely asked you to."

"So . . . this isn't your version of foreplay?"

Paige's lock on his arm tightened just enough to force a squeal out of him.

"Just kidding," he quickly said. "I get it. You made your point."

Slowly, she loosened her grip before finally allowing Cole to exhale. "You remember that Blood Parlor I mentioned? It's being run by Steph and Ace. Remember her?"

"Steph's kind of hard to forget."

"Well, she plays up that whole sexy vampire act for a reason. If you're going to do anything against the Nymar or anything else that's out there, you can't be suckered by such simple bullshit. We're headed into some rough times, Cole. I need to make sure you're with me."

"If I didn't want to be here, I wouldn't be here." Rubbing his shoulder, Cole added, "Believe me, it's too late to turn back now."

"That's right. A few shapeshifters have already tracked you down, and every Nymar in Chicago knows who you are. We can't kill them all, but we need to keep them in line.

They've got enough supernatural tricks up their sleeves, so don't make things easier for them."

"This is different."

"Is it?"

"Yeah," Cole fumbled. "You're . . . well . . . you. I've handled myself pretty well in spots where someone tried to distract me."

"Like when we raided that club where the Nymar were feeding on college kids over on Lawrence Avenue?"

"You're never going to let that go," he grumbled. "Some blonde made me look away for a second, and I still managed to back you up when you shot your mouth off."

"Barely. And that blonde wasn't even very hot. All she had to do was flash you some fake boobs to get you to do exactly what she wanted."

"All right, you caught me. I'm a guy who looks at women when they expose themselves. I also happen to blink before hitting them in the face. And, every now and then, I may pause for a second when a *very* hot blonde opens her robe and touches herself in some *very* interesting ways. File a lawsuit."

"You're not just some guy, Cole. And we're not just some people who carry sticks. We're doing a dangerous job and can't afford to act like everyone else."

"No nookie for Skinners, huh? If I'd known that, I might not have signed on."

Even though Paige was nearly a foot shorter than him, she carried herself as if she was merely keeping her head down before making her big move. Stepping up to him, she said, "It's got nothing to do with nookie and everything to do with expectations. Have you seen any other Skinners around here checking out the hot Nymar babes?"

"Ever since Prophet left, I haven't seen any Skinners at all."

"Prophet doesn't count. At least, not completely."

"Then I guess I haven't seen anyone but you."

"Exactly," Paige said. "As far as I know, we're the only ones within four states who think of vampires and werewolves as something other than characters in one of those games you design. The only thing keeping all Skinners alive is the fact that nothing out there knows the whole story about us.

"If the Nymar knew how few of us there are, they'd pull themselves together and take us out. If they knew they could get one of us into bed or hooked on God knows what they've cooked up in their drug labs, we wouldn't stand a chance in hell of keeping them in their place. We're a threat and a mystery to them. The second we become something less than that, we lose our fight. Understand?"

He let some of his pride go along with the breath he'd been holding and said, "Yeah. In my defense, though, I've been taking a lot of bumps to the head. That could explain some dumb behavior."

"And maybe you'd get hit less often if you didn't tap away on that computer when you should be practicing."

"That computer brings in the money, lady. In case you haven't noticed, *Hammer Strike* has been doing well enough for me to pay some bills around here."

The weapons in Paige's hands shrank back down into normal batons like melting candles. "We've been down here for three hours," she announced as she picked up the shirt she'd discarded.

Cole looked around and saw nothing but gray block walls and greasy stains around him. "Did you finally put a clock up down here?"

"No."

"Oh, great. Am I going to have to hone my awareness of time as some goofy part of my training?"

"You could." Lifting the little item that had been on the floor beneath the shirt, she added, "Or you could buy a watch, Mr. Moneybags. Show me a twitch and we can call it quits for the day."

"A twitch, huh?"

"That's all that stands between you and dinner."

Knowing it was useless to bargain with her, Cole extended both arms as though offering Paige his weapon. He tightened his grip around the spear and winced as the thorns dug into his palms. Even though the sharpened protrusions were less than half an inch long, they felt as if they'd bored tunnels all the way up to his elbows. In many ways they went a lot deeper than that.

After a few quiet seconds, Cole glanced up to find Paige standing with her hip cocked and her hand resting upon it. Her hair was long enough to be pulled back in a tail, but several strands always came loose no matter how hard she tried to keep them under control. A single bead of sweat emerged from her forehead to trickle along the crooked side of a nose that still looked cute despite having been broken long before he ever met her. The sweat dripped off her chin and made a wet spot upon the inviting slope of her breasts. When she absently dabbed it away, he muttered, "I'm feeling a twitch or two right now."

"If I see anything other than that weapon move, I'll put it down real quick," she told him while slapping her baton against her open hand.

Cole pulled in a breath and focused upon the forked spear in his hands.

"Concentrate, young one," Paige said in the bad kung-fu master impression she always found to be amusing.

Just as Cole was about to chalk up his poor performance to being tired, he heard the spear creak.

"That's it," Paige whispered.

It wasn't much, but the spear bowed inward just enough for him to feel the movement.

Paige's eyes widened and she moved in closer to him. "There you go. Just like that."

Cole's mind drifted further away from what he was trying to do and ventured into the area of what he *wanted* to do. The spear in his hands creaked like a board getting ready to snap, but he couldn't exactly appreciate it.

"That's the way, Cole," Paige said encouragingly. "Keep doing that."

"Stop it, Paige."

"What?"

"You're making it hard to concentrate."

Smirking, she asked, "I'm making it hard?"

After using the back of her hand to wipe the remaining sweat from her brow, she lifted her right leg so she could slip her baton into the leather holster attached to her ankle. The moment her foot touched down again, she smiled and placed her hand upon Cole's shoulder. "Sorry. You really are doing well."

"Better than the other eight people you trained before me?"

"Yeah. Sure."

"Now you're just jerking my chain."

"Maybe," she said with a shrug while her hand slid down along his arm. "You're putting on some muscle, though. I'll get you into shape yet. Who knows? Before too long, I may not be able to resist."

As Paige spun around to head for the stairs, the weapon in Cole's hand creaked again. The spear bowed, but it was tough for him to tell if the wood was changing shape or if he was about to snap it in half.

It had been eight months since Cole first met Paige Strobel. In that time, he'd also met vampires, werewolves, and a few other things that he didn't quite know how to categorize. He still had an apartment in Seattle, but was currently leasing it to one of the level designers at Digital Dreamers. The sporadic rent checks he received were enough to help pay for some expenses, but not nearly as much as his salary when he'd headed the team responsible for building video games like *Hammer Strike* and the ever-popular Sniper Ranger series. Digital Dreamers was also behind *Zombie House,* versions one through four, *Puzzle Cube,* and plenty of others. Although Cole never wanted to be one of the corporate guys, he would have picked that over getting beat up in a basement any time.

On the upside, he'd definitely lost some weight. There was a mirror hanging from the wall of the walk-in freezer that had been converted into his room, but he was too tired to get up and look into it. Instead, he peeled off his workout clothes, looked down at his somewhat flat belly and gave it a few appreciative slaps.

"Not quite a six-pack, but I'm up to at least a two."

The longer he sat on the edge of his cot, the more exhausted Cole felt. Rather than watch his stomach expand as he relaxed, he looked up and rubbed his hands over the top of his head. His hair wasn't much more than stubble sprouting from his scalp. It was cool in the Chicago heat and easy to take care of. His clean-shaven face was thinning a bit as well, but still ached from the hits he'd taken during his frequent sparring sessions.

Paige's timing was impeccable. The very moment he thought about how great it would be to take a hot shower, he heard the water start to run in the restaurant's only bathroom. Technically, there were two other bathrooms in what used to be the main dining room, but those were filthy enough to discourage homeless people from wandering into the place. A good portion of the dining room had also been rigged with traps to keep the local monsters at bay.

Monsters.

Cole still couldn't quite get over how many times he used that word in legitimate sentences. The supernatural creatures out there had not only knocked him out of his happy, video-game-designing existence, but even sucked the fun out of the simple things. For instance, the shower he so desperately wanted would only be ruined by the soap Paige forced them to use. The stuff was supposed to keep their scent from being detected, but it smelled like old tires and felt like a brick of oatmeal. Despite the fact that it didn't even do a very good job of masking their scent from the things that hunted them, Paige insisted on using the stuff. It was also cheap.

Cole's room wasn't bad, as far as renovated freezers went. It was quiet, there were plenty of shelves for his stuff, and it contained more than enough outlets for his computers and recharging needs. Ironically, however, it wasn't nearly as cool as the other rooms in the place. Since the actual refrigeration unit was gone, the aluminum plated walls were real good at holding in whatever kind of air was left. In the middle of summer, that air was hot.

Paige took her time in the shower, so Cole decided to get to work. Rather than switch on his laptop, he picked up the forked spear and held it in both hands. He'd found it was easier when he didn't think too long before sinking the thorns into his palms, so he simply gripped tightly and exhaled as the sharp little buggers dug into all the familiar places.

Every inch of the spear was varnished to a dull sheen using a concoction that Paige had taught him how to brew. He applied another coat every two or three days, so the spear was pretty much soaked through by now. Since the varnish was mixed using shapeshifter blood, the weapon would eventually change shape on command. If he hadn't seen Paige pull off the trick, he never would have believed it was possible.

"Come on," he snarled as he held on and stared at the petrified weapon.

The longer he begged and threatened the spear, the less it moved. Finally, he couldn't even bend the damn thing using brute force.

"Honestly, honey," he mumbled. "This has never happened to me before."

If the spear hadn't been attached to his hands, he would have thrown it into the corner. He made do with setting it down gently and kicking it to the other side of his freezer. Cole looked down at his hands to watch the puncture wounds seal themselves up. That part had something to do with the varnish as well. Nymar saliva was another ingredient that naturally sealed puncture wounds to keep victims alive while they were being fed upon. Nymar proteins were also used to make a powerful Skinner healing serum. If those freaks were good at something other than sucking blood, it was healing.

"Nothing's ever easy," he grumbled as he straightened up and walked over to the stack of plastic crates he'd been using as a desk. When he got his laptop warmed up and started typing, he realized it had only hurt a little to walk. After a nice shower, he might even be back to normal.

"Bathroom's all yours," Paige hollered from another room.

Cole waited for it.

"Hot water's gone, though," she added.

And there it was.

Chapter 2

When Cole had arrived in Chicago to meet Paige for the first time, the city felt like a different place. The sights and smells were comforting. Driving down West Cermak, he looked at the same city and saw another beast completely. Instead of something that was just there to be sampled, consumed, and abused, Chicago stared back. It dared him to spend too much time in its dark places and enticed him to venture into the most delectable spots that he had yet to peruse.

At the moment, however, the only thing Cole wanted was a White Castle hamburger. White Castle wasn't exactly confined to Chicago, but he couldn't get them in Seattle. Some grocery stores carried frozen versions of the burgers, but those were simply blasphemous and cruel to anyone who'd ever tasted the real thing. Real White Castles were warm, squishy, about the size of a coaster, and were steamed all the way through with pickles and onions. His ex-girlfriend Nora swore a recipe she'd found online allowed her to make them, but those weren't the same. After making the mistake of sparing her feelings with an approving thumbs-up, he was forced to eat the false idols every couple of months.

Cole hung a right onto South Cicero Avenue and grinned as he caught sight of a White Castle which he loved despite the damage it consistently did to his intestinal tract. When he drove around the newly remodeled fast food joint, he kept his window rolled down to fill Paige's car with the glorious scent that hung like a cloud over the gleaming white building. The line at the pickup window was long and moved a bit too slowly, but brought him to a kid wearing a blue visor who handed him paper sacks stuffed with pure joy. Hamburgers contained in little cardboard castles were stacked on top of flat rectangular boxes stuffed with fries and onion rings. Still sifting through the food to make sure his order was correct, Cole managed to turn back onto Cicero and start his journey toward Twenty-fifth Street.

Between the hot touch of summer reaching in through his window and the heavenly aroma seeping through the car's interior, he almost missed the group of vampires loitering in the narrow alley between a bank and a small industrial supply company. The three didn't look like monsters. They barely even looked like trouble, but they did cause a reaction to the scars left behind by his weapon, which felt like spiders crawling under his palms. After having so much of the potent varnish introduced to his system, he could feel that reaction through both arms by now.

Only vampires made him itch like that. Actually, they insisted on being called Nymar. Applying the V word to them was like calling a large percentage of the human population "brown people." It wasn't inaccurate so much as just plain ignorant.

He slowed down but didn't stop. While turning onto Twenty-fifth, he took out his cell phone and called Paige. She answered on the third ring.

"Did you forget my order?" she asked.

"It's not that," Cole said anxiously. "I just saw three Nymar hanging out on Twenty-fourth Street."

"What were they doing?"

"I don't know."

"Were they feeding on anyone?"

"No," Cole quickly replied.

Upon hearing her sigh, he had no problem picturing the annoyed shift of Paige's facial features. "Then why are you so worked up?" she asked. "I'm hungry."

"Aren't you the one who told me there shouldn't be any Nymar this close to us?"

"Yeah, I told you that. I just didn't think you'd remember. Why don't you go and see what they're doing?"

"That's more like it. How long before you get here?"

"I'm staying put." After a few seconds of dead air, she added, "Think of it as practice. You didn't think I'd be around all the time to wipe your nose, did you?"

"No," Cole said defensively. "I'm just not done training. I can't even do the fancy stuff with the spear yet!"

"You've got your weapon with you, right?"

He reached back to pat the length of petrified wood resting behind the passenger seat. "Wouldn't leave home without it."

"And the .44 is still in the glove compartment. Tuck one under your belt, keep the other where the Nymar can see it, and you should be fine. Before you get too cocky, remember that you don't have nearly enough room in your pants for that spear."

"One last jab before sending me out to die, huh?" Cole grunted. "Classy."

"Come back without my cheese fries and you'll be dead for real." With that, Paige hung up.

Cole tossed his phone onto the seat, where it immediately slid beneath the warm sack of burgers like a rodent burrowing for refuge beneath a stump. He made a right onto South Fiftieth Avenue, another onto West Twenty-third Street, and yet another to head south on Cicero. It was late, but not late enough for the streets to quiet down. There were a few people walking along the sidewalks and cars sharing the road with him, but he wasn't distracted by any of that. Instead, he allowed the itching to guide him toward his destination.

When he spotted the trio of figures huddled exactly where they'd been on his first pass, he was vaguely disappointed. If they'd taken off, he could have just driven around for a while before heading home to enjoy his food. He parked at the curb near the corner of Cicero and West Twenty-fifth Street, hoping the Nymar would just bolt when they figured out who he was. That would be a nice little boost to his ego.

The engine of Paige's battered Chevy Cavalier rattled to a stop like a wheezing old man who'd been smoking for most of his life, which wasn't far from the truth. He took a deep breath, propped his spear on the floor against the passenger door, and reached into the glove compartment to find the .44 revolver right where it should be. Tucking the pistol under his belt, Cole stepped out of the car and pulled his shirt down to make sure the gun was covered.

"I shouldn't be doing this," he muttered. "I should make Paige come down here with me. I should just go back and tell her there's nothing to worry about."

But there was something to worry about. That's why he was getting his ass kicked every day in a basement while learning how to fight with a petrified stick. If things were all well and good, there wouldn't be monsters loitering on Cicero Avenue.

The three figures standing at the mouth of the alley all turned to face Cole. One of them looked to be in his early thirties, with light brown hair styled into a mullet. The second was a younger guy with a full beard and short black hair. Both of them were dressed in clothes that could have been pulled out of any department store in town. Not too fancy and not too tattered. The third was a girl who appeared to be somewhere in her late teens. She was cute in a naughty kind of way and played that to the hilt by pulling her dark hair into pigtails and wearing her blouse open to display a lacy bra.

The guy with the mullet stepped forward and asked, "What's goin' on? Help ya find anything?"

Cole nodded and stood with his feet planted shoulder width apart and his thumbs hooked over his belt. The more he hoped to keep his cool, the more he knew he was blowing it. Before he started to shake, he said, "I was about to ask you the same thing."

The other three chuckled and looked back and forth at each other. In those few seconds, Cole was able to pick out the black markings beneath their skin. Nymar were named after a growth on their heart that fed off of human blood. That growth spread through its host's body using black tendrils that showed up like veins. At first glance the black markings looked like tattoos. A second or third glance was usually enough to reveal that those supposed tattoos were slowly writhing just beneath the skin's surface. There were ways to tell how old or powerful a Nymar was by studying those markings, but Cole couldn't think about them now. It was all he could do to hold his ground as the three moved in closer to him.

"What's that supposed to mean?" Mullet asked.

"I was going to ask if you needed any help," Cole replied.

The girl nudged the bearded man aside so she could reach out to tug the front of Cole's T-shirt as if straightening an invisible tie. "Help with what, cutie?"

Her arms were slender and the black marks stretching under her wrists were thin. She was Nymar, but hadn't been one for long. The tendrils were dark enough to show that she'd fed recently.

Before he could think of anything better, Cole said, "Maybe you're lost."

Mullet narrowed his eyes and scowled in a way that allowed Cole to see his teeth. He hadn't extended any fangs yet, so the guy must have just been a mouth breather. "Are you a cop? We're just standin' here."

"Yeah," the bearded guy chimed in. "We're not doing anything wrong."

Cole leaned to one side so he could get a look farther down the alley. The space between the two buildings wasn't wide enough for a car to drive through, but there was plenty of room for things to happen back there.

Putting herself squarely in Cole's line of sight, the girl with the pigtails asked, "What are you looking for? You must've stopped for something. Maybe you'd like me to nibble on you and you're just too shy to ask."

Cole tried to think of what Paige might say. After that, he thought of about a dozen reasons why he shouldn't say what Paige would say.

Slowly, the girl in pigtails smiled. When she did, she stared at him in a way that nobody her age should have been able to pull off. There was confidence without cockiness. Some arrogant little teen would have written him off already, but she watched him like a predator that was as aware of herself as she was of her prey. "Look at him," she said softly. "He *is* shy."

Mullet stepped up so he could bump his shoulder against Cole's. Some people walked along the sidewalk toward the alley, glanced at Cole being surrounded by the other three and quickly crossed the street to give them some space. He could sense their fear, but the Nymar could practically drink it down.

"You want her to suck you or not?" Mullet asked. When he didn't get an answer right away, he reached out to grab Cole's shirt. "Then move the fuck along."

Cole slapped Mullet's hand away out of pure reflex and shoved the Nymar back with a move that had been one of the first Paige taught him. While Mullet was recovering his balance, Cole turned to the girl and asked, "You belong to Stephanie, right?"

"Why do you want to know?"

"I'm a friend of hers."

The girl shook her head just enough to wiggle her pigtails. "Mister, you don't know what you're talking about and you sure don't know Stephanie. If you want to party, just say so. There's no need for all of this testosterone to be flowing."

"I know Steph well enough," Cole said. "Is she still keeping Ace on a short leash? I mean, she's got to be the one who insists all of her girls wear those pigtails. If it was up to Ace, you'd probably be branded or something."

All three of them took a step back, eyeing him as if committing every detail to memory.

"If I look in that alley, will I find out you three have been feeding in the open?" Cole asked. "You know that's against the rules."

At first Mullet looked surprised. His slack-jawed expression quickly gave way to a snarl. When he curled his lips back, the big set of upper and lower fangs slid out from his gums. Cole knew there was a third set of fangs in there, but the Nymar wasn't laying all his cards on the table just yet. "So you're the new Skinner we've been hearing about?"

The Nymar with the beard crouched down a bit while keeping his eyes fixed upon Cole. That one did extend his other set of upper fangs. The thinner, curved teeth dropped into place, where they were framed by the thicker set used for feeding.

"Take it easy, Sid," the girl said. "Even a Skinner might want a bit of lovin'."

"Oh yeah," Cole chuckled. "You're one of Steph's all right."

Her smile didn't fade in the least. She reached out to let her fingers wander along Cole's chest. "All kinds of normal people pay us good money to feed on them, you know. I've got more regulars than I can handle, and we only just set up shop here a week ago."

"You shouldn't have set up shop here at all. You've been warned to stay away from Cicero."

"Warned by who?" Mullet asked. "Gerald was the only real Skinner around here, and that old man's dead. I hear his skinny little partner got killed too. That only leaves some short broad, which sure ain't you."

That dredged up some bad memories, which Cole couldn't keep from showing on his face. The instant he felt the warm flush run through his cheeks, the Nymar took note.

"You knew Gerald?" Mullet asked.

This time Cole didn't have to dig down to put an edge into his voice, and he didn't have to try to make his anger seem convincing. "I knew Gerald well enough, and if you've been feeding in the open, I'll do Gerald proud by kicking your asses all the way back to the Levee."

"We conduct our business where we please, Skinner," Sid growled. "That is, if you even are a Skinner."

The girl's fingers encircled Cole's wrist. Before he could pull away from her, she twisted his hand up to get a look at the scars on his palm. "He *is* a Skinner. Looks a little fresh, but—"

"Show me the alley," Cole snapped as he pulled against the girl's thumb just as Paige had taught him. Even if the Nymar was stronger than him, she still had a weak point in her grip, just like anyone else who walked around using all the human bits and pieces.

Clenching her hand into a little fist, she stepped back and

allowed the other two to stalk forward. "You want to look down that alley?" she asked. "Be our guest."

Cole glanced up and down the sidewalk. There were a few people here and there, but none of them were anxious to have any part in what was going on near the alley. Suddenly, he thought of something that didn't involve walking into a cramped spot with three Nymar bloodsuckers behind him. Surprisingly enough, his idea didn't involve running away either.

"It's all right," he shouted toward the alley. "You can come out now."

A dog barked somewhere. Farther up on Cermak, someone blasted their stereo loud enough for the bass to rattle Cole's back teeth. Other than that . . . nothing.

"Nobody's going to hurt you," Cole added. "No charges will be filed if you just come out right now."

Before the bass line up the street could shift into another song, another figure emerged from the alley. Unlike the ones that had caught Cole's attention in the first place, this figure wasn't sporting any black marks on its neck or wrists. It also wasn't wearing any pants.

"I don't want any trouble," the guy said. "I was just waiting for her to . . . " He was somewhere in his forties, with a full head of hair and a gut that would have hung over a belt if one had been around his waist. Grabbing at the rolls on his hips, he suddenly realized what was already painfully obvious to everyone else. "I . . . don't have my pants. Can I just—"

"Get out of here," Cole snapped. "And whatever you were doing before, don't do it again."

The guy looked around quickly and then scampered off in the direction with the fewest people to gawk at him.

"Another happy customer," the girl said with a grin.

"Take your business where it belongs," Cole warned. "Right now."

"Or what?" Mullet challenged.

The Nymar with the eighties hairstyle might have been posturing, but his buddy meant business. Sid crouched down and bared all three sets of fangs in the supernatural equivalent of taking a gun from its holster and thumbing back the hammer.

One of those Nymar was going to pounce at any second. After that, the others would follow. Since turning his back on them wasn't a smart idea, Cole knew he only had one alternative. He filled his lungs with warm night air, catching a whiff of the hamburgers waiting for him on his front seat, then grabbed the closest Nymar by the front of his shirt. Mullet seemed surprised to be targeted, but twisted to get away while also attempting to swipe at him with his right fist.

One of the first lessons Paige had taught Cole about fighting was to use movement and momentum to his advantage. She'd tested him relentlessly, landing punch after punch until he had learned to anticipate and adjust to every swing. Now that it really mattered, he did exactly what he was supposed to do.

When Mullet pivoted to swing his right fist, Cole tightened his grip on the Nymar's shirt and turned in that same direction. That way, it took a minimum of effort for Cole to spin his opponent around and slam him against the car. Mullet hit the Cavalier hard enough to dent the door, which wasn't nearly enough damage to stand out from all the other ugly spots on the vehicle. While Mullet tried to figure out what had just happened, Cole hit him in the face. Other than being very satisfying, the punch only resulted in Cole ripping open his own fist against the Nymar's upper fangs. Fortunately for him, they weren't the slender, snakelike fangs. The venom from those would have knocked him out faster than a kick to the head. Thanks to Paige's sparring sessions, he was all too familiar with being kicked in the head.

Sid let out a snarling hiss as he jumped toward Cole's back. Having expected that from the start, Cole hopped aside to catch only a glancing blow as the bearded Nymar slammed against the dented Cavalier.

Cole staggered back a few steps, slow to make another move simply because he was surprised to be doing so well in the fight. He wanted to get to his spear, but there were two Nymar pressed up against the door. As much as he would have loved to run around to the driver's side, he didn't want to give the others a chance to catch their breath. Putting every bit of muscle behind his left arm, he twisted his body around and drove that elbow into Mullet's face.

The Nymar's head snapped back and his knees started to give. Sid had wound up closer to the hood of the car after inadvertently body-slamming his partner, so he wasn't close enough to get to Cole just yet. Before that situation changed, Cole fumbled for the pistol wedged under his belt. It was a sloppy draw and, if the .44 was anything but a clunky revolver, could very well have turned him into a eunuch. The gods were smiling on him and his goods because he managed to take out the .44 and drive the barrel straight into Mullet's chest.

"You guys may not be afraid of guns, but we all know how much damage a shot at this range can do to the little buddy stuck to your heart," Cole said.

"You'd better be real sure about that!" Mullet replied.

Cole thumbed back the pistol's hammer. "What do you think my odds are? Fifty-fifty?"

Inching his way around the front of the car, Sid hissed, "Do it and we tear you apart!"

"Shut up, asshole!" Mullet barked.

Although Sid was still baring his fangs, his beard covered all but the pointed tips.

Nodding slowly, Cole looked around to find several small groups of people scattered farther down the street. He looked over to the Nymar in pigtails and said, "You stayed put through all of this, so you must not want things to get worse. Wanna tell your boys to back off, or would you rather wait for the cops to get here?"

The girl had her arms crossed and her lips parted just enough to show the top two sets of fangs extending from her gums. The thicker canine teeth slid against the thinner venomous ones in a way that somehow managed to look sexy. The calm expression on her face and the commanding tone in her voice made it clear she was well past the age she projected.

"You two," she said. "Heel."

Mullet and Sid weren't happy about it, but they obeyed.

Uncrossing her arms to hold them out as if she was expecting a hug, she asked, "Is that good enough for you?"

"All of you know better than to be in this part of town unless you're looking for us," Cole pointed out. As an afterthought, he asked, "Were you looking for us?"

"We sure as hell found you, didn't we?" the girl mused. "But we'll find somewhere else to play. How's that?"

"As long as it's away from here, suits me just fine."

"Good. Are you Cole?"

Upon hearing his name, Cole felt a twitch in the corner of one eye. Fortunately, he was twitching in too many other places at the moment for that one to stand out. "Just get the hell off of my street."

He had been waiting a good portion of his life to say something like that. Rather than soak up the moment while imagining tough background music, he tried to keep his glare from cracking and prayed the other three would just go away.

They did.

Once the trio of Nymar disappeared down the alley, Cole kept his head down and walked around to the driver's side of Paige's car. The seat was still warm from when he'd last sat in it, but it felt like a week and a half had gone by since he was driving along fantasizing about eating his little hamburgers. Although technically trivial when compared to possibly getting his throat shredded, those burgers brought a smile back to his face.

The taste of victory in a little cardboard box.

Chapter 3

Cole hadn't felt comfortable anywhere since he'd seen his first werewolf, but the gutted old restaurant off of South Laramie Avenue was a spot where he could sometimes let his guard down. At one point the restaurant had customers, employees, and a real name. Now, all that remained of the place's former glory was a sign painted onto the front wall that had been partially worn away by the elements and who knows what else. The letters that could still be seen were: RAZA HILL. He parked along the side of the place, collected his bags of food, and hurried in.

"You'll never guess what happened," he sputtered the moment he caught sight of Paige sitting on a stool in the kitchen.

She glanced over to him and asked, "Where are my cheese fries?"

"Remember those Nymar I called about? There were three of them, and I chased them away without any help. Hey, wait a second. You seriously weren't planning on coming to help me?"

"What makes you say that?"

"You're planted on that stool like nothing happened! What if I got hurt?"

Shrugging, Paige replied, "If you can't chase off three Nymar, then you'll never be any help to me. Where's your weapon?"

"Oh, I left it in the car."

"But you brought in the food? At least you've got your priorities straight."

"Don't you want to hear about the Nymar?" Cole asked.

Paige swiveled around on her stool, placed her hands on her knees, and gave him one crisp nod. "Yes, Cole. I want to hear all about the Nymar. After that do I get my cheese fries?"

He dumped the fast food bags onto the counter. "Here you go. The fries and everything else is in there. I'll go get the rest of my stuff and we can eat."

"Do you know how cute you are when you pout?"

"Save it."

After taking his weapon from the front seat, Cole stomped back into the restaurant. He slapped the spear down, grabbed a double cheeseburger from the pile, and tore into the steamed little miracle.

"There," Paige said. "Feel better now?"

"Yes."

"Me too. Now I'm ready to hear about the Nymar."

Cole looked over to find her holding a handful of gooey cheese fries that had all been bitten off in the middle. That same cheese was smeared over a good portion of her mouth, and a few drops had fallen onto the front of her nightshirt. With her hair pulled back into a messy tail, she was anything but glamorous. Somehow, she still managed to get that twitch she'd been after.

Launching into his story while stuffing his face, Cole went through the whole account. By the time he was finished, most of the cardboard burger boxes were empty. Most of the food that hadn't been eaten was soaked into the front of Paige's clothes.

"So they weren't feeding in public?" she asked.

"The guy in the alley was paying for it, but he was out of sight."

"That's not a killing offense, but the Nymar are supposed to stay around the Levee or near the Loop. There must be more of them coming back into town after that business with Misonyk was cleared up."

It had been a while since that name was mentioned. The Nymar were worried about dredging up old demons, and the Skinners were simply glad to be rid of the lunatic who'd used an infected werewolf to try and make a name for himself in Chicago and the adjacent states.

"Things have been quieter than usual since Misonyk was killed," Paige continued, "but it's stupid to think that would last too long. Most of the Nymar that left town will be coming back to pick up where they left off." She picked up one of the onion rings from the two remaining boxes on the counter and then dipped it into some partially hardened cheese from the second container. "Others might come here thinking we're still soft from what happened before," she said amidst a pungent, greasy spray. "You said that girl had her hair in pigtails. Were they tied back with bands that had little cats on them?"

"Huh?"

Waving her hand impatiently, Paige said, "Never mind. She was one of Steph's girls, all right. They all have the same attitude and like to push their luck."

"What did you mean about those cat bands?" Cole asked.

Paige hopped down from her stool and tapped his forehead. "Know your enemy, young one. Steph and Ace's working girls all wear their hair in pigtails tied back with bands that have cats on them. Haven't you ever noticed that?"

"They're scantily dressed vampire hookers that flash their goods every chance they get and you think I'm looking at the bands in their hair?"

"Did you at least notice the pigtails?" she asked hopefully.

Cole perked up as he replied, "Oh yeah. I noticed the pigtails."

"We need to pay Steph and Ace a visit. They know better than to cross the border we laid down, so that means they're either testing us or they've got reinforcements to back them up. We'll go to that new Blood Parlor tonight after the crowds die down."

Cole watched Paige hop off her stool and walk out of the kitchen. He'd been around her enough to know just how long he could study her from behind before getting caught. When the timer in his head went off, he pretended to look at something else. Paige shot a quick glance over her shoulder but had no reason to break her stride.

"Too slow, dragon lady," he whispered in his own kung-fu impression. "Time for young one to polish his stick."

Cole's spear leaned in the corner of his walk-in refrigerator, gleaming with a fresh coat of the varnish that was mixed using an old Skinner recipe. Although Skinners tended to hand down their teachings through word of mouth, Cole desperately wished Paige would just give him a damn list of ingredients. Instead, she'd forced him to mix up dozens of batches until he finally got it right. Since he actually had some time for himself, he abandoned the Skinner stuff in favor of something from his own century.

The laptop was his own little tricked-out piece of home, which had recently been upgraded so it could handle Sniper Ranger multiplayer without locking up every ten minutes. Running a connection into the sealed metal box hadn't been easy, but it was worth it. That and the signal booster he'd rigged for his cell phone turned the freezer into a work space that was slightly better than the first cubicle he'd ever been assigned in the real world. As soon as he logged in to play a few rounds of *Sniper Deathmatch,* an instant message popped onto his screen: CALL JASON.

Jason Sorrenson was a friend, which meant his messages were usually a bit more colorful. Rising to the upper echelons of a prosperous game designing company hadn't turned Jason into a corporate jerk, so whenever he even slightly sounded like one of those jerks, something was wrong. Cole flipped open his cell phone, pushed the button to dial his old work number, and sifted through his mental list of all the reasons Jason could be pissed at him this time.

"Digital Dreamers."

"Why the formalities?" Cole chuckled.

"Who is this?"

"Aw Christ, I haven't been gone that long. Besides, dumb shit, you just IM'd me to call you."

"Pardon me?"

For Jason to be this serious, something was definitely wrong.

"This is Cole."

"I'll patch you through to Mr. Sorrenson."

Then again, another good explanation was that the person who'd answered the phone wasn't the head of Digital Dreamers. As if to make Cole feel even more out of place, the person on the other end of the phone asked, "Cole who?"

"Cole Warnecki. I work there. Jason's expecting me, so just patch me through!"

Having tapped into his mean streak already that night, Cole was able to repeat the trick well enough to get the lines of communication unclogged. There were a few clicks, followed by a ring tone and then another voice that sounded a whole lot like the previous one.

"Jason?" Cole asked cautiously.

"Yeah, Cole. I'm surprised you responded to the message so quickly. I've had a hard time getting in touch with you."

"Maybe your new assistant has been handling all your business. Nobody'd know the difference."

"I know. I've been trying to talk differently to avoid confusion."

"You really need to learn how to throw your weight around more," Cole chuckled. "What's up?"

"How's that downloadable content for *Hammer Strike* coming along?"

"I've put a few more things together. The game's only been released for a couple months."

"People on the forums have been clamoring for it," Jason replied.

Cole let out a haggard sigh that he hoped translated fully through the cellular connection. "People on the forums are always clamoring for something. When we announced there would be downloadable content for *Hammer Strike,* they wanted to know what it was and when it was coming. When we released that first batch of stuff, they all bitched that it wasn't enough. When we announced that the new multiplayer maps were coming, they bitched about the release dates or the price."

After a slight pause, Jason said, "That first batch was just a bunch of different clothes for the characters and new designs for the weapons."

"Yeah, I know."

"The new designs didn't even change weapon performance, and we charged three dollars for each download."

"I know!" When Cole sighed again, it was less for dramatic effect and more to get some actual air into his lungs. "That first batch was rushed. I know it was crap. I made the crap. I check the forums, so I realize everyone else out there thought it was crap too. Still, it sold pretty well."

Jason didn't voice his impatience, but Cole could feel it as if he could see his boss rolling his eyes to examine the underside of the Mariners cap that was always stuck on his head. "We've got some loyal fans. They buy our games because they know they'll be good, and they download the extra content because they think it'll be just as good. I let that first batch slide to test the waters, but it didn't go over well. Not well at all."

As always, Jason was being kind. Cole had worked on *Hammer Strike* since the game was nothing more than an excited conversation over some hastily drawn sketches. Since then both of them had been hip-deep in creating the characters, enemies, fighting mechanics, level design, background rendering, and anything else it took to turn ideas into a functioning video game. When Cole took off for his vacation to Canada, *Hammer Strike* had been almost ready to be pressed onto disks. That was before he knew what a Skinner was or that monsters were real. After *Hammer Strike* had been released, it was all he could do to keep up with the project he'd started.

"Maybe I shouldn't be on this team anymore," Cole grumbled.

"That's what I was calling about."

"What? You really think I should be off the team?"

"No," Jason said. "I could tell you've been having your doubts. Before you left Seattle, you ate and breathed *Hammer*

Strike. You were supposed to come back to fix the remaining bugs, remember?"

"Yeah."

"You never came back and just threw together a patch on your laptop. What the hell happened?"

Rather than try to lie to his longtime friend, Cole simply replied, "I told you what happened."

"First you told me there was family trouble you needed to work through. Then you said you had to stay in Chicago for personal reasons. The only way those excuses could get more generic would be for you to send them to me written in black ballpoint on a brown paper sack."

"I know."

"And I'm not trying to get into your personal business. If you need time away, you can have it. If you want to keep working for Digital Dreamers, you can, but I don't usually allow someone at your level to work remotely. I don't care what kind of a laptop you've got, you need to be here with the rest of the team to hash out new ideas and put together a functioning build for the next *Hammer Strike.* We need something to show at the next Electronic Gaming Conference."

"So there really is gonna be a *Hammer Strike 2?*" Cole asked.

"Not if we keep churning out garbage like that first batch of downloadable content. Come on, Cole. Did you really think a few new color sets for the weapons would make fans happy?"

Suddenly, Cole felt like a kid being scolded by the principal. What made it worse was that he knew he had it coming. "No, Jason," he sighed. "I didn't."

"Have you heard the new slang floating around the review sites?"

"Yeah," Cole laughed. "When this year's NFL game came out, they tried to make people pay a few bucks more to unlock the bonus stadiums and a few different touchdown dances for their characters. Someone called the patch 'Hammer Paint.' To be honest, though, that first content I submitted was more than just different colors."

"There were a few new shapes for the weapon handles too. Whoopie. The point is that whenever anyone online thinks they're getting ripped off by some shoddy crap pushed out by a game company, they call it 'Hammer Paint.' That does us no favors, buddy."

Cole winced at that. It was one thing to catch grief from fans. Hearing it from a friend and his boss was bad. Since both of those people were wrapped up into one normally soft-spoken guy, it was doubly bad.

"What are you working on now?" Jason asked.

"You haven't gotten my latest?"

"No. That's why I called."

Frantically, Cole tapped on his laptop to see when he'd sent his last e-mail to Digital Dreamers. "Aw hell, Jason. I thought I sent it to you a week ago."

"What is it?"

"You'll love this," Cole said as he leaned forward in his chair. "Not only have I worked out some new multiplayer arenas, but I've incorporated shifting day and night patterns that affect which monsters are out at what times. And get this—after they download the patch, if snipers camp in the same old spots for too long, those monsters will sniff them out. Some of the urban areas will have collapsing buildings or new areas attached to the perimeter of the play area. It'll breathe new life into all the popular maps!"

"Okay," Jason said in a favorable tone that probably came along with a nod. "What else have you got?"

Relieved by the reaction he'd gotten, Cole said, "I've designed some new enemies as well."

"More monsters? Do we really need that?"

"These monsters aren't just new character models. They're the old monsters that transform into bigger, stronger, or faster ones. It's a real evolution of the game and it'll only require a few more animations to go from one to the other. Trust me," Cole added. "I've researched them thoroughly and they'll kick our players' asses. I've got everything drawn up and laid out as far as how it all fits together. It sounds like a mess right now, but it'll be so cool."

"Sounds like it." This time Jason seemed genuinely pleased.

"But wait," Cole added in a voice pulled straight from a late night infomercial, "there's more. I wrote up some tweaks for the now infamous painted hammers that will upgrade the stats."

"You mean the different colors and handles won't just be pretty?"

"Nope. I came up with ways to modify the weapons so anyone who bought that first batch of downloadable content will do more damage or get more attacks or even—"

"I get it, Cole. Will it be easy to implement?"

"The changes should just fit right into a patch that—" Knowing Jason was more concerned with the bottom line, Cole cut himself short. "It'll just be another download. I thought we could make it free as a show of goodwill."

"And a way to apologize for the first bunch of crap we put on the market."

"My way didn't sound so brutal, but yeah."

"Send what you've got as soon as you can," Jason said.

"I just did. Hopefully this will keep me employed for a little while longer."

"I wasn't going to fire you, Cole. Well, not yet anyway. Apart from the whole Hammer Paint fiasco, you've been turning in better content than any of our other part-time contractors."

Part-time contractors. A fancy name for the guys who sent in pages of ideas to get a small commission. He might not have clawed too high up the corporate ladder, but the part-timers didn't even have a rung. Now it seemed he was down there with them.

As if picking up on the gloom settling in over Cole's head, Jason asked, "How's Paige?"

"What was that?"

"Paige. You mentioned her in a few of your other e-mails a while ago. It sounded like she might be something more than just a friend, but you hadn't quite . . . you know . . . sealed the deal."

Jason was never good at guy talk. He knew the basics, but couldn't commit enough to the subtle banalities to be truly fluent in the language.

"She's been kicking my ass," Cole grumbled.

"I hear you, man. Women."

"I'm going to stop you before you try to call me bro."

"That's probably for the best." Jason shifted enough to make his chair squeak and then said, "The e-mail just arrived. It looks like some good stuff. Your old job is waiting for you whenever you decide to come back to Seattle, but don't take advantage of our friendship. Another Hammer Paint fiasco will sink our download division for good."

"Read through everything I sent you. If you still want to scold me after that, I'll bend over and take it like a good cell mate."

Chapter 3

Kansas City University of Medicine
Kansas City, Missouri

Lisa Wilson knew better than to walk by herself at night. Not only had her parents drummed that into her head ever since she was young enough to have strangers offer her candy, but she had enough common sense to avoid certain spots after the streetlights came on.

She'd enrolled in the University of Medicine because it was located in a section of town she knew well and, thanks to a few student loans and a partial scholarship, the tuition was within her range. The little apartment she shared with a roommate was a short walk from the university on Highland Avenue, and Lisa knew how to get there without straying into any danger zones.

There were always some potheads hanging out near the buildings between school and home, but they were more hungry than harmful. A few bums shuffled across the street, and Lisa smiled at the dirty, familiar faces. That smile faded a bit when she pointed it at a man slouched against a light pole bordering the parking lot where she kept her red Nissan. The man sat with his skinny legs bent and his lanky arms resting upon his knees. His back was against the pole and the color of his skin made it look as if he'd spent a lot of time under a rock. Lisa politely turned away from him and kept walking.

"Hey," the man shouted in a guttural English accent. "Got time for a chat?"

Rolling her eyes, she shook her head and kept moving. Between the Jehovah Witnesses, Mormons, and countless other religious salesmen roaming the apartment complexes near the university, she'd gotten lots of practice in the art of courteous apathy.

"Hey!"

The sound cut through the air like a shovel that had been swung at the back of her head. It stopped her in her tracks and got her heart racing within her chest. She turned to see what the man was doing and found him standing upright with his back to the light pole, watching her silently. His gleaming eyes looked vaguely attractive, but were framed by a sunken face and a leering smile.

Suddenly, Lisa was very aware of what she was wearing. It was hot and humid, but perhaps the denim shorts she'd chosen were too short. Maybe she'd been stupid to make the walk to her apartment wearing the Kansas City Chiefs shirt that barely made it down to her waist. If she moved in the slightest, her bare belly could be seen, along with the little shamrock tattoo she'd gotten over the last spring break. Nervously fidgeting with her short, light brown hair, she almost ran away. Then she spotted a few of her friends gathered around a white pickup in the nearby parking lot. One of them was a big sports medicine major named Ryan. The other guy was Ryan's roommate, and he was with a tattooed girl who carried pepper spray in her purse.

"Come here, girlie," the skinny man by the light pole said. "I got somethin' for ya."

She might have been nervous, but she wasn't going to be abused by some freak on the street. As much as she wanted to give the guy a swift kick, she knew better than to go near him. Instead, she dismissed him with a backward wave and hurried toward her apartment building. "Whatever!"

"What's the matter, dude? Couldn't find any hookers to yell at?"

Lisa glanced over her shoulder to find Ryan strutting toward the English accent freak in typical macho fashion:

chest puffed and arms out. She did not usually find that sort of thing appealing, but it was more than welcome now.

"You wanna yell at someone?" Ryan asked. "How about you yell at me?"

Lisa turned around to ask Ryan to walk her to her place. The freak looked even bigger and bulkier now that he was standing up straight. He reached out to grab Ryan's arm, then pulled it from its socket with a loud crunch. Ryan let out a high-pitched scream, which was immediately washed away by a wail from the freak that seemed like a primal mockery of the younger man's pain.

The man was even larger than he'd been a second ago, and his clothes were suddenly consumed by a coat of black fur that spewed from his skin. His cheeks were still sunken, but he'd grown a long snout and pointed ears that were flattened in a way far more menacing than Ryan's puffed chest. The creature that had once been the freakish man opened its mouth and let out a rasping gurgle that almost matched the sound Ryan made after his throat was torn open.

The fatal motion had been so quick that Lisa barely saw it. The creature pulled Ryan closer and then swiped its claws under his chin to send a bloody spray through the air. Once that was done, the only thing left for Ryan to do was bleed. All the while, the creature hacked as if gagging on his own drool.

"Your turn . . . little lady."

It leaned forward to step toward her, stretching both arms out before dropping onto all fours. By the time it started running at her, the thing had shifted into a hulking animal with the frame of a wolf but the mass of a bear.

A blanket of cold fear dropped onto Lisa's shoulders. One of the guys in the parking lot was yelling something but seemed unable to do much else. The girl with the tattoos was fumbling with her cell phone, so Lisa turned and ran.

Highland Avenue felt crooked beneath her feet. Her breath came in quick, frantic gulps. Her ears filled with the churning of the air and the pounding of her heart. When she got to her apartment building, she stuck her hand in her pocket to fish out her key.

If she made it just a little farther, the thick metal of her front door might hold the thing back until the cops could get there. Surely, her friend in the parking lot was calling for help.

The footsteps padding against the concrete behind her seemed light and heavy at the same time, brushing and stomping the ground in a rhythm that blended almost seamlessly with the panicked chorus inside her own body. Little cries fluttered at the top of her windpipe. A strained wheeze rattled within her chest as something pounded against her back.

Then Lisa was shoved face first to the sidewalk as though she hadn't even been moving. When she tried to crawl away, all she could do was scrape her fingers against the cracked cement and kick one leg against the ground. Her other leg had crumpled beneath her, snapping in three places. Before she could wrap her mind around that, bony spikes stabbed through her shoulder.

The werewolf picked Lisa up as gently as his current form would allow and carried her away so only her heels brushed against the cement. Cars sped toward him, but the creature warned them away by curling his lips up to bare the teeth that were halfway sunken into Lisa's shoulder. Driving his fangs in deeper and holding her with them, he crouched down and launched himself into the air. Another couple of jumps put a few blocks between himself and Ryan's bloody remains. The screams were quickly left behind in the short time it took for the creature to find a nice quiet spot at the easternmost end of North Terrace Park.

Dragging Lisa behind a row of trees, he panted anxiously. His breaths churned back and forth like hot wind passing in and out of an old set of bellows. He kept his head low and twitched at every little sound. Then the beast slowly opened his jaws to let her slide off its teeth.

Lisa Wilson was brought back from the edge of unconsciousness when she fell on top of her broken leg. Choking back the agony that came when she moved her arms, she sobbed while trying to pull herself to safety. North Terrace

Park was thicker where it bunched up around North Chestnut Trafficway, but there were usually people hanging out in the thinner section bordering Cliff Drive and Gladstone Boulevard. The trees were thick there as well, providing plenty of natural cover from the few cars and trucks that ambled through the area. But if she could scream, she would be heard by someone. *Anyone.*

Only a few feet away, the beast dug into the wet soil. Its tongue lolled out the side of its mouth and its paws tore at the earth in a frenzied blur.

In a short, agonizing chain of motions, Lisa turned away from the creature and filled her lungs. Before she could expel the breath she'd collected, however, it snapped its head down to aim a pair of perfect, multifaceted eyes at her. The teeth it bared were coated in slick layers of her blood. Thick rivers of saliva flowed from its gums.

The warning snarl lessened and its gaze lowered to the cracked bones protruding from her ravaged shoulder. When a sudden, burning stab of pain shot through Lisa's upper body, the creature cocked its head ever so slightly. After that, it clawed at the ground a few more times to uncover a pit-sized hole that had been hastily covered with chunks of earth.

Just as Lisa was about to pass out, her wounded shoulder was invaded by what felt like two rows of crooked steak knives. Fangs tore through her tender, shredded flesh and sank into the splintered bones below so the beast could lift her from the ground and toss her into the hole with a casual flick of its head.

Lisa was dropped into a pit that reeked of decay and feces, and was shoved inside until the earth pressed against her cheek. At first she thought the shape beneath her was a log. When the log shifted and let out a shuddering breath, she realized her mistake.

She heard the rustling of a thick coat and felt a claw scrape against her face. Although the thick bony finger didn't move, the claw twisted to curl delicately along her chin. Too weak to protest, she allowed her head to be moved again, and whimpered at the pain sent through her torso, to die in her numbed legs.

The creature looked down at her. As it drew closer, the black fur covering its face was sucked back into its pores to reveal distorted human features. A white patch sprouted from a deep scar that ran along the bridge of his nose and straight down to his left cheek. "Be quiet now," he said. The words came quickly and were sharpened by a leering cockney accent. "I can make it hurt worse, you know."

"Please don't," Lisa gasped. "Whatever you want to . . . just . . . please don't."

"Your mates seemed to like you. If they got the salt to come this far, maybe you'll have some more comp'ny down there."

Cars raced along a nearby street. Sirens drifted through the air like pets that started barking after a burglar had already cleaned out the house. The beast lifted his scarred nose to the fragrant air, pulled it in and mused, "Maybe they'll find you. Maybe they won't. It don't matter now, luv. If I was you, I'd get comfy down there with your new friends. Always nice to have an ear to bend, eh?"

As he began to cover the pit's opening with chunks of solid earth, he sighed and grumbled, "Good an' quiet in there. I envy you, luv. Damn humans can't go anywhere or do anything without makin' noise. As for the lights, there's no escaping them."

"Please stop," Lisa sobbed. "I want to . . . go home. I won't tell."

Something twitched inside Lisa's body. It writhed, flailed, wrapped around her innards and squeezed a pained grunt out of her.

As dirt was heaped over the pit's opening to blot out the distant sirens, different sounds skittered into her ears. One of the other bodies stuffed into that hole grunted a few unintelligible syllables. Muscles tore loose and became wet mulch, only to be stuck together again. Bones strained to the breaking point, held, and then snapped within their quivering, tortured shells.

Sickness poured in from where she'd been bitten and

seeped into her bones, tugging at the very frame of her body to shape her into something else.

One of the others choked on a pained cry.

When Lisa Wilson realized she was too broken to stick her hand out through the dirt wall piled in front of her, she cried too.

Chapter 5

Chicago

It was well past two in the morning, but there were plenty of night owls riding the Eisenhower Expressway. Paige was behind the wheel of the Cav and he sat beside her. With the amount of fidgeting he'd been doing, he probably could have jogged across town in less time than it took to drive.

"What's that smell?" he asked.

Paige took a quick sniff, which turned into a grimace. "About four weeks' worth of greasy little hamburgers."

"Not that."

"Then those fried tacos you insist on buying by the dozen."

"Not those either. It smells like vinegar and . . . sweat?"

Chuckling while weaving between a few slow cars with Iowa plates, she said, "That brings us back to those tacos."

Cole unbuckled his seat belt so he could twist all the way around and reach into the backseat. "No, seriously! It's stronger back here." After digging through all the garbage, newspapers, and supply kits in back, he found a cheap black plastic trash bag that gave off the offending odor in waves. "Good Lord, Paige, what's in this bag?"

"Some critter I scraped off the road. Since you like those fried tacos so much, I thought you might be able to make your own if you just had the right meat."

"Leave those tacos alone! You never even tried any! This isn't really . . . ?"

"No, it's nothing like that. Remember the Mongrel that tracked you down when you first got here?"

"Jackie, the cat lady. I remember her."

Looking over to him, Paige asked, "What's with the sloppy grin? Do you already know where I'm going with this?"

"No, I'm just remembering what she looked like under all that fur. I mean, when she was visible."

Paige shook her head and let her eyes settle back onto the expressway. "Yeah, well you remember how she could bend light or something to turn almost invisible?"

Cole nodded. "She had some sort of grease or oil in her fur. That stuff came in real useful once we got some of it for ourselves. You still have that crap? Good Lord, it's been months since you wiped that stuff up!"

"This isn't the exact same stuff. I sent some of it to a friend of mine and he was able to make more. Apparently, it's not too hard to reproduce. The only thing is, the artificial stuff doesn't last very long unless it's soaked into something. Once it gets on your skin or out in the open air, it evaporates real quick."

"When did you do all this?" Cole asked.

"While you were typing and hunched over that laptop for the last couple of weeks."

He plopped back into his seat and placed the bag on the floor between his feet. "So what's in here?"

"A little something that should help me get inside the Blood Parlor to back you up. I've been told the security there is pretty tight."

"By the way, are you going to tell me what a Blood Parlor is?"

"It's a place where the Nymar can feed on humans so it's not out in the open."

"And . . . we encourage this?"

"Not exactly, but we can't stop it." Veering off to the exit that led to the Kennedy Expressway, Paige said, "Nymar like to talk about being these big vampire kingpins, but they don't run much of anything, apart from their mouths. There's a lot of them and they can be dangerous, so Skinners have been keeping them in check. Part of that is making a few deals that work out for the greater good. One of those deals is us allowing them to feed on willing participants and make a living doing it. Well, I guess you could call it an un-living."

Paige laughed at her own joke, but cut it off once she saw Cole dryly looking back at her.

"Stephanie and Ace run a good chunk of these places," she continued. "It's basically a prostitution ring with teeth."

"What kind of people pay to get bitten?"

"Normal folks pay to have a lot kinkier things done to them. You should know that. Aren't you the one who spends so much time on the Internet?"

Without a good answer to that, Cole just shrugged.

"Blood Parlors started off as fancy names for blocks of hotel rooms that Nymar rented so their paying customers could have some privacy," Paige continued. "The hotel rooms were traded up for suites and the suites for blocks of rooms at the fancier places downtown. A month or so ago Ace and Stephanie bought the upper floor of a building on North Rush Street."

"Lots of good bars up there." When he saw Paige glance over at him, Cole said, "What? I get out every now and then."

"You're right about the bars," she said. "There are also some clubs and plenty of other places to attract the sort of creeps who might want to pay to get bitten on the neck by sluts wearing black lace and garter belts."

"That does sound kind of intriguing."

"There's an ATM along the way. I'm sure Steph would offer a nice discount so you could lay back, close your eyes, and let some parasite tear into your arteries. Who knows? A friend of one of the Nymar we've had to put down might be the one drinking from you. I'm sure they'll pull out before you run dry."

"All right. Scratch that idea. How many Blood Parlors are there?"

"This is the only one I know about in this part of town, but there's got to be more. It's been getting a whole lot of rave reviews."

"Nymar brothels get reviewed?"

"Once again, thank you, Internet," she grumbled. "That reminds me, since you're so big into computers, I want you to take over our local research. It involves a lot of trolling through fetish websites and those kinky 'meet someone local for a quickie' matchmaking services. Lots of willing food sources on those sites."

"Yowza."

"Yeah," Paige grunted. "Anyway, I've been wanting to visit this new Blood Parlor for a while, but I've been busy training my backup. Between setting up shop out in the open like that and sending her little pigtail girls nosing around our part of town, Ace and Stephanie are getting cocky, and I don't like it. Plus, we need to introduce ourselves to any new arrivals. Everyone needs to be reminded of why it's a good idea to work with us rather than against us."

Paige parked the Cavalier on Superior Street not far from where it intersected with Rush. Some of the bars had closed, but there were still plenty of pedestrians milling from one spot to another. Although Cole got a few puzzled glances when he walked toward the corner with a curved spear strapped to his back by a harness that was slung over one shoulder and hooked to the back of his belt, the reaction wasn't quite as big as he'd been expecting.

"You really think I should wear this in plain sight?" he asked.

"Yep. We're flying the flag here, so wear that harness so it can be seen. If any cops ever ask you about it, just say it's firewood or a prop for something. Nymar will know what it is, and to everyone else you're just some weirdo carrying a big stick."

"Can I at least bring the .44?"

Paige shook her head before he'd finished the question. "Tight security, remember? The last thing we need is to set off a bunch of metal detectors."

"So I'll walk in to threaten a bunch of Nymar with a stick. Could be worse," Cole said as he looked Paige up and down. "I could be dressed for leather night at the gym."

She stopped and looked down at herself. She wore a black leather top that was a cross between a corset and a camisole: Too durable to be lingerie and too intimate to be body armor. It didn't even come close to matching the gray sweatpants that were cinched tightly around her waist and ankles by elastic bands. "The sweats are just what I'm wearing to get in. Once I'm inside, I want to blend in."

"Good luck with that."

Before they got to the corner of Superior and Rush, Paige stopped and pushed Cole against the flat brick section of a parking garage with a deli on the bottom floor. Before he could get a word out, he felt her lips press against his. It wasn't the most original ruse, but he topped it off by placing his hands on her rounded hips. A small group of club hoppers walked past them without taking notice of the spear scraping against the cement wall of the building.

When she came up for air, Paige whispered, "That building on the corner is the Blood Parlor."

Now, Cole could see a slick-looking man in front of the parlor looking in his direction. Since Cole's back was to a wall and both he and Paige were obviously preoccupied, the man turned and walked back inside.

"You go in through the front," Paige said. "Ask for Ace or Stephanie and flash that weapon. One of those should catch a Nymar's attention. While you lay down the law about those three that were on the wrong side of town, I'll sneak around back."

"By yourself?"

"Some high-tech security would be the perfect test for this invisibility gunk. I'll get a look around to see what's in this place and then jump in if you need help."

"*If* I need help?" Cole asked.

She patted his arm and nodded confidently. "You can handle yourself."

"This may sound stupid, but that place looks like it might be closing. Will I be able to get in through the front door?"

"Brothels don't keep bankers' hours," Paige replied while giving his cheek a gentle tap. Her fleeting smile displayed an equal mix of affection and pride. That last part caught him by surprise.

Slipping away from him, Paige jogged into the alley that led from Superior Street to cut between the Blood Parlor and the parking garage. Now that he took a closer look, Cole was stricken by the contrast between those two buildings. While the closest one was a gray, multilevel block, the Blood Parlor was a mix of urban elegance and medieval architecture. Dark brick flowed up into a steeply angled roof and several pointed gables. Sharp rectangular windows looked down over an entrance that looked more like an old sandstone cottage. To complete the ornate mix, several of the lower windows had neon beer signs hanging in them, while one of the upper panes was covered by the stencil of a rose dripping what was probably supposed to be blood onto the sill.

Once she was in the shadows of the alley, Paige opened the garbage bag that Cole had found in the car a few minutes ago. She pulled out a hooded sweatshirt that matched her sweatpants. At least, it probably matched the pants before it had been covered in a dark, greasy substance. "Anyone out there?" she whispered.

Since there were only a few people wandering along the street, and none of them were taking any interest in him, Cole replied, "Nope."

Paige stuck her hands into the hoodie and pulled it inside out. When she slipped it on over her head, it looked as if a torrent of water flowed from nowhere to wash over her entire torso. Even though Cole had seen the stuff put to use by the shapeshifter who'd used it to bend light around herself, it was even more impressive to see Paige recreate the trick. The stuff shimmered for a few seconds before rendering her all but invisible, leaving a pair of gray sweatpants below a blank spot with a head above it.

"Watch the upper windows," she said.

Cole nodded, but couldn't help watching her as she pulled the hood up and lowered her head so everything from her waist up was now a mirage. With the speed and agility of someone used to changing in dirty sheds at public pools, she whipped her sweats down, flipped them inside out, and hopped back into them. Seconds later her legs, along with a good portion of her feet, began to fade. The effect wasn't perfect, but if he hadn't known she was there, he could easily have mistaken Paige for a ripple of heat coming off the sidewalk.

Before he became completely entranced by watching the blur in the alley, Cole did what he was supposed to do and checked the upper windows. Most of them were covered by bars on the outside and frilly curtains on the inside. A flickering light from within the place cast just enough light to project a few shadow figures, but none of them stayed still long enough to be of any concern.

An older man wearing an expensive suit pushed open the door to the Blood Parlor and stepped outside. His arm was draped around a girl dressed in a dark red top with thin straps and tight jeans that rode dangerously low on her hips. The scars on Cole's hands had started itching like crazy since they'd gotten within sight of the Blood Parlor, so he couldn't rely on that as his only warning system. Since the woman wasn't wearing pigtails, and neither one of them had any black markings on display, he let them pass.

Still nobody at the upper windows.

About halfway down the alley, near an alcove that must have been one of the parlor's side doors, pinpoint laser beams emanated from a security device somewhere in the alcove. The lasers looked as if they'd been shot through dirty water, and when they hit the substance in Paige's clothes, formed a dim bubble around her. No alarm sounded and nobody rushed out to check on the alley, so none of those beams registered as having been broken.

He watched those lights for a second and then glanced around to make sure nobody else had noticed them. A car had pulled up to the curb in front of the parlor, thumping a bass line from a cheap set of speakers, so most of the attention inside the building was probably focused upon it.

Once Paige was through, the flickering stopped. There was a creak followed by the brief glow of interior light spilling into the alley before she stepped inside and shut the door behind her.

"Well," he muttered, "time to fly the flag."

Chapter 6

The entrance to the Blood Parlor was just what anyone would expect after looking at the outside of the place. There was a bar covered in coasters representing different brands of beer, foreign and domestic. A couple dart boards hung on the far wall, music from some college band Cole had never heard of drifted from a large jukebox, and a couple televisions hung from brackets on either side of the room. He wasn't allowed to take more than two steps inside before he was blocked by the slick guy he'd spotted earlier. Up close, Slick was a little taller and a lot beefier than Cole had expected.

Extending one arm to put his hand flat against Cole's chest, Slick said, "If you're with those jackasses, you might as well go home with them right now."

The man had a dark, East Indian complexion and spoke with a cultured British accent. His straight black hair was primped to the far edge of masculinity without quite crossing over to the fairer side, and hung just over his ears. When Cole tried to push forward another step, he didn't even move the man a fraction of an inch.

The jackasses in question were being herded from a staircase at the back of the room to the front door. A bunch of young guys and even younger girls were escorted outside by bouncers in suits that looked to be cheap knockoffs of Slick's. After a whole lot of grunting and swearing, the jackasses piled into the car with the thumping bass and rolled down Rush Street.

"I'm not with them," Cole said. "I'm here to see Stephanie."

"No one here by that name. Come to think of it, we're closing."

"Closing?"

"Yeah," Slick said. "So hit the bricks."

Cole turned at the shoulders as he scoped the inside of the bar to make sure the doorman or one of the others could see the flag that was being flown.

The doorman with the borderline hair was on his game. "What's on your back?"

"Ask Stephanie. She should know all about it."

"Let me see your hands."

Although Cole took half a step back, he wasn't retreating. He just wanted some extra room in case things got interesting. He held both palms up and out so the doorman could have a look.

When Slick saw the scars on his palms, he took a full step back. "Where's the other one?" he asked.

"Who should I say is asking?"

Just then, descending the back stairs as if she'd been waiting for the perfect moment to make her entrance, Stephanie announced, "His name's Astin. Forgive him if he's being rude, but he's new in town."

Stephanie wore a black dress with red polka dots that cut straight across the top of her breasts and was held up by a single strap that looped around her neck. The strap was the same red as the polka dots, which was the same color as the ribbon that went around the middle of the dress and the narrow strip of lace along the hem. Her shoes were shiny, black, high-heeled numbers that brought her up to within an inch or two of Cole's height. She walked through the bar with her chin held high and her dark red hair pulled into ponytails that dangled on either side of her head. She eased her shoulders back as if to display her chest every bit as much as the thick black markings that snaked up along her neck. Thinner black tendrils ran through her arms, and only a few reached down to one ankle.

"Hello, Cole," Stephanie said as she grinned and extended an arm to him. "Last time I saw you, you were swinging a piece of wood at me. Ahh," she purred as she glanced over his shoulder. "I see you've still got wood. Must be my new heels."

Cole glanced down at the hand she offered and said, "If you're waiting for me to kiss that, you're going to be standing there a long time."

"Maybe you can kiss something else," Stephanie snapped as she turned on the balls of her feet and then clacked across the hardwood floor. "I suppose you came here to see my Blood Parlor?"

"That and to have a word with you." When he tried to follow her to the stairs, he was stopped once more by Astin's thickly muscled yet tendril-free arm. "Do you know what she is, Astin?"

"She's the one that pays my salary," the doorman replied.

Hanging onto the railing of the staircase, Stephanie turned to show thin, curved fangs extending from her upper gum line just enough to scrape against her bottom lip. "I'm also the one that hands out freebies to my employees when they do good. You did real good, Astin. Let the nice Skinner through."

Astin lowered his arm and took a step back. Judging by the way he ordered the others in the bar around with a few clipped words and some hasty pointing, he was more than just a doorman. Cole fell into step behind Stephanie and swore he could feel more eyes upon him than there were faces in the room.

The farther up the stairs she got, the bouncier Steph's movements became. "I didn't think you'd ever get here. We were all ready for you and that little partner of yours to show up on opening day and you never did. Don't tell me you two are losing touch with this town."

"Not at all. We just thought we'd give you a chance to get things rolling before we paid a visit."

"That's cute. If you or that little bitch—"

"Watch your mouth," Cole snapped in the most convincing growl he'd done all night. "She's my partner."

Stephanie arrived at the top of the stairs, kept her fingertips on the banister, and did a slow turn to clear a path while coming around to face him. "Sorry," she said with an unconvincing pout. "Maybe I'm just jealous that she gets to spend so much time with you."

Cole stepped away from the stairs and positioned himself so his back was to a wall. "Yeah. I'm sure that's it."

At first the upper floor seemed bigger than the one downstairs. That was mostly because the lower level was sectioned off into the bar and other rooms used for storage or office space. The top of the stairs opened to a room that was about the size of the bar and stretched from one side of the building to the other. Several windows were built into the walls of what looked like a newer addition that extended the main room out over the sidewalk. A hallway stretched all the way down the length of the second floor, with doors to private rooms on either side. At the far end of the hall was what looked like another, narrower staircase.

Stephanie strutted through the room as if she expected an entourage to appear and kiss her feet. The burgundy carpeting was thick enough to silence every step. Two sofas and several chairs were set up at the front of the room, each padded in colors that were only slightly different from the carpet. Lace curtains hung over the windows and candles were set upon little tables that also held magazines and several binders.

"This is the waiting room," she said as she bent down to rub her hand along the cushion of the nearest sofa. A well-dressed man in his late forties sat there watching her as if silently praying her hand would come his way. "Our customers make their selections, settle their bills, and get all revved up for their sessions out here. It's all very civil."

"Looks that way so far."

Stephanie answered the waiting guy's prayers by lowering herself onto his lap. Kicking out one leg and smiling without showing any fang, she said, "Doesn't this whole place just make you want to curl up with someone?"

"Oh yeah, the decor is great. It does feel like it's missing something, though." Cole snapped his fingers and added, "Maybe a big pipe organ and some dude in a cape hanging from the ceiling! You're not going to make this poor guy dress in some frilly shirt before he gets fed upon, are you?"

Stephanie hopped off her living prop's lap and walked over to Cole. The man on the couch made the best of her sudden departure by gluing his eyes to her naked shoulders. When she got close enough, Stephanie took hold of Cole's wrist and tried dragging him down the hall. Since she was obviously used to men following her like puppies, he held his ground.

Letting go as if Cole's arm had turned into a decaying tentacle, she lowered her voice to a hissing whisper that could barely be heard over the soft piano music piped in through hidden speakers. "Look, this is a business. You want a tour? Fine. You want to talk? I guess that's fine too. Just don't come in here and try to drive off my customers."

"You gotta admit," Cole replied in a voice just as low as hers, "you do seem to be laying it on kinda thick in here."

"Well, we can either hunt the way we're supposed to hunt or play it up a bit to have them come to us. There are Nymar clubs in plenty of other places that do the same thing. Some are bondage dungeons, some are spas, some give customers a private booth where they can get bitten and feel someone drink from them. Since you came all the way down here to single us out, maybe you should try it for yourself." With a smile that showed the lower quarter of her feeding fangs, she added, "I'd do you for free."

"Why don't we start with a tour?"

She wrapped her arm around his and led him down the hall. "Do you really think you need that stick?"

"Yes."

"Then will you at least cut the smartass comments when we're around my customers?"

"I suppose that's fair."

"These," Stephanie announced in a normal tone of voice, "are the rooms where our customers have their experience." The first three doors had red ribbons tied around the handles, so she passed them up. Upon reaching a door with a bare handle, she opened it and stepped inside. "As you can see, there's nothing out of the ordinary."

For the most part, she was right. It was a fairly plain bedroom that had been decorated as though large doses of lace and velvet were legal requirements to appease the Cook County fire inspectors. A full-sized bed in the middle of the room was covered with velvet blankets. A small table, chair, and nightstand were all trimmed in lace. The air, which smelled like incense mingling with the subtle remnants of pot smoke, made Cole think back to his college days.

The moment Stephanie sat upon the edge of the bed, he shut the door and scooped up a chair to wedge under the handle.

"Big mistake, bruiser," she said. "There's a camera in every room and any one of us could punch through that door."

"And scare away the customers?"

As if to prove him right, there was a quick series of taps on the door instead of a Nymar fist exploding through it. He grinned at Stephanie, who shot him a tight-lipped scowl in return.

"There a problem?" someone asked from the hallway.

Stephanie began to speak, but cut herself off when she saw Cole reach over his shoulder to pull his spear halfway from its harness. Locking eyes with him, she said, "I'm fine. Just go back to the security room."

With every inch of the second level floor covered in such thick carpeting, it was impossible for Cole to hear if the people in the hall walked away or not. He looked up and couldn't find the camera, but did pick out a few cheap little sculptures along the edge of the ceiling that could easily hide an eye in the sky.

"The last time we met, I probably didn't make a very good impression," he said.

She smirked and replied, "You tried to hit me with a trash can lid and then pushed me into the sunlight. Hah. And you're the one calling me cliché?"

"What was your girl doing in our part of town?"

"My who was where?"

Cole narrowed his eyes and stepped closer to the bed. "You know goddamn well what I'm talking about. All of your girls are marked with pigtails tied back with the little cat bands. One of them, some asshole with a mullet, and a guy named Sid were caught sucking businessmen in an alley."

"Did they tell you who they worked for?"

"The one with the mullet did some talking, especially after I cracked his skull against the side of my car."

"Yeah," Stephanie said as she stood up and took the single step required to put her within a foot of Cole, "but did they tell you they worked for *me*?"

When she was that close, he could smell the fruity scent of whatever she used in her hair. He could see the subtle texture of the tendrils that slowly writhed beneath her skin, and felt the heat emanating from her body. Apparently, that stuff about vampires being cold was as big a myth as the one about them burning up in the daylight.

Her eyes looked brown or possibly dark green from a distance. From where she stood now, Cole thought they had a slight purple hue to them. Those eyes silently assured him that they could pick up any lie he tried to float past her. Of course, there was one surefire way to test that theory.

"Yeah," he lied. "Mullet boy brought your name up once or twice."

Without skipping a beat, Stephanie raised her eyebrows and shrugged her shoulders. "I guess you got me. Seems like Paige really has whipped you into shape. Tell me something. Have you fucked her yet?"

"There's the Stephanie I remember."

"You haven't, have you? I can feel that much just like I can feel, well, this much."

Before Cole could do anything about it, Stephanie slipped her hand between his legs. She squeezed a bit too hard, as if to remind him who was in control, but eased up quickly and started rubbing him back and forth. "You've been with her all this time and no action? What's the matter? Oooh, I can tell it's nothing to do with your plumbing. Must be her. Is she freezing you out?"

Cole shook his head, intending on saying something but not quite getting there.

"I may have been a little rough on you when we first met, but you've shaped up since then." Placing her hands upon his arms, she squeezed them and smiled. "You've been working out."

Trying to distract her as well as himself, he asked, "Do your customers even know what you are?"

"I doubt it."

"What about those?" he asked while tapping the thickest black line on the side of her neck. "Don't they notice anything strange about those? I mean, sometimes they move."

"They move a lot of the times, but we keep the normals too busy to notice. We tell them they're tattoos, and that's good enough. I told one of my customers something of the whole story when he put some of the pieces together about what's actually going on. You know what he said? He said it was weird. Can you believe that? A guy who paid me to make him bleed and lick the wounds actually called me weird!"

Pulling the strap of her dress over her head, Stephanie wriggled just enough for the garment to slide off her body. A few more well-practiced shimmies and the dress was bunched around her high heels. "I mean, see for yourself. Do I look so weird to you?"

Cole knew he shouldn't look at her. Stephanie might not have been his favorite person if she was human, and being a Nymar only cranked her attitude up to unbearable degrees. She knew just how to roll her eyes or curl her lip in a way that made him want to wrap his hands around her neck and squeeze. Even so, with her standing naked in front of him, he had to remind himself over and over again why he shouldn't like her.

She was a Nymar.

She admitted to sending more Nymar to scout a few blocks from where he and Paige called home.

She'd threatened their lives more than once.

She . . . looked damn good wearing nothing but black heels and a grin. The markings beneath her skin didn't cover her entire body, but radiated from the middle of her chest. Spots along her stomach and waist were perfectly smooth and clean, while sections of her neck, arms, and thighs were marked in a way that resembled standard black tribal tattooing. As he examined her, he could see the tendrils writhing slowly inside of her. With his eyes already below her waist, he couldn't help but notice the way she'd trimmed her pubic hair into a design that resembled more tendrils running between her legs. That was a little unsettling, but she made it work.

"I'm not the same woman I was a few months ago," she purred. "I was angry and things were so bad with all the trouble that was going on. But you stopped that."

"Paige and I stopped it."

"Right. You stopped it and I'm so grateful. Your partner just wants to fight. If she has her way, there won't be any progress."

"Progress?" Cole scoffed.

"Look around you, sweetie. This place ain't some alley. This is a real business. Do you know how much money we pull in every week?"

"No, but I bet you're going to tell me."

"Or . . . " she said as she eased her hand up along Cole's stomach and chest, "you could find out for yourself."

"Why would you want to give me such an opportunity?"

"Because the two of us could make things in this town run smoothly. I could keep the Nymar in line and you could—"

"I could be the one to take out anyone who you don't like," he cut in.

"You could take out the troublemakers. Isn't that what Skinners do already?"

Pushing her hand away, Cole said, "You're not supposed to come down to Cicero. You were warned, and I suppose you needed to see if Paige and I were really paying attention. We are, and if anyone wanders where they're not supposed to go, we'll shut down all your places. Starting with this one."

Stephanie put on a hurt expression as she tugged at Cole's belt. Somehow, she managed to get it open in a matter of seconds. "There are other fringe benefits," she said as she took his hand and guided it to the front of her body. "And the first one's free."

Cole tried to pull his hand back, but lost the will to struggle when he felt just how soft Stephanie's body was. Her breast was firm and her nipple rigid with anticipation. Even the Nymar markings added a smooth, ridged texture to her flesh. Soon, her leg was rubbing against his and he could feel the warmth between her thighs through his jeans.

He knew damn well what she was doing, and thanks to some of his more recent sparring sessions, wasn't so eager to partake. "Get away from me, Steph."

"You don't mean that, sweet stuff."

"Yeah," Cole snapped as he shoved her away. "I do."

The slightest hint of confusion drifted across her face as she grabbed his waist. She struggled with him as if she'd forgotten she wasn't wearing a stitch of clothing, holding on using the strength that set her well above human norms.

Breaking her hold with more force than he would have normally used for any woman, Cole took Stephanie by the wrist and tried to shove her aside. She was Nymar and he knew that well enough, but it still went against his grain to treat a naked girl like that. Even with his clear thinking and extra effort, he was only able to move her a foot or so in the other direction.

Rather than admire the way the black tendrils framed her upper and lower assets, Cole looked at her mouth. Like any Nymar being threatened, the fangs were starting to show. Instead of just the two upper sets, however, the lower ones were also making an appearance. Those thicker bottom fangs were only used when they needed to dig in deep and keep their prey from getting away during feeding. Showing them meant Stephanie was gearing up for a fight.

Cole reached over his shoulder and removed the spear from its harness. "Stay the hell away from Cicero," he snarled. "And keep your whores in their kennel."

She crouched down and scooped up her dress. Pressing the clothing against her chest, she looked up at one of those sculptures along the upper corner of the wall and said, "Are you going to keep watching this bullshit, Ace, or is someone gonna kill this jackoff?"

Chapter 7

As Cole kicked the chair away from the door, he wondered if he might have pushed things just a bit too far. The simple truth of the matter was that Stephanie had a knack for pissing him off. All she thought she had to do was strip and whisper a few things to get her way. What made him even madder was that the simple, age-old tactic had almost worked.

When he pulled open the door, Cole saw two Nymar racing toward him. One wore a black suit and the other looked more like a bouncer from the bar downstairs. He gripped his spear in both hands, brought the weapon across his face to protect himself, and then snapped it forward to crack it against the chin of the Nymar in the suit. That one twisted around and hissed loudly as he bounced off the wall. The bouncer ducked down and sent a quick uppercut into Cole's stomach. Fortunately, Stephanie had been right about one thing: he had indeed been working out.

The punch hurt, but mostly just bounced off tensed muscle. He still had his spear held high, so he brought it around to swat the Nymar's hand away to create an opening just big enough for him to bring his right leg up into a simple straight kick. His foot pounded against the bouncer's hip and sent the guy staggering back a few steps.

More footsteps pounded up the stairs from the bar. A second later Astin was in the waiting room and looking for something to damage. He didn't have to look far before spotting the commotion in the hallway.

"Astin!" someone barked from the opposite end of the hall.

Astin, Cole, and both of the other Nymar looked toward the sound of that voice to find a wiry guy with a partially shaved head strutting toward the fight. The guy appeared to be somewhere in his early twenties and wore a dark gray suit that looked as if it had been tailored to fit a teenage girl. His black markings stretched all the way up from his neck to his cheek, but didn't quite make it to the symbol shaved into the left side of his scalp. It was a diamond. The last time Cole had seen Ace, the symbol had been a club.

"No need for things to get worse," the wiry Nymar said. "You'll upset our clients."

Astin understood exactly what he'd been told and took his hand away from whatever was holstered under his arm.

Stephanie didn't hit the brakes so easily. In fact, she exploded from the room, still barely covering herself with her dress as she shrieked, "Nobody treats me like that, Ace! If someone doesn't shred this Skinner motherfucker soon, I'll do it and then work my way through the rest of you!"

That made the customer in the waiting room squirm more than anything else.

While most of the Nymar reflexively backed away from her, Ace held his ground. "Put some clothes on, Steph," he said. "You look ridiculous."

"Ridiculous, huh? You want to see—"

"Everyone's seen more than enough," Ace cut in. "Don't ya think?"

Stephanie bared her teeth, but her fangs were actually slipping back up under her gums. While drawing her mouth into a tight line, she pulled her dress on over her head and twisted it around so she could fit the straps on properly.

By this time several of the other doors along the hallway were opening and girls were peeking out. A few anxious men and women were trying to get a peek as well, but were being pulled back inside by their Nymar hosts. Farther down the hall, one of the doors near the back staircase opened and a woman sauntered through.

"Hello, Ace," Cole said without lowering his guard. "Glad to see you can still rein in your girl, here."

"I don't want my place busted up, that's all," Ace replied. "That don't mean you're about to walk out of here without sportin' a couple fresh bruises. This about Rita wandering too close to Cicero?"

"If Rita rides along with someone named Sid and another guy with hair from the Reagan era, then yeah. She was *in* Cicero."

Ace shook his head and clucked his tongue. "Aw, Steph. That's not good."

Tugging at the sides of her dress to fit it back into place, Stephanie growled, "Give it a rest."

"Did you make him the offer?" Ace asked.

"Yes. He refused."

"Astin?" Ace asked.

"Customer's gone," Astin said. "Gave him twenty percent off his next visit and sent him on his way. Bar's clear too."

"Good," Ace said as he reached under his suit coat to remove a pearl-handled .38 from where it had been holstered. "The rest of our guests are regulars. They don't mind a little noise, so that means we can get back to the good stuff."

Not all of the Nymar drew guns, but they were all baring fangs. The bouncer had the pinched face and tight lips of someone who was about to spit. Since some Nymar were known to deliver their venom that way, Cole went for him first. Anticipating that move, the bouncer grabbed his arm and nearly pulled it from its socket when Cole used his weapon to push him into a wall. As the air was forced from his lungs, venom sprayed from the tips of the bouncer's thin, snakelike fangs. Being all too familiar with the paralyzing effects of Nymar venom, Cole brought his spear straight up so the middle of the weapon caught the bouncer squarely on the chin. Nothing fancy, but it was enough to dim the guy's lights and send the poisonous spray over his head. The blow also drove the thorns in the handle deeper into Cole's palms, sending pain through his system like a hundred espressos mainlined into his arteries.

He turned toward Ace, knowing the skinny prick had a

gun. Ace was still holding the .38, but appeared to be distracted by something else. Before Cole could make another move, that .38 was pointed directly at him.

There were things Paige had taught him to do in that situation, moves he'd practiced and tips he'd been given, but they all just coagulated into a cold lump and dropped to the bottom of his stomach. No amount of training would allow him to just shrug off being at the wrong end of a gun.

The first thing he thought to do was stab Ace with his spear. His reflexes were enhanced by just enough panic and adrenaline for him to step aside and drive his weapon forward as the pistol went off. A round hissed past his temple as his weapon made contact with its target. If the pointed end of the spear had been facing forward, it might have impaled the Nymar's hand in a very impressive way. As it was, Ace's wrist was wedged within the forked end of Cole's spear.

Slowly, Ace's lips formed a grin. "Nice try, Skinner."

Cole had wanted to strike with the single sharpened end.

The sharpened end of his spear was the one he'd meant to use.

Not the forked end!

The sharpened end!

Single. Sharpened. End.

The spear in his hand twitched. He thought to pull it away before someone took it from him, but couldn't move it back. When he pulled a bit harder, Ace staggered forward. That's when Cole noticed that the forked end of his weapon had snapped shut like a pair of wooden scissors. It wasn't what he'd had in mind, but he was now looking at a single sharpened end that had enclosed around the Nymar's gun.

For the first time since he'd strutted down the hallway, Ace looked worried. His hand was stuck within the makeshift clamp and getting squeezed hard enough for his gun to be angled toward the spitting bouncer. When Ace tried to adjust the angle of the gun, his hand was twisted painfully against the joint.

Cole twisted the spear a little more, turning Ace's arm the wrong way and bringing the skinny Nymar to his tiptoes. "Drop the gun," he demanded.

"I . . . can't!"

"Then take your finger away from the trigger."

It took some doing, but Ace got his finger outside of the trigger guard. "What about her?"

"If Stephanie makes one wrong move, I'll—"

"Not her," Ace snapped as he nodded toward the rear staircase. "Her!"

Careful not to take his eyes away from Ace for too long, Cole glanced down the hall. At first he only noticed Stephanie, a few of the Nymar bodyguards, and one or two of the girls who must have worked at the place. Something about one of those girls seemed familiar, so he glanced again. The familiar girl had her black hair tied into pigtails so it brushed against shoulders that were bare thanks to the black corset she wore. "Paige! Where the hell have you been?"

Paige stood between Stephanie and the bodyguard in the black suit. She had a sickle in each hand, holding the weapons up to press the curved blades against both Nymars' throats. Although Stephanie looked ready to pounce, her bodyguard cringed at the touch of Paige's sharpened blade and allowed the barrel of his small submachine gun to droop toward the floor. "You seemed to be doing pretty good until these chickenshits pulled out their guns." Pulling the sickles in a bit tighter, she added, "This is about to get really messy, Ace. Sure you want to stain this tacky new carpet?"

Even though she was at the business end of a very sharp blade, Stephanie pointed out, "They're not gonna kill us. If they were, they'd already be spraying that antidote shit all over the place."

Cole realized then that he didn't have any of the Nymar antidote. One of the first Skinner innovations he'd ever seen was a serum that directly counteracted the infection that changed a human into a Nymar. When injected directly into Nymar tendrils, the stuff might as well have been acid. It was the most effective weapon the Skinners had against Nymar, and he hadn't been given any when sent into a building full of them. Paige was definitely going to hear about that.

"I've got some antidote on me," Paige pointed out.

A tight scowl came across Cole's face. Insult . . . meet injury.

Stephanie rolled her eyes. "Such a bad bluff. Kind of pathetic, really."

"You're so cute, Steph," Paige said. Just then the sound of creaking wood drifted through the air and Stephanie's eyes widened. Without moving her hands, Paige willed the sickle blades of both weapons to extend and wrap around the throats of both Nymar. "You'll be perfect once I make one little adjustment."

"She's right!" Ace quickly said. "I mean, your boy here said he just wanted to deliver a message."

"Hey!" Cole said in his own defense.

Ace couldn't have been quicker to correct himself. "Cole. His name's Cole. Sorry about that, man. It's just that he said he wanted to deliver a message. Stay away from Cicero. We got it. We'll stay out of Cicero. Okay?"

"You've said that before," Paige pointed out.

"I know, but we just had to test the waters, you know? Let Steph go and we can call it a night."

But Paige was having too much fun to let it drop now. Cole could tell that much by the mischievous glint in her eyes as the sickle around Stephanie's neck cinched in a bit tighter. "I don't know. I mean, we did come here to take a look around and have a little chat, but then you went and tried to hurt my partner. You threatened our lives and we can't let that pass. I mean, that just wouldn't look right."

In an instant Ace's concerned expression shifted to impatience. "Wouldn't look right? You wanna come into our place, kick around our people, threaten to cut our heads off, and you wanna talk about what looks right? How about this? Get outta here while you can. You wanna do some damage to us? You won't live long enough to—"

"Someone's after Daniels," Stephanie blurted.

Ace's eyes narrowed into angry slits and his upper lip curled into a snarl. "Bitch, you'd better shut your mouth and let me handle this!"

Stephanie met Ace's glare and then some. "You're the one who wanted to send Sid and that other asshole along with

Rita! I told you my girl could scout just fine on her own, but you had to send those two shit stains along with her! They're the ones that brought the Skinners here!"

Cocking his head to one side, Ace raised his eyebrows and patted the air with his free hand. All the anger and impatience that had been on his face suddenly evaporated as he said, "We don't know that. Even if it was their fault—"

Cutting Ace short by twisting his spear, Cole growled, "Let her talk."

"Yeah," Paige said. "Who's after Daniels?"

"Some guy from New York. He's been asking about him and it got back to us."

"What's he want?"

"I don't know," Stephanie whined.

"I think you do."

"Maybe, but it's really hard to think with whatever the hell that is wrapped around my neck!"

Paige let out a controlled breath, which allowed her to ease the sickle blade away from Steph's neck just enough to let her turn her head.

"All he said was that he wanted to find Daniels," Stephanie said

"So you talked to this guy yourself?" Cole asked.

"Maybe," she squeaked.

"Say everything there is to say about him so we can get the hell out of here," Paige announced. "How's that for a plan?"

"The guy is from New York," Ace replied. "At least, that's all we've heard. If you want a home address, you're out of luck. He asked about Daniels, but we weren't gonna give him up without meeting the guy face-to-face."

"What about a name?"

Staring at Cole, Ace replied, "Burkis. That's the only name he gave. Mr. Burkis. He came to town asking about one of us, so of course we heard about it."

"Daniels doesn't work for you," Paige quickly pointed out.

"He's Nymar," Ace told her. "We own this town. Someone pokes around about one of us and we all know."

Cole didn't have to try too hard, but Paige did a pretty good job of keeping a straight face through that particular line of garbage. Despite the appearances they liked to put on for anyone who looked in their direction, the Nymar were more of a loose association than a real organization. They had numbers and some assets throughout some major cities, but so did the National Association of Hot Dog Vendors.

Raising his eyebrows, Ace added, "He also asked about you."

"What's this Burkis guy want with us?" Cole asked.

"Just you," Stephanie replied as she locked her eyes on Cole as though he was once again on the menu. "He said you had some knife before Daniels got it."

"Knife?"

"Maybe just part of a knife. He only mentioned a blade."

Paige looked at Cole for a fraction of a second, which was enough to let him know they were both thinking the same thing. Once the moment passed, Paige moved her sickles away from the Nymar throats. "If we need anything more, we know where to find you."

"What about me?" Ace asked.

"Let him go, Cole."

Suddenly, Cole felt like he was in one of those dreams where he was supposed to deliver a speech in front of his Spanish class but could only remember one word of Spanish. He stared down at the spear in his hands the same way he would have stared down at all those blank note cards. After a bit of mental screaming, the end of the weapon creaked and snapped apart to form the forked end he'd carved there in the first place.

Ace pulled his hand away so quickly that he dropped his gun. Either that or his fingers were too numb to hold the pistol any longer.

"Any chance of you giving me this Burkis guy's number?" Paige asked.

Rubbing his wrist, Ace stood against the wall like he was exactly where he wanted to be. "Any chance of you telling us what knife he's asking about?"

"I don't need knives," Paige told him. "Just ask Miss Crushed Velvet and Anguish over there."

"Hey!" Stephanie yapped.

Before the fight was started all over again, Ace steered things back on course. "So we're done here?"

"Sure," Paige said while looking around as if daring one of the Nymar to make a move. "Unless one of you still has an itchy trigger finger."

Finally, Stephanie announced, "We've got more customers coming in a few hours and we need to cover the mess you made in here."

"Just throw around some more red roses or bat statues," Paige quipped. "Nothing says 'eternal torment' like bat statues."

Chapter 8

"That was great!" Paige said while steering the Cav onto Ontario Street. "If you were saving that for a surprise, it sure worked because it was a hell of a surprise!"

"You mean the surprise where I almost got beaten to death or the surprise where I almost got shot?" Cole asked.

"The second one. Since when could you get your spear to do that?"

Cole knew the truth, but didn't want to tarnish something that had gone over so well. "Oh, I've been working on that for a while."

"Well, good job. I was worried you wouldn't be able to hold off until I got there."

"Yeah, speaking of that, where the hell were you? And why do you smell like antifreeze?"

Paige brought her arm up to her nose and took a few quick sniffs. As she did, the lights from the street played off her skin with a glistening effect. "The grease from that sweatshirt doesn't dry too well. It kept me hidden for a bit longer than I thought it would, and I didn't want to waste an opportunity to do some sneaking around in there."

"You mean you didn't know how long it would last?"

"I tested it a few times back home, but not the way I did tonight. It seems to really stick to loose cotton like sweatshirts and -pants. Once it starts to evaporate, it really goes fast."

Suddenly, something about the odor struck a nerve. "Wait

a minute," he grumbled as he sniffed some more. "I've smelled that before. Back at Raza Hill."

"I told you I tested it."

"In my room!" Cole snapped his fingers and added, "In my room three or four nights ago. I was on my computer and I smelled it. I looked around but didn't see anything."

"There you go," Paige quickly told him. "The stuff really works well."

"You were in my room? You were spying on me!"

"Testing, Cole. Testing."

"What did you see?"

"Nothing," she said while raising her eyebrows. "Nothing at all."

"Oh, Jesus."

Paige laughed and patted his arm. "The only time I went in there, you were hunched over a picture of some warehouse with guns on the floor and flags posted at either side."

"That's one of the new *Hammer Strike* maps," he breathed with a sigh of relief. "Don't mention anything about that to anyone, by the way. It's under wraps."

"Yeah, Cole. With everything we do, I'm more anxious to leak your game levels to the Internet."

"So what did you find out while I was so expertly distracting everyone?"

"That side entrance led to a back room in the bar. There wasn't much in there, other than a secret door that opened to some back stairs leading up to the parlor. On the other hand, the monitors in the security room were interesting. Their customers are either into some nasty stuff or Ace sprung for the deluxe S and M channels. He walked right past me without noticing a thing, though. He might have smelled me, but he didn't see squat. It was great."

"Did you happen to see me and Stephanie on a monitor?"

"Yeah, but don't worry. There was a lot more action going on in the room next to yours. Anyway, I got the addresses of other Blood Parlors opening up around town along with a list of new employees. Since Sid's name was on the list, the others are probably Nymar or potential converts. I jotted down some names and phone numbers, so we'll be able to keep real busy for a while." Paige veered to the right, cutting off a blue Lincoln in her haste to get to the ramp onto I-94. "Speaking of getting busy, you should hope you didn't pick up anything while that skank was grinding on you."

"Sounds to me like you're jealous."

Her pigtails whipped against her cheeks as she glanced at him. "You *wish* I had a naked chick grinding on me," she chuckled. "I saw the kind of websites you visit." Looking back at the road, Paige got another face full of hair. She nearly tore some of it out in her haste to remove the bands that kept it tied up.

"I warned her against going to Cicero," Cole said in a desperate attempt to change the subject, "but I don't know how seriously she took me."

"Did you do anything I might have missed from the security room?"

"No."

"Then she took you seriously. Trust me, women who strut and flaunt like that are used to guys dropping to their knees and doing whatever it takes just to get on their good side. If you'd caved to that, she wouldn't have listened to another word from then on. You'd be just another one of her toys. If she had some fake boobs and a sex tape, she'd be in some good celebrity company."

"You should leave the pigtails in when you bare your claws like that. It's hotter." For once, he'd been the one to fluster her. Before she could fire back at him, he added, "Sorry about the fight, by the way. It seemed like she was getting ready to spring something on me, so I thought I'd make a play of my own. I figured you'd be waiting for something like that."

"I was waiting for something more along the lines of yelling or you getting slammed off a few walls, but you handled yourself really well. I hung back until things got bad because you needed practice other than sparring. And what you did with your weapon was . . . well, that was impressive."

"It was an accident," Cole grumbled.

"I don't care. It was just what we needed. The whole reason Skinners haven't been killed off by now is because the Nymar and all those other things out there see *us* as the freaks. You threw them a curveball with that little trick. Everyone back there will be talking about it for weeks!"

"I don't know if I'm excited about being the topic of Nymar conversation, but there it is. What's next? We're obviously not headed home."

"We're paying Daniels a visit."

"You think we should go there right after we heard about someone looking for him? What if one of Steph's people follows us?"

"First of all, nobody's following us," Paige said confidently. "Second, Steph already knows who Daniels is because she mentioned him by name. The Nymar may not have this city as wired as they say they do, but they can probably track someone down if they want. If she knows where he is, she'll make a play for him right away. If she doesn't, then we've got nothing to lose by driving there now."

"Do you think they know Daniels has been helping Skinners come up with new weapons?"

"If they did, he would have been dead a long time ago. What concerns me is that Ace and Stephanie might just call this Burkis guy to let him know we were there so he can give us some grief. That's why we need to get out to Schaumburg as soon as possible, which would be even easier if *someone learned to use a turn signal*!"

Paige had stuck her head out the window to aim those last few words at an old man in a new Honda four-door. After leaving him in her dust, she calmly said, "Maybe you should call MEG while I let Daniels know we're coming. Could be that someone else has mentioned someone named Burkis."

Cole dug into his pocket and removed his new phone. It still had the clear plastic film over the touch screen, which would stay in place until it either fell off on its own or got too smudged to see through. He cradled the phone in one hand and began swiping through his screens with gentle, loving motions of his finger. "I've got all the MEG branches on speed dial," he said proudly.

"Take them off."

"What? Why?"

"Because you only need to know a few phone numbers, and you should have them memorized. Anyone who gets ahold of your phone could find out all of your business. Right now your business is my business, so delete those numbers."

"Fine. As soon as I hook into my computer and update the software so I can make changes to the system, I'll do it."

"Real convenient phone you got there. Is that the one you borrowed all that money for?"

Rather than answer that question, Cole dialed the number. He even used the speed dial to really show her who was boss.

After a few rings a woman picked up and said, "Midwestern Ectological Group Branch 40. How can I help you?"

"Hi, who's this?"

"Midwestern Ectological Group Branch 40."

"I know that. Where's Stu?"

Although there was a touch of tired aggravation in her tone, the woman at the other end of the line was far from flustered. Being an organization that searched for ghosts by following creaks in people's attics and flashing digital cameras at cold spots in the middle of dark, empty rooms, MEG got more than its share of strange calls. "If you have an instance to report or a sighting to document, you can log onto our website. If you need to reach someone in particular, I can pass along a message."

Cole knew all too well that the woman wasn't even close to writing anything down yet, so he spoke quickly before she hung up. "His name's Stu. He usually always answers the phones. Just tell him it's—"

Swatting him on the arm, Paige whispered, "Use your number."

The first time he'd called the paranormal investigation society, Cole needed to pass along an identification number belonging to a Skinner named Gerald Keeley. A lot had changed since then. Gerald was dead and Cole had his own identification number, but he was on such good terms with the guy who usually haunted MEG's main phone line that he never needed it.

Pressing his phone against his shoulder, Cole used his free

hand to pat his pockets. "I can't find my card," he whispered to Paige.

Gnawing on the inside of her cheek, she grunted, "You don't keep *that number* on you, but you program in all the phone numbers that are plastered all over those MEG websites and that stupid cable show they keep rerunning?"

"Sir? Are you still there?" the woman on the phone asked.

"Yeah," Cole said. "Hang on. I've got a number for you."

"All right."

The frantic expedition into his pockets turned up nothing but forty-two cents and a faded coupon. His socks contained his feet and a little over two hundred bucks, which only left one more place for him to look. Lifting his butt an inch or so from the seat, he slid his hand along the space where the backrest met the bottom cushion. That's when he struck pay dirt.

"All right," he said triumphantly as he plucked the card from where it had been wedged. "Here we go." He read a string of numbers from his card as Paige busied herself with her own phone. When he reached the final digit, he heard a definite shift in the voice at the other end of the long-distance connection.

"Cole Warnecki?"

"That's me."

"I didn't realize you were one of those . . . I mean . . . I've never talked to anyone who—"

"I know. I get that all the time," Cole said, even though he rarely had anyone seem remotely impressed with his name. This was actually one of the few times a newcomer had even pronounced it correctly.

"You still want to speak to Stu? I'm sure I could help."

As much as he wanted to draw out a conversation with a voice as sweet and promising as hers, he was hesitant to comply. There was more to think about than just getting on the good side of an interesting woman. Surely, the end of days was nigh.

"I'd kind of like to talk to Stu if that's all right," he said.

Quickly, the woman replied, "Sure. That's fine. Let me

get him for you." She didn't sound annoyed or upset, just a little disappointed to be passed over. Now he really felt like an ass.

There were a few clicks, some static, and then a few more clicks before a familiar voice drifted through Cole's new phone. "If you want me to retract what I said about those painted hammers on the Digital Dreamers forums, I won't do it."

"Hey Stu, it's not about that. Wait . . . couldn't you possibly consider—"

"No! What do you want?"

"I need to know if you guys have heard anything about someone named Burkis."

"First or last name?" Stu sighed.

"Probably last," Cole told him. "He's supposed to be from New York. At least, that's what my sources told me."

"How reliable is the source?"

"Just look it up."

The MEG guys were known as a lot of things. A small group of rabid fans called them brilliant scientists, but closed-minded folks used some more colorful and less favorable terms. Everyone else along the middle of the spectrum either didn't know about them at all or found them mildly interesting. Their videos of grainy footage taken from inside supposedly haunted locations sold well enough to keep them stocked in batteries for their meters and cameras, but their real funding came from several private investors who didn't bother hassling the Midwestern Ectological Group about unproven techniques or making up words to fit an anagram. Most of those patrons were Skinners.

Skinners were generally a very low-tech crowd. People who lived and died hunting monsters also tended to be a little paranoid. To that end, they weren't quite on board with the notion of taking their communications online with the rest of the planet. That's where MEG came in. The branches of paranormal investigation teams had their communication network well in place before they'd ever crossed paths with a Skinner. Cole often wondered how funny it was when that first ghost chaser tried to get a hardened warrior to pose for a picture in front of a freshly killed werewolf.

Stu's fingers rattled over his keyboard and he muttered incoherently into his headset. Then again, Stu did seem the type who might also wear one of those obnoxious little wireless earpieces. "There's a couple Burkises mentioned, but those were in Ontario," he finally said. "Oh, that was one of our cases."

"You guys are doing investigations in Canada now? Congratulations."

"Yeah. After all the commotion when Gerald and Brad's bodies were found, it's been a real hotbed up there. Uh, no offense."

"None taken. What happened with those bodies?"

"They were buried in a private ceremony. Apparently someone claimed them and arranged for it all. No pictures, but it was probably real nice."

"Yeah," Cole said as he looked over to a certain brunette who used to work with Gerald before the old man was killed. "I'm sure it was."

"You got your own number issued, huh? Congratulations right back at ya. Let's see . . . Burkis in New York. There are a few listed in phone directories and stuff, but nothing connected to any notes from you guys. I'll keep checking. Honestly, I thought you called about whatever killed those people in Kansas City."

"What people?"

"Don't you watch the news?"

"Between sparring and sleeping, when the hell am I supposed to read or watch anything?" Cole snapped.

"Bring it in a notch, killer. I thought you might have seen it online. Four people were killed in Kansas City and plenty more have gone missing."

"Wouldn't that be the cops' problem?"

"They were torn apart. The news started off by saying there was a pack of pit bulls running lose, but that was before the pictures started coming in."

"What pictures?"

"You really have been out of touch," Stu grumbled.

"We've been putting them up on our site. Lately, the news and police statements have latched onto the idea of some sort of rottweiler-bullmastiff mix, but we've got eyewitness accounts and some cell phone pics that point to a bunch of those skinny werewolves you guys like so much."

"Half Breeds," Cole muttered, as if afraid of saying the words too loudly.

"Right. There's also a few blurry shots of the other kind. One of those big ones."

That didn't set well. "Can you send those pics to me?"

"Not on that fossil of a phone you're using."

"That one's history," Cole beamed. "I've got one of the new touch screen models."

"The new ones from four months ago or the new ones from last month?"

"The *new* new one."

"Man, you're lucky," Stu gasped. "I waited in line for hours and still didn't land one. Tell me how these pics look."

Within seconds an icon started flashing on Cole's phone. He tapped it and brought up a set of three pictures sent by Stu. The quality was okay, but the lighting was terrible. Even so, he could make out the hulking form of a full-blooded werewolf with black fur stalking through a park. The other two pictures were of leaner creatures racing along nearly deserted streets. They'd been moving so fast when the pictures were taken that they weren't much more than blurs. Even so, he would have bet they were Half Breeds.

"How do those look?" Stu asked.

"Not good," Cole sighed. "Not good at all."

"Well, they were probably taken on one of those—"

"Keep looking into that Burkis guy," Cole interrupted. "And e-mail me whatever you've got on what's going on in Kansas City."

"Yeah. Okay. Is everything all right over there?"

"As good as it ever is."

"Oh," Stu said gravely. "I'll let you get back to it, then."

Cole ended the call and tapped his phone to enlarge the picture Stu had sent him. A few seconds later Paige snapped her phone shut and said, "Daniels is home, but he's hiding. He says some Nymar are waiting for him outside his place."

"We need to get to KC," Cole told her.

"I'm not about to run away just because Ace and Stephanie got their prissy little noses out of joint."

"Not that." Showing her the picture on his phone, Cole said, "Because of this."

Paige studied the blurred picture for about a second before nodding and shifting her attention to the interstate. "Looks like a Full Blood. Could be the one that found us in Wisconsin, but I'm not certain."

Cole turned his phone around and studied it so closely that he nearly pressed his face against the smooth touch screen. "What if it's Henry?"

"Even if Henry is recovered from all the crap he was put through, he was too crazy to hit and run like that. When he resurfaces, there won't be any doubt it's him. And look at the color of the fur. Full Bloods change shape, but they can't change their fur. If anything, that's the one that came to take Henry away from us. Yep," she added after another quick glance at the picture. "See the white patch on the nose?"

"You can't possibly see all that from this picture!"

Nodding as if she was accepting an award, Paige said, "It's a gift. Once you see a few more of these bad boys, you'll pick up on the details too."

"So what if these other things are Half Breeds?"

"Oh, those are Half Breeds," Paige replied.

"How could this get by us?"

"I've seen some stuff on the news about dog attacks in KC, but that was a few days ago. Since then all the attention was shifted over to the people who went missing."

Already sifting through different screens on his phone, Cole shook his head and said, "I'm looking at news reports online right now. This isn't good at all. Two cars were found alongside a highway last week. One of the drivers was busted up beyond recognition and the other was never found. More people have turned up dead or gone missing. Some college girl was dragged away by . . . well, this says it was a rottweiler, but come on! Aren't we supposed to be on top of this crap?"

"We'll look into it."

"It's all right here, Paige! I did a search for Kansas City dog attacks and ten pages came up."

"Those are Internet search pages," she reminded him. "How much of that is porn?"

Since the answer to that wouldn't have helped his cause, Cole settled for a stern glare in her direction.

"There are real dog attacks and plenty of missing people," she said. "We can't investigate every last one on the off chance of a Half Breed turning up. Now that we know there's a problem in KC, we'll go there. If a Full Blood is still there, we'll need what Daniels is working on anyway. Read off some more of those search results."

"I can't," Cole snarled. "My battery just died."

"How long did you wait in line for that new phone?" Paige chided.

"Shut it."

Chapter 9

It was a long drive to Schaumburg, but thanks to an over-priced car charger for his phone, Cole had plenty to keep him busy along the way. As Paige drove to the Chicago suburb with her arm propped on the window and the night breeze shaking her hair back into its normal shape, he sifted through dozens of online news sources. The reports ranged all the way from syndicated articles about the supposed rottweiler-bullmastiff mixed breeds roaming Kansas City to conspiracy blogs that compared the attacks to the incident in Wisconsin commonly known as the Janesville Massacre. Cole and Paige had been in Janesville to see the massacre firsthand, and there were more Nymar there than were-wolves, but the blogged reports were a little too close for comfort.

Then Cole spotted something to perk him up. "Hey! I think I found someone in KC who might help us."

"Don't trust anything you might hear about Skinners or their locations. I plant all sorts of lies on the Internet to cover us. If another Skinner was nearby, I'd already know."

"This isn't a Skinner. It's a cop. The story is only two days old and says he hit one of those mixed breed dogs with his car. Apparently he still has the body and is trying to sell it on—"

"We're here," Paige announced as she nodded toward a cluster of buildings on the right side of the road. "The rest will have to wait for later. If there are Nymar watching this place, I don't want to miss them."

Cole tucked away his phone and took the revolver from the glove compartment. They'd left the interstate and were cruising through a quiet apartment complex that looked as if it had fallen out of an expensive mold. The buildings weren't quite fancy enough to have an electric gate around them, but were clean, well lit, and inhabited by people who had impressive taste in cars.

"This is where a Nymar lives?" Cole grumbled.

"Sure beats your freezer, huh?"

"It beats the place I used to live back when I was pulling in a real salary."

Paige drove along a road that led into the middle of the apartment complex where a clubhouse glowed with blue, wavy light reflected from the nearby pool. Pointing to the third of five identical buildings, she said, "Daniels lives in that one."

"Why is it so important that we see this guy right now?"

"Because he does a lot of good work for us, and you should be introduced before Ace and Stephanie hand him over to some asshole from New York." Slapping the Cav into Park and cutting the engine, Paige added, "Plus he's got the Blood Blade. If we're going to KC, we're gonna need that. He's been using it to put together a nice little surprise that should also come in handy."

"What surprise?"

"You remember that project I had him working on after we chased Henry out of Wisconsin?"

Cole furrowed his brow and rolled his eyes toward the roof of the car. If he'd stashed any notes around, that wasn't the spot. Finally, he said, "No. I don't remember."

She sighed and pushed open the car door. "You'll just have to wait, then. Look out for any Nymar lurking in the parking lot."

"Will we be able to spot them?"

Rather than say anything else as she walked to the narrow sidewalk cutting across a well-tended lawn, Paige simply tapped the palm of her hand. The cuts from his weapon's thorns had long since healed. He'd sat and watched the gashes close up once, but found it more disturbing than interesting. Since he didn't feel the prickly itch caused by the reaction of the venom in the weapon's varnish with the Nymar that produced it, Cole knew there weren't any of them nearby.

"Take this," Paige whispered as she placed a syringe of the Nymar antidote in his hand. "I've got more if you need it, but try wearing them down before you inject them. Remember, aim for the biggest, fattest tendril you can find. The gun's already loaded with the special rounds, so don't be afraid to use it. If there are Nymar watching this place and they're taking orders from Steph, I doubt they've been told to go easy on us."

The apartment complex was pleasantly quiet. There were no dogs barking, no loud music, and, Cole noticed, no drunken idiots screaming at three in the morning—more advantages of this place over his old apartment. He could hear traffic from the nearby interstate, but it was more like the tide of a mechanized ocean. Following the sidewalk to the third building, he looked up to see nothing but windows and porches framed by thick wooden beams. A cool breeze rolled in from the north to brush past a set of chimes hung by a resident on the top floor.

Paige walked up to the main entrance of the building and tried opening the double doors. They rattled a bit in their frame but didn't budge. Shifting her attention to the row of buttons beside the entrance, she pushed the one marked 303.

Almost immediately a squeaky voice came through the little speaker set into the wall above the buttons. "Yes?"

"It's Paige."

"Who else is with you?"

"My partner, Cole."

"The delivery guy left a package down there. Bring it in."

Paige found a parcel near her feet that was about the size and shape of a brick and wrapped in plain brown paper. Just as she picked it up, the door buzzed. She tried pulling it open but wasn't quick enough to get there before the buzzing stopped. "For Christ's sake," she muttered. "Every damn time." Keeping her hand on the door, she waited for the next quick buzz and finally got the door open.

Cole watched the parking lot for a few more seconds. He felt a slight reaction in his palms, so he checked to make sure his spear was in its harness as he followed Paige inside.

After climbing the first set of stairs, they turned the corner on the second floor landing to continue up. Suddenly, the door to apartment 203 opened. "Hey. Stop."

Paige glanced toward the door the way she glanced at anyone who tried to bug her with stupid questions like, "Where are you going with those sticks?" or "Why are you chasing that big, wild dog?" But instead of a curious bystander, she spotted a familiar face peeking through the crack of a partially opened door.

"Daniels?" she said as she stopped with one foot perched on the next set of stairs. "I thought you were on the third floor."

The door swung open, but the man inside stepped away from the opening. Peeking around the door like a cartoon mouse sticking its nose out for a big triangle of cheese, he waved frantically for them to come inside. Paige turned while smoothly drawing one of the batons from her boot holster and walked in. Cole followed her lead by taking the spear from where it was strapped across his back. No matter how many times he'd practiced to make that look good, he still got the forked end snagged before the snap on that loop popped open.

The apartment was sparsely furnished but stuffed to the rafters. Boxes of all sizes were piled into neat pyramids, and bookcases reached as close to the ceiling as the little owner of the place could reach. Daniels stood just under six feet tall, but his posture was so bad that it made him seem smaller in every way. Not only was his back stooped, but he held his head low and twitched at every sound Paige or Cole made as they tried to find a place to stand where they wouldn't knock something over.

"When did you move in here?" Paige asked. "What happened to the old place?"

"I still live upstairs, but I rent this apartment too," Daniels said. "And one of the apartments beneath this one."

"Why?"

"I've always wanted to do that," Cole mused. "Fewer neighbors."

Daniels had walked up to Cole and extended a hand to be shaken. His friendly grin and rounded face looked like they'd been taken from the kindly malt shop owner of any 1950s sitcom. Long arms sprouted from a lumpy body that came complete with a spare tire. He wore a pair of khaki pants that might have been tailor-made to fit a buoy, and a sweat-stained navy blue dress shirt with sleeves that were rolled up past his elbows. Daniels's skin fit poorly on his skull, but not because of anything supernatural. His Nymar spore had probably just changed him from an ugly, lumpy human to an ugly, lumpy vampire.

Just when Cole thought he'd adjusted to the strange man in front of him, he noticed something even stranger. At first glance Daniels's stringy, light brown hair seemed to be capped by a toupee that was several shades too dark. Now that he was closer, Cole could tell the narrow band around the back of his scalp was actually hair and the toupee was really a solid cluster of Nymar tendrils gathered at the top of his head and the base of his neck. He had seen other Nymar with tendrils clustered on their heads, but those seemed more like prison tattoos. Daniels's tendrils, like almost everything else on him, just didn't fit.

"Go on and shake his hand, Cole," Paige urged. "He won't bite."

As Cole finally completed the awkward greeting, Daniels's feeding fangs drooped halfway from his gums. It was difficult to tell if that was a warning or the Nymar equivalent of leaving his fly down. The fumbled attempt at a smile didn't help much.

"Howdy," Daniels said.

At least that cleared things up. Not even cowboys said that when they were trying to scare someone off. Cole nodded and shook the other man's hand just to get it over with. "Hi."

"So what's the deal with all the apartments?" Paige asked as she strolled through the cluttered living room and into what was supposed to be a dining area.

Daniels's head snapped around and he rushed ahead of her to protect one of the stacks of boxes. "Watch your step. There's a lot of delicate equipment around here."

"This is where you do your work? How come I've never been here? Is that a hole burnt into the ceiling?"

Craning his neck to look up into the closet that Paige had found, Daniels replied, "Yes. I used a torch to burn through the ceiling just as I did to put a hole in the floor of the bedroom. That way I can climb freely between all three apartments."

"Kiss that deposit goodbye," Cole chuckled.

"For your information, when I leave this place there will be no need to settle any contracts. I have made arrangements to clear my path and have set aside any funds needed to compensate the management for damages."

"He's just flapping his lips again, Daniels," Paige said as she moved around to get in front of the Nymar inventor. "Tell me, though. Why haven't I ever been down here? You've obviously had this set up for a while."

"It wouldn't be secret if I told everyone."

"Why bother with it at all?"

"Do you know how many times my previous residence was broken into after I started working for you?"

"That was back in the St. Louis days," Paige said.

But Daniels barely skipped a beat. "Lots. So when this apartment came up for rent, I took it and used it as a storage space. Burning through the ceiling was easier than you might think. It's a crude access point, but very functional. Whenever someone comes around that I don't want to speak to, it's just a simple matter of climbing through the floor of one apartment and pulling a rug over that hole. If someone happens to come in here, I just shut the closet door."

Cole peeked into the large closet, which was probably meant to hold a washer-dryer unit. Now, it held a ladder and a charred hole in the ceiling. "You could just pretend you're not home."

"Pretend?" Daniels sputtered. "What kind of solution is that?"

"And there's another hole in the bedroom?" Paige asked.

Daniels nodded and ran his hand over the top of his head. His fringe of hair shifted a bit, but not as much as the black tendrils beneath the rest of his scalp. "I got that one for a steal, seeing as how I was already renting these two."

Paige stopped her pacing at a large freezer that looked more like a plus-size coffin. "You mean the rental office knows you've got all three apartments?"

Daniels nodded.

"So if someone wanted to kill you and they asked around your rental office, they'd find out you rented three apartments?"

"Do you really think someone would go to all that trouble?"

The patience in Paige's tone was no longer there when she asked, "If you thought your would-be attackers were so stupid, why burn through your floors?"

That stopped Daniels cold.

Rather than wait for a response, she waved her arms and stomped toward the door. "Is your lab still upstairs?"

"Yes, but someone's watching that apartment. Why do you think I pulled you into this one?"

Paige turned and tossed the package from the front porch at the Nymar. Placing her hands together at chin level, she said, "Daniels, I'm begging you. Please tell me you're not going to make us hide here until some car leaves the parking lot. I'm tired and you knew I was coming. Is the new stuff here?"

"No," he replied while still trying to recover from clumsily catching the package. "It's upstairs. I just didn't want you being watched."

She looked to the closet and stomped across the floor. "Fine. But before I climb this thing, tell me whether the stuff's ready or not."

"It's . . . sort of ready."

"Good enough." With that, she climbed to the next apartment with a series of sharp, clattering steps on the molded aluminum.

Daniels watched her ascend through the crooked, blackened hole. Tilting his head to keep her in sight as long as possible before she disappeared into the upstairs apartment, he whispered, "Why is she dressed like that?"

Even though Cole was right beside the closet, he wasn't watching Paige. One of the banker's boxes was open and something inside had captured every ounce of his attention. Without looking up, he said, "We went to see Stephanie before coming here."

"Is Paige working for Ste—"

"For the love of God," Cole said quickly, "don't finish that question." Shifting to look up to the top of the ladder, he didn't speak again until he knew the coast was clear. "Is this what I think it is?"

Stretching out his hands like a monk preparing to grasp an idol that had been sanctified by his favorite higher power, Daniels replied, "It's very valuable and very delicate. Please . . . just put it back."

Cole started to lower the object back into the box from whence it came, but couldn't bring himself to let it go. Reverently, he raised it up again and gazed upon its divine wonder. "This looks like a pristine, twelve-inch, fully posable Boba Fett figure. Is that—" He snapped his head forward so the toy in his hand wouldn't have to be moved too abruptly. "Is that a Wookie scalp hanging from his belt?"

Having been fully prepared to use any means necessary, Nymar or human, to get that figure away from Cole, Daniels snarled, "Yes. It is. I don't have the original packaging, but those are all the original accessories."

"I used to have one of these," Cole said. "And not one of the newer ones they made for the re-release of the trilogy. I'm talking about one just like this." Slowly rotating the plastic bounty hunter, he lovingly soaked up every detail. "I was about ten years old and I had all the Star Wars toys, but only one figure this size. I couldn't play with it along with all the other smaller figures, so I traded it to my friend for one of those plastic light sabers with the flashlight in the handle."

"The red one or blue one?"

"Red."

Daniels nodded. "Nice choice."

"That's what I thought. I got it home, ready to start kicking some butt, and my dad takes it away from me. He says I'll knock stuff over, so he took it to his workshop, sawed the tube in half, and covered the end with masking tape."

Daniels's eyes widened as if he'd just witnessed a puppy being tortured.

Cole sadly shook his head. "The light still worked and the stumpy tube lit up, but it just wasn't the same. I'd traded my Boba Fett with the real Wookie scalp for a light saber neutered by a piece of masking tape. I love my dad and all, but I'll never forgive him for that."

There was compassion in Daniels's eyes, but he still reached out to take his figure back. "I feel your pain. This one's mine, though."

"What else do you keep down here?"

"Besides the work stuff, there's every issue of the X-Men dating back to 1963. I've also got some model kits from the original Star Trek and stamps that come from—"

"Is anyone else coming up here or do I have to pull you both up through the floor?" Paige shouted from upstairs.

Daniels reflexively stepped toward the closet, but stopped and bowed his head. "After you, Cole." When Cole started climbing the ladder, Daniels placed the action figure into the box in much the same way he might tuck a newborn into its crib. Just to be safe, he stuck that particular box under a different pile than the one where Cole originally found it. Then he scampered up the ladder.

Having just crawled up through a hole that had been burned through the floor, Cole was surprised to find himself in a very comfortable, very normal apartment. The living room contained a television, couch, easy chair, and coffee table. The kitchen was sectioned off by a counter and a few stools. All the appliances looked to be the ones that had come with the place, and the floor was covered in clean beige carpeting. A short hallway presumably led to a bedroom and bathroom, but his attention had been caught by the wire racks of video games next to the flat screen television. "So," he said after Daniels had emerged from the floor, "what do you think of *Hammer Strike*?"

Daniels nodded approvingly. "I guess it's all right."

"Just all right? What about the Cerberus level?"

Paige walked down the hallway, pulling a Chicago Bears jersey over her head. If she'd been wearing regulation shoulder pads, it would have still been a little loose. She walked straight to the kitchen and began sifting through the cabinets. "You'd better answer him or he'll just keep bugging you. He designed the game."

"Really?"

Cole nodded proudly. "And you really seem to know your way around this guy's closet."

Glancing down at the jersey she'd thrown on, Paige let out a single snorting laugh. "I left this here before I had a place of my own."

"You did?" Daniels asked.

"Under the bathroom sink. Remember, back when the Mackey brothers were trying to chase me and Gerald out of Chicago? That was before you started burning through the floor like some sort of mole."

Growing increasingly uncomfortable with the conversation, Daniels shifted his eyes toward Cole and said, "Maybe you could tell me how to unlock the Rotary Saw Bracer."

Paige ripped open the chips she'd found and perched upon a stool near the counter. "No time for all of that."

"Oh," Daniels sighed. "Then let me just amend my previous statement by saying I like *Hammer Strike* a lot."

"Good," she grunted through a mouthful of half-chewed snack food. "Introductions made. We're all friends. You two got beat up a lot in high school. Now that all that's established, let's get to the reason we're here. How's our project coming?"

Daniels straightened up and clapped his hands together. When he grinned, the fangs that had been hanging lazily from his gums snapped up to disappear completely. "It's been coming along great! I think I've actually come up with a way to get your idea to work. At first I thought it was impossible, but now it looks like we're close to really pulling it off!"

Cole tried to mimic the other two's excitement. "What project?"

"Remember the Blood Blade?" Paige asked.

Cole nodded warily. "That's the magic knife I brought to you from Canada. The one that can cut a werewolf."

"Not just a werewolf," Paige reminded him. "A Full Blood. And it cuts through them because they're charmed, not magic. The question is, charmed with what? Why does the Blood Blade hurt a Full Blood when everything else from fire to automatic weapons leaves nary a scratch? As far as we know, those creatures may be immortal."

"Full Bloods," Daniels said, "like all supernatural creatures, can be harmed by other supernatural creatures. That's why those weapons you carry work after that varnish mixture is soaked all the way through the wood. The shapeshifter and Nymar blood—"

"You can skip that," Paige told him. "Get to the good part."

Daniels gritted his teeth and shook his head as if he was physically grinding through his gears to skip to the next section of what he wanted to say. "I took samples from the Blood Blade to try and find out how it was forged."

"That way," Paige interjected, "we could make our own instead of trying to buy or steal them from the Gypsies that make the damn things."

"Is that slang or a racial slur?" Cole asked.

Paige squinted and let out a short, snorting laugh. "Gypsies? They're people. Just relax."

Anxious to dive back into his lecture, Daniels paced and twiddled his fingers as if operating a very intricate, very invisible, piece of machinery. "A Blood Blade is made from metal that's bonded to shapeshifter blood so precisely that it becomes more effective than your wooden weapons. While most Skinners already knew this, they don't know *how* the two were bonded. Turns out there are elements within the metal that I couldn't identify, so I couldn't duplicate a Blood Blade well enough for it to be put to use. I discovered that within a week or two after I got the blade. "

Cole looked over to Paige, only to find her nodding and

clapping the dust from the chips she'd just eaten off her hands.

"I could, however, figure out how the metal was bonded to a peculiar element," Daniels explained. "In that aspect, the Blood Blade isn't much different than your sticks. It's just a matter of binding the sample to metal instead of soaking it into wood. Obviously, that varnish mixture you use won't work on metal, although I could try if I had a sample to analyze for myself."

Paige shook her head at Daniels and said, "Not gonna happen. We gotta keep some things secret for the ones who signed on for the full membership package."

Being one of those members, Cole actually felt kind of proud. The feeling was boosted when Daniels looked over at him with genuine envy. That'll teach him for not sharing his toys, Cole thought.

"Anyway," Daniels sighed, "I've recently been able to come up with a way to bond a small sample of the blade with a viscous substance that can be thinned down to a more manageable liquid. More shapeshifter blood is required, but that's a lot easier to come by. At least . . . it is for you two."

"You mean this stuff you made is like the varnish for our weapons?" Cole asked.

"Almost," Paige told him, "but not quite. Our stuff is more of a concoction, and this is a . . . dispersed . . . how did you describe it?"

"It's along the lines of a colloidal dispersion." Not at all surprised by the dumbfounded expression on Cole's face, Daniels went on to say, "Although I don't know the specifics, I gather the mixture you use for your Skinner weapons must be replenished or at least added in so many layers before its effect becomes permanent."

Cole knew that well enough. Since the night he first whittled his spear down from a freshly cut sapling, he'd lost count of how many fresh coats of the rancid varnish he'd applied.

"This particular colloidal dispersion," Daniels explained, "is a substance that can be directly applied to other medi-ums. The substance becomes so potent that its qualities are transmitted to its new medium in a ratio somewhere in the vicinity of six to one."

Rolling her hand as if she was guiding a car into its parking spot, Paige said, "Which means?"

"Which means, in the case of the substance I devised using the Blood Blade, traits of the biological element will be directly passed on to a biological recipient in a manner similar to when those traits are passed on to the mediums of metal or wood."

Paige hopped off her stool and started pacing. "Blood Blades are forged using some special Gypsy metal and shapeshifter blood just to give the metal a supernatural charge."

"Charge isn't the best term," Daniels muttered.

Continuing as if Daniels hadn't even spoken, Paige said, "Our weapons can change shape because they're alive, or they used to be. They're not as strong as the Blood Blade because we have to use wood instead of metal."

"Metal with the special mystery element," Cole added sarcastically.

Paige snapped her fingers and pointed at him. "Exactly! When raw, pure shapeshifter blood bonds to living things, it allows them to do things like grow fangs and claws, run from one end of a state to the other, throw big stuff . . . you know."

"I think so," Cole said as some of the fog in his head started to clear.

As she went on, Paige reminded him of a professor feeding a slow student his lines and hoping he caught on. "But if the shapeshifter blood bonds directly with the blood of a *person* . . ."

"They become a Half Breed," Cole said.

"Yes."

"Either give me a sticker or get to the point," he grumbled.

Daniels stepped in. "The natural bonding process has bad side effects, as you mentioned. The bonding process used for your weapons requires so many treatments that the same side effects would be passed on to any living thing that's more complicated than a stick. The process used on the Blood Blade, however, is different because it uses another element as a buffer. I don't know exactly what the element is, but I did manage to separate it from the samples I've been given."

Cole's hopes for a simple explanation were dashed, so he looked back to Paige.

Leaning on the edge of her stool with elbows planted on her knees and the jersey hanging down low enough to show the top of her leather corset, she looked like she was calling for a very interesting huddle. "The stuff we use on our weapons is basically varnish. It would kill you if you tried to mix it with your blood. Whatever is used on the Blood Blade acts like a gateway between the shapeshifter blood and whatever it's bonding to."

"How did you come up with all of this?" Cole asked.

"I've been kicking it around for a few years. The details don't matter," Paige said dismissively. "The tricky part has been getting a Blood Blade to someone with more chemistry know-how than me to work on it. Now, after a few tests, we'll be able to use this stuff to safely bond shapeshifter blood directly with our blood and use their power against them."

Cole froze for a second and leaned forward, as if being closer to Paige and Daniels would help their words sink in. "Wait. You mean you could get the powers of a shapeshifter without becoming one?"

"Bingo!"

Daniels was quick to step in before either Cole or Paige could get worked up. "No. Not bingo. Not yet. I said certain traits could be passed along, not all of them. It's got to be tested, but with all that's involved in the distillation process, I can guarantee it won't be a perfect conversion. I believe my ratio was in the vicinity of six to one, meaning any powers that are passed along will be six times weaker than the source. Most likely, only the basic predominant qualities will be passed along for a short time before being weakened by that same ratio."

Cole felt the proverbial lightbulb start to glow over his

head, but knew it was forty watts at best. "So, this stuff might make someone become just a little bit of a were-wolf?"

"Actually," Daniels said with a wince, "a full bond would be needed for transformation. With this process, only pre-dominant traits like strength or endurance of the specimen would be passed on in a diluted form."

"So if I injected this—"

Daniels shook his head and waggled his hands as if going into convulsions. "No direct injection into the bloodstream. That would be too dangerous. Paige has suggested an-other means of introduction into the system that might just work."

When he looked over at Paige, Cole was surprised he didn't see canary feathers dangling from her bottom lip.

"I sure did," she said proudly. Being in the football frame of mind, Paige motioned for a pass from the Nymar, and had to scramble to catch the brick-sized package before getting hit in the face. Even that near miss wasn't enough to dampen her spirits. She ripped off the brown paper to reveal a cardboard box, which she also tore open. Inside, wrapped in bubble wrap and plastic bags, was a cylindrical grip, some long needles wrapped in more plastic, and a piece of machinery that looked like a strange amalgam of spooled wires, small pistons, and metal brackets.

It wasn't until Cole saw the heading on the receipt that he had any clue what those pieces were supposed to form. "Mustache Pete's Tattoo Supply? Are you serious?"

He'd never seen a smile so wide on Paige's face. "It's per-fect," she insisted. "The stuff can't be injected, so it doesn't go into a vein. This is a way to get it right where it needs to be without going too deep!"

"You know how to use that machine?" Cole asked.

"I'm not making a real tattoo. I'll just be drawing lines on arms or legs. It doesn't matter what it looks like because it won't even last. Right, Daniels?"

Daniels rolled his eyes and reluctantly nodded. "Every test I've run has resulted in the entire sample degrading over a relatively short amount of—"

"It breaks up, burns off, fades away, whatever you want to say," Paige cut in. "I've seen it!"

"You've seen it on a pig," Daniels corrected. "A *dead* pig! It's not the same."

Winking and grinning at Cole, she said, "He also tested it on himself."

"I'm not exactly the same as you two," Daniels said.

"But he's still got human muscle tissue . . . Well," Paige groaned, "a little muscle tissue. This stuff he tapped into his arm gave him enough of a boost to move his furniture without breaking a sweat. After a few minutes the stuff just faded away. It was beautiful!"

"Tapped in?" Cole asked.

"Old school Polynesian method," she said. "Real tribal. Very manly. It worked pretty well, but he wanted to refine it some more. I gave him another week and here we are."

"You're two days early!" Daniels snapped. And just when it seemed he couldn't be more annoyed, a grating buzz filled the apartment. "What the hell?" he muttered as he scurried to the front door.

Paige flew across the room to grab him by the shoulder. "Don't let anyone in," she hissed.

Matching her harsh whisper, Daniels told her, "I wasn't. That's the buzzer from the security door."

"Are you expecting anyone?"

He shook his head.

Cole walked over to stand next to the television, which put him between the front door and the kitchen. He'd just spotted the panel in the wall next to the door when the buzz came again. From that distance it was loud enough to rattle his back teeth. "Maybe it's just someone downstairs hitting the wrong button."

"Maybe it's those two that have been sitting in their car watching the building," Daniels suggested.

"Can you point the car out from here?" Paige asked.

Daniels raced from the buzzing panel to the sliding glass door that opened onto one of the patios Cole had spotted from the parking lot. Daniels stopped there and gingerly pulled aside one of the vertical plastic strips covering the door. He peeked through the narrow opening and then eased the strip back into place. "They're gone," he whispered.

"Are you sure?" Cole asked.

Daniels nodded. "The car's still there, but it's empty."

"Someone leaving their car unattended in a parking lot isn't what I'd call suspicious," Paige said.

Daniels had already caused a mild reaction within the two Skinners, but something else triggered a dull heat that ran from Cole's scars up to his elbows. Paige met his eyes long enough to let him know that she'd felt it too.

Whoever was downstairs tapped on the button two quick times, like the friendly beep of a car horn.

After Paige nodded solemnly and stepped back, Daniels reached out to push the speaker button. Setting his jaw as if there was a camera attached to his door, he said, "What do you want? It's late."

"My name is Burkis. I think you know why I'm here."

Chapter 10

Paige's hand locked around Daniels's wrist to pull his finger away from the button.

"Do you know anyone named Burkis?" she asked.

Daniels shook his head as he replied, "Is he the one from New York?"

"So you do know him?"

"No, but I've heard someone from New York has been trying to find me."

"And why didn't you say anything?"

The fleshy pockets around Daniels's eyes pulled back and his lips twisted into a gaping frown that displayed one and a half sets of fangs that had slipped from their sockets. "I *always* tell you there's people after me! Why do you think I paid for two extra apartments and burned escape routes into them?"

The buzzer went off with a prolonged, impatient stab of the downstairs button.

Before Paige could answer that, Cole leaned forward and asked, "Can you see the front door from the first floor apartment?"

"Yes," Daniels replied. "Well . . . sort of."

Cole looked to Paige and raised his eyebrows with another unspoken proposition. She picked up on it immediately and nodded. "Good enough," she said. "Daniels, keep this guy talking while we go down and have a look. Any trouble, you come down to us. Where's the Blood Blade?"

"It's in a safe in the apartment right below us. Bedroom, under the throw rug."

She ran to the closet and slid down the ladder. Cole was about to join her when Daniels snapped his fingers to catch his attention.

"The ladder to get to the first floor is in the little closet in the hall where the water heater should be," the balding Nymar told him. When the buzzer sounded again, Daniels answered right away. "Sorry, I was checking my contact list. Who sent you?"

Cole couldn't hear the answer, but the voice that came through the speaker had the low pitch and stern tone of a parent dealing with a bothersome kid. Grabbing onto the sides of the ladder, Cole slid down and hit the floor on the balls of his feet. He went straight to the hallway closet and motioned for Paige to follow. Sure enough, instead of a water heater, there was another rough hole in the floor with a ladder extending down from it. Cole and Paige were a bit more careful to keep quiet as they descended, but were still quick to get to the front door of apartment 103.

Since he was the first to arrive, Cole placed his eye to the peephole. Within seconds Paige was behind him. He expected to get pushed out of the way but instead felt her hand press firmly on his back as she whispered into his ear.

"Do you see him?" she asked.

Not only was the apartment door a bit to the side of the building's main entrance, but the lens of the peephole made everything look like it was projected onto the rounded surface of a bubble. "I don't have a good angle," Cole grunted as he twisted and squinted to try and improve his view, "but I can make out the front door. Looks like there's more than one out there."

"How many?"

"At least two. Maybe three."

"Let me see," Paige said as she tapped him eagerly.

Cole stepped aside and let Paige take a look. Pretty soon she was doing the same wriggling dance to see more through the little hole. Stepping back, she said, "Keep an eye on them. Hopefully Daniels keeps them talking long enough for me to get the Blood Blade."

"Hold on," Cole hissed. "I can see one of them."

Now that he'd stared through the warped lens for a while, he could see the man at the speaker lean over to look through the tall window beside the building's front door. He was no more than six-two or six-three and dressed in a plain, dark suit that hung loosely over broad shoulders and a thick torso. The man turned to stare directly at the peephole, making Cole reflexively jerk away from the door.

"What's the matter?" Paige asked. "Who's out there?"

Steeling himself to look outside again, Cole replied, "Just get the blade. Whoever's out there is getting antsy."

Keeping his eyes fixed on the door to 103, the man outside leaned against the entrance to the building as two more figures stepped up behind him. There was no doubt the man in the suit was Burkis, because Cole recalled the other two, Mullet and Sid, from his eventful trip to White Castle. The expression on Burkis's face didn't change in the slightest as he pressed against the main door and broke whatever bolts had been holding it in place.

Burkis walked into the building and glanced at 103. Shifting his eyes to the stairs, he waved toward the ground floor apartment and started to climb. Whether they'd been given silent orders or just understood Burkis's signal, Mullet and Sid grabbed the handle of the door and started shaking it.

"They know we're here," Cole announced as he backed away and drew his spear from the harness on his back. "Burkis and those two I saw in Cicero."

"Can you hold them off?"

It hadn't taken long for the Nymar thugs to stop jiggling the handle and start pounding on the door itself. Judging by the amount of plaster that cracked around the door frame, they wouldn't have to pound for long.

"I'll try," Cole said, "but you'd better get in here!"

" 'I'll try!' " Sid shouted in a squealing mockery of Cole's last statement. The door came loose and was flung open. It slammed against the wall of the entryway as Sid rushed inside. All three sets of fangs were on display as he opened his mouth and let out a breathy snarl.

Cole reflexively brought his spear across his chest as Sid

charged into him. Since he couldn't keep from being driven backward, he bent at the knees, rolled onto his back, and straightened his arms. Sid's teeth clamped together loudly as he was tossed over his prey and into a tall stack of narrow white boxes.

The move went pretty well, but Cole didn't have time to be impressed with himself. He scrambled to his feet and whipped around to find Mullet standing in the doorway. Compared to Sid, the guy with the bad hair looked tired and pale. He spat a quick obscenity into the apartment and then dashed down the hall that led to the neighbor's door.

"Paige! He ran next door. I think he wants to feed!"

Nymar were strong enough already, but they had a nasty habit of grabbing a quick meal when faced with a fight. Apparently, Mullet hadn't expected to face anyone stronger than Daniels and needed a quick shot of energy.

Paige bolted from the bedroom, weaving between small stacks of boxes and dodging Cole while plucking the baton from her right boot. As she raced from the apartment, her batons creaked into full combat mode: sickle blade on one end, with the handle sharpened down to a stake.

Like most animals desperate for its next meal, Mullet moved quickly and tore through anything that got in his way. One of those things had been the door to apartment 102, which Mullet knocked completely off its hinges. Paige stalked over the door laying flat upon the floor and cautiously moved inside. The apartment was dark, except for a trickle of light coming in from the newly busted front doorway. Paige didn't need night vision to know where Mullet had gone. She could hear screams coming from the bedroom and the sound of something heavy slamming against the walls. She jogged as quickly as she dared while her eyes adjusted to the darkness. By the time she reached the bedroom, she could see one shadow pouncing upon another.

She reached out with her right hand to swat the wall beside the doorway. Finding the switch, she flipped it and bathed the room in the soft glow of a single lamp. It was a woman's bedroom, filled with mirrors, a couple small dressers, and a queen-sized bed. The woman in the bed was middle-aged and wore an oversized T-shirt that had twisted around her as she squirmed and tried to crawl to the other side of the mattress.

Mullet had one foot on the floor and the other propped upon the edge of the bed. He reached out with both hands, clawing at the blankets and mattress in his frenzy to get at the woman. One hand slapped against her shin and thick fingers closed around her ankle in a grip that brought a pained yelp to the woman's lips.

With Mullet reeling the woman in, Paige only had enough time to land one blow. She drove the end of her sickle's blade into Mullet's hip, leaned back and pulled. The Nymar snarled loudly and hung on. Even as he was dragged toward Paige's side of the bed, he brought the woman along with him. She stretched out and managed to grab hold of her nightstand. It wasn't heavy enough to keep her from moving but worked nicely as an anchor once it became wedged against the side of the bed. Now that she had something to hold onto, the woman pulled herself away from Mullet and kicked his head with her loose foot.

Paige dug her other weapon's blade into Mullet's side. "Come on now," she growled. "Wouldn't you rather have a girl who's ready and willing?"

Once the frightened woman scrambled out of his reach, Mullet slid off the bed and twisted around to face the Skinner. Paige's weapons tore through his flesh, which brought an angry snarl from the back of his throat. Hungry, desperate, and now wounded, the Nymar let out a sound that wasn't even close to human. The black markings on his neck and wrists stood out as though the tendrils inside of him were about to emerge from his flesh and wrap around the first warm body they could find.

After a few wild swings with his fists and some jerky twists from his upper body, Mullet ripped free of Paige's weapons. The soft light from the lamp made the foamy drool dangling from his lips seem more like something that had been excreted from an insect and hardened onto his face. Now that his full attention was on her, the Nymar alternated between trying to grab her and knock her out. The look in his eyes made it clear that he would feed upon whatever pieces he could tear off.

Paige was only human, so she couldn't move her arms at Mullet's speed. She stood her ground, kept her eyes focused upon the Nymar's center of mass and whipped her weapons around to block as many incoming swipes as she could. After batting one of Mullet's arms away, she prepared to block the next. Paige shifted her weight, bobbed her head, and leaned to dodge whatever she couldn't block.

The Nymar's hands and forearms met Paige's weapons with a steady stream of thumps that echoed through the bedroom. After clubbing Paige's shoulder with a two-armed swing, he knocked her back half a step and attempted to pull the weapons from her hands. Paige was able to twist both sickles away before they were taken, but not before Mullet snuck a punch through her guard.

His fist felt like a chunk of cement pounding against her stomach, and Paige folded around it while letting out a pained grunt. A second shot came right after that one and landed heavily on Paige's back. Because she'd hunkered down and braced for it rather than trying to get away, she caught most of the impact on muscle and bone instead of her neck or face. If she'd been dressed for a fight instead of an orgy, she would have been wearing something heavier than a football jersey over a corset. As it was, Mullet's fingernails cut straight through the layer of nylon to rake through the skin of her shoulder and start a flow of blood running down her back.

The instant she felt the warm trickle on her skin, Paige pulled away and snapped her left weapon up. The Nymar had been coming in to feed and wasn't even trying to block her strike, allowing the top of her weapon to crack solidly against his jaw. Mullet reared back and sent a spray of blackened fluid through the air to spatter upon the ceiling. Rather than come at Paige again, he sent a wild kick into her midsection that bounced her off a dresser. Mullet rolled off the bottom of the bed and landed on all fours. From there, the Nymar whipped around, lunged over the top of the mattress, and grabbed the woman who'd been trying to hide in the corner farthest from the door.

"Get over here, bitch," he snarled as he pulled the woman by her hair.

His eyes were glassy and clouded. His grip nearly crushed her arm. When she kicked and beat her fists against him, the woman only bruised herself. As her hair began to rip from her scalp, she seemed ready to tear it all out just to get away. A hand closed around her throat just under her chin. She grabbed and scratched at it but only managed to peel away a few layers of dead skin to reveal something dark, solid, and uncompromising beneath it.

The woman screamed and scraped her feet against the floor. She pulled and strained with every muscle in her body. No matter what she did or how hard she fought, she was unable to get away from the hungry Nymar that now came at her with venom dripping from the one curved fang that hadn't been cracked during the brawl.

Suddenly, there was movement at Mullet's neck. Something slipped around his throat and dug into the thick mass of muscles and tendons. The blade didn't do any damage, but it pulled his head back before he could sink his teeth in.

Paige appeared over Mullet's shoulder and growled with the strain of pulling the Nymar another inch or so from his intended meal. Just as he was about to lift the woman up to his fangs, Paige pulled back one more time. Muffled gunshots thumped from next door, but that didn't keep Paige from using her sickle to force his head back a little more. Her left hand was wrapped around a syringe, and she dropped it like a hammer onto the black marking that ran down the side of Mullet's neck. The moment the needle broke his skin, Paige sent the antidote through the tendril and directly to the spore attached to his heart. His grip on the woman was weaker than a baby's before the needle could be removed. Just to be safe, Paige dragged Mullet across the bed and dumped him onto the floor.

The trembling apartment owner stood with her hand pressed against her sweat-soaked nightshirt and watched as Paige bolted from the room. The monster who'd nearly ripped both women apart lay convulsing near the bedroom door. His limbs seized up and his pale gray skin settled upon his bones while something within his chest shuddered one last time.

Paige had just gone after Mullet when Cole attacked Sid with his spear. Unlike the times he'd sparred with Paige or swung the weapon at empty air, he wasn't just practicing a set of motions or concentrating on his stance. He was tearing through skin, scraping against bone, and the target was fighting back.

After getting stabbed three or four times in a row, Sid trapped the spear against his side and dropped his other arm straight down on the middle of the weapon. Any other stick would have snapped under the impact of the Nymar's fist. Cole's spear not only stayed in one piece, but tore open a long gash as it was pulled away. The Nymar howled in pain, flung himself back and tripped over a pile of boxes.

More fear than blood pumped through Cole's veins, but it was instinct that got him clamoring over the boxes to where Sid had landed. No innards could be seen within any of Sid's gaping wounds. There was just a writhing black mass that stretched little tendrils to the edges of each fissure to pull them shut. Cole drove the spear straight down toward the spore attached to the Nymar's heart, but Sid batted it away.

Allowing his weapon to flip around, Cole brought the forked end down and swung it like a broom. It caught Sid's forearm and scraped toward his hand until the Nymar's wrist was wedged in the crook of the weapon. Cole leaned behind his spear and pinned Sid's arm.

"What now, Skinner?" Sid rasped. "You wanna take a swing at me like a man or stand there and watch me heal?"

Cole's eyes dropped to what had been a series of messy open wounds in Sid's belly and ribs. Now, there were only a few cuts and a mess of oily, polluted blood soaked into tattered clothes. Sid lashed out with one foot to take Cole's legs out from under him. When Cole staggered back, the Nymar pulled his arm free and jumped to his feet. From there he slammed a powerful fist against Cole's ribs and followed up with a punch to his chest. Having absorbed plenty of punches over the last few months, Cole took those and swung his spear.

Sid was fast enough to clamp his hand around the sharp-ened end, and he used it to pull Cole into a straight, gut-level kick. Wrenching the spear out of Cole's grasp, he warned, "You'd better have a lot more than that, asshole."

"I do," Cole said as he drew the .44 from where it had been tucked under his belt. The pistol bucked in his hand and drilled a lopsided hole through Sid's body. The Nymar's innards met the antidote that was mixed into the lead of the bullet with an acidic hiss.

Sid dropped Cole's spear to claw desperately at the gun-shot wound.

Cole didn't have time to fish out the syringe Paige had given him. The Nymar's wounds were already closing and there wasn't enough antidote on that single bullet to do the job. "Damn it," he grunted as he jammed the barrel of the .44 into the wound and fired several muffled shots up toward the Nymar's heart. Every pull of the trigger caused Sid to flail and kick like he was being electrocuted. Cole recovered his spear and drove it into the smoking mess that was Sid's chest.

As soon as Sid stopped twitching, Cole raced out of the apartment to check on Paige. She exploded from the neigh-boring doorway and skidded to a halt with five or six inches to spare before running into the business end of Cole's weapon. When she saw the oily black and red Nymar blood dripping from the tip of the spear, she smiled.

"You got the other one?" she asked breathlessly.

"Pretty sure, yeah."

"Is Daniels upstairs?"

"One way to find out."

Cole bounded up the stairs and rounded the corner on the second floor to get to the next flight of stairs. Several other apartment doors opened to let a few curious faces peek out, but none of them were showing any fang. "Looks like we woke the neighbors," he pointed out.

Paige was right behind him. "Yeah. The cops will probably be here before too long. We need to make this quick."

The door to 303 was ajar but hadn't been kicked down,

which was a good sign. Cole and Paige entered the apartment to find Daniels backed against a wall with Burkis looming over him. That wasn't so good.

Cole's scars sent a deep burn through the tendons of his hands. Something about Burkis seemed familiar, yet different. If he was Nymar, he was unlike any of the others he'd encountered so far. He hadn't encountered many shapeshifters since getting bonded to his weapon, but Burkis wasn't quite like them either.

Not one for introspection, Paige snapped, "Just who the hell are you?"

Burkis stood next to the couch while Daniels pressed against the back wall of the living room. He carried himself like a man who was too powerful to be decked out in such a cheap suit. His thick mane of dark brown hair hung just a bit too low to be conservative and was shot through with several strands of gray.

"I was just about to complete a transaction with Mr. Daniels," Burkis said.

Scraping his hands along the wall behind him, Daniels looked ready to climb all the way up to the ceiling. "He wants the Blood Blade."

"Why do you want that?" Paige demanded.

Burkis merely glanced toward the front door, as if Paige and Cole were just a couple of strays who'd wandered in by mistake. "My business isn't with you."

"What about those other two?"

One of Burkis's eyebrows rose for a second as he subtly shifted his feet so his back wasn't exposed to anyone in the room. "It's very difficult to find one particular leech in a town that's crawling with them. Having never met Mr. Daniels before, a proper introduction was needed. Now that we've met face-to-face, I won't have that problem again. Unfortunately, the whore who contacted me insisted that those other two come along."

"That'd be Stephanie," Paige muttered. "I knew she'd screw us over."

"I suppose that was the intention," Burkis continued, "which is why I pointed them in your direction."

Cole's hands reflexively tightened around his weapon. "You knew we were here?"

Burkis looked from Paige to Cole and said, "Your scent has been masked but is hard to miss at this range." Then he shifted his focus back to Daniels. "We've talked long enough. Give me the Blood Blade."

"It's . . . not for sale," Daniels squeaked.

"It never belonged to you."

"It belonged to a friend of mine," Cole said. "And I say it's not for sale. Your Nymar bodyguards are dead and someone had to have called the cops, so just get out of here while you still can."

The side of Burkis's face twitched. He turned to look at the sliding patio doors a few seconds before Cole heard the wail of distant sirens.

"Give me the Blood Blade, Mr. Daniels," Burkis said dryly. "I know it's here. Hand it over and I may only kill the Skinners."

Paige took a step forward and held both weapons at the ready. "Come on, Daniels. You're coming with us."

"What about Sally?" Daniels asked while easing away from the wall.

Cole was getting more impatient with every word. "Who?"

"My girlfriend. She lives in 102."

"She's fine," Paige said. "A little shaken up, but fine."

"I need to make sure."

"Daniels!" Paige snapped. "We're leaving!"

Burkis didn't make a move to stop any of them from clustering together and heading for the door. He simply said, "I was hoping for this to be easier than Canada, but you Skinners should know you can't possibly move fast enough to get away from me." With that, he pulled in a breath that caused his chest to swell beneath the layers of his cheap suit. His torso kept expanding until the material strained and ripped. When his head drooped and his lips curled back, the man's skull crunched as if it had been trapped in a vise before swelling out to form a thicker brow and a long, squared snout.

Cole felt as if he'd suddenly pressed his hands flat against the engine block of a running car.

"Jesus," Paige gasped. "We need that Blood Blade." Grabbing Daniels by the arm and pulling him away from the sight that had stopped the Nymar in his tracks, she screamed, "Grab everything you need for our project and get to my car. *Move!*"

Cole inched toward the door one tentative step at a time. Fear and panic soaked into his body like weights tethering him to the carpet.

Burkis's muscles had exploded under his skin, reducing his cheap suit to shredded rags hanging from his shoulders and waist. His mass had become great enough to force him down onto all fours. Once there, he twisted his head back and forth as long ears stretched out from the sides of his face and teeth sprang from his jaws to scrape against each other and rip through his cheeks. As the snout took shape, Burkis lifted his head and cried out in a voice that shifted from smooth, deep tones into an even deeper roar.

Cole wanted to run, but he couldn't. He was scared, but that wasn't what kept him in the apartment. At that moment not even Paige's iron grip on his wrist could pull him away.

"We need to get to that Blood Blade!" she shouted over the creature's roar and scraping of claws against the floor. "He'll kill you!"

Burkis's legs shot out from the remains of his trousers, snapped in half to bend against the knees, and grew to nearly twice their original length. Every move he made brought up sections of the carpet along with a few pieces of the floor itself. The man from New York arched his back as his spine rippled in a shockwave that started at the base of his neck and rolled all the way down to his newly formed tail.

"We can kill him," Cole said.

"That's a Full Blood! We need the—"

"I know what it is," Cole snapped. "He's still changing. We can kill him before he grows to full strength. Like those Half Breeds we found in that den in Wisconsin, remember? We got to them before they changed all the way and we can do the same with him but we need to hurry!"

Paige thought it over for less than a second before she nodded. When she lifted her hands, they were each wrapped around shorter versions of her sickles, which allowed for stronger blades. "You ready for this?"

"No, but let's do it anyway."

Burkis was now somewhere between human and animal. It wouldn't be much longer before he was one of the most dangerous creatures in the world. Cole just hoped there would be one less in the world before the night was over.

Paige got to Burkis first and sank both curved blades into his back. Since Burkis's muscles were still expanding, she was able to pull the right one out, but was having trouble getting the left one free.

Cole wasn't able to build up much steam, but what he didn't gain from momentum he more than made up for in adrenaline by driving his spear into the shifting meat of the werewolf's side like a soldier delivering a killing blow with a bayonet. Judging by the howl that exploded from him as he shook his head and arched his back, Burkis felt the weapon hit home. A second later fur flowed out of every one of his pores as if to entangle the weapon before it was reclaimed.

With one sweep of a massive arm, Burkis knocked Paige off her feet. When the creature stood upright, Cole was almost hoisted off the floor. He pulled his spear free, dropped to his feet and was immediately knocked toward the sliding glass door when the creature pivoted toward him.

Burkis's face was now completely changed. A low, ridged brow had settled in above a pair of crystalline, gray-blue eyes. Fur flowed from him like water trickling over his skin after a hard rain. As the creature's frame settled into its final shape, he hacked up a bellowing roar, kicked aside the couch and lashed out with both hands.

Cole was just quick enough to drop and roll away from the window before those claws shattered the thick glass of the sliding door. When the creature turned, it howled and staggered to knock away a sizable portion of the door frame. Only then did Cole see Paige hanging from the sickle that was still lodged in its back.

Seeing her hang on with every bit of strength she had, Cole thought back to the isolated cabin in Canada where the first two Skinners he'd ever known were killed. They were good men who'd put up a hell of a fight before being torn apart by the same Full Blood that was seconds away from ending Paige's life. It had been the better part of a year since that happened, but Cole still smelled that blood and heard those screams in the back of his head as he threw himself into a fight that no reasonable human being could ever hope to win.

Every swing of his weapon drove the thorns farther into his own flesh. One of those hits must have landed in a soft spot, because the creature dropped to all fours and shook Paige off. She pulled her weapon free but landed awkwardly and was about to hit the floor on her back when Cole caught her.

"We're not doing anything but pissing it off," she said. "We need to get downstairs."

"That's the Full Blood," Cole wheezed.

"I know. That's why we need the Blood Blade!" She grabbed Cole by the back of his collar as if dragging an uncooperative mutt by the scruff of its neck.

Resisting Paige's efforts to get him moving, Cole held his weapon in front of him and watched the thing that scrambled to get disentangled from the broken patio door frame. Outside, the sound of police sirens drifted from the direction of the main parking lot. "No. That's the Full Blood from Canada. The one that killed Gerald and Brad."

Paige took a moment to look the creature over, recognizing the color of its fur as well as the patches of gray on its chest, thanks to Cole's past descriptions. Burkis even had some familiar scars that could now be seen through spots where its coat had thinned out a bit. "Run," she said.

"We need to kill it."

"We're chipping the surface but not doing enough damage. We need something other than what we've got."

If Burkis had been hurt in the slightest by their attack, it was recovered now. Baring its teeth, it glared at the Skinners and unleashed a demonic howl wrapped around the vestiges of a human scream.

"Run!" Paige shouted.

Chapter 11

Paige jumped through the hole in the floor that led to apartment 203 and shouted for Daniels. The Nymar was gathering things from a pile of overturned boxes and shoving them into a large gym bag he'd strapped over his shoulder. Seconds later Cole dropped through and knocked the ladder down behind him. The Full Blood quickly appeared to stick its gnarled face through the opening and snap its jaws at him.

"The cops are here!" Cole shouted as he hopped away from the closet.

"Hopefully they'll just find a big dead body," Paige replied in a rush. "Where's that package, Daniels?"

"Already packed it," the Nymar replied. "Along with the mixtures of ink, my burner, and my notes, so I can—"

"Get the Blood Blade and bring it to me. You never told me the combination to that damn safe!"

Gripping the edges of the opening that had been burned between the second and third floor apartments, Burkis tore away chunks of the floor and ceiling like he was digging a hole in the ground. Wood, plaster, and metal formed a heap in the closet as the werewolf forced its way down.

Daniels collected a few plastic containers and stuffed them along with some other knickknacks into his bag. After that he raced down the hall and disappeared through the next hole.

Standing beside Paige, Cole asked, "Have you ever killed one of these things?"

"I don't know if anyone's really killed one. There's been stories, but nothing solid."

"Can we kill it?"

"We can try."

Burkis hit the floor and exploded from the little room that had contained the ladder. As soon as he saw Paige and Cole, he roared and batted aside the piles of heavy boxes as though they were all empty.

Paige distracted the werewolf with a few swings of her weapons as Cole backed toward the hall where the water heater should have been. Racing down the ladder without being fully aware of what his arms and legs were doing, he felt the touch of panic lapping at the edges of his mind. He managed to keep moving and was soon joined by Paige in apartment 103.

The flashing lights and sirens of the police cars were getting closer. Cole only cast a quick look toward the approaching commotion when he felt Paige shove him into the living room. Burkis didn't do any digging this time. Instead he shoved his face through the opening to rip directly into the first floor apartment. His thickly muscled frame was solid enough to crack the ceiling and send chunks of plaster to the floor. He hit the ground and immediately lunged forward to clamp Paige's arm between his teeth.

She let out a short, piercing cry that contained as much surprise as pain.

Although Cole made some sort of noise as he rushed toward the werewolf, he couldn't hear it over the drumming of his heartbeat and the dull impact of his spear being driven over and over into the tough meat along the side of Burkis's neck.

The werewolf's jaws hadn't quite closed, but its face showed the strain of working to that end. Even in the dark hallway its eyes caught the stray bits of light being cast from outside to reflect it inward through a blue-gray prism. Tendons along the side of its mouth drew taut. Muscles sprouted where they were needed and its jaws strained a bit closer toward closing time.

Cole shifted his aim to keep from hitting the creature anywhere that might force it to bite down harder. He landed plenty of blows along Burkis's shoulder and side, but didn't have the power to push the spearhead in more than an inch or so. Suddenly, Burkis's eyes snapped open and he let out a choked snarl. As the creature swung its head back, Paige pulled her arm free. Instead of the bloody stump Cole had been expecting, she dragged out a double-ended stake that had kept the werewolf's jaws from closing while also digging into the top and bottom of its mouth. When it came out, the weapon brought a few of Burkis's fangs along with it.

The werewolf howled and lashed out with a paw powerful enough to collapse a section of the hall. Dropping the moment she'd broken loose, Paige barely managed to dodge the swing. When Burkis jerked his head to one side, Cole saw Daniels hanging from something he'd stuck into the Full Blood's cheek just below its right eye. The Nymar was flung into the closest wall, where he bounced and then dropped into a heap on the floor.

Since Paige was closer, Cole grabbed her by the left arm and tried to pull her away. "Wait, wait!" she said while tearing her arm from him. Swiping her hands along the floor as if looking for a contact lens, she picked up the broken werewolf teeth, showed them to Cole, and triumphantly announced, "Dibs!"

Although Burkis started to stand up, he staggered before making it all the way to his feet. Cole took the strongest stance he could and stuck the werewolf in the chest. It would have been a devastating blow on most anything else, but Burkis's torso might as well have been rock covered in several inches of leather. The creature ignored him completely and gingerly touched the jagged piece of gleaming metal from which Daniels had been hanging a few seconds ago.

Since Paige couldn't have trained him for this exact moment, Cole fell back on what little knowledge he had on the subject. In any video game, when the big strong thing was hurt, you needed to hit a spot that had already been damaged. Normally, Cole and every other game designer was kind enough to mark that soft spot by a patch of glowing red or some sort of blinking light. In the real world, however, his only beacon was a charmed blade protruding from a monster's face.

Peeling his hands from the grip of his spear, Cole held the weapon more like a sword and swung it at Burkis's wounded cheek. The hit landed with all the impact of a whiffle bat on the creature's fur, angering it even more. But when Cole swung again, the forked end of the spear scraped against the end of the Blood Blade and drove it deeper into the meat of Burkis's cheek.

The roar that followed was something civilized man might have never heard before. It shook all there was and sent a dizzying fear through Cole that hit him like a battering ram. It might have actually been the Full Blood's paw that knocked him to the floor, but something else dragged him toward the front door. He was still dizzy when he somehow got to his feet and raced from the apartment building.

"Cole! You with us?"

It was Paige's voice. She was running at full speed and pulling him along with her. He snapped his head back and forth to find Daniels outpacing them by several yards. Considering all the crap the Nymar was carrying, that was a pretty impressive feat. Lights from the cop cars filled the air of the adjacent parking area.

"Where'd it go?" Cole asked. "Where's the Full Blood?"

Paige had been breathing heavily, but her next few gasps were relieved sighs. "Daniels hurt it and then you hurt it more. It knocked you down and was gonna take your head off, but I pulled you out of the way. I think you hit your head on the wall because you were out of it for a little bit."

"Where's the Full Blood, Paige?"

They'd cut across a courtyard to arrive at the lot where the Cav was parked. Daniels was hopping around it like a six-year-old waiting for the bathroom door to open.

"After he took you out, Burkis jumped through the patio door," she said as she unlocked the car and pulled open her door. "You two must have done a real job on him because he sure as hell didn't want to fight anymore."

Daniels dove into the backseat and Cole climbed in to sit up front next to Paige.

"Is he still here?" Cole asked.

Paige got the car running in a matter of seconds. Just after that, she pulled out of her space and threw it into gear. "The cops were shooting at him, but he's got to be gone by now."

"How can you be so sure?"

"Because the cops are still making a lot of noise. Dead men are a little quieter than that. Well, mostly."

Now that he was sitting down and able to catch his breath, Cole could see more than just a few steps in front of him. The apartment complex had several little parking lots, and one of them swarmed with curious residents and some very anxious police officers. More sirens blared from the distance, which meant reinforcements were winding their way through the crooked streets of the subdivision.

Being careful not to get too close to the police, Paige circled around just enough to get a look at where the first two patrol cars had pulled in. Neither vehicle was in one piece. The front end of the car closest to Daniels's building was flattened, and lights flashed at odd angles due to structural damage to the frame. The second car's roof was sloped in a way that clearly marked where Burkis had stepped down onto the pavement. Remains from both windshields lay scattered on the surrounding pavement. Four uniformed officers stood near their cars. One motioned for the encroaching residents to stay back, while another spoke into her radio. The other two were still standing with their guns drawn, feet planted in a firing stance and gawking in the direction that Burkis must have gone.

Cole's entire body felt fractured. Dull, throbbing pain swelled up from his right side and quickly bled into the rest of him. As if she'd read his aching thoughts, Paige asked, "Are you hurt?"

"Just banged up."

"You're bleeding. Reach under the seat for that kit. Take a dose of what's in there just to be safe."

Cole was just about to point out some of Paige's injuries but she was already looking a little better. He reached under his seat, found the small leather pouch and unzipped it. The pouch had probably been a travel kit for nail files and that sort of thing, but now held several small syringes. Since the labels marked with an N were Nymar antidote, he took one of the others, which contained the special concoction Skinners used for healing.

Perhaps it was the kit or the syringes, but he couldn't help feeling like a junkie. "You sure I need this? I'm feeling okay."

"You need to let it absorb into your system. Once you start producing it on your own, you won't need half as many injections."

Pausing with the needle poised over his arm, Cole asked, "Can't I get addicted to this stuff?"

"Only if you take too much when you're not hurt. Just do it."

The syringe was half the size of a pencil and not even half full. The needle was about as thin as a hair. He didn't feel so much as a sting, but could definitely tell the solution was doing its job after the injection. The breaths that followed were easier to pull in. The sore spots where all those punches had landed weren't aching so badly, but his headache stayed put. Nothing was perfect.

Once she'd put the apartment complex behind her and pulled onto I-90, Paige floored the gas pedal.

"Shouldn't we look for that thing?" Cole asked.

Daniels leaned forward and grabbed the backs of both seats. "The hell we will! We're going back for Sally and then getting the hell away from here!"

Paige turned around to look directly into Daniels's face when she said, "Both of you, shut up! Burkis got what he wanted and left, just like Canada. He's long gone by now."

Cole was still anxious. He looked in the mirror a few times, but there was nothing bounding down the street behind them, and the burning reaction from his scars had completely cooled off. Finally, he let out a sigh and slumped into his seat. "Right. Just like Canada. He was after the Blood Blade."

"And Daniels gave it to him," Paige said.

"No I didn't."

Ignoring the squeak from the backseat, Paige continued, "Cole, you happened to be in the spot where Gerald and Brad were picking up two of those blades and the Full Blood came to get them. You brought one back, so he tracked you here and came to get the second one."

"If Blood Blades can kill those things, why would Burkis follow it around?"

"Probably so nobody else can have it."

"But," Daniels mumbled, "he doesn't—"

"It's not your fault," Paige said as she tossed a wave over her shoulder. "We're not angry. You did the best you could."

The Nymar's meek voice gained an edge when he said, "I saved your lives."

Cole took a quick look back to find Daniels sitting with his arms crossed. "He's right, Paige. Burkis was there for the Blood Blade and he got it, right in the damn face. Maybe the cops haven't found him yet because he changed back after he lost too much blood. He may even be dead."

"He's not dead," Paige said.

"How do you know?"

"Because," she replied as she steered toward an interchange that led to I-80, "that would make things too easy."

"I want to go back," Daniels announced. "It's the least you can do for me."

Paige lifted her chin to look at him through the rearview mirror. "Your girlfriend is fine. I made sure of that myself, and Burkis has no reason to go back there. If you want to call her, go ahead, but we're not going back there either."

"Where are we going?" Cole asked. "Back to Raza Hill?"

Keeping one hand on the steering wheel, Paige dug out her phone with the other. "Nope." Before Cole could ask another question, the call she'd made had already been answered. "Hey, Steph! How's it going? . . . Yeah? . . . Well I just thought I'd give you a quick call to let you know we got the gift you sent . . . Oh, come on. You know the gift I mean. That guy from New York with the matching set of assholes from your own personal collection . . . Don't give me any of that. I know you sent them . . . Uh-huh." When she paused this time, Paige looked over to Cole and made the yapping gesture with her free hand.

Cole chuckled uncomfortably and looked out the window. The weight of everything he'd done started to mash him into his seat like a bag of rocks the size of Minnesota being slowly lowered onto the back of his neck. He had some trouble drawing his next breath, so he rolled down the window.

"Why would they come on their own, Steph? Tell me that," Paige said. "Can't think of a reason why they'd do that? That's because they *wouldn't* come on their own. They're your buddies, and you're the one who knew about the man from New York." Paige listened for a few seconds and nearly clipped a minivan as she swerved into the next lane. "That's better. It feels good to 'fess up, doesn't it? Hey, speaking of confessions . . . "

The bag of rocks pushed down on Cole a bit more. Conversely, Paige was doing her best not to keep her smirk from bleeding into her voice when she said, "You know those two Nymar I was talking about? They're dead . . . Yeah, we're sure. Dead as Abe Lincoln. And that guy from New York? He's a Full Blood. Send anyone you like down to Schaumburg or you could just flip on the news. You'll hear all about it. What's that? . . . "

Cole pulled in one deep breath, held it, and then let it out. It helped, but not a lot.

"You're sorry?" Paige laughed. "About the Full Blood or the guys you sent to kill us? . . . Oh, I see. Well, since the only time Full Bloods generally deal with Nymar is to pick them out from between their teeth, you'll be real sorry before too long. Just thought I'd keep you in the loop, sweetie. Tell Ace me and Cole say hi . . . Huh? . . . Oh, well screw you too, then. 'Bye." Paige snapped her phone shut and threw it toward the backseat. When she heard Daniels yelp, she looked into the rearview mirror and asked, "Wasn't that great?"

"What did she say?" Cole asked.

"Oh, first she tried to say that Burkis came on his own and must have gotten the other two to come along with him.

After I told her the news, she got all pissed and said she'd called Burkis and sent all three because we made her look bad in her parlor. When I told her about the Full Blood, that really got her."

"Almost got all of us," Daniels muttered.

She leaned over to Cole and said, "Nymar don't like Full Bloods."

"Is it the old 'vampire versus werewolf' feud?" Cole asked.

"Not really. Do *you* like Full Bloods?"

"No."

"There you go. There's more to it than that. Way back when, a few Nymar got lucky and killed some werewolves in Philadelphia. Whoever did that kept the ball rolling and tried to set themselves up like lords in a stronghold. The Nymar never really controlled the place, but they kept strutting to make themselves look good, and the Full Bloods have just stayed out of the cities since then. Cole, see if there's anything new about KC on the Internet and then call MEG. After that, you can sleep for a few hours."

"I can stay awake until we get home."

"We're not going back to Raza Hill. I already told you that."

"Wherever we're stopping, I can make it there and then crash when we get home," he insisted.

"Well, we'll probably stop for gas in a while, but we're headed to Kansas City."

Both Cole and Daniels sat up and said, "What?"

Paige nodded and tapped the wheel to a song that could barely be heard over the radio. "We chased away one Full Blood, but there's another in KC. If we don't do something about those Half Breeds, the whole city will have one hell of an infestation."

"No," Daniels snapped. "I've got appointments. Research to do. *Your* research! And I need to get back to my apartment before police and who knows who else starts poking around in there."

"I told you to grab all the stuff you needed to finish that research," Paige reminded him. "Did you?"

Reluctantly, Daniels said, "Yes."

Bouncing her eyes between the road and the rearview mirror, Paige shifted her voice to a softer tone. "I didn't intend on kidnapping you, Daniels. Honestly. That Full Blood was a surprise, and you're too valuable for me to risk him getting to you again."

"Didn't you just say there's another one in KC?" Daniels asked. "How much safer am I going to be there?"

Wincing at how quickly he'd arrived at that, Paige replied, "All right. I'm going to need you to finish the work on that ink. Without the Blood Blade, we'll need some other advantage to swing things in our direction."

"He didn't get the Blood Blade. If you listened to me before, you would've heard me when I told you that."

Cole spun around in his seat. "What are you talking about? I saw the blade sticking out of that thing's head."

"As I've been trying to tell you, that was the sample I've been using to work on Paige's project. This," Daniels said, as he dug around in his overstuffed gym bag, "is the Blood Blade."

Daniels stretched his arm out between the two front seats. Cole recognized the gleaming, ornate weapon clutched in the Nymar's fist. It was the blade he'd brought back from Canada all those months ago. The surface was still smudged with the blood that had been melded into the metal, but a good portion of the blade had been chipped off from the hilt all the way to the tip.

"I grabbed this as soon as I got to the first floor," Daniels said. "Rather than risk losing it when you were both going to be ripped apart, I used the sample on that creature. It seemed to do well enough."

"Yeah," Cole said. "It sure did."

"Now," Daniels snapped, "can I use someone's phone to call my girlfriend?"

Chapter 12

Westbound on I-80

A sharp rattle snapped Cole out of a heavy, dreamless sleep. He sat up, looked around, and saw a few smudges of pink and purple in the sky. The ground was flat and barren enough that he wouldn't have been too alarmed if Paige was asleep behind the wheel with a brick holding the gas pedal down.

She was awake, although the bags under her eyes made it clear she was struggling to stay that way. Taking notice of him, she looked over and said, "Welcome to Iowa."

"What time is it?"

"Early. You want some breakfast?"

Just as he was about to give Paige a hard time for always wanting food, he realized his stomach was gurgling almost loud enough to be heard over the engine and radio. Something from the sixties was coming through the speakers, but he was too groggy to think of the singer's name, and Paige had the volume down low enough to keep him from hearing anything more than a few murmured melodies. "Breakfast sounds good. How about some sort of muffin-egg sandwich from somewhere?"

"Perfect."

"How long was I out?"

"About two and a half hours."

"That's all?" Cole growled. "No wonder I feel like I could drop off again."

"Well, you've got until I find somewhere to stop for breakfast. I need some sleep too and it's not a lot further to KC."

Cole stretched his arms and looked behind him. Daniels was lying on his side on the backseat. His arms and legs looked strange curled around him, but not as strange as the blackened bald spot that took up most of his scalp. "I don't suppose he can drive?"

"He's only just gotten to sleep," Paige said. "He was on the phone most of the night, talking to his girlfriend. He's gonna be working hard once I get him set up, so it's best if he gets all the rest he can."

Lowering his voice, Cole asked, "So Nymar really have girlfriends?"

"I only met her once, but she's really nice. She was almost a quick snack for another Nymar last night, so she needed plenty of comforting."

"I never pictured a Nymar having a girlfriend. That just seems so . . . I don't know . . . normal."

"Lots of Nymar are pretty normal. They feed on people they know, or work out some sort of trick for hunting. When I was training, me and another guy found this Nymar in St. Louis who used to run a three card monte game outside of a pool hall. He'd let himself get caught cheating just to start a fight. During the ruckus, he'd scratch and bite and get enough blood to hold him over for a few days."

Cole winced. "Feeding in public, huh? That's not good."

Shrugging, Paige told him, "We let it pass. He was on the receiving end of most of the beatings, and they were handed to him by loudmouthed jackasses who had something to prove outside of a pool hall. None of them wound up dead, and the Nymar was actually pretty slick. Creativity should never be discouraged, especially when it involves creatively beating up loudmouthed jackasses."

It wasn't much longer before Paige pulled off of I-80 to fill the gas tank and snag a few breakfast sandwiches from a drive-through window. Before heading back to the highway, Cole got behind the wheel so she could curl up to get some rest. Daniels woke up for some coffee and then got to work on his laptop. Twenty minutes later Daniels needed to stop for a bathroom break.

"Vampires still need to use the can," Cole grumbled. "Learn something new every day."

The car was quiet as it idled in front of a rest stop. Cole closed his eyes, brought a foam cup to his lips and held it there so the coffee steam could make its way to his nose.

"You ever fight a puppy?"

Paige asked the question in a soft, breathy voice that made Cole think she was talking in her sleep. He tipped the cup back and sipped his coffee.

"Cole?"

"Yeah."

"Have you ever fought a puppy?"

"Why?" he asked. "Are they running wild in Topeka?"

She coughed and nestled into her seat. Just when it seemed she was going to drift back to whatever she'd been dreaming, she said, "Sure you have."

"Do you realize you're saying this out loud?"

Lifting her head from where it had been resting upon her folded arms, Paige turned toward him, but not enough to actually look at him. "You know what I mean. Haven't you ever wrestled with a puppy or let a kitten swat and scratch your hand? They've got those little soft teeth and their claws don't have enough muscle behind them to really do any damage."

"I had a kitten that used to climb up my leg," Cole told her. "He went all the way up to my shoulder and laid there. Once he got bigger, he really tore me up trying to do that."

She fell silent for a second, keeping her head raised and her eyes cast toward the window without really seeing through the glass. "Puppies just sort of gnaw on you," she mused. "Their teeth feel like rubber or wet plastic. It's cute, but you can see the concentration in their eyes. They really think they're goin' to town and messing you up. That's how I felt last night. Fighting that Full Blood, I was just some puppy with bad intentions and no teeth. It's been a long time since I felt that way. I didn't like it back then and I hate it now."

"Well, for a bunch of puppies, we did pretty good," Cole told her. "The last time two Skinners were in the same room as that Full Blood, neither one of them made it out alive."

"We're only alive because of Daniels."

"True, but he's not at all like a puppy."

"Because he's Nymar?" Paige asked.

"No, because he's bald and stabs people in the face."

Paige's head drooped back down to where it could rest against the door. Her shoulders seemed to curl up around her ears, which made Cole wonder if he'd picked the wrong time to make a lame joke. When he heard her start to laugh, he felt a lot better.

Daniels was set up in a hotel just off of I-35 in Kearney, Missouri. It was on the outskirts of the greater Kansas City area, which was only a short drive to the southwest. The room wasn't much, but it had enough space for him to work. After promising some results later that night, he turned his back to Paige and shuffled into the room. Nymar might not melt in the sunlight, but this particular member of the species looked as if he really wanted to.

"You can talk to Sally if you want," she told him. "Just make sure she doesn't find out where you are. And don't use the room phone."

That perked him up a little, but not much.

Before long Cole was driving head first into the moving jungle that was morning rush hour in Kansas City. Even after trudging along for almost an hour, they didn't make much progress. As if the sheer number of cars and crazed drivers wasn't enough to contend with, he had another set of obstacles strategically placed around the multiple lanes of traffic. "What the hell is the deal with the construction?"

"Potholes don't fix themselves," Paige said as she dialed another number on her cell phone.

"I know that, but we've been sitting at a dead stop for half an hour. I see blinking lights. I see cones. You know what I don't see? Workers! Is anyone out here doing anything?"

"They're somewhere."

"Sure," Cole griped. "That's what they want you to believe."

"And if you paid taxes here, you'd have every reason to complain. Since you don't, just shut up and let me make my call."

After a few minutes of choppy conversation over her phone, Paige snapped it shut victoriously. "We've got an appointment!" she declared.

"With who?"

"Remember that cop named Stanze? The new girl answering the phones for MEG got a contact number and I finally got a message through to him! We're set to meet him for lunch. He even said he'd take us around to the spots where those animals were sighted."

Cole nodded. "I could have gotten the number for you, but whatever. So what do we do until lunch?"

"Let's worry about getting downtown before you start trying to ration your free time."

The traffic inched along all the way to Crown Center. It would have taken a row of topless bikini models lining the streets to make it a destination worth the hassle of getting there, but it was a nice place all the same. The buildings along Pershing Road had a futuristic, glassy look to them complete with walkways crossing above the street in several places. Cole couldn't take in many more sights than that because he had his hands full trying to drive without getting killed. By the time he found a spot to park, he practically had to peel his fingers from the grooves they'd dug into the steering wheel. For someone who'd become accustomed to driving in Chicago, that was saying a lot.

As soon as he turned the engine off, heat seeped into the Cavalier from all sides like an invading army that had been waiting for the right moment to make its big push. "Where to?" he asked.

Since the air conditioner barely managed to turn the air lukewarm, Paige hung her arm out the window. "He said he'd come by to pick us up." Before long her phone rang. She answered it and immediately perked up. "Officer Stanze? We're a little early, but we're here . . . That's right. The Cavalier with the Illinois plates . . . All right. Thanks." Hanging up, she looked over to Cole and said, "He's almost here."

When Cole saw the red and blue lights flashing nearby, he swore under his breath. There were no fire hydrants or important signs nearby, but the police cruiser separated itself from the traffic on Pershing and headed his way.

"Just take it easy," Paige said as she patted his arm. "If anyone asks, we are *not* carrying firearms in the glove compartment."

After pulling to a stop behind the Cav, a policeman who looked to be anywhere in his late twenties to early thirties stepped out. He had the build of a football player and carried enough gear on his belt to make a superhero jealous. Judging by the spotless uniform and friendly smile he wore, one of his powers was immunity to the summer heat. "Is Paige Strobel in that car with you?"

"Yes," Cole replied.

"I'm Officer Stanze. We spoke on the phone."

Paige leaned toward the driver side window. "Officer Stanze? That was quick."

"My shift's over, so I was just waiting for you to get here."

"Oh. I was expecting someone a lot more . . . never mind. I'm Paige."

"Right. So you two are with the Ectological Group?"

"Yep. I've been with MEG for a few years and Cole's new."

"Cole, huh?" Stanze asked as he offered his hand. When Cole tried to shake it, Stanze shook his head and asked, "Mind if I see some ID?"

"We don't carry badges or anything," Cole said.

Paige took something from her pocket and placed it into Stanze's hand. It was one of the few business cards she carried around that she hadn't designed herself. Apparently, MEG offered more benefits than a phone service. "You can call the number on there if you like," she said. "Just ask for Jarvis."

Taking the card from her, Stanze examined it for a few seconds and then tucked it into his shirt pocket. "That's the same number I called when I spotted that UFO a year or so back. Sorry if I seem suspicious, but messy cases attract all sorts of crazies. Not that you or your friend are crazy, but would you mind answering a question for me?"

"Ask away," Paige said.

"What's the stick for?"

Cole reflexively glanced toward the spear propped within his reach behind Paige's seat when she answered, "It's a divining rod. You can find anything, from spiritual activity to a well, from a hundred yards away."

"A divining rod, huh?" Stanze said. "Takes all sorts, I guess. That's Penn Valley Park over there. Some of those strange calls we talked about before came from there. Most of 'em were weird animal sightings, but we haven't been able to spot anything ourselves. There's a good amount of nutcases living in that park, so the calls are probably just them trying to get some attention."

Paige found a notepad somewhere among the garbage on the floor at her feet and flipped it open. "What kind of animals were sighted?" she asked in her best reporter impression.

Stanze glanced toward the park. Only a few trees could be seen from where they were, but he pointed as if the place was laid out in front of him. "Some homeless guy named Alvin swore a giant dog with big teeth ran past him over at the west end of the park. He said it moved like a cougar or some sort of mountain lion, but the animal I found definitely has a snout like a dog."

"Like one of those pit bulls on the news?" Cole asked.

Shaking his head, Stanze replied, "That's in North Terrace Park and it's not a pit bull. My cousin Terry has pit bulls and they're not as big as the things these people are seeing."

"You think this is connected to the people that were killed?"

Stanze pulled in a breath and chewed on it for a second. "Hard to say. People tend to get crazy during the summer and this is a hot one. We've been establishing a solid presence in the areas where those attacks happened, but haven't turned up any more bodies than what was on TV."

"Have you found any suspects?" Paige asked.

"It's an ongoing investigation," Stanze replied. "Everything I've told you has already been released and I can't say anything more. I can show you where those animal attacks happened, though. You can finish your interview back at the station, where I'm keeping that body, and then we can catch some lunch. How's that sound?"

Paige flipped her notebook shut and said, "That would be great. I'll come with you while Cole has a look at this park."

Glancing down at Cole as if he'd forgotten about him, Stanze grinned and said, "I wouldn't suggest drinking from any wells you find with that stick."

"Thanks," Cole said uneasily. "Should I bother looking for this Alvin guy?"

"Sure. He's not hard to find. Hangs out in the southeast corner of the park under a little bridge that crosses Penn Valley Drive. Long hair. Approximately a hundred and fifty pounds. Caucasian. Early fifties. Lots of black tattoos on his neck and arms."

"Black tattoos?" Cole asked.

"That's right. No real pattern. Just a bunch of lines that're probably covering a whole lot of needle tracks. He's not dangerous, though. Just some poor old junkie. You have any trouble, just give us a call."

"I should be fine."

"So you're riding with me, Paige?"

"Sure thing."

Officer Stanze gave them a curt nod and walked back to his car.

After the policeman moved away from the window, Paige said, "He seems nice. A lot younger than I thought he would be. I know I haven't slept much, but I don't look too bad, do I?"

"No," Cole grunted. "What interview was he talking about?"

"I told him I was coming to interview him for the MEG newsletter," Paige said as she fussed with a few stray pieces of hair sticking out from the mostly disheveled whole. "He's a fan, so that worked out really well. I asked him to show us where those people were supposedly attacked by dogs so I can write up a story. It was when you were bitching about the traffic. Check out that park and see what you can find. If there are Half Breeds around, that's the sort of place they'd make a den."

"You seriously want me to look for Half Breeds in this park. Alone?"

"This park and the other one, North Terrace Park." As Cole fumbled for something to say, she told him, "You're gonna have to be on your own sometimes. Remember that run we made to Indiana?"

"Yeah, but that was just one little Chupacabra and it only ate dogs," Cole said.

"But you found the den, so you know what to look for. You can handle some sleeping Half Breeds."

"Oh, so they'll be sleeping?"

Climbing out of the car, Paige said, "They don't like the sun, remember? We need to find as many as we can before more people are killed or turned. You're ready to head out on your own for a bit, so just wander the parks and use your radar to zero in on any hot spots."

Stanze poked his head through the window of his cruiser and asked, "You want to do this some other time?"

"No," Paige replied. "I'll be right with ya." She gripped the Cav's door as if she was going to tear it off. "All right, Cole. Let's see if I can spell it out for you. There's a park over there where a bunch of animals who look like inside-out Dobermans have probably made a den. Where do you think you should look for them? Under a picnic table where a bunch of kids would have already found them? What about by a water fountain? Maybe they're on the swings!"

"All right, all right. I get it."

"You've seen Half Breed dens. Just look for a hole by some trees off the beaten path. It'll be big enough for a man-sized thing to crawl into and is probably hidden by leaves or branches or something. Use what you already know and let the scars do the rest. It's just something you've got to go out and do, Cole, so go out and do it."

"What if I run into trouble?" he asked.

"Deal with it."

He gritted his teeth and was about to snap back at her when he realized he was just looking for someone to hold his hand. As soon as he thought of it that way, the little drill instructor voice in his head called him a few degrading names and then everything was fine. "All right," he said. "I'll look around, but I'll save the good stuff for when you decide to stop flirting with the cop. What about Alvin?"

"He should be easier to find," Paige said as she moved away from the window. "Just listen for the high-pitched singing." By the time she'd walked to the cruiser, Officer Stanze was holding the door open.

Chapter 13

Werewolves came in a variety of flavors. In his short time
with Paige, Cole had found out this little fact firsthand. Full
Bloods were the worst of the lot. Mr. Burkis was one of those,
and if reports from other Skinners were to be believed, there
weren't many more like him. Half Breeds were another story:
part shapeshifter and part unnaturally occurring plague.

As Cole picked his way through the more heavily wooded
sections of Penn Valley Park, he ran over what he knew
about the creatures he was hunting. As far as the moon
cycles were concerned, Hollywood had gotten it partially
right. Half Breeds liked their moons full, but that didn't
mean they were limited by them. And they did like to sleep.
That was most likely due to the pain.

When Half Breeds changed from human to werewolf,
there was no changing back. That was another thing the
movies had gussied up. Full Bloods could shift back and
forth just fine, but Half Breeds were pulled apart and forced
into their animal form. Changing a human skeleton to that
of a four-legged monster required every bone to be broken,
reshaped, and then held together by knots of muscle. Not
only did this make Half Breeds flexible, but it tended to put
them into a perpetual state of being pissed off. The only
transformation they went through after that was into a resting state where most of their fur was sucked back under their
skin and their muscles relaxed. Paige called that the "peeled

grape stage," and it was a fitting name. The first Half Breeds Cole had ever seen were in that stage, which made it very easy to understand why they kept out of the sunlight during that time.

Half Breeds tended to be only slightly smaller than when they'd been human and burrowed into the ground to make their dens. This meant he had to look someplace where a hole could be dug and the creatures could come and go without being seen. If they'd picked a spot near the portable bathrooms or next to the road, they would have been found already.

Strolling away from the main path in the park, all Cole found was several dozen yards of open, grassy park broken up by the occasional tree. Some teens in baggy shorts and freshly faded T-shirts were gathered at one of two picnic tables. As soon as they caught him studying them, the group flicked away whatever they'd been smoking and meandered to their second favorite spot.

In the end it was the application of common sense to uncommon circumstances that brought Cole to a patch of uneven ground at the west side of the park. The presence of shapeshifters caused the scars in his hands to burn. That pain was almost constant within the city, but had grown even worse with every step he took toward a wall of trees separating one spot from the rest of the park. At the base of two of the bigger trees, almost covered by an overhang of loose turf, he spotted a hole that was slightly bigger in diameter than his head. Approaching it, he was reminded of another fun fact regarding Half Breeds: they stank.

Wanting to make sure he hadn't simply found a rabbit's final resting place or garbage that had been collected by raccoons, Cole got onto his hands and knees for a closer look. He almost reached out to pull up the turf awning but was stopped by another bout of common sense. It was a big enough relapse for him to reach for his weapon, but not big enough to do the truly smart thing and drive to some other city.

"All right," he muttered as he slipped the forked end of the weapon under the earthen flap and lifted it. "Let's see what we got here."

The hole's covering was thick with moisture and heavier

than it looked. Keeping the flap propped up, he pressed his head against the ground, peered inside, and was almost knocked out by the stench that drifted up from below.

The odors of wet earth, animal urine, and rotten meat all washed through his nose to drip down the back of his throat. He lifted his head, took a few breaths of cleaner air, and then gazed down into the hole again. The second time wasn't quite as bad, but half of putrid was still pretty damn awful. All he could see were a few shapes that could very well have been wet rocks. One problem with that theory: wet rocks wouldn't be panting.

Keeping his ear pressed against the ground forced Cole to acclimate to the stench. Clawed feet scraped against the dirt as the shapes inside the hole huffed and wheezed. Before too long he could see a little better in the dark. "Ahhh," he whispered under his breath. "There you are."

The den was smaller than a decent-sized television set, and two Half Breeds were curled up in it. They squirmed every so often or twitched when one's paw touched the other in a tender spot. Considering that both of the creatures were slick masses of exposed muscle and protruding nubs of bone, every spot had to have been pretty tender.

Cole eased the turf back down. Gritting his teeth and holding his breath, he prayed his stomach wouldn't growl loud enough to catch the attention of the Half Breeds. Just when he allowed himself to exhale, the phone in his pocket started wailing the hard rock song he'd forgotten he'd downloaded for one of his caller-specific ring tones.

Scooting away and scrambling to his feet, he ripped the phone from his pocket and stabbed the answer button just to shut it up. "What?" he asked in a snarling whisper.

"Damn," Stu replied. "Let me guess . . . you're in Kansas City getting hassled by some cop named Stanze."

Cole looked around, but didn't know what he was expecting to find. Other than the teens who had resumed their smoking farther down the path, there were only a few other people sitting with their backs against trees or wandering across the grass. None of them seemed to be spying on him. "How'd you know that?"

"Officer Stanze called the main MEG number and asked about you."

"Why?"

"Just checking to make sure someone was supposed to be with Paige. Jarvis told him she liked to travel with some doughy reject carrying a stick."

"Nice," Cole grunted. He'd put some distance between himself and the den, so he felt more comfortable talking. "Is that it?"

"Just thought you should know he's got his eye on you. By the way, should I bother downloading that *Hammer Strike* pack?"

"What? No. Actually, wait until it gets updated. Before then, it's just—"

"Just another coat of paint. Gotchya."

Now that his heart had settled back into its normal spot, Cole sighed, "So who's that new girl?"

"Which new girl?"

"The one who answered the phone over there the last time I called."

"Oh, Abby? She's not new. Normally, she's in the field, but she broke her ankle on an investigation and has been downgraded to answering phones and sifting through videos and EVPs for a while."

"Is she cute?"

Stu chuckled and then said, "I guess. See for yourself." After that he heard some movement on the other end of the line followed by a high-pitched tirade that ended with something heavy cracking against the phone in Stu's hand. "There's a file on the way, but don't ask me to take the picture again."

Recognizing the voice that had been yelling at Stu, Cole snarled, "Jesus, she's right there?"

"Uh-huh. Right little spitfire too." Something rustled as the phone was covered up. The voice that had been screaming before now spoke in an excited chatter.

"What the hell's going on over there?" Cole grumbled. "Are you guys really that bored?"

"Do you know what EVP tapes are?" Stu asked. "They're hours upon hours upon *hours* of air and our own voices played from three different angles with only the occasional

groan or raspy voice to break up the monotony. Sometimes, I'd rather kill myself than listen one more time to
Jarvis asking the same freaking thing. 'Is there someone in
this room with us?' 'Are you angry?' 'Does my tech crew
stomping around in their big boots in your quiet house dis-
turb you?' 'Can you please flick my ear again?'"

Cole felt a laugh brewing, but held it back because he knew
that would only add fuel to the fire. An e-mail arrived to
send a quick tone through his earpiece, and when he opened
the file, he was treated to a picture cropped at the bottom by
something that had to be Stu's thumb. The rest of the frame
was filled with a long table covered with tape recorders and
computer monitors. Sitting behind that was a woman who
looked to be in her early thirties. It was hard to nail down a
more exact age due to the way her light brown hair and glasses
covered her face. Her eyes and mouth were wide-open in an
expression of shock and anger. One hand was balled into a fist
and the other was in the process of throwing a stapler.

She was cute.

"You get that pic yet?" Stu asked.

"Yeah, just now. Looks like you're catching hell."

"What do you think of our little Abby?"

Cole smiled and tapped the icon on the phone to save the
picture instead of erase it. "I think you should let her answer
the phones more often."

"You wanna talk to her?"

"I want you to let me get back to work. Also, send me any
more pics you guys have from the animal sightings in KC."

"One step ahead of me," Stu said. "I was just about to ask
if you wanted those."

"Send them to my regular e-mail instead of the phone.
Can you get them to me by tonight?"

"I'll get them to you in an hour."

"Perfect. Also, try not to post any more of them to the
MEG site."

Stu pulled in a labored breath that sounded unintentionally pornographic over the phone. "Ohhhh . . . ahhhhh . . .
I don't know about that. We kind of have an obligation to
report whatever we can."

"Handle this right," Cole added, "and I'll see if I can get you an exclusive once we're through with this Kansas City business."

"Really? I can't censor the site, but I can delay posting to it. That good enough?"

"That'll do."

"Oh and one more thing. Abby says she loves you."

That was immediately followed by another shouting match and the impact of something heavier than a stapler cracking against Stu's head. As fun as it would have been to continue his little tour through grade school with those two, Cole hung up. He was still grinning when he spotted the tall, lanky figure dressed in dirty khaki pants and a suit jacket staring him down from the tables where the stoner kids had been sitting. As casually as he could manage, Cole lifted the flap of earth to get another look down the hole. The Half Breeds had shifted a bit but hadn't moved.

Considering what he knew about the creatures, he wasn't surprised they were such sound sleepers. Then he considered finishing off the werewolves without waiting for Paige. Sooner or later he would need to do the dirty work himself. Picking up his weapon, he shifted his hands onto the grip so his palms scraped against the bloodstained thorns. With a quick squeeze, he could sink the thorns in and stab those Half Breeds before they woke up. Whoever those creatures had been before, they would surely thank whoever put them down.

But there was always the chance he might miss.

Even if he killed one, the other would surely wake up. Those things might have looked like a mess, but they could move when they needed to and could take a lot of punishment. Cole was pretty sure he needed to hit them at the base of the neck for a one-hit kill. Or was it the spine? Could he even see the bases of their necks?

"Damn it."

At that moment, he couldn't decide if he felt more like a trainee or some helpless little kid who needed to wait for Mommy to show up. He swallowed all of those bitter morsels and lowered the earthen cover back onto the hole. He had to be real sure and real quick if he was going to kill them. Otherwise, some innocent people in that park would be real dead. It was no time to take wild stabs.

Sometimes, Mommy did know best.

"I, uhhhhh, wouldn't go there if I were you."

Cole swung around toward that voice and reflexively brought his weapon up to point at whoever had just spoken. Not only had the man in the khaki pants and rumpled suit jacket gotten to within a few feet of him, but he'd done so without making a sound. If he wasn't already feeling the burn from being so close to the Half Breeds, Cole might have noticed the subtle itch caused by the presence of a single Nymar.

The man was tall, somewhere in his fifties, and had plenty of marks along his neck and arms. If Officer Stanze's description had been a little dry, it was sure accurate. Cole lowered his spear, even though the Nymar didn't seem too threatened by it. "Alvin?" he asked.

The Nymar nodded, which seemed to rattle his eyeballs within their sockets. Even after he'd stopped moving his head, he continued to shift his nervous gaze between Cole, the Half Breed den, the sky, the ground, and every point in between. It looked as if the secondhand suit was the only clothing he owned because his sunken chest was exposed under the jacket and bare feet stuck out from the tattered cuffs of his slacks. "Are you a cop?"

"No," Cole replied cautiously.

When he held his hand out to show Alvin the scars on his palms, the Nymar glanced down and grumbled, "You probably shouldn't shake hands with me. There ain't no more soap in the Porta-John."

"Are there a lot of you around here?"

"Some other folks live in this park. Times is hard."

"No. I mean . . . Nymar."

While Alvin had been tentative at first, he now took a cautious step back.

"You know," Cole insisted. When it was obvious that Alvin didn't know, he bared his teeth and tapped the spots where the upper two sets of fangs would be. "Others like you. Vampires."

It felt strange to say that word to a Nymar and not catch

hell for it, but Alvin's face lit up and he rushed forward as if to wrap both arms around him. He stopped before running into the spear and asked, "How'd you know about that?"

"I just know." It was a lame response, but seemed to be enough for Alvin. When the Nymar quietly nodded, Cole said, "You know about the things sleeping in this hole?"

"Sure I do. I seen 'em dig it."

"How long ago was that?"

"Few days," Alvin replied without hesitation.

"Are you sure?"

He nodded vigorously. "Only time I stepped away from here was to talk to the cops. They didn't believe me when I told 'em I saw those things come runnin' through this park and they didn't believe me when I showed 'em that hole. 'Course it was empty when the cops was here. They said they'd come by to take another look, but they never did."

"Has anything else been running through here?" Cole asked.

Alvin shook his head. "Just them sorry lookin' dogs, but they mostly sleep."

In the time that had passed since Alvin started talking, the scents of cheap wine and beer permeated the air. "How do you feed?" Cole asked. "Do you hunt people that walk through this park?"

"No! I eat whatever I can get. I ain't no killer!"

Judging by the Nymar's sunken features, bony body, and pasty skin, he hadn't drained enough blood from anyone to do much damage. Even the tendrils under his skin were shriveled and faded. "Do the others like you in town help you out?"

"Others? There are others like me?"

"Never mind. Just make sure not to hurt anyone, all right? If I find out you're hunting people in this park, I may have to do something about it."

"I ain't no killer," Alvin insisted. Lowering his voice to a haggard whisper, he added, "I mostly bite the drunks or potheads that fall asleep aroun' here. Even then, I can't take much before they wake up an' take a swing at me. I used to go after joggers, but they're . . . you know . . . fast."

"Yeah. I guess they would be. Thanks for the help, Alvin."

Chapter 14

It was past eleven-thirty by the time Officer Stanze drove past the last crime scene and brought Paige to the Police Station on Locust Street. The building was a typical government brick: fairly clean outside, more than a little cluttered inside, and filled with the ringing phones and muted conversations of any office.

Stanze grinned and paused with his hand resting upon the handle of a door. He'd led her down a few halls as if he was in a race, but now stopped to announce, "Here's the final stop on our gruesome tour." With that, he pushed open the door to reveal a stairwell. They only went down one floor, but the hallway on the other side of that door seemed to have led them into another building entirely. Unlike the bustling, somewhat organized upper floor, this one was obviously not meant for the public. It had the rumpled, lived-in quality of a break room except without as many vending machines.

Even though he was wearing a uniform, Stanze had to pause and sign in before getting all the way to the room at the end of the hall. "When I actually got a reply from those ghost guys, I thought it was a joke," he said as he shouldered open a door that led back outside. "Half the calls I got after I posted those pictures were cranks, and the other half were from crazies. You don't even wanna know what kind of people are bidding to buy the thing I found."

"I can imagine," Paige chuckled.

The door they'd just used had deposited them into something of a dugout. The main entrance was on the opposite side of the building, which had been built into the slope of a hill. That way, both the entrance and exit they used opened to ground level. Paige looked around to see a long row of metal tables, a few dirty basketballs lying around the perimeter of a patch of cracked concrete, and some water coolers. "So, that thing you found," she said. "You keep it out here?"

"I brought it inside to stay out of the heat, but it got booted out here. It's a good thing you came out today or it might've been gone altogether." As he'd been talking, Stanze walked over to an upside-down cooler that was big enough to hold several pizza boxes, a few six-packs, and plenty of chips. Judging by the smell that filled the air at the moment, it wasn't holding anything so inviting. "You ready?"

"And waiting."

Reaching down to the cooler, Stanze pulled in a deep breath and then lifted it to reveal a large, dark green garbage bag. The odor Paige had smelled before was just a trickle. Once the garbage bag was open, the real flow began.

This wasn't the first time she had been around a Half Breed carcass. Compared to how they smelled once they were cut open and salvaged for parts, this one wasn't all that bad. Even so, she placed her hand over her mouth to at least play the part of a normal person.

"Ever seen anything like that before?" Stanze asked.

"No," Paige lied. "Can I take some pictures?"

"Go right ahead. I took plenty already."

The Half Breed carcass inside the bag was twisted up like a meaty, bony, rancid pretzel. Its head was turned around at an odd angle and all four of its legs were practically knotted into a bow. Its torso wasn't much more than a mass of flesh marred by ribs jutting out at odd angles. Paige removed her cell phone and took a few pictures. "Has anyone tested it?" she asked while reaching in to push aside some of the wiry fur from its upper forepaw.

"Tested?" Stanze asked.

"You know, like its blood or hair. DNA? That sort of thing."

Stanze laughed and swatted one of the dozens of flies that had found their way to the exotic carrion feast. "Oh, hell no. I wanted to, but it was all I could do to keep from having Animal Control cart it off with the rest of the road kill. Some more people were attacked after I hauled this one in, so they figure it isn't the one we're after. Even if this one did hurt someone, one science boy told me it's just some big dead dog. I tried to call in a few favors, but I don't know anyone who owes me enough to cover the cost of a DNA test."

"Where did you find it?"

"I shot it," Stanze corrected her proudly. Just then the door opened and a pair of cops in plainclothes stepped outside carrying bottles of water. They looked over at Stanze and immediately started to laugh. Before the comments could start to fly, Stanze muttered, "Well, I hit it with my car and then shot it. Damn thing messed up my vehicle so bad, I may be forced to cover the cost myself. I sure won't hear the end of it from the rest of these clowns."

"And where did you hit it?"

"Right across the ribs and the side of the head," Stanze said without cracking a smile. He maintained his composure for another few seconds before removing his cap and nervously patting down a section of his hair. "Oh. I was on an access road off of westbound I-70. It was a few days after that first guy was declared missing. Rothbard was his name."

"You think this thing hurt any of those other people?" Paige asked while carefully watching Stanze's reaction.

The cop furrowed his brow and looked over to the other pair as if expecting them to jump in at any time. "Sure I do. I've heard of pit bulls attacking people and even trying to drag some little kids away, but nothing like what's been going on lately. Now the press is saying the animals running wild are some sort of mixed-breed rottweiler. Does that look like a rottweiler to you?"

She looked down and shrugged. "It's so mangled, it really doesn't look like much of anything."

"Yeah, I guess. Maybe I should have his stomach pumped."

Paige's smile was subtle but genuine. At least Officer

Stanze was trying, while the rest of his department seemed content to make fun of him for it. To maintain her reporter act, she took a few more pictures.

"What do you think it is?" Stanze asked.

"It's dead," she told him before flashing him a little grin.

Stanze ate it up, but quickly steered things back on course. "Yeah, but is it anything you or the other MEG guys have seen before? Maybe a really rare animal or some unknown species? Somethin' like that's gotta be worth something." He leaned in a bit closer to her and lowered his voice. "Maybe I could just get some credit on your website or a mention on one of those cable shows? Some recognition would go a long way. I'm dyin' here. Every cop in this building thinks I should be tossed into the loony bin."

"I can arrange something along those lines," Paige assured him. "But I don't know about auctioning it off. Have you gotten any serious bids?"

"Like I told you, there's been plenty of e-mails and offers." Fidgeting from one foot to another, he added, "Most of the responses I got are cranks. I deal with enough of crazies to know that much."

"Well, I've seen plenty of things like this alive and dead, so it's sure not as rare as you might think." After the time she'd spent with Officer Stanze, Paige was glad to be completely honest with him. "Let me get another look just to be sure." She stuck both hands into the garbage bag so she could see the rest of the Half Breed.

Stanze had the beginnings of disappointment on his face, which was quickly replaced by disgust. He wasn't quite ready to fill a barf bag, but he was more than a little surprised at how dirty Paige was willing to get. "What . . . uhhh . . . what're you doing there?"

Flicking her head back to move a stray piece of hair from her face, she ran her hands along the dead thing's sides and around the base of all four of its limbs. "Just checking its muscle mass." Quickly, she added, "To make sure it's not a coyote or stray dog."

Obviously, Stanze had heard that comparison before. "It's no coyote," he said while looking over to the cops loitering near the building. "I looked it up, and coyotes don't have snouts like that. They're also not so big."

Paige reached in a little farther to push aside a slick clump of fur on the creature's abdomen. There was a dark green smudge on the Half Breed's skin, which looked like a burn or possibly some sort of stain. Pressing her fingers on the perimeter of the smudge, she drew the skin together until it looked less like a stain and more like a shape with four curved lobes. She took a picture of the symbol, a few more of its teeth, and then pulled her hands out.

"Could you get me a description of those missing people?" she asked as she lifted her hands from the bag and held them in front of her. "Any stuff about distinguishing marks or tattoos would be helpful."

"Why do you need that?"

"Oh, nothing to do with this critter. The MEG website gets a lot of hits every day, and I thought I could post some notices about those missing people. Might as well put all those amateur investigators to work looking for something other than glowing mists, right?"

Stanze blinked a few times and then nodded. "Yeah. That would be helpful. We've already got some notices and press releases printed up. I'll get them for you."

"Great, you do that. I'll run to the ladies' room to wash my hands and we can go get some lunch."

"You still want to eat?"

"Yeah," Paige said. "Your offer is still good, isn't it?"

"It sure is. Follow me."

As Paige walked toward the door of the building, one of the two plainclothes cops raised her voice. "Hey!" barked a tall blond woman with a face that had probably soaked up more than its share of cheap moisturizers. "What did Stanze tell you about that thing?"

Too far away from the door to get inside without obviously ignoring the question, Paige replied, "I'm just here to take some pictures."

The other plainclothes cop was about Stanze's age and had a clean-shaven face that made him look like a kid. "Hope you're not some sucker he got to buy that freak show exhibit."

"Don't worry about it. I need to wash up."

"It's a fake, you know. Stanze doesn't know his ass from a hole in the ground."

Paige stopped with her hand on the door. Even though she'd endured a lot worse, the condescending tone in the cop's voice got under her skin. It went beyond confidence and into the realm where anyone who disagreed with the speaker was obviously an idiot.

"Maybe it's fake, maybe it isn't," Paige said. "Have a good one."

The two cops snickered to each other just loud enough to be overheard. Paige looked back at them and smiled. When she opened the door, she made certain to smear plenty of Half Breed juices onto the handle for them to enjoy when they decided to wrap up their break.

After washing her hands, she found Stanze in the hall. The two plainclothes cops were needling him on their way to the stairs that led up to the main floor, which left a sour look on Stanze's face. By the time he walked back to Paige, all of the enthusiasm that had been there before was totally drained from his face.

"You said it's some regular animal, right?" he muttered. "I'm just gonna dump the thing. If you want it, you can—"

"I'll give you two grand for it," Paige cut in.

Stanze blinked and then shook his head as if he'd heard disembodied voices. "If you want it, just haul it away."

"Two grand is my final offer." Seeing the confusion in Stanze's eyes, Paige removed all the traveling money she had in her pocket. The funds came from a pool of donations from thankful civilians who owed Skinners their lives, as well as some winnings from lottery numbers picked with the help of a psychic independent contractor known as Prophet. "I'll need some help getting it to my car, and you're still treating for lunch, so don't try talking your way out of that."

"Let me write out a receipt," Stanze said. "For the monster corpse and nothing else." Dropping his voice to a mumble, he said, "It's not a great idea for me to accept money inside the station like this."

Paige tucked the money back into her pocket. "Write up

whatever you need. Give me your address and I'll have MEG send you a check," she told him. "How's that?"

"That," Stanze said as his face lit up with a wide smile, "sounds great! Let's get that ugly bastard wrapped up and find your partner so we can eat!"

Chapter 15

Sometimes Paige would eat anything that wasn't trying to run away from her. When it came to hot dogs, however, she was much more particular. Knowing this all too well, Cole got a bad feeling about the place where Officer Stanze brought them for a late lunch.

Chi Town Hot Dogz grated against the Skinners' nerves right off the bat. First of all, Cole bristled whenever he saw something spelled with a *z* instead of an *s*. Second, it referred to Chicago as Chi Town. That one always rubbed Paige the wrong way, but not as badly as when a Nymar from Jersey used the phrase, "Chickey Ville." That hadn't turned out well at all.

Stanze got his hand on the door and was pulling it open when the radio on his belt began to squawk. After a few sentences came through, he keyed the transmitter attached to his shoulder and then let the door slip from his hands. "I gotta go."

"I thought your shift was over," Paige protested.

"It is, but I'm in uniform and they need backup, so . . . can you find your way without me?"

The Half Breed was already loaded into Paige's trunk and the Cav was parked outside, so she nodded. "Sure. I'll get back to you about that check."

"Great. Nice meeting you. Same with you, Cole. Tell whoever's at the counter that I sent you and you should get a free dog."

Cole waved at Stanze, who was already climbing into his cruiser. "Bribing cops now?" Cole muttered.

"Not that sort of check," Paige replied. "He's a good guy."

"Let's hope he knows his lunch spots. I'm hungry."

Chi Town Hot Dogz looked as if it had once been a fast food burger joint. Cole recognized the layout of the drink dispensers as well as the proportion of booths to tables. Looking over to Paige, he recognized the sour expression upon her face. "What's the matter? You look like you've already got a complaint for the manager."

Rather than answer that question, she stepped up to the counter with one of her own. "What kind of hot dogs are these?"

The guy behind the register kept his smile intact despite her tone. "Grade A, Chicago style," he assured her.

"No. Are they Vienna Beef? I don't see a Vienna Beef sign."

"You mean like that one?" the cashier asked as he hooked a thumb toward a plastic sign that was partially hidden by a Cubs pennant. It was the official yellow, blue, and red logo that Paige had been looking for, so she nodded and moved on.

"What about the buns?" she asked.

"They're fresh."

She pulled in a deep breath and let it out with a sigh. "The buns need to be poppy seed. The dog needs to be Vienna Beef, topped with pickle spears, tomatoes, peppers, relish, mustard—does any of this sound familiar?"

Unlike most of the food service employees Paige pulled through the wringer, this one kept his spirits up. "Sure. Check the menu and see for yourself."

Everything Paige had demanded was listed under the heading, #1 DOGZ.

"All right," she said. "I'll take one of those."

"You want any ketchup on that?"

Paige wheeled around and stomped for the door. "We're leaving."

They wound up eating lunch at a round metal table, sitting on metal seats that felt as if they'd soaked up the heat from a sun that had gone supernova ten minutes before they arrived. Since he'd passed about sixty-three signs advertising REAL KANSAS CITY BAR-B-Q, Cole dragged Paige to the closest one of those places and wouldn't accept any other suggestions. As always, once she had some food in her stomach along with some on her face and T-shirt, she was much better company.

"So what did you and Officer Stanze do while I was out crawling through the dirt?" he asked.

"He took me around to the spots where people were killed and others were supposed to have been dragged away or attacked by dogs."

"Fun date."

Pausing while in the middle of sopping up some greasy sauce with a hunk of white bread, she replied, "I bet he is."

"Well, I found some Half Breed dens," Cole announced before she could follow her previous train of thought too far. "Three, as a matter of fact. One in Penn Valley Park and two in North Terrace Park."

"Did you get a look inside or did you just spot a few holes and call it a day?"

Anticipating that reaction, Cole had a speech prepared. The three dens were pretty similar, so it didn't take long to fill her in.

When he was done with his presentation, Paige asked, "What about that Alvin guy? Did you find him?"

"Sure did. He's a Nymar, and a loopy one at that. He didn't even know there were any others like him."

Paige shrugged and grabbed the short corn on the cob that had accompanied her lunch. "There hasn't been a big Nymar presence here for years. Even in places like Chicago it's not unusual to hear about some Nymar living their whole lives thinking they're the only ones. Just proves they don't have their shit together half as much as they say they do."

"Otherwise, they'd have a better welcome package," Cole said.

Paige bit into her corn, accidentally squirted Cole in the face with it and said, "Exactly!"

"Alvin said the Half Breeds got there a few days ago."

"Good. That means they'll still be resting up from their first transformation. It takes them a couple days to recuperate."

"What about that thing in the trunk?" Cole asked. "Did you feed Officer Stanze a story or just swear him to secrecy?"

Paige shrugged and finished off her last piece of beef. "With all the Half Breeds running around this town already, there's probably hundreds of grainy pictures being taken by dozens of cameras. He's a cop so he's in on all the weird calls that have been coming in. He seemed like he's already seen and heard a lot worse than a screwed-up hunk of road kill."

"Learn anything on your drive?"

"We drove to those spots, but I only felt an itch at a few of them. We'll check those out after lunch. Everything he said makes it pretty obvious that the Half Breeds were out hunting and sniffing out their territory over the last few days."

"That doesn't sound good."

"Not good, not bad," Paige replied. "But it could be worse." Falling into the tone she used when teaching Cole a new attack, she explained, "Half Breeds are made when someone survives a really bad werewolf attack. You knew that much already. The first time they shift into that new shape, pretty much every bone in their body is broken. Muscles and tendons hold them together, but it kills the person in a bad way. All that's left is the wolf.

"They're pretty useless for the first day or two after they're turned, but the first thing a wolf in pain wants to do is crawl away somewhere until it feels better. Once it feels better, it gets hungry." Paige picked up a napkin and began the meticulous process of cleaning her face, hands, and clothes from the assault of barbecue sauce she'd endured. "Once the muscles harden around their broken bones, they can walk. Once they figure out they can walk, they're off. After that, they eat, run, eat, kill, and eat some more until they die. Those Half Breeds you found sounded pretty fresh, so they may be a little ways off from becoming a real problem."

"Their skin was still damp and there wasn't a lot of muscle around the ribs or legs." As he said that, Cole remembered the sight of those things in the hole. The smell came right along with that memory, and after that hit him, he grimaced and pushed away the rest of his lunch. "So do you think the ones from North Terrace Park attacked that girl from the university?" he asked.

"Actually, I think the one in the trunk *is* the girl from the university."

"How could you know that?" Cole asked.

"Well, to begin with, it's a female. They have shorter front legs and longer ones in the back. That makes them just a bit faster. The males are the other way around."

After pitching their garbage into a huge metal barrel, they went back to the car. Rather than start the Cav's engine, Paige walked around to the trunk and opened it. The stench rolled out like a kick from an invisible pair of hiking boots, but she ignored it as she peeled open the garbage bag and reached down to poke the dead creature inside. "Look for yourself," she said.

Once Cole's eyes stopped watering, he was able to point out a few things. "This carcass is pretty small. The descriptions of Lisa Wilson being run on the news say she was only five-five or five-six, so I guess this is about the right size," he pointed out. "And its fur is thick. Actually, the fur covers most of its body. I usually don't see that in the ones that are standing still."

Paige grinned and gave his arm a playful swat. "Very good, young one. This was killed while it was in full wolf form and on the prowl. Stanze said he hit it with his car and then shot it. Looks to me like he unloaded a whole clip into her. He was probably so freaked out that it wasn't dead from the crash, he just kept on firing. But look closer. Right . . . there."

Paige used the tip of her finger to push aside some of the fur to reveal the green smudge on its belly. "Oh shit," Cole grunted. "Not another werewolf infected by Nymar. Are these things gonna start popping up all over the place now?"

"That isn't Nymar. Stanze gave me a press release with descriptions of all the missing people. Under tattoos and distinguishing features, Lisa Wilson is listed as having a shamrock tattoo on her belly. This thing's skin is a bit stretched to see details, but check it out." Placing her fingers around the smudge as she had at the station, she bunched the creature's skin together so the symbol came together again. "See?"

Cole leaned in to get a better look. Fortunately, he didn't have to get much closer before he asked, "That's her shamrock tattoo?"

"Yep. Not so lucky for her, but it gives us a bit of a timeline. If this is Lisa Wilson, the first batch has hit the streets. She's got enough muscle to have fed, so that means there'll be more resting up somewhere."

"Wow," Cole said. "I'm impressed."

"Skinners have been watching these damned things for a long time. It's been a while since there have been this many in one place, and I've never even heard of dens being planted like this."

"Planted?"

Even though people were coming and going from the barbecue restaurant without casting more than a glance at them, Paige became uncomfortable. Cars flowed back and forth along the nearby street just as casually, but she didn't seem to like the looks of them either. "Let's get moving," she said as she slammed the trunk shut. "I'll talk and you drive."

It wasn't until they were pointed south and merging with the rest of the late afternoon traffic that she said, "Some of those pictures we saw before coming here, the ones from MEG, were of the Full Blood that came to drag Henry out of Wisconsin before we could finish him off."

"You think Mr. Burkis is here too?"

"The Full Bloods aren't known for traveling in packs. They're territorial, but I've only heard of them crossing paths every once in a rare while. If Burkis was the one you saw in Canada—"

"He was," Cole snapped. "There's no doubt about it. Maybe this is just like a meeting or some time of the moon cycle when the Full Bloods gather and . . . I don't know . . . howl."

Paige shook her head while checking the gun in the glove compartment. "You don't get it, Cole. Full Bloods don't stake out patches of woods or stretches of mountain ranges.

One Full Blood has been seen at different ends of this country and up into Canada only days apart. When they hit their stride, they move so fast that you can barely even see them. You can just feel it as they go by. Each one could stake a claim that's a couple thousand miles wide."

"Sounds like tall tales to me," Cole grumbled. "All hunters get that way after a while. I had uncles that used to hunt bears, and the tougher one was, the more they exaggerated when they told the stories. They really believed what they were saying, though. Same thing with fishermen. The easy ones to catch are just little fish. The ones that put up a fight are monsters."

Rather than try to argue, Paige simply emptied the rounds from the pistol into her hand. "We'll need to reload this with the heavier ammo. These Nymar rounds are just greasy lead to a shapeshifter."

"What did you mean when you said those dens were planted?" Cole asked.

Paige snapped her eyes to the road and pointed to the upcoming corner. "Turn right there and take another at Rockhill." After the first turn was completed, she went back to digging through the glove compartment. "Half Breeds make their dens wherever they can. They sniff out a hole, a basement, anyplace they can sleep while the sun's out. When there are too many Half Breeds to fit in one den, they either fight with each other or find a new one. They don't divvy up a city like this."

"Maybe they're not part of the same pack," Cole offered. "One got loose, tore up some people, and moved on. Then the new ones made a den of their own."

"If they're spreading naturally like that, why aren't they clumped closer together?" Paige asked. "Half Breeds are stupid and hungry. They don't strategically pick a different feeding ground each night. Not many animals do. When they find good pickings somewhere, they stay there until the food's gone or until it's too dangerous to go back." After she'd finished reloading the pistol, she said, "Pull over."

"Where?"

"Just stop. I need to show you something."

Cole pulled into a gas station and parked next to an over-priced, motorized air pump that was missing its hose.

Twisting around to the backseat, Paige removed a road atlas from the previous year. "Look here," she said while flipping to the map for Kansas City. "Here's Penn Valley Park. Here's North Terrace Park. This is Blue Valley Park, one of the spots that Rob showed me where there were a few supposed pit bull attacks."

"Rob?" Cole muttered.

"Officer Stanze."

"First name basis, huh?"

Shaking her head and waving at Cole the way she would shoo a fly, Paige pointed to another spot on the map. "This is where we're going now. Forest Hill Cemetery. What do you notice about all these spots?"

Cole squinted down at the map and watched Paige use the tip of her finger to connect all the dots scattered throughout the city. "Kind of looks like a rectangle," he said.

She nodded. "There are other spots as well, but none of them are as close as they should be to another one. Just the fact that so many popped up so close to all these people is strange. Usually, when Half Breeds get together and hunt, they're spotted and are either killed by us or taken down by regular people."

"People who take down Half Breeds don't sound too regular to me."

"Half Breeds are fast and mean, but they can be shot. It takes a whole mess of bullets or possibly getting run down by a car, but it can be done. Full Bloods . . . not so much. Since the cops don't know they're dealing with a fast moving creature that likes to burrow and hide underground, there's probably other dens that nobody's even found yet."

"Maybe the Half Breeds want to hit a spot with the most people."

Paige studied the map carefully. "All Half Breeds do is eat and run. Full Bloods are the ones who think and plan."

"And they can create Half Breeds whenever they want. This reminds me of a game that my boss was working on a couple years ago."

"Everything reminds you of some game," Paige snapped as she closed up the atlas. "Get moving."

Cole pulled back into the stream of traffic and resumed his course. "It was an RTS. That's real-time strategy, for those who don't know."

"I know what it is. I played *Dueling Warlords* through most of high school."

"Really? That's kind of sexy. I just picture you in a school uniform allocating resources, managing an army, and sending out attack forces—"

"Was there a point to this?" Paige asked.

It took a second for Cole to shake the imagery from his head, and it would have been a lot easier to do if a bit more time had passed since he'd actually seen Paige in pigtails. Finally, he said, "If you want to take over a fortified spot on the map, you set up your units wherever you can all around that spot. If you can sneak some bombs into the middle of enemy territory, that's even better. Could this be something like that? I mean, planting a Half Breed den in the middle of so many people could cause more deaths than a bomb. And considering a portion of the victims will turn into more Half Breeds . . . "

"That could make things a lot worse for a long time," Paige said with a nod. "Take Rockhill to Sixty-eighth Street and go left. So if that Full Blood from the pictures wanted to do a whole lot of damage, planting Half Breeds is a hell of a way to do it. If we don't clean out every last den, Half Breeds will roll through this city like an army."

Cole raised his eyebrows and said, "The last time we saw that Full Blood in Wisconsin, it said it was going to reclaim its territory. Maybe it meant KC."

"Or maybe this is just the first spot it's marking as its own." Shaking her head, she added, "It won't do us any good to try and think the way those things do. You'd have better luck figuring out what motivates a tornado. Let's just stick to what we know. The parks seem like a natural choice for dens, but Rob told me this cemetery is where the first sighting came from."

"Plenty of holes get dug around there."

"Yep. There are also caretakers who would pick up on something like a hole that doesn't belong or strange animals coming and going from it. If I don't find something on my own, at least I'll have someone to ask."

"While we're there, why don't we just clean them out?" Cole asked. "We've got guns and some better ammo. Let's hit them while they're sleeping."

"I think Officer Stanze liked me, but not enough to give me a pass if we get hauled in for shooting up his city. Even if we forget about the guns, the last thing we need to do is get a bunch of those things worked up and have one get away."

"Then what the hell are we here for?" Cole snapped while tightening his grip on the steering wheel. "People are already dead! I thought we came to help."

Paige didn't get angry and she didn't lose her patience. She simply placed a hand on his shoulder and replied, "We are here to help. Just ask yourself something. How long would a game last if you went charging into a fight before you knew what you were up against?"

Gritting his teeth, he replied, "Not very long."

"Right. We're scoping things out and taking a head count right now. Please tell me you'd do the same thing if you would have thought it over for a few more seconds."

"Yeah," Cole sighed. "I guess I would've gotten there eventually."

"Good. We've got weapons and tactics that have been working for a couple hundred years or so. I can immunize you against werewolf bites, treat Nymar infections, and even heal some ugly wounds, but we're not invincible. We need to think. That way, when it's time to fight, we stand a better chance of winning. Trust me, that time's coming soon enough."

Chapter 16

Forest Hill Cemetery was a large, sprawling property surrounded by a low stone fence. Paige and Cole stopped at a short section of broken sidewalk where one of the cement squares had been torn up to reveal what looked like a manhole. A larger portion of the ground behind that section had been pulled up as well, and the whole stretch was marked off with bright orange plastic fencing held up by a couple of iron bars.

Paige huddled down next to one of the bars at a spot where the temporary barrier had come loose. "Smell that?" she asked.

"Yeah," Cole replied as he pulled in a lungful of air tainted by the stench of Half Breed. "Makes me long for stuff like hot tar or dead skunk."

"Listen."

Cole stood on a square of sidewalk that was still intact and watched the few people in the cemetery along with the cars driving by on Troost Avenue. "I can't hear anything."

"Come closer to me."

Reluctantly, he took a few steps closer, but at her tug on his pants leg, dropped down to one knee beside her. Paige's hair had an almost imperceptible hint of strawberry scent from her regular shampoo. Whenever she got around to cleaning up after this long day, it would smell good enough to drive him crazy.

"Hear that?" she asked.

Fortunately, he heard something before he had to admit

he was either deaf or sniffing her hair. *Un*fortunately, what he heard was quick, heavy panting echoing from somewhere under the sidewalk. He nodded and promptly eased away from the opening.

"That's a big one," she whispered.

"Sounds like there could be a lot of them."

Paige led the way back to the car and jumped in. Once the door was closed, she spoke in an excited rush. "There's enough room down there for more Half Breeds than we can clean out right now, and the only thing keeping them in that pit is the sunlight. They're ready to run, which means there's not enough time for us to go all the way back to where Daniels is staying. We'd only distract him. Let's get a room somewhere around here and we can get to work. I've got mixing to do and you need to find us a good wide-open spot."

"What kind of spot?"

In a thick cowboy drawl, she told him, "A spot to make our last stand, pardner." Wincing, she added, "Bad choice of words, but you know what I mean. We need to bring these Half Breeds all together and take them out."

"How do we bring them anywhere?" Cole asked. "Drop invitations into their dirt pits?"

"Bait," Paige replied with a grin.

The first thing Paige had insisted upon when Cole signed up to work with her was that he pack a bag of clothes and supplies that would always be kept in the car. She had plenty of cases tucked away in the Cav, about half of which were hidden well enough to make it through most international border inspections. They didn't have to pass anything along those lines to check into the Holiday Inn on Westport Road, but Paige pushed her luck by insisting that Cole help her drag the dead Half Breed up to their suite on the fifth floor. The room cost an arm and a leg, and there was barely enough space for Paige to unpack everything she needed.

"Why do hotel clerks look at you like you're a criminal when you pay cash?" she squawked while dragging the stinking garbage bag the final couple of steps to a spot next to the luggage rack.

"Why do they insist on calling a room like this a suite?" Cole replied. "Some mysteries defy explanation."

"No, I'm serious. I paid cash, in full. He doesn't need to bother with a credit check. They've got all their money, but he looked at me like I was going to open a meth lab in here."

"Oh no," Cole chuckled. "Instead, you're going to cut up a dead werewolf. What could be wrong with that guy?"

"Fine, smartass. Just for that, you get to do the mixing while I clean up."

"What am I mixing?" he asked.

"It's an old Skinner recipe that Half Breeds can smell for miles in any direction. We'll need to place it around the city and near those dens, but it should bring them right to us."

"Somehow, that doesn't sound like a great idea."

"Sure it is," Paige said as she rooted around in one of the larger cases. "We get to pick our spot, draw those things away from where too many people will get hurt, and take them out. This is how Skinners have worked for so many years without everyone learning about us."

Cole stretched his aching legs and leaned back. "What would be the harm in that? I mean, why not just tell the cops about all this crap and let them deal with them? Half Breeds can be killed by big enough guns, and there's no shortage of those."

"Tried that once. Actually," Paige said as she straightened up and tapped her chin, "I think that's been tried three or four times. Once was in England a couple hundred years ago. There was a big Half Breed growth spurt, which led to one hell of a hunt that ended with a lot of rotting bodies of all shapes, sizes, and breeds. Apart from the people killed after those Half Breeds were whipped into a frenzy, the scientists of the day had a ball dissecting the carcasses to see what made them tick. All that unnatural blood and bacteria and Lord knows what else mixed with the air and water to make a whole new problem called the Black Plague. They didn't know that when you get that many dead werewolves in one spot, you gotta burn 'em."

"Bullshit," Cole said. "The Black Plague was caused by rats or fleas or something."

She shrugged, picked out a few containers that looked more suited for holding leftover veggies, and went right on. "Then there was a few of the smaller villages in the original colonies. Those Pilgrims ran into a little shapeshifter problem when they got to the New World and they did the proper thing by telling the authorities . . . or whatever they had for authorities. As far as we know, some of the creatures were killed, but not before most of the villagers were killed. They didn't do a complete enough job, got on the wrong side of a very bad thing, and got completely wiped out by whatever came by later to finish them off. The Natives only survived because they knew when to cut and run. They also knew you don't screw with a pack of monsters unless you know how to screw every last one of them into the ground so far they won't get up again."

"You don't even know what got them?" Cole asked.

"No survivors. All that's left to record the incident is a few pieces of a journal from a Skinner who was in training when he left England. Probably just a few pieces of that Skinner left too. Then," she said as she removed a scalpel from the case and walked over to the garbage bag, "there was the incident in New York."

"You're just making this up to scare me, right?"

"You can't be scared if it's just bullshit, right?" she asked. "Anyway, there were accounts of some kind of monster ripping through a few of the gangs that used to run New York City back in 1904 or so. As far as we can tell, it was a Full Blood. The gangs tried to protect their streets, the cops tried to rein in the gangs, and everyone got on the bad side of the Full Blood. By the time the bodies stopped dropping, they had to write the whole bloodbath off as a turf war."

A year ago Cole wouldn't have believed a word of any of this. But if Paige was making this stuff up, she was doing an awfully good job of selling it. "What happened?" he asked.

She stopped with her hands poised over the carcass and the scalpel ready to cut into the dead werewolf's stomach. "We don't really know."

"Weren't there any Skinners in New York back then? There had to be."

"Sure. At least two or three, but they didn't survive. Some letters were sent back and forth asking for help with some creature they called Standing Bear, but nobody got there in time. Those Skinners were never heard from again, a bunch of people were killed, and the survivors thought it best to cover up the whole thing and hope the Full Blood just went away."

Cole's eyes narrowed and he let half a grin creep onto his face. "I know there were gang wars in New York City back in the early 1900s. Those couldn't have all been Full Bloods wreaking havoc."

"Not *all* of them were," Paige assured him. "But *one* of them was, and it was a doozy. That's how all of this stuff gets lost or goes unnoticed. There's plenty of crazy, violent shit going on every day in every part of the world. Most of it's caused by humans, but some of it isn't. There's enough of the human variety for most everyone to accept a little more."

Grabbing onto the dead Half Breed's fur, Paige began cutting. The tone in her voice was the same as when she'd been picking barbecue from her teeth at lunch. "The simple fact is that we don't know exactly what makes one sort of infection cause cold sores and another cause someone to turn into a Half Breed. We understand more than most, but not all the way down to the real essence. Why do some growths turn into cancer and other ones turn into Nymar?"

"Magic? Well . . . shitty magic."

"Might as well be," Paige replied. "Skinners have been trying to figure it out for years. After a lot of trial and error, we can whip up some good stuff, but we just don't know all the specifics. We can pluck away at our research because there's no huge organization hounding us. If a government gets involved, they'll have bigger agendas. Eventually something gets leaked and someone else digs too deep for information, that stuff gets spread around and it causes panic. If it gets ignored, then there really wasn't any reason to break our traditions in the first place. Too many uninformed people messing around with stuff they don't understand causes very bad things. Until we figure out more of the bigger answers, it's best to just put out whatever fires we can and let nature take its course."

"Nature?" Cole laughed.

"Or magic or aliens or— There it is!" Suddenly, Paige's face brightened. "Come over here. Take a look at this." When Cole was close enough to see, she removed a small dark sac from the Half Breed carcass. It looked like sausage casing filled with glue. "This is what you're looking for when you're mixing up shapeshifter bait."

"Aww gawd," Cole moaned as he used one hand to squeeze his nose shut and cover his mouth. It was difficult to breathe that way, but with the stink that came up from the werewolf's innards, that didn't seem like a bad thing.

"Watch and learn, Cole. This is a time-honored tradition passed down through generations."

"Are you really trying to make this seem like a proud moment?"

"Yeah, sort of."

"It ain't working."

"Watch anyway," Paige snapped. "You need to mix up this crap while I shower and take a nap. There's a long night ahead of us."

In the space of twenty minutes the top spot in Cole's mind for "most disgusting life experience" was replaced about half a dozen times. Ten minutes after that he was sitting at a desk in a corner of the room, mixing ingredients from Paige's supplies into a bowl and kneading it into a paste with his bare hands. Every so often he had to squish some of the stuff from the sausage casing into the mix, knead some more, and then add water. The only saving grace was the distraction of Paige's warbling singing voice as she took a shower.

Hearing her through the open door, Cole took his hands from the bowl in front of him and reached for some water to add to the mixture. "To hell with this. I'm jumping in the shower next."

"You'll just have to get that stuff on you again. Besides, I'm the one that's been sweating like a pig in that damn leather for half the night."

"Then I at least get a nap! You can't be the only one to

get some rest." As he'd spoken, Cole twisted around to look at Paige. She stepped from the bathroom wearing a pair of faded jeans and a fresh shirt while vigorously rubbing her hair with a hotel towel.

"I was going to show you how to skin that Half Breed," she said, "but I could just do it myself and put some body armor together. It's not like there won't be plenty more for you to practice on when we're done."

"Why even bother with armor?" Cole grunted. "You said supernatural creatures can rip each other up, so what good is that gonna do anyway?"

"Their hides can still take a lot of punishment. Even if they just stop a few claws and teeth, it'll keep you alive longer than regular stuff. Kevlar might as well be toilet paper against a Half Breed."

"Yeah, yeah."

She stepped up behind him, dropped her towel and tapped his shoulder. "Go on and catch some sleep. You've got more than enough of this stuff mixed. I'll get started on the rest." When Cole looked at her freshly scrubbed face, she gave him a smile that had an apologetic curve to it. "You need to sleep," she said. "I can't have you trying to run on half a tank."

"What's the plan, exactly?" he asked.

"Well, we need to place that stuff you mixed around town so when those Half Breeds come out for the night, they come to where we want them to go instead of wherever they can take down a quick meal."

"Will they really come to us?"

"That stuff makes them crazy. It's a blend of pheromones that attracts Half Breeds to one another. We also need to find a spot to take them," Paige continued. "Once we do, we'll air out some more of that mixture and wait for our guests to arrive."

"But you already said there are more dens around than the ones we found."

"After all the casualties that have piled up, I'd rather take our chances in a hard fight than allow those Half Breeds to run wild another night. I've got some extra firepower in the car, and we're both ready to take out a good number without firing a shot. I've been watching you, Cole," she added while placing a hand on his shoulder. "You'll do great."

The warmth in Cole's chest was put there by the confident smile on Paige's face. After spending the day thinking about innocent people getting ripped to shreds and gazing into reeking pits, it was nice to have something to live for.

Cole slept for an hour or two and woke up when the sun was still shining through the window. Its light was a bit warmer and duller than it had been during lunch, which told him it wouldn't be around much longer. Paige was busy placing strips of Half Breed skin inside of harnesses resembling bulletproof vests that had been pulled apart, gutted, and re-stuffed.

"You still asleep?" she asked.

As much as he wanted to roll over and drift off again, Cole grunted, "No."

"I need you to find us a good spot to meet up with those Half Breeds."

After plugging his laptop into an outlet and switching it on, he asked, "What exactly am I looking for, here?"

Paige zipped the layers of the second vest closed, encasing the werewolf hide within it. "Someplace not too far away, but outside of the city. Lots of open space. Preferably somewhere we won't be disturbed."

After a few minutes of getting online and searching the local map pages, he asked, "What about a nature preserve? It says here there's one with primitive campgrounds and hiking trails."

"It really says primitive?"

"Yeah, it does."

"Perfect. How far away is it?"

"Uhhh . . . about sixteen miles."

She nodded, set the completed vest on top of the first one, and gathered a few empty baby food jars. "Very nice."

"What if there's people camping there?"

"We'll tell anyone we see that there's a storm coming. Tornadoes are good, because it'll be dark by then. If they don't start moving, we'll just act crazy and get them to steer clear of us. Once the Half Breeds arrive, any dumb-shit campers that don't get the hell out of there deserve whatever they get."

Marveling at Paige's infallible logic, Cole glanced at the blinking e-mail icon at the top of his screen. Clicking on the little envelope took him to a screen that listed the contents of his in box. There were twenty-six messages that had arrived over the last few days, mostly from work. Since he was almost done with his level designs and didn't have time to do anything else, he ignored those. Some of the messages were junk that had slipped through his filters, and a few were from MEG's e-mail server. The name of the sender of all of those was SpookyChik92.

Cole smirked and reflexively turned the laptop so the screen wasn't visible from where Paige was sitting. The first message read, "Sorry for cutting it short on the phone last time. Stu can be such a jerk. If you ever get time to talk, that would be nice. Later, Abby."

The second message was sent an hour after that one and read, "Not that I just assumed you wanted to talk. I know you guys want to keep to yourselves. I've always wanted to talk to one of you guys and you seemed pretty cool. Plus, the whole Digital Dreamers thing is beyond cool. Maybe we could play some *Hammer Strike*. Abby."

The third had been sent earlier that night: "I'm not stalking you. Honestly. Stu told me you were asking about me and that's weird because I've asked about you when he mentioned you. Not that he blabs about you guys or anything. He's full of carp so nobody pays attention to him anyways. Abby."

The last message was Cole's favorite. It simply read: "Crap. I meant he's full of crap. I'll stop embarrassing myself now. A."

In response to the last message, Cole typed, "Sorry. I've been busy. I'll definitely give you a call when I get some time. I know what you mean about Stu. It may not be carp, but there's definitely something fishy about that guy."

Unfortunately, he sent the e-mail before he could come up with a better joke for the end.

Shattering his comfortable frame of mind, Paige said, "Take a look in those bags over there for some shotgun shells. If I'm out, we'll need to hit a sporting goods store on our way to that campground."

Cole set his laptop aside and rummaged through the bags lying closest to him. "Hey, uhh, what're the odds of any Full Bloods showing up tonight? Will they smell that bait?"

"Full Bloods can smell damn near anything for miles in any direction. If there's one anywhere near KC, they'll already know we're here."

"Are we equipped for Full Bloods?"

"*So* glad you asked," Paige replied. "Remember when Burkis nearly bit my arm off?"

"Yeah."

"Well," she said with a nasty grin as she screwed the lid onto one of the jars she'd filled with Half Breed blood, "I got me a few souvenirs. Check out your new weapon upgrade."

"Speaking of weapon upgrade, did you ever find those level forty *Fire Mace* sketches I lost?"

"Forget that video game stuff," Paige scolded. "This is important."

Cole walked over to where his spear was propped against a wall. Since the forked end was at the bottom, he didn't have any trouble spotting the bony spike that had been attached to the main spearhead by several layers of leather cording. "Is this one of those teeth you knocked out of Burkis's mouth?"

"Oh yeah," Paige said proudly. "Full Bloods can chew through damn near anything, so that stick of yours can now do the same. The one on my baton keeps it from fitting into its holster just right, but that's okay. Just don't smack it against any brick walls and your upgrade should stay put for a while."

"And I get one of those vests, right?" Cole asked.

Paige nodded. "These babies are gonna go over real well at the party tonight."

Chapter 17

Cole had never felt so scared and so stupid at the same time. The concoction that he'd put together at the hotel had been split into three squeeze bottles designed to hold mustard or ketchup. Each bottle contained a mixture that ranged from weak to strong on whatever scale was used to measure bait for Half Breeds. Paige drove to the were-wolf dens they already knew about so he could hop out and squirt some of the gunk onto a sign or post where it could get the most air. The most diluted stuff had the consistency of jelly and hardened into a crust in a matter of seconds.

Having started at the tail end of rush hour, they managed to drive from point to point without getting snarled up in too much Kansas City traffic. Every so often Cole dashed from the car, looked around for cops or the occasional concerned citizen, then vandalized a public spot with foul-smelling pheromone paste. He got plenty of surprised looks and a few harsh words from people who saw him at work, but nothing bad enough to slow their progress.

As they worked their way east, he switched to the more potent mixture. That stuff took some getting used to. It started as a thicker paste, splattered against whatever he'd chosen as his target, and hardened into a brown shell. Not only did it befoul whatever property caught his eye, but it polluted the air just as badly. People gathered to look up at a lot of those spots, but were driven away by the smell before they figured out a way to clean it off. Just to be safe, he and Paige made several other stops along the path to Highway 24 over the next hour or two.

Outside the city's limits, Cole switched to the heavy-duty mixture. The instant he removed the stopper from the last squirt bottle, the car filled with a sweaty, bitter odor that stuck to the back of his throat in the same way the jelly from the other two bottles had stuck to any available surface around the city.

"I kind of feel bad about this," he said after hanging his head out the window. "KC seems like a pretty nice place and we're spraying this crap all over it."

"The Half Breeds will be coming out . . . " She paused to stretch her neck toward the windshield and get a look at the moon, which was just full enough to be seen through the fading sunlight. " . . . any time now. As far as I can tell, this is the night when things would have really gotten interesting if we weren't here. The first batch have probably already gotten some sneaky patterns down pat, and the fresher batch will be raring to go. All of the Half Breeds are pretty young, though, so they should be a lot easier to bait."

"You're so smart," Cole chided with an exaggerated twang. "And purdy too."

She slammed on the brakes and pulled onto the side of a rough road that didn't look to be in the best part of town. "Cut the shit and do your job."

Cole opened his door and made a mad dash to a light pole just ahead of a convoy of pickup trucks and SUVs. For a second he was worried that the stuff in his squeeze bottle had completely solidified. After rolling the bottle between his hands and unscrewing the top, he worked enough of the gunk out to fling it up high onto the metal pole. It had the consistency of cookie dough, but smelled as far from that heavenly of all substances as another substance could get. It plopped against the steel, slid down less than an inch, and turned into a rust-colored lump.

Slamming his door shut after hopping into the car, Cole tried not to look at the old man yelling at him from the other side of the street. "I just thought of something. Are we coming back to clean this stuff off?"

"No, why?"

"First of all, it's gross. Second, it'll just keep attracting Half Breeds, won't it?"

"Nah," Paige replied. "It stops smelling in about twelve hours. By tomorrow it'll have dried up and blown away like any other glob of snot."

Cole held the bottle up next to his face. "Eco friendly and full of fiber. Operators standing by."

Paige was still shaking her head when her phone rang. Digging it out of her pocket, she looked at the screen and then flipped it open. "Yeah?" After a few seconds she shook her head even harder. "I don't need to hear this right now." She listened and furrowed her brow. "If you don't have anything specific, save it for later. This isn't the time for half-assed predictions."

"Who is it?" Cole asked.

Paige looked over and mouthed the word *Prophet*. Then she barked into the phone, "I don't care what you dreamt!"

Sensing the approach of a hang-up, Cole asked, "What's going on?"

"Here, talk to Cole. I'm driving." With that, Paige slapped the phone against his chest.

He took it from her and was instantly bombarded by the loud thumping of dated techno music pounding through the phone's little speaker. "Walter?" Cole shouted. "Are you there? Can you hear me?"

"Yeah, Cole. I can hear you. Hey, after the hell we went through in Wisconsin, you can call me Prophet. What's up?"

"Where are you?"

"Some little place outside of Minneapolis."

A chorus of whoops and hollers came through the connection after a DJ announced that someone named Candy Mounds was coming to the main stage. That gave Cole a pretty good idea what sort of place it was. Actually, he wouldn't expect much else. "Another strip bar, huh? How's the buffet?"

"Actually, damn good," the bounty hunter replied. "It's all

Chinese food. I don't know if it's always like this or if I just lucked out."

"Don't try to get too lucky," Cole warned. "You might get arrested. Are you on a job or just trying to unload a bunch of folded dollar bills?"

"Little bit of both. Remember Shimmy's?"

That one word was enough to bring a smile to Cole's face. "Whenever I can."

"Little purple A-frame in the middle of nowhere, right? Guess what this place looks like?"

"Purple A-frame?"

"Yeah! You know what's even weirder?" Walter asked.

"The fact that you care about the food they serve?"

"No, there's a nymph working here too. Three of them, actually. I think it's some sort of nationwide organization or something. It covers a few states at least. This is the fifth strip club I found in a purple A-frame, so I'll be sure to call when I got more to report."

"That's great. Now, what did you do to piss Paige off so bad?"

"Considering how that last batch of lottery numbers hit, she shouldn't yell at me like that."

"What big hit? The last one I got was just over twenty bucks!"

"Ask your partner about it," Prophet told him. "She's the one handling the money in Chicago. While you're at it, remind her that I know what the hell I'm talking about. The dream I had was one of the good ones, but she still doesn't wanna hear about it."

Candy Mounds must have done something extraordinary because the noise from the crowd became loud enough to drown out the thumping music accompanying her. Cupping his hand around the phone, Cole shouted, "What dream?"

"That stuff going on in Kansas City. Have you heard about it?"

"Yes."

"There's more than just some people getting killed. I think there's something more like what we saw in Janesville. You know, like that big werewolf?"

"I know, Prophet," Cole sighed. "You're a little late on that prediction."

"Well, I've been busy. Also, tell Paige to keep a good eye on that little bald guy."

"You mean Daniels?"

"I don't know his name," Prophet said. "She needs to watch him close so he can finish. Or maybe he wants to finish something. I don't know much more than that, but they were both in a hell of a bad spot."

Suddenly, Cole knew why Paige had been close to hanging up. Although Walter Nash's psychic talents were good enough to earn him his nickname, they weren't one hundred percent. If they were, Prophet's lottery predictions would allow the Skinners to travel in something a lot classier than a piece-of-crap Chevy. "All right, then. Anything else?"

Prophet's voice came through, but was intended for whoever was on stage. Finally, he asked, "Did you say something?"

"No. Talk to you later."

"Sure. 'Bye."

Paige pulled in a deep breath and let it out with a hiss. Having just turned onto a dumpy two-lane road headed north, she pulled over next to a gas station that looked like it had nothing but dust in the cashier's booth and rainwater in the pumps. "I don't want to hear any more of whatever he was babbling about. Give me the phone." After Cole handed it over, she told him, "Now slap some bait on the side of that building. Use a lot. We want the scent to carry."

"The scent from this crap could carry this whole freaking car into Kansas."

"Just go."

Having already squeezed some of the disgusting paste to the top of the bottle, Cole stepped outside, flung the clump toward the roof, and heard it slap against the wall. Paige barely waited for his butt to hit the seat before pulling away and heading north.

"What did Prophet say?" she asked.

"Something about Daniels being in trouble and you screaming at him to finish."

"I've only been screaming at him to finish that damn ink for a week, and if he'd called us about that *before* we'd gotten to that apartment, we might've had a good heads-up regarding Mr. Burkis. Instead, he wasted time at some nasty buffet in some nasty strip bar."

"He did say there could be a group using nymphs to lure people into a trap or something."

Rolling her eyes, Paige groaned, "The purple A-frame theory again? I swear that guy only comes up with that shit to justify hanging out at those bars. If he thinks he's luring me to another one of those dives, he's got another thing coming."

"Shimmy's wasn't a dive," Cole pointed out.

"Tell you what. Survive the next few nights and I'll let you stuff your money into some g-strings with Walter. Okay?"

"I can taste the Chinese buffet already."

"Prophet found a strip bar that serves Chinese food? Good Lord, what has this world come to?"

Paige glanced back and forth between Cole and the back road she was using. It was getting close to eight o'clock, so there wasn't a lot of traffic to get in her way. There also weren't a lot of cops along that route to prevent her from introducing the gas pedal to the floor of the Cav. After steering off the main road in favor of an even smaller one, she said, "We need to clear out as many of these Half Breeds as we can tonight. So far, there's only been a dozen or so deaths. Maybe a little more, maybe a little less."

"'Only' a dozen or so?"

"As the rest of those things get strong enough to come out of their dens and hunt, they'll shred through entire neighborhoods before anyone puts them down. Plus, you've gotta think about the panic that will cause. Enough people are already carrying guns around here. What's going to happen once they have a reason to twitch at every strange shadow?"

Trying not to give in to his own panic, Cole said, "That's true."

One glance was all Paige needed to see the layer of sweat that had suddenly appeared upon his chalky skin. "If it makes you feel any better, I've never seen Full Bloods and Half Breeds fight together. Half Breeds are too wild to follow a leader, so that should be all we get tonight."

Cole let out some of the breath he'd been holding and looked out the window. The houses, gas stations, and fast food restaurants that had dotted the road so far gave way to open spaces and low hills stretching out for miles under a blanket of scorched grass. "So, you've been able to survive a night like this on your own?"

"Yep," Paige said with a nod.

"You baited a bunch of Half Breeds and wiped them all out?"

"Sure did."

"How many were there?"

She crinkled her forehead and twisted her mouth into a thoughtful, crooked line. "Three."

Feeling as if someone had found the release valve in his chest, he asked, "You think that's all that'll be coming?"

"Oh no," Paige laughed. "Considering all those dens we found, there'll be a lot more than that. And with all the bait we put out, we may even attract some from the neighboring county."

Cole's mouth hung open, but he forced it shut before he asked another question. Any more encouragement from Paige and he might just throw up.

The nature preserve outside of Kansas City was a strip of open land about two miles long. There were a few campers set up here and there, but Paige drove until she spotted a place that suited her needs. It was flat, away from the road, and had a minimum of trees on the side facing the city.

Cole spotted two campsites that were situated a bit too close for comfort and wondered what Paige would do about them. She took the easy route by passing out enough money to pay for hotels all around plus a little more. It was a hot enough night for the campers to gladly accept the bribe and agree to eat their s'mores under the stars some other time. While they were packing up, Paige scooped out some spots in the dirt to set up a little camp of her own. She removed a few heavy packages from her trunk and buried them under a shallow layer of dirt. "Watch out for these spots here," she told him.

Sitting hunched over a metal bowl and mixing up another batch of bait using a powdered mixture that didn't smell quite as bad as the fresh stuff they'd spread all over town, Cole looked up and asked, "Why?"

"Bear traps," she replied while pointing to all five mounds of dirt. "Hopefully, we can hobble a few of the Half Breeds before they get to us."

"Can you mark the traps with little flags or sticks or something?"

"Can't you remember where they are?"

"I've got a lot on my mind here," Cole snapped. "Just put some damn sticks in the ground. It's not like a bunch of rampaging, wild animals are going to sidestep a few suspicious twigs."

Paige marked the buried traps with sticks, and by the time she was done a wispy cloud of putrid steam drifted up from Cole's bowl. After that the only thing left to do was gather their ammunition, divvy out enough to fill their pockets, and scatter the rest in strategic locations they could get to in a rush. Cole took the shotgun and Paige took the revolver. Even though he wound up with his preferred weapon for most of the games he'd created, he wasn't feeling any better. Not even the metallic clack of the shotgun's pump could light a fire in him.

The sun lingered like an oblivious houseguest before finally dipping out of sight. He and Paige sat just outside of the campfire's glow. Her pistol was tucked away and his shotgun was strapped across his back. The thorns of Cole's weapon pressed against his palm without breaking the skin, feeling oddly comfortable and familiar. Paige had her knees bent and pulled in close to her chest. One baton was propped against the toe of her boot and she tossed the other casually in the air to catch it on the end without the thorns.

The fire crackled.

A slow wind blew.

Every so often a car or truck engine rumbled in the distance.

Cole craned his neck to look at the stars directly overhead. "It's nice out here," he said, doing his best to avoid looking at the moon.

She didn't take her eyes off the urban glow illuminating the sky to the west. Tossing her baton into the air created a subtle whooshing sound as the weapon turned end over end. The varnished wood slapped against her palm and she tossed it up again.

"I never camped much," Cole continued. "It seemed fun, but I didn't want to go through all the trouble. You know . . . bugs. Rain."

"No outlets," Paige added.

"Yeah," Cole said. "That too." He sighed and tried to pick out a few constellations, but was inevitably drawn to the moon. That pale light steered his eyes to the yellowed electric glow being sent up by Kansas City to wash out the stars in that section of sky. His next inhalation was tainted by the bait stewing over the fire. It smelled like exhaust and garbage.

"I think we're downwind of that stuff," he said.

Paige slowly shook her head and caught her baton with another loud slap. "That won't matter. Half Breeds aren't dogs. They can smell it just fine no matter which way the wind blows."

"And you think they'll follow it here all the way from the middle of KC?"

Slap. "Yep."

When he thought about the Half Breeds he'd seen, his weapon felt a lot lighter than it had a few seconds ago. He swung the front end down to draw a few shapes in the dirt near his feet using the newly modified tip. "What did you want to be when you were a kid?"

"What?"

"You know. When you were growing up? I wanted to be a pilot. Then I wanted to be in the Navy. Then I wanted to be a Navy pilot. When I got to be recruiting age, I realized I'd just watched too many movies and didn't seriously want to go through all of that stuff."

Slap. "This is why I don't like camping. Everyone feels

like they need to tell stories. They sell the trip with a lot of promises of peace and quiet, but then they either bring a freaking CD player or won't stop talking about hopes and dreams."

"All right, then. Let me guess." Cole snapped his fingers and said, "You wanted to be a short order cook. That's why you live in a restaurant."

Slap.

"Are you even listening to me anymore?"

After another *slap*, Paige said, "I was in school to be a veterinarian."

"Seriously?"

"Yep. That was before, though."

"Before," Cole muttered. That word reminded him of days spent at a keyboard when his biggest worry was hitting deadlines for new game concepts or level ideas. His nights might not have been full of parties and wild sex, but he hadn't spent them crouched on a patch of dirt surrounded by bear traps and spare shotgun shells. Suddenly, he started to laugh. "You know what? Maybe this isn't too far off from how it was before. Instead of watching a guy in a game hide somewhere in the dark with boxes of bullets scattered all over the place, I'm actually living it."

Paige tossed her baton one more time, caught it, and stood up. "Come here."

He went to her and couldn't help but notice how the moonlight caressed the curves of her body as she reached back with one hand to gather her hair and clip it behind her head. The pale glow coming from above worked nicely to make the lines of her neck stand out. Even the crooked shape of her broken nose looked cute when bathed in that light.

"Close your eyes," she whispered.

Cole did as he was told.

"Hear that?"

He listened for a few seconds but couldn't pick up on any sounds that hadn't been there before. Finally, he asked, "Hear what?"

Just as he was losing hope, he felt her hand press firmly against his chest. Despite the roughness of her palm and the fact that her fingers felt like iron bars wrapped in a thin glove, Paige's touch felt soothing as she slid her hand along his chest and to his side. Once there, she turned him a bit in one direction and said, "There. Just listen."

The sappy, expectant grin that he couldn't hold back froze in place when he heard a rush of movement beneath the malodorous breeze of the incoming campfire smoke. The sound churned with a power of its own. It wasn't thunder, but more of a current being pumped through a nearby pipe.

After another second or two he could hear panting snarls being forced from several sets of unnaturally powerful lungs.

A few cars honked in the distance as tires screeched against pavement.

Something heavy was knocked over.

By the time he picked up on the snapping of twigs and low hanging branches, a dry creaking came from Paige's batons as they stretched into curved sickle blades. Cole's hands wrapped around the thorny grip of his spear and tightened until the sharp little spikes punched through his palms.

"How many do you think there are?" Cole whispered.

After a pause that was just a little too long, Paige replied, "More than I expected."

"Should we still do this?"

She stood beside him so the side of her foot brushed against his shoe. "Just tear them up as much as you can and don't ever let go of your weapon."

The snarling breaths and scrambling paws drew closer. Cole blinked away a bead of sweat, which allowed him to make out the shapes of lean animals racing at him from the surrounding dark. Wide eyes glinted in the moonlight, and the panting became intermixed with a series of frenzied barks.

"Paige, I—"

"Save it, Cole. Here they come."

Chapter 18

The first two Half Breeds exploded from the shadows amid a flurry of claws and teeth. Their long legs and lean bodies gave them such a gangly appearance, it seemed a wonder they could move at all. As soon as they spotted Cole and Paige, the creatures adjusted their course and charged at them even faster.

A few more werewolves followed the first two and three more came after them. There were more on their way, but Cole was too rattled to take a head count. He guessed the closest ones were about a hundred yards from where he and Paige stood. Before he could finish choking on the breath that had lodged in his throat, the first wave was nearly upon him.

A few feet away, Paige gripped her batons and said something that was lost in the chorus of raspy barks. The Half Breeds racing toward her weren't like the ones that had been curled up in their dens. At rest, those creatures were gnarled tangles of limbs and broken bones held together by knots of muscle. These Half Breeds were in their element. Long, lanky bodies were covered in tangled, sweaty fur. Powerful limbs were in constant motion, and claws curled out from the tips of stubby fingers. They kept their ridged chests close to the ground as their vaguely canine heads pumped back and forth like pistons in an unstoppable engine. With most of their body mass clumped toward their shoulders, the creatures' hind ends were narrow and bony, with short, ratlike tails dragging on the ground.

Ducking down over one knee, Paige snapped her right arm straight out to drive the pointed end of her weapon directly into the eye of the first Half Breed that reached her. The tooth fixed to that end of her weapon drilled straight through, hit home with a wet thud and dropped the creature to the dirt. Cole could only see that much from the corner of his eye as he braced himself for his first customer of the night.

The Half Breed that got to him before any of the rest looked about five and a half feet long. Extending both sets of legs all the way out, however, nearly doubled that length. It came at him with its teeth bared and a hungry snarl erupting from deep within its throat. Cole reflexively raised his weapon to protect himself as the werewolf leapt with enough force to knock him onto his back.

His blood burned with the proximity of so many of the creatures. The pain of getting those thorns driven so deeply into his hands caused him to grit his teeth and push the Half Breed away before it could tear off a piece of his face. Powerful jaws snapped shut less than an inch from his cheek. When the thing reared its head back to take another bite, Cole shoved it to one side and rolled to the other. The Half Breed compensated by twisting its neck at the impossible angle required to hit its mark. Jagged teeth tore through Cole's upper arm and sent a spray of blood into the Half Breed's mouth. Seeing the hunger that had grown to overtake the creature was enough to get Cole on his feet to defend himself.

He swung the forked end of his weapon at the Half Breed. One of the sharpened ends dug into the creature's back, so he drove it in deeper to hold it against the ground. The Half Breed yelped and tried to get free. Its claws kicked and dug little trenches into the dirt but remained pinned. Before Cole could decide what to do from there, Paige buried one of her curved sickle blades into the Half Breed's forehead.

"Don't wrestle with them," she snapped. "Kill it and move on." Then she knocked away a snapping bite from another creature, tore the weapon free from where it had been lodged, and cracked the side of that blade against another Half Breed's skull.

Cole heard paws thumping against the ground, whipped around and saw a werewolf racing toward him. It would have pounced if its rear leg hadn't been caught between a set of iron jaws that popped up through a thin layer of dirt. Letting out a high-pitched yelp, the Half Breed fixed its gaze intently upon him. When the chain connecting the bear trap to the ground reached its limit, the creature's front end flopped down and its chin smacked against the earth.

Raising his spear, Cole drove the single pointed end into the Half Breed's side. Thanks to the tooth attached to the spearhead, it drilled all the way through the creature's torso and sent another yelp ripping through the air. He turned toward the sound of more scampering steps to find a trio of Half Breeds running at him from another angle. He ducked down and allowed the group to leap through the empty air over his head. Using a scooping motion to reclaim his weapon from the trapped werewolf's torso, he opened a wound wide enough to put the creature down for good. As an afterthought, he glanced down at the arm that had been bitten only a few seconds ago. The wound was there but had already stopped bleeding. When he flexed those muscles, he felt a coolness flow through him that normally only came after he'd been given a dose of Paige's healing serum. Apparently, he'd taken enough injections for the stuff to be in his system. Even so, he hoped the pain and adrenaline wouldn't stop. They were all that kept him moving.

"Paige, behind you!" he shouted.

Having taken a low, wide stance, Paige held her arms out so both weapons were well in front of her. Another one of the traps had caught a Half Breed's front paw, forcing it to scramble and contort any way it could just to get to her. One of her blades punched a neat hole through the base of its neck, which killed the thing instantly.

She whirled around to meet one of the three Half Breeds circling around to rush at her from behind. The blunt end of her weapon knocked against the first one's chin, temporarily stunning it. When that Half Breed flopped onto its side, it cleared a path for another to spring forward. Paige swung at its neck, but the Half Breed twisted its head away at an angle that made it look like a broken movie prop. After the sickle passed by the creature, it snapped its head back around to try and sink its teeth into Paige's ribs.

The teeth sliced through the outer shell of her body armor and were snagged in the underlying layer of werewolf flesh. The Half Breed's weight pulled her to one side, as if she'd caught a bullet. Hanging from her vest as its limbs swatted at the ground, the Half Breed desperately tried to regain some balance.

Seeing that Paige had been bitten, Cole took a swing at the creature that was still gnawing on her. His spear caught the werewolf in the neck, glanced off bone and ripped open a gash from its shoulder blades down to its tail. Hanging limply from teeth that were still snagged in her vest, the creature somehow managed to twist its head upside down, tear free of Paige's armor and drop onto its side.

Cole buried the modified spearhead into its chest, but didn't feel much resistance. The weapon seemed to drive through leathery skin while everything inside shifted to avoid being damaged. At the same time, the Half Breed folded its lower end until the spear ripped from its skin like a stick through a thick spider's web. Flopping over until all four paws were beneath it, the werewolf snapped its head back from that unnatural angle and bared a full set of teeth at Cole.

Even as its long, thick fur bristled and stood on end, the Half Breed wasn't as burly as a Full Blood. When he attempted to stab it with his spear, the creature scampered around in a semicircle and folded its torso like a jackknife, avoiding another strike from Cole's spear. As soon as his weapon slammed into the dirt, the Half Breed lunged.

Cole dropped to one knee in a well-practiced set of movements that brought the forked end of his weapon up and around while his back leg braced for impact. The Half Breed came at him like a drooling battering ram, taking both points into its underbelly. After that, the creature's own weight and momentum were enough to drag itself over the spear and spill its innards onto the earth.

Getting all that blood on his hands ignited a primal fire in Cole's body. With another werewolf bearing down on him, he pivoted on one foot and swung his weapon across his upper body. The single spearhead caught the nearest Half Breed flush in the side of the neck and sank in until Cole's fist thumped against its fur. From there, he forced it toward the ground until the spearhead emerging from the other side of the Half Breed's neck dug into the dirt.

The creature refused to stop moving. Its legs slapped at the earth in what appeared to be death throes, but its claws grabbed on so it could find its center of gravity. With its head still pinned, the Half Breed got all four legs under it and slashed Cole's shin. The thick denim of his jeans absorbed some of the punishment, but the werewolf's claws shredded through the material and ripped into his flesh. He stepped back to remove his leg out of the Half Breed's reach before too much damage could be done. When the cool flow of healing serum in his system kicked in, a light-headed sensation rolled through him like a reward for remaining on his feet.

Howls filled the air. When Cole looked to see if another wave was coming, he saw several more Half Breeds gathering around the simmering bait, nipping at each other in their haste to get to the mixture. His attention was brought back to the creature he'd pinned to the ground when it swiped at his ankle.

After clipping him with a paw, the Half Breed tensed the muscles in its neck and pulled until its own flesh gave way. The spear remained in the ground as the creature tore loose. Flaps of skin hung open at its neck, exposing the cracked bones of its shoulder, which moved like snakes trapped within layers of muscle. The creature sucked in a deep breath and jumped at Cole before he had a chance to brace himself.

Attempting to swing his spear at the Half Breed, Cole only managed to smack the weapon flat against its side. Some of the thorns from the handle snagged the werewolf's skin, but it barely seemed to notice. Cole rolled to one side as its teeth brushed past his shoulder and its paws pressed against his upper body. He realized then that in another second or two he would be the one pinned to the ground.

But then the Half Breed grunted and twitched. Cole opened his tightly clenched eyes and saw Paige's legs a few inches away as she pounded on the werewolf's ribs. She hit the Half Breed again, even harder, and the creature stepped off him with a yelp. Since he didn't have room to swing his weapon, he reached over his shoulder, got hold of the shotgun and wrangled it so he could use the barrel to push the creature away. His struggle, along with Paige's continued assault, bought him another inch or two, which was enough for him to place the business end of the shotgun firmly against the Half Breed's chest and pull the trigger.

There was a muffled thump that sent the Half Breed flying and sprayed blood across both Skinners. Paige's T-shirt had been completely ripped away, exposing the body armor she'd crafted back at the hotel. The vest was shredded, and the hide inside of it looked like stuffing that had been pulled from a broken toy.

"Hit it again," she said while grabbing his arm and lifting him to his feet.

Cole blinked as the adrenaline and serum racing through him threatened to overwhelm his senses. He looked down at the Half Breed he'd just shot and saw it struggling to get to its feet. The creature's fur was singed and a good-sized hole had been blown through its rib cage, but its muscles had come together just enough to keep it moving. Hacking breaths shook its twitching body, but turned into strong panting when the Half Breed got another look at the prey that had eluded it. A slick, pointed tongue lolled out from between unevenly spaced teeth that resembled rows of broken stalagmites on a cave floor.

Taking quick aim, Cole fired the shotgun again. The wave of hot lead slammed against the Half Breed's face, knocking it to one side. While it staggered as if shaking off a hard punch, Paige stepped forward to deliver a chopping blow that cut through the rest of whatever was keeping its head connected to its body.

More Half Breeds were still gathered around the campfire. Some were trying to tear each other apart, while others curiously sniffed at the stew pot. Cole fired again and again at the ones that were more interested in live bait. Although the shotgun blasts didn't kill everything they hit, the encroaching werewolves were either wounded or forced back a few steps.

"Are you hurt?" Paige asked.

"Yeah, but I can't feel it yet. That serum is in me, just like you said."

She was bloodied and torn open in several spots, but was still swinging her weapons. "Shock's got something to do with it, but we'll worry about that later."

"Looks like they're backing off," Cole gasped as he reloaded the shotgun. "This was a little easier than I thought."

Paige didn't take her eyes from the campfire. Shaking her head, she told him, "That was just the first wave of runners. When too many Half Breeds get together, they get reckless. The pack mentality makes them stupid. Just like humans. Once they snap out of that, they get really nasty."

Cole counted nine Half Breeds near the fire. Three of them were fighting with each other, while the other six shifted their gaze toward the Skinners. Then the werewolves displayed their teeth as they hung their heads and fanned out.

"We can't let them flank us," Paige whispered. "How's your body armor?"

Patting his hand against his torso, Cole found his vest was in even worse shape than Paige's. The last few minutes had flown by so quickly that he hadn't realized just how much punishment he'd taken. "It can probably take a few more hits," he guessed, "but I'm starting to feel it in my arms and legs. Aw, shit! That looks worse than I thought."

Both Cole and Paige looked down at his left leg, which had a set of deep, bloody tracks starting just above his knee and running almost down to his ankle.

"Can you stay up on your own?" Paige asked.

"I think so."

"If not, drop to your knees and fight from there." Once she'd dispensed that tidbit, Paige locked eyes with the closest Half Breed and took half a lunging step forward. The feint was just enough to set the creature off, and it charged straight at her, with a second one following close behind. There was a good amount of ground to cover, but the Half Breeds practically flew over it. Cole fired in the general direction of the creatures and dropped the closest one chin first to the ground. It skidded a few feet before its companions jumped over it and continued on.

"Son of a bitch," he grumbled as the remaining Half Breeds scattered and bolted into the shadows before he could fire another shot.

Paige turned to keep her current target in front of her. The Half Breeds near the fire moved away from the blaze, using legs that weren't restricted by joints. One of them crab-walked with its belly pressed against the dirt to climb over the bodies of its fallen brethren. A rasping growl issued from its chest, stuck in its throat, then came out in a huffing bark that made the remaining Half Breeds snap their heads up and look toward the Skinners. One of the werewolves that had scampered away from Cole's shotgun reappeared, to come at him from another side, and was brought down by one of the hidden bear traps.

Meanwhile, another Half Breed launched itself at Paige. Hitting the ground with one knee, she swept her weapon up and across, to slash its face and stop it with a jarring crack of petrified wood against its temple.

Cole jumped in to help her by snagging the Half Breed by its neck with the forked end of his weapon. Doing his best to pull it off Paige's back, he managed to give her enough room to wriggle free and slash at two werewolves that had crept closer to them. Her left hand whipped toward the werewolf that Cole had pulled away, if only to knock aside a claw before it dug into her. She snapped her right hand out to try and decapitate another Half Breed, but only ripped through a few layers of fur before the creature twisted around in a way that should have snapped its spine in half. Before it could straighten itself again, Paige drew her revolver and fired two shots at its head. One shot grazed the creature's skull and the other only clipped its ear. Since neither wound was bad enough to put it down, the Half Breed shook off the effects and stalked around her to find another angle from which to attack.

Cole, still pinning one werewolf by its hind quarters, tried to do something more than annoy it. Just as the creature pulled away, he jabbed the forked end toward its neck. Both sharpened points stretched out less than a quarter of an inch before snapping shut, but the Half Breed had bent its head back like it was about to dispense candy from its throat.

Putting all of his strength into one motion, Cole flipped his weapon so the spearhead swept up and out, digging a messy trench through the Half Breed's shoulder. The creature staggered and tried to get away, but wasn't fast enough to escape before Cole swung again. This time he stabbed it in the side and twisted the weapon before it came loose. The Half Breed contorted just enough to slash at Cole with its paw. He defended against the first swipe, but another Half Breed joined the fray, to create a flurry of teeth and claws. Cole kept his spear in front of his face and chest, pivoting often to answer with a few jabs of his own.

Teeth scraped against the collar of his body armor and ripped away a little piece of his chin. One set of claws sliced less than an inch away from his eyes, and another set shredded the waistband of his jeans. One Half Breed finally reared up and placed its front paws upon his shoulders.

Cole could feel his legs start to buckle and realized that he wouldn't have the strength to stay up if the werewolf pushed against him with all of its weight. Out of sheer desperation, he brought the spearhead up to impale the creature through the bottom of its jaw. The Half Breed craned its neck to pull away, but not before the modified spearhead dug a tunnel straight up and through its brain. With a quick push, Cole shoved the creature back and then let it drop.

As soon as he stepped back, another creature hit the ground. He turned and saw Paige place her boot on that werewolf's back and drive her weapons into its sides. Even then, the Half Breed continued to drag itself toward Cole. Paige put a stop to that by pounding the sharpened handle of her weapon through its skull.

"That was a stubborn one," she said.

There were still a few other Half Breeds nearby, but they seemed hesitant to approach. In fact, they were backing away from another werewolf that had a thicker, meatier frame and larger, longer ears that lay flat against its head. It was tough for the Skinners to make out the details of the bigger creature since its fur was so black that it absorbed shadow as well as the bit of light cast by the campfire. Once Cole saw the crystalline eyes glittering in the firelight, however, he knew exactly what they were dealing with.

The Full Blood was shorter than he remembered. Despite a more compact frame, raw power exuded from the beast like it would from a hurricane or a black wall of storm clouds. The burning that crackled through Cole's scars ran like a live current all the way up to his shoulders.

"That's not Burkis, is it?" he asked.

Paige shook her head. "No. Wrong coloring. That's the one that took Henry away from us in Wisconsin."

"Yooouuu waaaaant Henrrrry?" the Full Blood snarled, using words that were crudely fashioned from growls and forced out through a latticework of fangs. Unlike the daggerlike protrusions that cut through Burkis's face, this one's teeth laced together neatly but prevented its jaws from fully closing.

The few remaining Half Breeds were getting impatient. When two of them huffed and began to rush the Skinners, the Full Blood stretched its body forward and opened its mouth to let out a quick, roaring bark. Upon hearing that, all of the Half Breeds pressed their chests against the earth and slunk away.

As his lips came down and his snarl faded, the Full Blood lowered his shoulders and lifted his chin. When he spoke again, it was through a muzzle that had shortened just enough to accommodate a more human voice. "Henry used to ask about you, Paige."

"Good," she replied as she adjusted her grip on her weapons. "Tell him to come see me. I've got a couple presents for him."

The Full Blood's lips curled into a savage grin. "I thought you'd already gotten to him, but now I see he's simply run off."

In the distance, car engines revved and faded as headlights swung wildly down a path leading through the nature preserve.

"It probably won't be long before the cops or a ranger shows up," Cole whispered to Paige.

"This'll be over long before the cops make it out here," she replied.

"Oh, I hope not," the Full Blood said in an English accent that tarnished his voice the way rust corrupted glistening steel. "Your founding father didn't show his face, but I'll still have plenty of witnesses to see what happens to murdering ghouls like you."

"Founding father?" Paige asked. "What the hell are you talking about?"

The Full Blood drew in a lungful of passing breeze as if sampling a finely aged wine. "I thought he would come to your aid, but I guess I was mistaken. That changes nothing. I warned you to clear a path for my kind the last time we met. If you refuse to step aside, then I'll just have to remove a few more Skinners from this world. Funny," he added with a tilt of his growing head. "I thought more of you would come to defend this piss hole of a city. Perhaps there are fewer of your kind than we thought. How interesting."

When the Full Blood lowered his chin and dug its claws into the earth, Paige raised her weapons. "Take one more step and I'll gut you just like I gutted your friends!"

"Thaaat's it," the dark Full Blood snarled. "If you scream loud enough, you'll catch someone's attention."

"Who else are you after?" Paige asked.

Standing upon two legs but keeping his body hunched over, the Full Blood approached and stared at her with his unnaturally clear eyes. The upper portion of his skull settled into a more human shape, and his snout retracted to a mildly protruding nose. "The one that's hiding like a tick wedged in the middle of this continent."

"I'm the only partner she needs," Cole said.

The shadowy beast lifted his chin and then cocked his head to one side. His eyes narrowed before widening into glittering circles. "You know what? I believe you really don't know about the man I seek."

"Honest mistake, so I'll give you one chance to leave,"

Paige said. "If you go back to your forest or wherever you were before, we'll call it a night. If not, then—"

"Then *what*?" the Full Blood roared. "I warned you when I collected Henry to stay away when we came to reclaim our territories! This is where all old debts are repaid, Skinner. The diseased leeches who spit their venom from their bloody cities will be gutted soon enough. Tonight, I send a message to all of those who think they're strong enough to hunt us. It's too late to save this place, so do what you can to save yourselves. The only chance you have is for you to tell me where I can find the others of your kind." Baring his teeth, the Full Blood added, "All of them."

The Half Breeds stood in the shadows, swaying on their feet and panting with anticipation.

When Paige spoke, it was in a snarl that rivaled the Full Blood's. "You wanna do more than bark? I'm right here."

The single puff of air that came out through the Full Blood's nose was as much of a chuckle as a growl. He stretched out both arms and dropped back down into his compact, barrel-chested form. The challenging smirk remained on his face as his teeth nearly doubled in length. Barely another second passed before he bolted forward.

"Paige! Look out!" Cole shouted as he dove to push her out of the way.

Both Skinners were human, which meant neither of them was fast enough to avoid what was coming. Just when he thought he could shove her to the ground, Cole felt a rush of air as Paige was snatched away from him. Cole landed on his side, rolled over and popped back onto his feet with his spear raised in front of him. He didn't expect the Full Blood to be close enough to reach out, grab him by the shirt, and toss him through the air.

Being whipped around like that took away his perspective. The ground rushed along the edges of his vision, and the moon flew by in another direction. His feet knocked into his legs. His arms flailed through empty air, and just when he thought he'd figured out which way was up, he was proven wrong. He hit the ground on his back, expelling all of the wind from his lungs in the process. Paige wasn't in sight, but the Full Blood was only a few inches away.

Cole knew he needed to move, but he couldn't. The Full Blood loomed over him, gazing down and drizzling saliva onto his arm. When Cole dug the business end of his spear into a huge paw, the massive creature seemed genuinely surprised. "I see you've already met Randolph," the Full Blood said as he reached down to grab Cole's weapon. "Either that, or he's losing his teeth in his old age. Needn't worry about that from me."

Cole rolled away as the beast's claws dug a row of trenches through the ground where he'd just been. When he felt the brush of a twig against his backside, he stopped rolling and scrambled to his feet. The Full Blood stood upright, flowing easily into his taller form. While this one looked a bit smaller than Mr. Burkis, he made up for it with speed and ferocity. Even with a burst of panic-induced strength coursing through him, Cole only barely managed to deflect a powerful swing with his spear, then felt the shock wave of the creature's attack rattle all the way up to his teeth. Somehow, the petrified weapon remained in one piece.

Unable to get a look at Paige, Cole had to assume she was holding her own against the Half Breeds that snarled and clawed at her several yards away. Even if she wasn't, he knew he couldn't do anything to help her. The Full Blood roared and swiped at him again and again. When the beast finally delivered the overhand swing he'd been waiting for, Cole jumped aside. The thump of its massive paw against the earth was followed by the clang of iron jaws of a bear trap snapping shut around the Full Blood's wrist. When it reared up and pulled the trap from the ground, Cole drove his modified spearhead into its chest.

The creature's entire face twisted into a mask of pure rage. Although the tooth attached to Cole's weapon pierced its skin, the bone beneath its flesh was like an iron plate. Cole leaned into the strike, but knew he'd reached his limit. After plucking the weapon free, he aimed for the stomach and stabbed the outermost layer of thickly banded muscle. The Full Blood pivoted on its feet and slapped the weapon away. Cole's hands were nearly torn apart, but the thorns in the spear's handle kept it rooted within his grasp. After that, he could only run away before the fury of an unnatural cataclysm rained down upon him.

Cole knew he'd never moved so fast in his life. He barely even felt his feet touch the ground until he dug in and skidded to a stop beside the campfire. The Half Breeds had nudged the kettle away from the flames when they'd sniffed at it, but there was still some of the concoction inside. Cole grabbed the kettle by its handle and hurried to retrace his steps. Heat from the handle would have burned a whole lot more if he didn't already have a thick layer of blood and scar tissue on his palm.

The Full Blood ran toward him in easy, loping strides, the bear trap rattling from one wrist like a grisly accessory. It gripped the earth using all four paws and panted expectantly at the sight of its next meal.

Cole veered to the left, planted his feet, grabbed the bottom of the kettle and tossed the contents toward the Full Blood. Since the hulking werewolf hadn't slowed down, Cole also slammed the kettle against its nose. Scorched iron met snout with a muted clang. The Full Blood snapped his head from side to side and huffed angrily through both nostrils.

Working his jaw only seemed to aggravate the beast. It arched its back and erupted with a bellowing roar as muscles swelled to form a thicker shell around a growing, two-legged form. Even as he brought his forepaws up to hold them like arms, the Full Blood was too enraged to act as anything other than an animal.

"Come on," Cole whispered. *"Come on!"*

Just when it seemed that he had made the worst call of his short fighting career by goading the huge creature, smaller footsteps scrambled in from all sides. The Full Blood glanced to his right and spotted a trio of Half Breeds baring their teeth. Some more of the leaner werewolves closed in, while most of the ones fighting Paige left her to attack the Full Blood that was now covered in the bait mixture.

The Full Blood leapt back, but wasn't able to get far enough away before the Half Breeds clamped onto his legs.

One of the wretches bit down on the bear trap and was tossed through the air when the Full Blood finally shook loose of the metal jaws.

As much as he would have liked to watch the bigger were-wolf wrestle with those things for a while, Cole had already spent too much time separated from Paige. She was still tangling with one Half Breed, but a straight, solid jab from Cole's spear was enough to back it off. When that werewolf turned to face him, it caught a sickle blade straight across its jugular.

Paige grabbed the Half Breed's ear, pulled its head back and nearly sawed it from its shoulders. Recognizing the glassy look in her eyes, Cole pulled her away and said, "Come on! We need to get out of here."

She blinked a few times as if looking at the campgrounds for the first time. "How'd you get those Half Breeds off of me?"

"I sicced them on the big guy."

Paige had no trouble spotting the Full Blood. It contended with the Half Breeds by wildly swinging his arms to toss the smaller werewolves into the air or ripping them to shreds. When one refused to be shaken loose, the Full Blood gripped the gnarled creature by the head and slammed it down while letting out a bellowing howl. As he ground that creature's skull into paste, the Full Blood cast his eyes at all the other Half Breeds and roared in a way that forced them to scamper back while twisting their heads aside to bare their throats to him. The minute he ran out of breath, the Half Breeds again caught the scent of the bait mixture that was on him and renewed their attack.

"Let's get the hell out of here," Cole said.

Paige dusted herself off and discovered several gaping wounds in the process. Grabbing a plastic syringe from her belt, she injected the healing serum and growled, "We're not leaving." She waited for a Half Breed to get ripped apart and ran in to attack the spot on the Full Blood that the gangly werewolf had been chewing.

The huge, ebon creature started to climb onto its hind legs, but was dragged down by the weight of the Half Breeds. He howled a command for the Half Breeds to back off, which gave Paige a chance to drive her modified weapon in again. This time Cole lent his spear to the cause. Twisting around to bat away the two humans, the black beast left himself open to the persistent Half Breeds. When one of the wiry animals sank its teeth into the spot where the Skinners' modified weapons had hit, the Full Blood lifted his head to the moon and screamed. Every Half Breed tried to join in with howls of their own, which turned into frenzied yelps as the Full Blood launched itself into the air.

By the time its paws hit the ground, the Full Blood had already shifted to its more compact form. It disappeared in a thick blur of motion, taking the last of the Half Breeds with him.

"God *damn* it!" Paige shouted. "Grab one of these bodies and take it to the car. Bring back that lighter fluid from the trunk."

Cole surveyed the area, now a bloodied landscape of gnarled bodies and sprung bear traps. The soil had been churned up by so many different sets of claws that the ground itself looked completely different from when they'd arrived. Even the campfire was a sputtering relic of what it had been an hour ago. "How the hell do we explain this?" he asked. "What do we say to the cops? They'll be here after all that shooting! *Some*one had to see what happened!"

Stepping up to glare directly into Cole's eyes, Paige told him, "We didn't come here to explain anything to anyone. If someone saw what happened, they can explain however the hell they want. If the cops get here quick enough to stop us, we tell them we were attacked by wild animals. There's no law against that."

"How do we answer all of their questions?"

"We won't have to if you get that lighter fluid and help me torch the rest of these things!" Paige snapped. "Now pick up a damn body and drag it to the car!"

Cole didn't have much to say to her after that. After pulling in a few deep breaths and wiping the sweat from his eyes, he picked up a damn body and dragged it to the car.

Chapter 19

The closest thing to a cop that Paige and Cole passed on their way out of the nature preserve was a terrified park ranger sitting in a state-owned SUV. The ranger flashed his lights, hopped out of his vehicle, and waved his arms like he was cleared for takeoff. "You headed into the campgrounds?" he asked after Paige rolled down her window.

After all that had happened, she did an admirable job of looking like she was out for a drive and not hauling a dead werewolf. "No," she said. "I heard shooting coming from back there, so I just wanted to leave."

"There's a hell of a lot more than shooting. Some pack of animals tore through here and overturned a Winnebago. If you see anything along the roads, don't stop. Just keep moving and get to the highway. The police are on their way. Jesus, are you two hurt?"

"I think there's a fire back there," Paige told him. "You might want to take a look at that." Even though the ranger had something else to say to her, he let it go when he caught sight of the flickering glow coming from the nearby camp-site. When he looked back at her, Paige had already rolled up her window and was driving away.

Cole twisted around to look behind the Cavalier at the park ranger gawking at the fires they'd set and fumbling with his radio. There weren't many carcasses in one piece, but they were all ablaze thanks to the lighter fluid that had sprayed on them. "He might have taken down our license plate."

"Let him. We'll change them when we pick up Daniels. Give him a call to let him know we're coming. Also, tell him to have everything ready to go. We need to find somewhere else to stay."

"You think the fire will get too bad?" Cole asked.

"That ranger will get to it before any of it spreads too far. Werewolves are too damn greasy to burn for very long."

"So that's it, huh? I guess we just wait a few days and bait the rest of those things to some other field? Do we at least get a few days off?"

She glanced over at him and grumbled, "Sometimes I don't know when you're kidding."

"What if I'm not kidding?"

"Then you're just an idiot. Here, take this and get to work."

Cole nearly cleared his seat when he felt the knife fall onto his lap.

"Now let's see how well you skin that Half Breed," she said. "Get at least two good-sized pieces of hide from its body and pull as many teeth as you can. I'll take all the claws too." She grinned and looked over at him. "Dumping that bait on them was a hell of an idea."

"It didn't work as well as I thought it would. I was kind of hoping for a lot more ripping and tearing and not so much bowing and whining from those Half Breeds."

"It was enough that you got us out of there," she said. "Right now, we've got other stuff to do. Make that call and get to skinning."

"Yes, ma'am."

Cole phoned Daniels to let him know they were on their way and then climbed into the backseat to take his first crack at cutting apart a dead monster. Normally, something like that wouldn't have set too well with him. The smell alone was enough to bring the bottom layer of his stomach contents up to the back of his throat. At that moment, however, with the campsite behind them and getting farther away with every second, he didn't mind a little dirty work. It meant he was still alive.

* * *

A few hours later Cole was still in the car staring out the front passenger side window. Daniels was packed into the backseat, along with most of his and Paige's gear. The Nymar had one shoulder wedged against the window behind the driver's seat, due to the fact that his left leg was draped over a flat case. His feet were resting on top of more cases, which practically forced him to eat his own knees. Judging by the expression on Daniels's face, he wasn't at all happy with the arrangement.

"Why don't you just throw me in the trunk?" he griped. "I'd be able to stretch out more."

"Do you mind sharing space with a pile of dead Half Breeds?"

Daniels winced. "You Skinners truly are disgusting ghouls."

"Hey, for a guy who stank up his motel room as badly as you did, I'm surprised to hear any complaints."

"For your information, I had a breakthrough in my research."

"Yeah?" Cole asked. "It smelled like burnt hair. Didn't I see a cleaning lady leaving your room right when we got there?"

"She took an unfortunate fall and lost some blood," Daniels muttered. "As for the smell, I needed to use the heating element in order to—"

"You knocked out the cleaning lady so you could feed?" he interrupted.

Daniels pondered that for a second and then flashed him a smug grin via the rearview mirror. "Oh, no. That would be wrong."

Since the cleaning woman had been able to walk and wasn't screaming at the time, Cole let it slide. The wound running along the side of his leg was still tender. Paige had helped him wrap it up as Daniels was collecting his things. She'd patched her own wounds as well, but in a way that seemed like the medical equivalent of fixing an oil leak by slapping some tape onto the wet spots.

"You both look pretty torn up," Daniels said. "Shouldn't you go to a doctor or something?"

"We'll rest up as soon as we're done making these rounds."

"What rounds might those be?"

They were parked along Cliff Drive, which bordered North Terrace Park. It was late, which meant the street was relatively quiet and the nearby University of Medicine was mostly dark. This was the fourth stop they'd made since racing back into Kansas City, and Cole was beginning to feel as though he'd made the entire trip on foot. "We found a bunch of Half Breed dens scattered around the city," he explained. "She's checking them now to see if we cleaned them out or not."

"What if the things are out hunting?" Daniels asked. "It's that time of night."

Absently brushing his palm with his fingertips, Cole felt nothing more than the rawness that came from having the thorns rip through his skin and the minor irritation caused by Daniels. "They're not around the city. At least, there's not as many as there were before."

"The moon's out. They run real fast."

"Yeah, Dan. I know."

"It's not Dan."

"What?"

Leaning forward from the backseat caused a shift in the delicate balance of all the crap piled around the Nymar passenger. "My name is Daniels."

"Oh, and I suppose that big bald spot is just a temporary hair migration?"

Daniels leaned over and looked in the mirror. He started to run his hand over the top of his head but stopped as if his skull was an eggshell that had already been cracked. "That was mean."

"Sorry."

The driver's door was pulled open then and Paige dropped in behind the wheel. She landed with a strained huff, which became a wince when she turned the key in the ignition. "What are you sorry for this time, Cole?"

"Nothing. You find anything?"

"There was one Half Breed way in the back," she replied. "Just a day or two old by the looks of it. I put it down and knocked in enough dirt to bury it. Considering that's the only Half Breed we found in any of those dens, this was a pretty good night."

"I'll say it was!" Daniels chimed in as he grabbed the backs of both seats and pulled himself forward.

"Watch it!" Paige snapped. She started to turn around but flinched and settled back into her seat. "Just don't knock those cases around so much, okay?" She put the car in gear and drove away. "I want to stay somewhere outside the city. If any authorities saw anything, they'll be looking for those werewolves, but I don't want them to get lucky and stumble upon us."

Daniels slumped back and allowed the piles of cases and other supplies to slide over him like a slow motion avalanche. "We were set up just fine before."

"And if anyone was following us before, they'd head straight for that place," Paige said. "I'll bet there's at least one cleaning lady at that hotel that's got some interesting stories to tell." Taking a deep, obviously strained breath, she headed for I-35.

"Tell us about the breakthrough," Cole said.

For a few seconds Daniels sulked by pushing around as many of the cases as he could reach. When he was done with that, he leaned forward again. "This," he announced while extending his hand to display a heavy square attachment that had been soldered onto the tattooing machine, "is one of them."

Paige looked at the machine and then shifted her attention back to the road. "Isn't that the same thing I unwrapped at your apartment?"

"Yes, but the device you ordered requires a separate power supply. This battery pack not only allows you to use the machine wherever you like, but it even makes the necessary adjustments in speed and has a life of several hours."

"So that's what you were burning in your room?" Cole asked.

Daniels slumped back and grumbled, "I also needed to use my heating element to melt down shavings from the Blood Blade. After that, I was able to further isolate the medium that bonded the shapeshifter blood to the specially forged metal. That is, of course, after I separated the shapeshifter proteins and such from the plasma."

"Is it ready for use?" Paige asked.

Reluctantly, Daniels scooted away from her side of the car and replied, "Not yet. We should be able to start our first trials after I iron out a few more wrinkles."

"What sort of wrinkles?"

"The sort that transfers properties of the metal to the recipient along with the shapeshifter properties you so desperately want, no matter how many times I tell you the entire process is too dangerous to be considered."

"Gotchya," Paige said as she reached for the radio dial.

They drove north on I-435 until it changed into I-29 about halfway to St. Joseph. Cole savored the fresh air that blew in through the window to wash away the lingering stenches of Half Breed and the gunk that attracted them. Before long Paige pulled to a stop outside a quiet, three-story hotel advertising satellite TV and an indoor swimming pool.

"I see you guys spring for the nice places when *you* have to stay there," Daniels grunted on the way up to the second floor.

"Yeah," Paige sighed. "It's a huge conspiracy. I'll check on you in a while."

Cole followed her with cases hanging from both shoulders, under his arms, and in both hands. Like any good pack mule, he kept his head down and his feet shuffling until he was told to stop. When he looked up again, he was in a room that smelled like air-conditioning and deodorizer. Compared to how he'd spent the earlier part of his night, it was a little whiff of heaven. On that same train of thought, he noticed something else about the room. "There's only one bed."

"Yeah. It's all they had. Find my medical kit and pile the rest wherever you want."

The medical kit was a large tackle box that had been modified to hold all manner of goodies in little compartments divided among the main container and two upper trays. By the time Cole had set everything else down, Paige already had the kit open and was selecting several different items from her collection.

"Take your pants off," she said.

Cole stopped right where he was. "No dinner first?"

"If you want to bleed some more, crack a few jokes while I patch myself up. That scratch on your leg looked pretty bad, so I thought I'd start there."

The scratch she'd mentioned had gotten bad enough to cause most of that leg to go numb below the knee. The feeling returned quickly enough when she started poking him. "Why don't I just go clean it up first while you—"

"Oh, for Christ's sake," Paige grumbled. "You must be the only man to think twice after a woman tells him to strip. I must really look like shit."

"No," Cole said as he watched her peel off the cotton button-down shirt she'd thrown on in order to look a bit more presentable to the front desk clerk. "It's not that."

Technically speaking, Paige should have looked a lot worse than she did. Her clothes were stuck to her skin thanks to all the dirt, sweat, and blood they had absorbed at the campground, and her face was tired and dirty. But somehow she managed to make him forget about all of that just by dropping her voice a little and raising an eyebrow. "All right, then. You want me to go first?"

"Sure," he said. "Go right ahead."

She lifted one leg and crossed it over her knee. From there, she eased the boot from that foot and daintily lowered it to the floor. "You next."

Sighing, Cole unbuckled his belt, pulled open his jeans and shimmied out of them.

Within seconds after Paige's eyes dropped down below his waist, she started laughing. "Are those rabbits?"

It was useless for Cole to try and hide them from her, but he couldn't bring himself to look at the cartoon bunnies plastered all over his boxers. "They were on sale."

"Oh no they weren't! The ugly stripes and polka dots go on sale. The solid colors go on sale. Those cute ones are always more. You paid extra for those!"

"I'm bleeding, you know. Weren't you going to help me?"

Tugging at the leg of his boxers, she giggled, "And it looks like there's a whole little garden on there too. Is that a carrot?"

"Yowza! Watch where you're reaching, woman!"

Paige's hands may have drifted a bit too close to the carrot printed over the fly of his boxers, but she wasn't so quick to move it. "What other critters have you got hiding in there?"

"You're about to find out if you're not careful."

Leaning in close only caused her hand to drift a bit higher up. "I haven't been careful all night. Why start now?"

Cole was wounded, bleeding, and more tired than he thought he could be without passing out. He was also close enough to smell the natural scent of Paige's skin and feel her hair brush against the side of his face. Pulling in half a breath of her was more than enough to push his mouth against her lips and for him to grab hold of her with both arms.

Paige let out a soft, sighing groan as she pushed him onto the bed and took the kiss to a whole other level. Her lips parted and she teased him with her tongue as she swung her leg over and straddled him. The instant that leg fell into place, it brushed against the wound that ran down the length of his calf.

"Oh my God," Cole gasped. "You're gonna have to get off of me."

Tracing her fingers down his chest, she was about to say something when she snapped her attention to his leg. "Oh no! I'm sorry," she said as she climbed off. "Does that hurt?"

Every part of his body wanted to tell her he was fine and that she should hop aboard to pick up right where they'd left off. Well, some parts more than others. As he tried to move his leg, he grunted, "Yes. It does."

"Let me just fix you up and we can get back to business."

"That would be . . . that sounds . . . I mean . . . yes. That sounds good."

Paige had already gotten up to head for the bathroom. When she came out, she tossed a few towels to him and said, "Clean off that wound first."

He pressed the towel against his leg, but found that most of the blood had already hardened into a sticky crust. Rather than tear the coating off and create a gruesome mess, he wiped away as much as he could from around the wound.

When he looked up again, he was just in time to watch Paige trade her filthy T-shirt for a fresher sleeveless version.

Noticing he was watching, she walked over to him and said, "Good enough. Now hand me that turkey baster."

In one of the top trays of the kit, he saw several long plastic tubes filled with clear liquid, sealed with plastic caps at one end and rubber bulbs at the other. "Which one?" he asked.

"The one with the stuff to keep you from turning into a Half Breed." Since Cole hadn't reached for any of the tubes, she added, "One of the ones marked HB. It doesn't look like you got hurt bad enough to have a serious problem, but better safe than sorry."

He grabbed one of those tubes and handed it to her. She popped off the cap and squirted some of the clear blue fluid onto his wound. The stuff might have looked like windshield wiper solution, but soaked in with a cool touch. Paige emptied the rest of the large baster on every open wound both she and Cole had. The treatment left them looking like they'd been in a wet T-shirt contest, which Cole didn't mind one bit. It all soaked in or evaporated within a couple minutes.

"Now hand me the epidermic paste."

"What?"

"The tube near the bottom of the kit."

Cole found the tube and handed it over. He wasn't quite sure what the stuff was and didn't think to ask her about it, since Paige was slowly lowering herself onto her knees in front of him. She took the tube from him, popped it open, and looked up with a sly grin on her face.

"Are you ready for this?" she whispered.

"Oh God, yes."

Reaching out with one hand to brush her fingers and thumb along the side of his wound, she asked, "Are you sure?"

Feeling a rise in the carrot patch, Cole leaned back and told her, "Go for it."

Thanks to the numbness spreading once more through his leg, he didn't feel it when Paige pressed her hands against the skin alongside his wound. His calm frame of mind was shot to hell when she pinched the torn skin together and covered it with the stuff from the tube. His hands dug into the mattress and his butt lifted an inch or so up to send the rabbit right back into hiding.

"What the fu—" was all he could get out before the next wave hit him. Paige slid her hand all the way down the length of the wound, pinching it shut and sealing it with the clear, quick-drying glue. She set the tube aside a few seconds later, but the pain in his leg was a gift that kept right on giving.

She leaned forward, brushing against him while reaching for one of the syringes she'd taken from her kit. "Hold still, Cole."

"Hold still? I can't believe you tricked me like that!"

"Did that hurt?"

"Fuck, yes it did!"

"What about this?" she purred as she leaned forward again so her breasts rubbed against his other leg. "Is that better?"

Even though it was all he could do to pull in a breath, he replied, "A little."

"Just think about how nice that feels." As soon as she saw the first trace of a contented smirk drift across Cole's face, Paige buried the syringe's needle into a spot at the top of his wound. With a swift, crisp motion, she turned the needle under his skin so it pointed downward and then pressed the plunger.

The healing serum flooded through Cole's leg like ice water, to banish the numbness below his knee and replace it with a whole new kind of pain. While smaller wounds and infections were treated with thinner needles attached to smaller syringes, this one felt like a marker being shoved into his aching shin. "Damn, you'd make a good vet."

"What made you think of that?"

"The way you distract me right before the hammer drops makes me feel like a dog getting his vaccinations."

"Just wait until I fish out my rubber gloves."

"Don't even joke about that," he warned.

"Were you hurt anywhere else?" she asked.

"Feels like I was hurt everywhere else, but it's not too bad." That was a lie, but he could see the wound on his leg was bleeding less than a few seconds ago.

"Normally, that'd be a bit too much serum for such a short amount of time, but you were hurt enough to burn most of it off. If you have trouble sleeping, take this," she said while handing him one of the smaller syringes. "Now, do me."

"I thought I'd ease back into it a bit more, but . . . " Paige turned her back to Cole and held out the tube of skin sealant she'd just used on him. He took it and sat on the bed behind her.

Peeling her shirt off and holding it against her front, she said, "There's a few cuts on my back I couldn't reach. Pinch them shut and cover them with that stuff. Then give me an injection from that small syringe. I don't need much."

Cole took his time working on her. There were plenty of scratches, bumps, and bruises, but nothing half as bad as the set of three slashes that ran all the way across her ribs and wrapped around to stop abruptly near her spine. "Looks like something got to you," he told her. "Your vest caught some of it, though. You ready?"

"Just do what I told you."

There was a little bit of stuff in the turkey baster, so he added that to what she'd already drizzled over the cut. The process of sealing the wound wasn't much different than using a glue stick to put a few pieces of leather together. Since Paige didn't even squirm, he got it done with a minimum of fuss. Placing his hand on the darkened yet smooth skin of her ribs, he asked, "Doesn't that hurt?"

"Yeah. I may have busted a few when my shoulder was knocked out of joint."

"Should I wrap it up or something?"

She looked back at him, wincing less than when she'd been steering the car down I-35. "They *were* busted, Cole. By now they're probably just bruised. I knocked my shoulder back in place during the fight and it's just a little sore now."

"Damn, you're tougher than I thought."

"True, but it's not all because of good genes and a perfect diet."

Cole chuckled and placed his hand on her ribs again to verify what she'd told him. He was no doctor, but her ribs felt smooth and rounded just like they're supposed to. The rest of her felt much the same way.

"A few more doses of that serum and you'll toughen up," she told him. "Just remember to take it only as you get hurt so your body uses it right away. After a while your system makes enough to heal a lot of wounds on its own. You won't be able to shake off a bullet, but you won't have to crawl to a hospital after every fight."

"How about you shoot me up with that stuff before the fight?" Cole asked. "Wouldn't that make more sense?"

"Sure, if you want to become an addict. Trust me, more than a few Skinners have learned that lesson the hard way. That feels nice."

"That's what all the junkies say."

"No, what you're doing with your hands. That feels nice."

With his hands so close to Paige's bare skin, he'd reflexively begun to rub her sides and work his way around until his fingertips brushed along the edges of her stomach. The rush of moving his hands up a little higher until he felt the bottom of her breasts against his thumbs was just as good as when he'd felt up Karen McKeag back in the eleventh grade. The big difference came when Paige rested her head back against his shoulder instead of jumping like she'd stuck her toe in the cigarette lighter of his dad's hatchback.

"I'm feeling dirty," she whispered.

Cole started to chew on her ear, but paused so he could ask, "Is this another test to see if I'll let my guard down?"

"You already passed that one. This is a test to see how badly you want to take a shower with me."

Before he could think of a cool response to that, the phone on the bedside table jangled loudly.

Paige sighed and said, "It's probably Daniels." She reached over, picked up the receiver and snapped, "This'd better be good . . . Excuse me?" She straightened up and gripped the phone tight enough to turn her knuckles white. "I won't put a deposit down for anything else. Isn't my cash good enough?" Just when it seemed she couldn't get any madder, she said, "No, I won't be making any calls. I won't even be using this phone . . . What? *You called me!*" She slammed the receiver back onto its cradle, flipped her hair over her shoulders, and forced a smile onto her face. "Where were we?"

When the phone rang again, Cole lunged for it before Paige could knock it through a wall. "What?" he snarled.

This time it was Daniels. "I need something from one of Paige's cases. It's vital."

"Can't it wait?"

"Just one more thing and this ink may be ready for testing."

"Call back in an hour."

After a pause, Daniels grumbled, "Fine."

Cole slapped the phone down and found Paige lying on the bed with her legs pulled up against her chest and her arms wrapped around her knees. "Looks like you're awaiting corporal punishment," he mused.

"Would you be upset if I didn't want to do this anymore?"

"You mean . . . do *me* anymore?"

She slowly looked up at him with eyes that were sorrier than those countless times she'd cracked him in the head or hit him below the belt during their sparring matches. The rest of her looked about ready to collapse. "Yes, but I don't want you to think—"

Cole shook his head and held up his hand. Without another word, he walked around the bed, settled in behind her and draped an arm over her shoulder. Paige's body felt warm and softer than he'd imagined she could be. Letting out a contented sigh, she relaxed so completely that he could feel her steely muscles conform to him.

"That feels nice," she purred.

"Yeah. It really does."

Cole awoke suddenly as memories of blood, fangs, and claws assaulted his brain. The quick flashes were like a slap on the inside of his face and brought his head straight up. Beside him, Paige shifted and rolled onto her back, and he saw that she'd gotten dressed while he was asleep. The room was still lit by the cheap fixture hanging near the bed, and her eyes clenched shut reflexively against the glare. The prospect of drifting back to sleep was an inviting one, but his system was already moving too fast for that to happen.

Of course, there was some help nearby.

The little syringe was on the bedside table near the clunky old phone. Cole reached for it and justified its use with ease. Paige knew best, and she'd said he could have one more dose. Then again, there wasn't much call for it any longer. He was stiff and sore, but those sensations had soaked into his body like a coat of black and blue paint. When he flexed his leg, he resented feeling nothing more than the first aid glue tugging at his skin. The serum had already done its job. There was no good reason to have any more.

Still, if he closed his eyes, he could vividly remember the cool flow of the injection as the serum dimmed his lights while the healing took place. He imagined his senses would be dulled even more if he took the serum now. Without allotting too much of it to a wound, he could just lay back and drift away.

"Jesus," he sighed as he set the syringe down.

The thought that he'd almost injected a serum mixed with an extract from Nymar blood just to get some sleep made him sick. Rather than dwell on it, he put the syringe back into Paige's kit and rubbed his face. Not only was he covered in a crust of dirt, grime, sweat, and blood, but his senses were sharp enough to feel every last bit of it. Since he knew that getting back to sleep right away was an impossibility, he grabbed some spare clothes from his bag and took a shower.

Water flowed over his body in an uneven stream. The pressure was marginal, the massager setting didn't work, and the temperature never strayed far from the lukewarm range, but just getting rid of all that filth made him feel like a new man. He toweled off, threw on some clothes that were somewhat cleaner than the ones he'd left behind, and walked back to the bed. Paige had curled into a ball and looked too comfortable to be disturbed.

He went to his phone and found a text message waiting for him. It was from MEG, and all it said was: CALL WHEN YOU GET A CHANCE. He went to the window to get a stronger signal, tapped the icon to dial the callback number, and waited through a few rings.

"Yeah?" Stu grunted.

"Is that how you answer the official MEG Branch 40 line?" Cole asked.

"It is when it's just past four in the morning."

"I got your message. What's up?"

He couldn't be sure, but Cole swore he heard a keyboard get kicked around just before an empty soda can rattled against the floor. "Have you checked any news sites?" Stu breathlessly asked. "Or watched TV? Turned on a radio?"

Cole answered, "No," and was amazed by it. After spending so many years with a computer monitor in front of him, he'd always been connected to current events. Thanks to the little notes that popped up in the corner of his screen, he'd also known when a celebrity had a baby or which annoying asshole got voted off of which reality show.

"For being media stars, you guys are so out of touch," Stu mused.

"Hold on, I'll switch you to speaker." With that, Cole tapped a few buttons and opened the Internet browser on his phone. He scrolled down a little to find the local headlines and saw no fewer than three different stories ranging from LOCALS KILLED BY ROAMING PIT BULLS to FIREFIGHTERS MAKE GRISLY DISCOVERY AT CAMPGROUND.

"Did you see the one about the suspected ritualistic slayings?" Stu asked. "That's my favorite. What the hell did you stir up over there?"

"It's been a busy night," Cole said. When Paige rolled onto her side, he dropped his voice to a whisper. "Isn't there some sort of damage control for something like this?"

"There's never been anything like this. At least, not when I've been around to see it. A lot of pictures are making the rounds online, but so far there's just as many people saying they're fakes as there are who think the world's coming to an end."

Cole had just tapped to that section of the article. It took a few seconds to receive the pictures, but there were plenty to be found. Frame upon frame, collected from cell phones to pocket cameras, showed very blurry creatures moving like a swarm across streets and over open fields. For once, he was grateful the Half Breeds could run so fast. "I just washed the stink off and there's already pictures on the Internet," he muttered.

"I know. One time I posted a request for strategy on a *Sniper Ranger* fan site and I got three replies by the time I got back from draining the weasel."

"I knew you cheated on our death matches."

"Not cheating. Strategy."

"Have you posted any of these pics on the MEG site?" Cole asked.

"I'm . . . uhhh . . . not in control of everything that goes up on the site," Stu fumbled.

"What about debunking?"

His laughter sounded almost as hesitant as his reply to the last question. "I suppose we could try to shoot a few holes in this stuff, but that might only draw more attention to it. Maybe we should just leave it alone. Do you know how many pictures of the Loch Ness monster were proven to be genuine? We've posted plenty of disembodied voices and footage of genuine spiritual activity. You'd think that would be considered pretty important, huh? Life after death and all that? Other planes of existence. Nah. Most folks just go on with what they know and ol' Nessie drifts back down to the bottom of the lake."

Cole had stopped listening. While flipping through the pictures from Kansas City, he picked out a few favorites. "How much longer will you be there?"

"Just another hour. I can barely stay awake as is. Abby will be here soon, though."

"Does she like debunking?"

"Almost a little too much."

"Good," Cole said. "Then she'll love what I'll be sending your way."

Chapter 20

It was a nice house built on a quiet block in Overland Park, which was a pretty nice suburb of Kansas City. The neighborhood slept as the sun crested the horizon and paperboys made their deliveries. When one copy of the *Kansas City Star* slapped against this particular house, the impact knocked the door open an inch or two. It wasn't enough for the delivery boy to notice, so he kept going, and the rest of the city went about its morning routine.

A man in a cheap suit walked down the sidewalk with his hands stuffed into his pockets. His eyes slowly absorbed everything around him and his nostrils flared as he got closer to the house with the door that was ajar. Upon reaching the porch, he sniffed the air, shook his head, scooped up the paper, and walked inside.

The entry was very tidy, apart from a shattered coffee mug on the floor of the entryway and streaks of blood smeared on the tile. More blood led up a carpeted staircase to the second floor, where the coppery smell was even worse. A television was on up there, but played the music from a DVD menu that hit the end of its loop and began again. Mr. Burkis tightened his grip on the newspaper he'd brought in from the front step and scowled at the upper end of the staircase. The corner of one nostril twitched and his eyes snapped toward the source of the new scent he'd picked up beneath the odor of not-so-fresh kills. Someone had just opened a fresh can of coffee.

"'Morning, Randolph," chimed a voice from the kitchen.

Burkis seemed mildly uncomfortable to hear that name, but didn't refute it. He stepped over a hutch that had been knocked over, crushing some of the fine china that had spilled from it as he walked into a rustic dining room. A mess of splintered chairs and broken glass lay scattered near an upended, solid oak table. A chunk of the kitchen counter had been broken off, leaving the rest of the adjoining room mostly intact. A skinny man dressed in a baggy gray sweatsuit stood in the kitchen. He held a can of coffee in one hand, pulled the top off, and sniffed the plastic circle. A narrow smile slid across his sunken features as he said, "I've grown to love coffee since crossin' the pond. Care for a mug?"

Randolph narrowed his eyes and walked over to where the kitchen table had landed. He righted it with as much effort as someone might use to lift a box of cereal and slapped the newspaper down flat upon it. "What have you done, Liam?"

"Why, whatever do you mean?" the skinny man asked in a thick cockney accent.

Scanning the headlines for all of two seconds, Randolph slammed a finger down on a lower corner of the front page. "*This* is what I mean!"

Liam took the carafe from the coffee machine and filled it. Squinting as he scooped some grounds into a filter and put it all together in the machine, he asked, "Might you be referrin' to the gas prices or the construction?"

Randolph didn't move.

When Liam spoke again, his accent was smoother and more natural than it had been before. "They were bound to notice us sooner or later."

"Especially since you've been running down the streets and howling at the moon like an idiot!"

"That's fine talk comin' from you, Randolph. What about the street wars you instigated back in New York?"

"I didn't start those, and that was long before pictures and video could be spread so easily. For God's sake, there's hardly even a record of it! This," he snarled, while pounding his fist against the newspaper, "is even worse than your incident in Whitechapel."

Liam got the coffee brewing with the tap of a button and then glanced back at Randolph. "That was also over a hundred years ago. Besides, I've never been linked to those gutted whores."

Cocking his head slightly, Randolph narrowed his eyes to a point where the other man couldn't bear it.

Finally, Liam snarled, "All right, fine. I may have had a little something to do with the Whitechapel incident, but it wasn't just me killing a bunch of women for no reason. Those uptight constables had the gall to try and run us out of London! Don't you remember that?" Dark hair was plastered against his scalp and forehead in a way that would have seemed perfectly natural in the faded portrait of a banker from the eighteenth century. Even his facial structure seemed outdated. His bony shoulders and narrow limbs were built for old suits that hung in museums.

"Times are different now," Randolph reminded him. "Even if they weren't, what you're doing is unacceptable."

"Perhaps," Liam said as he raised his eyebrows, "you could have kept things in line if you'd been here. I did invite you, but you're so hard to find. I only recently learned the new name you've taken. Burkis, is it?"

The other nodded almost imperceptibly.

"Almost back to your roots, eh? I like it."

Randolph snatched up the paper and practically rubbed Liam's nose in it. "What do you hope to accomplish with this? You're *purposely* creating Half Breeds?"

"Yes. They're rather like machines. While I'm not altogether fond of machinery, it is nice to wind it all up and watch it go."

"Don't try to smooth this over with a bunch of prissy talk," Randolph snarled. "Do you actually hope to accomplish anything with this or are you just making another spectacle?"

Liam took the newspaper away fast enough to leave a few shredded scraps in Randolph's hand. After looking over the article, he let out an amused, snuffing breath. "Whoever wrote this is still blaming the deaths on dogs or criminals! There's been bloodier months when human criminals fight amongst themselves. You should know that better than anyone."

"Gang wars are started and fought by human gangs," Randolph said. "People know how to react to that. When those wars are over, everyone goes back to their lives. This can't possibly be forgotten so easily."

While Randolph spoke, Liam rolled his eyes and walked back to check on the coffee. "You weren't always such a stickler. In fact, didn't I hear about a bunch of hunters being slaughtered in a cabin that just happened to be in your stomping grounds?"

"Those hunters were Skinners."

"All of them?"

"No," Randolph replied. "One was a Mongrel in possession of a Blood Blade that was meant to kill our kind. Skinners should know to stick to the leeches in their cities or the Half Breeds that slip through the cracks. As far as Mongrels are concerned, I kill as many as I can find. The one I chased away from that cabin won't be a problem anytime soon."

Liam leaned against the counter and ran his finger along the side of the heated pad beneath the coffee carafe. "Oh, I see. When you kill, it's justified. Always against prey that should know better than to overstep your bounds. Didn't you hear the truth that Henry broadcast to the rest of us? Haven't you seen for yourself that the leeches don't rule the cities as we'd always believed? How the hell did we fall for that rubbish anyway? Doesn't that make you feel foolish?"

"I've lived in cities," Randolph said. "The leeches and Skinners can have them."

"Oh, sure. We get to live in parks or the little green patches of woodlands that the humans rope off like fucking zoos!" Liam roared. With every word, his voice swelled to fill more of the empty spaces within the house. "The days when we can live where we please are fading, Randolph Standing Bear. Just ask the Natives who gave you that name."

"Our arrangement has worked just fine. We can't—"

Slamming his fist down hard enough to shatter the countertop, Liam shouted, "There is *nothing* we can't do! We are Full Bloods! The only reason we scampered into the forests while the humans built their cities was because we *allowed* it to happen! I warned you about the Skinners, Randolph. I *warned* you they would figure out new ways to poison and kill us, and look what's happened! At least the Gypsies show some craftsmanship with their Blood Blades. The Skinners are grave robbers who prod us with sticks."

"You can stuff your warnings," Randolph said. "I'm the one that's been thinning the Skinner herd while you've been out spilling blood for no good reason. If you truly wanted to help, you'd help me remove the thorns in our sides without creating more of them to deal with. What purpose could such public slaughter possibly serve?"

The fist that he'd used to break the counter now unfolded so Liam could gently sweep away some dust that had settled next to the coffee machine. He grabbed the carafe and poured the fresh brew into his mouth. Leaving his chin up and his eyes locked upon a spot on the wall, he swallowed and said, "They should fear us. This whole world would be much better if people had the good sense to fear. It'd be quieter at least."

"What kind of manure is that?"

"Humans are arrogant. They strut about, flapping their gums, making their noise and tossing about idle threats because they're not afraid anymore. I'm not even talking about a crippling fear of the dark. I'm talking about that bit of common sense that warns them against walking into dangerous places or provoking someone who might do them harm. You know what humans do when they make a mistake or bite off more than they can chew?" After swigging some more coffee, Liam said, "They sue. Some idiot spouts off, gets beaten for it, and they sue. Another moron ignores a sign, stumbles under a load of bricks, and they sue.

"If they see something greater than them, they need to challenge it. If something is sacred to one group, another group just has to knock it down to show their will is *more* sacred. When these damned fools find something dangerous, they seek it out just for the thrill of it! There used to be a time when creatures that stupid were wiped out through the good sense of a harsh natural order. We're that natural order, Randolph."

"And humans are the arrogant ones?" Randolph scoffed.

But Liam shook that off with ease. "When a species becomes too large, they are culled by predators or disease.

Humans hide behind machines and suck down drugs to combat disease. They've cheated their way through an existence that should have been ended hundreds of years ago. We're the predators made to do the culling."

Randolph straightened up to his full height, which put him several inches over Liam's head. "All you want is to restore the natural order?" he said with sarcasm dripping from every word. "You're so much nobler than I remembered."

"At least I'm doing something, you self-righteous prick!" While Randolph's tone had softened, Liam's took on more of an edge. The longer Randolph looked at him with his wide eyes and friendly smile, the more Liam's teeth crept down to form the start of rounded fangs. "The humans may be too fucking stupid to ever admit their place in the real pecking order, but the Skinners know all too well. What I'm doing here will bring those killers to us instead of allowing them to hide and plot and build in the dark just like their whole cowardly species has done for so goddamn long."

"I've only smelled two of them throughout this whole state."

"Which must mean there's precious few of them left," Liam pointed out. "When they're gone, there'll be that many less thorns in our sides. And after the events I've started, Skinners will gather here from across this continent and probably others. They'll come looking for us, and if we can't snuff them out, we truly do belong skulking in the woods."

Randolph nodded slowly. "You've done some real culling, eh? If you'd killed even one of those two Skinners, you would have bragged about it by now. Instead, you're wincing when you move and favoring one side over the other. Those arrogant humans probably just snuck in a lucky shot, right?"

Leaning to get a better look at the right side of Randolph's face, Liam replied, "You've got no room to talk. That wound's new and has the looks of one that will never heal. Blood Blade, I'd guess. With your rugged Celtic looks, I bet that just drives the girls crazy."

Although Randolph didn't move to touch the thick, jagged scar that ran from his right cheek down to his jaw, he twitched as if that part of his face was about to leap away from his skull.

"Who did that to you?" Liam asked. "Was it a little brunette with the tight ass or the fellow who looked ready to piss himself?" Liam waited for a second and then nodded. "They're very creative, you know. I wouldn't be surprised if another one of their kind was somewhere scooping up our droppings to mix into some sort of potion."

The expression on Randolph's face would have been enough to force a lion back into a dark corner, but Liam only acknowledged it with a wary chuckle.

"You know it's true, pretty boy."

"I have the blade now," Randolph growled. "That's all that matters."

Liam's narrow features were made even sharper by the cruel grin that took them over. "Carried it away while it was embedded in your face, huh? Great plan, my friend. Since you'd probably like to get some more Skinner flesh under your nails, you can help me pick off the ones that did that to you. They flocked to this place thanks to me, and if there's more of them anywhere nearby, they'll come too."

"So that's your real reason for all of this?" Randolph asked. "Force the Skinners into a fight and bring me here to join you. What about that other stray you found?"

Drawing back as if preparing to defend his young, Liam said, "Henry is a Full Blood who knows more about our enemies than either of us."

"He's tainted by the Nymar."

"Not anymore. The Skinners saw to that. They cut it out of him and killed it using a Blood Blade and some of their own witchcraft. It was quite a sight to see. Now that the leeches are out of him, Henry can focus the gift that vampire gave him." Flashing a grin that was just a bit too wide, Liam proudly added, "He's a Mind Singer. Unfocused, but the gift is in him."

"And where is he?"

For the first time since he'd started the conversation, Liam faltered. He glanced toward a glass door that was mostly covered by a set of white vertical blinds as he replied, "Haven't seen hide nor hair of him for weeks. He buggered off to find one of the Skinners that hurt him and I ain't seen him since.

He's still alive, though. We may not be able to sniff him out for whatever reason, but we know he's alive."

"He is a Mind Singer," Randolph grunted. "The world's gotten loud enough as it is, but I still hear his song when I'm not even listening. As do the Mongrels. He's told us the Nymar aren't as organized as we thought, but the chatter never stops."

"Try havin' a conversation with the poor bastard."

"Wherever he is, he can stay there. Just as we've stayed out of the cities because everything moves along smoother that way. That's how it should remain."

"No," Liam snarled. "*You* stayed out for convenience. The rest of us were chased out by cowards and held at bay by a bunch of bragging leeches. It makes me sick knowing that our kind runs and hides from anybody. Once word spreads about what I've done here, every Full Blood will see just how easy it is to stake a claim of their own."

"Word has already spread."

"Ahh," Liam sighed contentedly. "Machines can be good for somethin'."

The closest machine at the moment was the one that had produced the coffee. Randolph let out a measured breath and let his eyes wander from that machine to the others in the kitchen and eventually to the entertainment center in the living room. Lowering his gaze toward the bloodstained carpet, he asked, "What about the family that lived in this house?"

"They're brewing into another batch of reinforcements. Half Breeds may be a pain in everyone's collective arse, but they work cheap and bring plenty of friends."

"The children?"

Liam set the carafe down and stepped up to stand toe-to-toe with the other man. Even though he wasn't nearly as burly as Randolph, he stuck his chin out and balled his fists as if hoping for a confrontation. "After all the decades of being hunted, of hiding, of being exiled, of scampering away from the idiots in these cities, you're going to question how I go about my affairs?"

"I merely asked about the children who live here."

"How do you know there were children here? Can you smell 'em? Some might consider that a little peculiar."

"There's crayon pictures on the fridge. Little bowls and little plastic spoons in the sink. Should I bother looking for toys?"

Liam blinked, stepped away, and took another swig of coffee. "Whatever children that live here must be away. They'll sure get a nasty surprise if they come back, eh?"

For a few seconds Randolph was quiet. The breaths that rolled through his chest were growls that simmered much like coffee in the machine next to Liam's hand had. When one of those breaths reached fruition, it spilled out of a mouth that was beginning to form into a snout. Abruptly, Randolph turned and headed for the door that led from the kitchen and opened to a set of stairs leading down. The door was nearly ripped off its hinges as he stomped down to the basement.

Liam moved toward the doorway at a leisurely pace.

Randolph stopped at the bottom of the stairs, which was far enough for him to see the broken cement, dirt, and other refuse that had piled up when a large hole had been dug into the basement floor. The hole was just big enough for three Half Breeds to lay curled up in a bundle of gnarled flesh and had the stink of a den, but was empty.

"Where are they?" Randolph growled.

"I planted them somewhere near a snack for whenever they get hungry," the skinnier man replied from the kitchen. "Even if you do find them, you won't be able to get to all the others. I had quite a busy evening."

Just to be certain, Randolph checked the rest of the basement. "If you want to force the humans' hand," he shouted from the musty space, "do it yourself. Don't drag any other Full Blood into it and don't make any more Half Breeds! If we were ever to have a curse, those wretches are it. Creating them to fight your battle is—"

"Is what?" Liam chided. "A sin?"

"It's a disgrace."

"Not the noble crusade like your fight against the Skinners?" Liam sneered in a quiet voice he knew the other Full Blood could hear. "However many you've killed, it'll never be enough. They're humans, so they'll only reproduce until you're smothered in a blanket of them. But it's not just you being smothered. It's all of us. Something needs to be done to wipe them out or put them in their place."

"And you think this will do the job?" Randolph asked. "Have you truly lost your mind?"

Liam stalked down the stairs, raking his nails along the wall while using his free hand to tap his forehead as if he was sending code. "I'm using my brain! You've never understood strategy, Randolph. I'm drawing as many of our enemies to one place and then doing whatever I can to tear that place to *fucking pieces*!"

For the first time since he'd arrived, Randolph grinned. The movement not only gave his fresh scar a curl, but displayed some of the rounded teeth that had extended halfway out from where they'd lain dormant beneath his gums. "Sounds like a hell of a war. Too bad you're too gutless to fight it on your own."

Although Liam shook his head and waggled a finger at the other man, the hand he'd pressed against the wall tore chunks of it away as if the structure was made from cheap plaster and balsa wood. "Don't try baiting me. You know damn well we work better together instead of when we butt heads."

"We haven't worked together for a very long time."

"Back then, you knew I had things to teach you. At the very least, you listened to me. Do you even know that these two Skinners have claimed Chicago as their home? Wasn't that your territory at one time?"

"Most of this continent is my territory," Randolph growled. "If you truly are this crazy, maybe it's time I claimed the rest."

"More blood will be spilled, but all for a good cause," Liam replied with an offhanded wave. "And with your help, the fight will be that much shorter. You may not believe me, but the Skinners cannot be allowed to run loose. Listen to the Mind Singer. Lord only knows where he is, but when he dreams, he shows everyone what horrors the Skinners are capable of. He's seen them firsthand. He was there at the start of their so-called science. He's a product of it!"

"There's no way you'll convince me to stand aside while your wretches fight our battle," Randolph said as he nodded toward the pit as though he was regarding a crudely dug latrine. "You'll dispose of them, as well as any others you've buried around this city."

"Don't get hasty. Wait until you've heard what else Henry has to say."

Randolph's nostrils flared and the seams of his suit were tested by the bulky mass of his growing torso. Thick brown fur sprung up from beneath his collar and slid out from his sleeves, but not enough to completely shred the cheap fabric. "I'm putting an end to this," he snarled through a mouthful of daggerlike teeth.

"You like chewing up Skinners so much, I thought I'd just—"

Leaping up the stairs, Randolph grabbed Liam by the face and slammed him against the closest wall. "You didn't think," Randolph barked. "You *never* think. You didn't think when you threw London into a panic by eviscerating those women and you're not thinking now."

"To be fair, we were both a little out of control in London," Liam mused as he dusted himself off.

When Randolph swiped at Liam, his claws slashed through empty air and dug a row of trenches through the wall. The skinny man with the greasy hair landed on all fours and had already replaced his sweats with a thick black coat.

"I don't care about your reasons for doing any of this," Randolph said. "Just clean up the damned mess you've made. I'm through dealing with you, and I'm through treating the Skinners like respected enemies. Either one of you pushes me again and I'll scatter your remains from one coast to another!"

"That's more like it! There's the wild fellow who stumbled in from the forests all those years ago!"

After letting out a snarl that quickly rose to a frustrated growl, Randolph eased back into a human form. He lowered his head, stomped away, and left through the front door.

"Welcome back, friend," Liam sighed. "I truly missed you."

Chapter 21

Paige twitched a few times, rolled onto her back, stretched her arms, and then peeled her eyelids open just enough to get a look at the outside world. Although her face instinctively drifted toward the sunlight, she snapped it right back to the crooked table where Cole was hunched over his laptop. "What are you doing?" she asked as she swung her legs over the side of the mattress and tried not to fall off.

"Nothing. Working."

"How long have you been sitting there?"

"You're so cute when you flop around like that. I mean, most people are a little groggy when they wake up, but you border on disabled."

"Yeah, yeah. Get back to your game before that computer gets wedged up your ass."

"Aaaand she's back," Cole announced. "Try not to walk into any walls on your way to the shower."

"If you're hoping to wash my back, you can forget it. That train has sailed."

"I don't care how the soap gets on you anymore, just so long as it does. You're stinking up the room." Cole looked up just in time to catch the dirty gesture Paige flipped in his direction. After that came the slam of the bathroom door and the running of shower water.

It was just past ten o'clock, and Cole had been sitting in his chair long enough to mold the cheap foam cushion into the shape of his butt. His back was stooped and he squinted at his glowing screen while scribbling his finger over the mouse pad of his laptop. It was the closest thing to a reunion with his normal life that he could get.

In the hours since he got up, he had done plenty of work. But instead of tweaking the *Hammer Strike* multiplayer maps, he'd used his graphics and shading programs to touch up the pictures that had become such a recent Internet phenomena. Before he looked up again, the shower had been turned off and Paige was dressed and drying her hair.

"What's that?" she asked.

Cole proudly turned his laptop around so she could see the screen. "Little bit of work on some pictures you may or may not recognize."

"Are those Half Breeds?"

"Yep. They're all over the Internet and more are popping up every couple of minutes. Most of 'em are copies or forwards, but the bunch we saw the other night must have torn right past a whole lot of people with a whole lot of camera phones. There's even one video on HomeBrewTV.com that's pretty damn cool."

"Please don't tell me you're putting more pics on the Internet. I'd at least like to get some breakfast before I smack the living hell out of you."

"No, no, no. Look closer." Standing up and reaching over the screen, Cole tapped a spot on the current picture where a pair of Half Breeds raced past a light pole. "Right there. See anything weird?"

Paige stared at the screen, glanced up at Cole, stared some more and then scowled.

"Look at the part of the pole above the Half Breed compared to the part below it," he urged.

After studying it, Paige said, "It's a little blurry, but I think there's a sign on there. Is that an ad?"

"No! They don't line up! Can't you see that?"

"Ohhhh . . . uhhh . . . sure. So?"

A vein started to rise on Cole's forehead as he rushed around to look at the monitor from Paige's side. "Check out the tail of this one here," he said in a rush. "See how it doesn't reflect any light being cast onto it from the store?" He flipped to another picture of werewolves running in a blur of motion. "What about this one?"

"Oh yeah! That's one of the gas stations we baited."

"No! Look at the placement of their feet. Can't you tell they're just a little too high?"

"No."

Cole took a deep breath and started flipping through several more pictures. "You may not notice all of this, but people who scour websites for this kind of stuff will. They'll see that the shading on some of the fur was the wrong shade of gray or a reflection doesn't show up in a window quite the way it's supposed to. When they pick out little flaws like that, they'll be tripping all over themselves to claim this whole thing was a hoax or some sort of stunt."

"People are dead, Cole. Some doctored pictures won't change that."

"I know, but it'll cool off the talk about monsters racing through Kansas City. Isn't that a good thing? You know, to avoid panic or plague or whatever you were talking about before?"

Turning on the balls of her feet, Paige dried behind her ears and walked back to the sink. Just because she'd started brushing her teeth didn't mean she was through with the conversation. "Sho, you get a few pictures out there and shay they're fake. What about all the real ones?"

"They'll still be out there, but *they'll* look like the doctored ones. Trust me. People are more willing to believe they've spotted a phony than admit this stuff is real. That's the beauty of it. By the way, do you know how difficult it was to make these pictures look just the right sort of fake?"

Paige spat in the sink.

"Not only did I have to figure out a bunch of little things that might show up in a doctored picture," Cole continued, "but I had to use all my design expertise to put those ideas into action. A little shading here, a little misalignment there, some displaced objects in the foreground that don't match up with the background. I'm telling you I'm one hell of an artist."

Walking out of the bathroom while dabbing at her face, Paige said, "All right. I guess it sounds like a good idea. Post those pics on your website or stick them onto a discussion group and see how far they get circulated."

Cole grinned and waggled his eyebrows in a way that was excited and unintentionally creepy at the same time. "And now for the next step in my beautiful plan. I'm not posting these. MEG is."

Pausing with the towel against her chin, Paige finally looked at the laptop as if she truly knew what Cole was talking about. "You're sure they'll do that?"

"I talked to Stu and Abby about it while you were still asleep."

"Who's Abby?"

"The field investigator who's answering phones because of a sprained ankle. She's really funny and sounds cute." Before he was cut short, Cole quickly added, "She's got enough experience to know that MEG couldn't just pretend these Half Breed pictures weren't out there. They wouldn't go so far as to purposely debunk something real, but they will post my pics just like they'd post anyone else's." Dropping his voice to a whisper even though nobody else was in the room, he added, "I even know a few conspiracy buffs at Digital Dreamers who live to spot this kind of stuff. I mean, we're gonna take care of things here anyway, so who cares if rottweilers or escaped coyotes get the blame, right? This will defuse some panic and let it blow over when we're done."

Paige looked genuinely stunned. She squinted at the pictures on Cole's computer, went through a few different facial expressions, and then finally looked up at him to say, "That's a damn good idea! I can't believe you came up with that."

"I thank you for the first part and I'll write off the second part to you being hungry. How about we hit the free breakfast downstairs?"

"Two for two, Cole. If you think of a way to keep Daniels from whining over our bagels, you'll be my hero."

Breakfast was served in a room just off the hotel's modest lobby. There was a TV bracketed to the wall, a coffee machine, some bins of cereal next to a pitcher of milk, and a few plates of pastries laid out for the guests. Since it was the middle of the week, Paige, Cole, and Daniels only had to share the room with an elderly couple reading a newspaper.

"I believe I've hit another snag in . . . " Daniels paused to shoot the old folks a suspicious glare, and then leaned across the table to whisper, "That whole ink idea may not be such a good one."

Paige leaned across and whispered, "You know, you draw more attention doing this than talking like a normal person."

Daniels sat back and ran his hand over the spot on top of his head where the Nymar tendrils gathered to blacken his scalp. "Since I take it the Full Blood got away, I suppose you'll want to take me home to continue real work on that project as soon as possible."

"What do you mean 'real' work?" Paige snapped. "What the hell have you been doing all this time?"

Sensing a definite turn for the worse, Cole asked, "How's Sally?"

Daniels nodded and smiled uncomfortably. "She's doing well. The pol—" For some reason, Daniels was still bothered by the little old man and lady who nibbled on sweet rolls while handing sections of the paper back and forth to each other. "She's been questioned about what happened, but didn't mention any names. Apparently, the authorities were called about the shots that were fired that night, but there's not enough of those two Nymar left to draw any suspicion."

"They probably just figure we were firing at the big thing that crushed one of their cars," Cole offered.

"Right. Sally told me some officers came by asking if an exotic pet escaped from one of the apartments and she went along with it. I suppose that's that."

Cole never thought he'd feel so apathetic about the police possibly looking for him, but he was starting to take on Paige's attitude about the whole thing: if the cops were good enough to put so many crazy pieces together, then good for the cops.

"So," Daniels said as he rattled his plastic stirring sticks around in his cream-filled coffee, "when do we head home?"

"You've got work to do," Paige told him. "I didn't bring you along to call your girlfriend and put together battery packs."

"I'm doing my best!" Daniels whined. "Perhaps you should accept the fact that this whole idea of yours may not be safe. The work I've done has definitely uncovered some theories that could be put to use elsewhere, but—"

Dropping her elbow onto the table so she could stab a finger within an inch of the Nymar's face, Paige said, "You'll put them to use where I told you to put them. If you need someone to test it, just tell me when to show up and you can test it on me. I need you to finish this here and now."

"That would be far too dangerous. You're talking about . . . " This time when Daniels glanced over at the old couple, they were glancing nervously back at him. "You're talking about injecting potentially hazardous, metallic elements directly under your skin. Even without the . . . *more exotic* . . . components, that isn't something to rush into."

Seeing the intense look in her eyes, Cole stepped in. "We need to drive around KC anyway to check on a few more dens, so you'll have some more time."

"No," Paige said. "It's too late for that. Even if the Half Breeds that showed up last night were the only ones, we know we didn't get them all. The Full Blood got away from us, and it could have made plenty more already."

The old couple shifted their eyes to Daniels, folded up their newspaper, and shuffled out of the dining room as fast as their slippered feet would carry them.

"Then we go after the big game," Cole said. When Paige didn't look up at him, he asked, "You do have a way to track down Full Bloods, right?"

"I can think of something," she replied. "Daniels, what will it take to finish up your work?"

"I'll cook up the next version of my mix, and try a few things."

Paige dipped a dry piece of bagel into her coffee. "Fine. Just do what you need to do."

"Then can we head back to Chicago?"

"As soon as we're done here."

"And what if those things get to us first?" Daniels asked.

Locking her gaze onto him, she replied, "If me and Cole get killed, you can fish the car keys out of my pocket and drive back. Good enough?"

Daniels winced, but tried to keep his face stern enough to match Paige's expression. Failing miserably at that, he got up and headed for the elevator.

Now that he and Paige were the only ones in the room, Cole asked, "You don't have a plan for what's next, do you?"

"A lot of the stuff that's happening right now has never happened before. At least, not on this scale. I'll come up with something."

He placed a hand on her arm and told her, "I've done plenty of big projects where time was a factor."

"This isn't exactly the same as designing a video game," she said.

"Have you ever been the one to tell a convention hall full of ravenous fanboys that the game they've all been foaming at the mouth for is being pushed back eight months? It can get ugly. One scary looking bald dude had the first release date for *Sniper Ranger 3* tattooed on his forearm. His *sniping* arm, is what he told me. When we canceled that date at an electronics expo, I was more afraid of him than any werewolf."

Paige's tired chuckle turned into more genuine laughter.

"We just need to break down what needs to be done into bite-sized pieces," Cole said. "That Full Blood isn't very subtle, so we probably would have seen him by now if he meant to track us down."

"He was hurt," Paige said.

"Those Half Breeds may have even finished him off."

"That would be nice, but I wouldn't bet on it."

"Okay, fine. We found the Half Breeds before. We can do it again. We'll check the dens, but I'm guessing the next batch will be in new ones."

"Yep," Paige sighed. "They could be anywhere. Parks were the easiest choices, but they could be in basements or abandoned buildings. Hell, considering how many of those ugly bastards showed up last night, we probably didn't even find all of the original dens in the first place."

"Too bad we can't just sniff them out directly," Cole said. Raising his eyebrows hopefully, he asked, "Can we sniff them out?"

"Not really." Paige was looking at the TV, which showed a local news break regarding the previous night's rash of "wild dog attacks." Fortunately, the only thing caught by a professional cameraman was a German shepherd chasing a rat.

Cole didn't even try to focus on the grainy amateur photos and frightened witnesses being interviewed. He had enough going through his mind without cramming in any more. Pressing his fingertips against his eyelids, he grumbled his thoughts as they drifted through his head. "They can track us. Those Half Breeds tore after that scent trail we left. Burkis probably followed me all the way from Canada."

"Don't forget Jackie. She's another little present you brought back from Canada."

Cole would never forget Jackie. In fact, there'd been many a tired and frustrated night in his walk-in freezer when he'd thought about her. Jackie was a shapeshifter known as a Mongrel. Where werewolves typically turned into something vaguely canine, Mongrels could look like any one of a motley assortment of representatives from the animal kingdom. According to Paige, there were were-leopards, tigers, snakes, and plenty more. Jackie was a cat of some sort. Her lithe body produced the substance that Paige had used to make herself invisible when sneaking into Stephanie's Blood Parlor. Apart from that substance and her fur, Jackie hadn't been wearing anything else when she introduced herself to him.

That was the part that kept his thoughts warm when he was feeling restless. The term "Mongrel" just didn't fit a creature like Jackie. In human form, her body was tight enough to make a professional dancer jealous. They had wrestled when they first met, but not in the good way. Now, as his thoughts pointed him in that direction, Cole slapped his hands down on the table and stared at Paige with wide eyes.

"I think I've got it," he said.

She smiled and angled her head toward a family of four that had wandered into the room to raid the cereal bar. Every other table was empty, but the middle-aged parents and their two eleven-year-olds just had to cluster around the one directly beside the Skinners.

Cole was too excited to worry about disturbing the new arrivals. "The Mongrels! They could track me, so maybe they can track a Full Blood!"

Paige got up, marched to the door and impatiently motioned for Cole to follow. He caught up with her at the elevator.

"What the hell are you talking about?" she asked while jabbing the Call button.

"Jackie tracked me from Canada. You told me she did at least some of that through scent, right?"

"Yeah."

"Half Breeds smell like ass, so they should be easier to track. And didn't you tell me Full Bloods and Mongrels fight like . . . well . . . cats and dogs? Those two must have a good way of keeping tabs on each other!"

The elevator doors opened and a couple in their early thirties stepped out. One was a guy with a shaved head and a long goatee dragging a black travel case. The other was a brunette with rosy cheeks and generous curves. As soon as they stepped out of the elevator, Paige and Cole stepped in.

"Mongrels are the only thing we don't have to worry about around here," Paige said. "Let's deal with what's already on our plate before we start thinking about the next course."

"Good Lord, you really don't play any sort of games do you?" Before she could answer that, Cole said, "It'd help you with your tactical thinking, you know. For instance, in all the games I've played or designed, there's always something that sets apart the grunts from the bosses. Bosses aren't bosses just because they're tougher. You've got to figure something out. They've got a weakness. It's either a soft spot or a pattern or something, but it's there."

"Why does everything come down to video games with you?"

He shrugged and considered that for a moment. "Would Star Wars analogies work better for you?"

"Forget I asked. I already know Full Bloods have weaknesses. That doesn't help us track them."

"We know that most supernatural things can be hurt by other supernatural things. Our problem is that we've just been using *dead* supernatural things."

The elevator's panel dinged and the doors opened to the second floor. Paige stepped out and said, "The live ones usually aren't very cooperative."

Cole tagged along with her, smiling and nodding like an idiot. Rather than say what was racing through his mind, he gave her a second to figure it out for herself. It was a good thing she was quick on the draw, because he couldn't have held out much longer before the vein in his forehead popped.

"They're not cooperative," she said slowly, "unless there's something in it for them."

"You just found the secret cheat code."

"Mongrels know how to find Full Bloods," she continued. "That's how they survive. If you find a Mongrel's home, you know it's a spot far away from Full Bloods."

"Are there any Mongrel homes within driving distance of here?" Cole asked.

"I'm not sure, but if another one of us found one, they would have let MEG know about it."

"You want to make the call or should I?"

Chapter 22

Cole sat in the car and tapped his fingers on the steering wheel while watching the sidewalk that ran along Forest Hill Cemetery. Paige had told him to hold off on calling MEG so they could focus on finding stray Half Breeds in the dens they knew about. Even though she was the one searching the section of broken sidewalk, he knew she wouldn't find anything. He could feel there were some shapeshifters about, but not anywhere close. Even with all the news regarding wild dogs and the charred remains that had been discovered at the nature preserve, the city just felt calmer than it had the night before.

His leg was bandaged, but the wound was scaled as if it had been healing for weeks. All the smaller cuts had faded, but the serum didn't do much for the bruises. Despite the ache that claimed nearly every inch of his body, he'd actually started to relax while watching Paige search the perimeter of the cemetery grounds. When his cell phone rang, he cleared his seat.

He plucked the phone from his pocket and was surprised to find Digital Dreamers, Inc. on his caller ID. "Hello?"

The voice that came through was familiar but distorted. His new phone might have had a nice, bright touch screen, but sometimes the reception was worse than a pair of cans connected by a string. "I just got finished with a meeting where you were supposed to be fired," Jason Sorrenson announced.

"Really?" Cole asked as a way to test the waters. "Maybe I should have showed up to that one."

"That might have helped when I went in to try and defend you to the other two directors. Fortunately, *Hammer Strike* is doing well enough that we want to get things rolling for a sequel, and those designs you e-mailed got here just before the meeting. Between that and the ideas you pitched to me earlier, you've still got a job. Thought you might like to know. When can you come back to Seattle?"

"I don't know, Jason. I really don't."

"Then I don't know if I can have you on the design team for *Hammer 2*."

Cole straightened up so quickly he nearly broke a rib on the steering wheel. "Hammer Strike is all me! You can't do the next one without my input. The players will know the difference, and it may just flop hard enough to squelch the whole series."

"Sending in tweaks and downloadable content from your laptop is one thing, but you can't truly expect to be a part of a real design team without even being in the same city as everyone else. At best, you could have a say on some of the creative aspects, but none of the technical stuff. It's too organic a process for any pivotal member to be so far out of reach. You know that, Cole."

Settling back into his seat, Cole glanced up and down the sidewalk and then spotted Paige strolling along the low rock fence. His services as a getaway driver weren't needed just yet, so he grudgingly said, "I know that, Jason. It doesn't mean I like it."

"Hey, I don't like it either. I don't want to start another Hammer without you. Whatever you're doing . . . wherever you are . . . it's gotta be good to keep you from refusing all the offers I've been making."

"Not refusing. Just taking time to think them over."

"Whatever you call it, it's getting old. Did I mention that we love those monster renders you sent?"

"Huh?"

"The shading renders for those werewolf things," Jason explained. "They're a little too close to the stuff that's floating around connected to those crazy stories coming out of Kansas City, but tweak those models a little bit more and we've got something. In fact, I'll bet we could build a whole new game around it."

Jason kept talking about the ideas that were sparked by what he'd seen, but Cole wasn't listening. He was too busy trying to figure out what the hell was going on. Then it hit him. He must have accidentally sent Jason some of the in-between renders he'd worked on while touching up those Half Breed pictures.

Out of pure force of habit, he had treated those pictures as he would any others he might use for his game designs. He'd turned the pictures into crude models, repositioned them and then reworked the models so they wouldn't hold up under close scrutiny. For video game character designs that weren't supposed to pass for real creatures, those rough sketches must have looked damn good. When he thought about it a little more, he realized he'd labeled the Half Breed sketches "HBtestpics," while his sketches for *Hammer Strike* were labeled "HStestpics."

"I'm a goddamn idiot," he grumbled.

"Not at all," Jason said. "You can fix that stuff next time."

"What stuff?"

"Weren't you listening to me?"

Since the truth wouldn't earn him any points with his boss, regardless of how long he and Jason had known each other, Cole deflected that question with another one. "You really think we could get a whole new series going?"

"Hell yes!" Jason replied. "There's tons of crap about zombies out there, plenty about vampires, and a few about werewolves, but we could do a hell of a game about whatever these things are."

Cole's brain swelled within his skull. Now, in addition to everything else that had been going on, he had a new project to worry about. He closed his eyes and rubbed them, struggling to come up with something to say. Before he could put any words together, he reminded himself to check the sidewalk for any suspicious people or rampaging monsters.

"Cole? You still there? Did that damn phone drop the call?"

"No, Jason. I'm still here."

"Good. So will you think about coming back to Seattle to work on this?"

Letting out a relieved breath, he took the lifeline Jason had thrown him. "Yeah. I'll think about it. Can I get back to you in a few days?"

"Take the week. This is a big decision."

"A week would be great. Thanks so much."

Shifting out of his executive voice and into friend mode, Jason said, "We've got a great thing going with this. It's what we've been working for all these years and it wouldn't be the same without you, Cole."

"I know."

Those two words seemed to be enough for Jason, because he accepted them and ended the call with a minimum of small talk. Cole didn't have any intention of letting his friend down or trashing his career, but there were any number of things that could prevent him from getting his work done. One of those things was on her way back to the car. Judging by the look on her face, the only animal Paige had found was the little dog taking a leak on the stone fence surrounding the cemetery. She opened the door, dropped into the passenger seat and ran her fingers through her hair.

"Did you call MEG?" she asked.

"Not just yet." As Cole drove away from the cemetery, he told her about his conversation with Jason. He steered away from the specifics, but the rest of the story was enough to hold her attention. That was pretty good, considering how she usually zoned out whenever the subject of programming was brought up.

"I thought you decided to stay with me," she said. "Now you want to head back to Seattle?"

"What if you came with?"

She reacted to that question as if it had been posed by a talking pizza box. After a few confused blinks, she shook her head and asked, "Are you kidding me?"

"Why? There's got to be Skinner stuff going on in Seattle!"

"We're all set up in Chicago! Look, just forget about that. We've got real work to do. You wanna call MEG now to see about that idea of yours?"

Gripping his phone tightly, Cole grunted, "Sure. Right now, I'd rather talk to anyone but you."

"Fine. Make the call, but don't talk for too long or Stu might just convince you to move to Idaho or wherever the hell Branch 40 is!"

Cole hit the speed dial as if trying to crack the screen. When his call dropped three times in a row, he nearly chucked the damn phone into traffic. Finally, he drove into a reception sweet spot and managed to stay there long enough for Abby's full greeting to be heard.

"Midwestern Ectological Group Branch 40, how may I help you?" she said.

"Hey, this is Cole Warnecki. You want my ID number?"

"No, that's okay. What's up?"

"Has anyone called in about Mongrel sightings? I'm looking for something as close to Kansas City as you can get, and I don't just mean one Mongrel. I have to find a den or a burrow or whatever you call the places they live."

Paige rolled her eyes and sighed.

"Ummmm . . . just give me a moment," Abby said. From there, she launched into a whole lot of typing. The pecking of her fingers against the keys didn't let up when she started talking again. "To be honest, I've never really dug into the files like this before. Usually we just log in names and locations, file a few accounts and that's that. We're real good at connecting calls, though," she said.

"Is there anyone else I can speak to who might help?"

The tapping on the other end of the call stopped. "Actually, no. Is something wrong?"

Suddenly, Cole felt like an asshole for using such an annoyed tone with her when he was upset with Paige. What made him feel worse was the realization that neither of the women had done anything to deserve it. "Sorry, Abby. This is just really important."

"I know," she replied. "Whether it's gangs, dogs, or a cult, it's gotta be crazy out there." When her typing resumed, her voice brightened. "Here we go! The last report we got about Mongrels is from someone named Rico. Do you know him?"

Cole covered the phone and asked Paige, "You know someone named Rico, don't you?"

"Yeah, why?"

"He checked in about some Mongrels."

"Great. Where?"

"Where?" Cole asked once he'd uncovered the phone.

Abby hummed a few off-key bars to herself and tapped on her keyboard some more. "Somewhere in the middle of Nebraska."

Cole laughed and steered around some construction cones that had been set up to close off the left lane. "Out in the boonies, huh? Think you could be a little more specific?"

"I was. The report was about a town in the middle of Nebraska."

"Oh, I thought that was just a saying, like Hicksville, USA."

There was a pause and then Abby said, "My grandma lives in Hicksville. It's a nice place."

"Aw hell."

Before Cole could kick himself too hard, he heard a cute little snorting laugh come through the phone. "Sorry," Abby said. "Just kidding. The town's called Valparaiso, but it really is in the middle of Nebraska. More or less."

"Is that the home of the Mongrels or your grandma?" As he asked that, Cole felt an impatient tap on his arm. Paige raised her eyebrows just enough to get her point across, but he didn't break stride to explain himself to her. He did, however, switch over to speaker so Paige could listen in.

"The Mongrels were in Valparaiso," Abby said. "There's not a lot in the report other than someone named Rico was looking into some big cat sightings. There are some pictures of a cougar-looking thing attached to the file. Looks more like a panther to me, but there's not supposed to be anything like that living in Nebraska, that's for sure. Anyway, this big cat was also supposed to be able to disappear whenever it wanted." She snorted again, but not in the cute laughing way. "That's real convenient, huh?"

"Rico loves chasing down urban legends," Paige scoffed. "He's a sucker for that crap."

"Is that you, Paige?" Abby asked. "How's the newbie training coming along?"

"It has its moments."

Suddenly, Cole felt like he was twelve years old and listening to a conversation about how cute it was that his voice was cracking and how he'd be a real lady killer once hair started sprouting from all sorts of funny places. "How about we save that for later," he said. "What about those Mongrels?"

Abby shifted back into her more official voice. It wasn't a whole lot different than the other one, but there was less snorting involved. "Rico said he tracked a few of the Mongrels down to a row of houses and they disappeared."

"Disappeared?" Paige asked.

"Yep. That's what they do, remember?" Abby tapped out a few more things and then went on to say, "He stuck around for a few days, but they must have really dug in because he lost them. He told us he couldn't find any rat holes— whatever that's supposed to mean—and he left. Since there weren't any more reports of injuries caused by anything that looked like a Mongrel, he moved on."

"Is that the closest Mongrel sighting to KC?"

"The only other reports over the last six months were in California, North Dakota, and Texas. Lots in Texas. There are a few others that could be Mongrels, but they're not specifically listed that way."

"When was Rico's last check-in?" Paige asked.

"Little over two months ago. Want me to e-mail it to you?"

Cole jumped in before Paige could utter another syllable. "Yeah, why don't you e-mail it to me? Got the address?"

"Yep."

"All right, then. I'll call you later if we need anything or . . . just to say hi. Whatever." After Abby said a quick goodbye, Cole hung up. Looking over to Paige, he recognized the half smirk that had taken residence upon her upper lip. "What?"

"Just to say hi? Real smooth. For a sixteen-year-old."

"I'm not exactly at my best here. What was that about rat holes?"

Paige chewed on her bottom lip and turned to look out her window. "That's what Rico calls Mongrel dens. Those things tunnel under buildings and floors to make their homes. Sometimes they just connect one basement to another so they can live wherever there's less chance of getting caught."

"Sounds like a fun time hunting them down."

"Try impossible," she grumbled. "Or damn close to it. Not only do Mongrels keep to themselves, but they can bolt when they need to."

"How quick are they?" Cole asked.

"We don't even know for sure. We do know they can be nasty when they're cornered, but they seem more content to go after other shapeshifters. It's not surprising Rico let them go. He's started to focus more on hunting for profit than tracking whatever he can find."

"Maybe he struck a deal with them. If Mongrels are so fast and so good at sneaking around, they'd make some mighty fine criminals."

Paige grinned and nodded as she glanced over at Cole. "I've taught you well, young one," she said in her kung-fu master voice. "Now you see past what you are shown."

"Oh boy," Cole sighed. "If I've become just as paranoid as you, what's next? Foil hats?"

She let out a comfortable laugh. "Sorry about biting your head off before. I'd really hate to lose a partner like you."

Today hadn't been the first time he'd considered moving back, but it was the first time he had mentioned it to Paige. The more he thought about it, the worse he felt for not telling her something that could affect her so much. If he left her in Chicago, Paige would have to fend for herself again. He wasn't about to kid himself into thinking he was keeping her alive, but he was doing his best to watch her back. The way things were shaping up, that job was becoming more and more vital for both of them.

"I'm just keeping my options open," he said. "Plus, there's still bills to pay. We can't just rely on Prophet's lottery numbers hitting all the time." When he didn't get an answer right away, he asked, "Right?"

"Sure."

"How much was the last hit, anyway?"

"Better than normal, but it was spread over plenty of other Skinners. Just leave it at that."

"So what do you think about the Mongrel idea?"

"I like it, but Rico's a damn good tracker. If he couldn't find them, we won't be able to."

"If the Mongrels are even still there," Cole pointed out.

Paige shook her head and gazed out the window. "They're homebodies. When they dig in somewhere safe, they stay there until it's not safe anymore. Since a Skinner came and went without finding them, that place is pretty damn safe." Her eyebrows flicked up and she turned to look directly at Cole. "I just thought of something! You and I may not be able to find a bunch of holes under some houses, but what if we had a tech team?"

"Skinners have tech teams?"

"No, but we know some folks who are already in on what we're doing and would *love* to be a part of it."

Cole looked down at his phone. The number he'd just dialed was still displayed in the corner of his touch screen. "MEG?"

"They go into places all the time with vans full of equipment. They're always rigging stuff up to try and catch a picture of a ghost or some cold spots drifting through a room. Would it be so hard for them to look for living stuff?"

"I don't think so. Haven't you seen their TV specials? Most of their gear is made to see in the dark and record stuff nobody can hear. One time, I saw a show where they found a bunch of mice living in a crawl space that a family didn't even know had been built right beneath their—"

"That's a yes!" Paige said quickly. She sat back in her seat, wearing the stunned expression of a lottery winner. More specifically, someone who didn't have to split her lottery winnings with a hundred or so other people. Since the car had come to a stop at a red light, she took Cole's head in both hands and kissed him squarely on the mouth. Unfortunately, she pulled away again before he could truly get into it. "Call MEG and see if you can arrange for one of their teams to meet with us. Where's my atlas?"

Cole hit Redial while savoring the sight of Paige's trim backside wriggling beside him as she fished in the back for her giant book of outdated maps. When Abby answered, he felt as if she'd caught him peeking into a dressing room. "Hi, it's me again."

In a droll tone, Abby said, "I'll need your ID number."

Rather than start in on the series of numbers he'd been forced to memorize, Cole just waited for the snort. When it came, it was just as cute and slightly obnoxious as ever.

"Just kidding again. What's up, Cole?"

"Are there any MEG offices close to that town in Nebraska?"

No tapping this time. "Sure. Branch 18 is in Omaha. It's only about an hour away from Valparaiso. Here's the number."

"So you've been there?" Cole asked after Abby recited the contact information. "Is it less than an hour away from Branch 40?"

"Not unless you can fly."

"Too bad. I was hoping we could get together."

"Maybe next time."

Making sure to keep his confident smile in place, Cole said, "Definitely. We've got plenty of work to do anyway. Take it easy."

"You too, Cole. Be safe and tell Branch 18 I said hi."

He hung up and tucked the phone away.

"Shot you down, huh?" Paige asked.

"So I'm a little off my game. Living in a freezer for a few weeks will do that. There's a MEG branch in Omaha that's about an hour's drive from those Mongrels."

"Maybe there's a sweet little thing answering those phones too. Try not to talk through that freaky smile you were using and you might just get somewhere this time."

Cole handed over his phone. "Why don't you make the call?"

Chapter 23

Omaha, Nebraska

It was about a three-hour drive into Omaha from Kansas City, so Cole and Paige arrived somewhere between lunch and rush hour. This city was much smaller, but felt like a breath of fresh air. One definite bonus, apart from the lack of festering Half Breed dens, was Omaha's user-friendly layout. Even Cole could have found his way around without having to rely on the navigational widgets in his phone, if his phone's battery hadn't died while skirting the Iowa border.

The MEG branch office was located in a strip mall on the corner of 108th and Maple streets that was built around a grocery store and a few restaurants. Branching out on either side of the grocery store was a Laundromat, a bar, a few specialty shops, an insurance office, and a modest place marked by a simple unlit sign that read: MEG BRANCH 18.

"Are you hungry?" he asked.

Paige tapped her stomach but kept her eyes on the prize. "We came all this way to conduct our business and get back. If Daniels knows how far away we drove, he might just try to sneak back to Chicago."

"There's a pizza place," Cole said in a tempting, melodic tone.

"Go to the MEG office."

"There's also a Mexican restaurant!"

"No."

"Oh, would you look at that!" Cole said as he parked the Cav in a spot a few doors away from MEG. "I tell ya, it's fate."

Paige only needed to look straight ahead to see a little place wedged in between the insurance office and a cellular dealer. CHICAGO DAWG HOUSE was spelled out in red neon hanging in the front window.

"Give it up," Paige grunted. "If we struck out so hard in KC, there's no way we'll find a good hot dog in freakin' Nebraska."

"We've got to eat."

"Business first."

Cole was hungry enough to feel a magnetic pull toward the door of the Dawg House. The only thing strong enough to override that attraction was his first glimpse through the window of MEG's local office. After all of the calls he'd made and all the times he'd visited the MEG website, he'd become more and more curious about what one of those places actually looked like. At times it seemed just as likely that MEG was run out of basements scattered across the country. Now was his chance to see for himself.

When Paige stepped into the office, her arrival was announced by a chirping beep triggered by a sensor on the door. There was a sitting area to the right that looked like it had been plucked from a dentist's waiting room, complete with two chairs and a stack of old magazines. On the left was a wall covered with a mural of grainy orb photos and blurry figures surrounded by newspaper clippings detailing local haunts and past hunts. A single, unoccupied desk was adjacent to the waiting area. Behind that was a short hallway that led to more rooms.

"Hello?" Paige said. "Anyone here?"

A skinny face covered in dark whiskers poked out from one of the first rooms down the hall. Judging by how high up against the door frame that face was, the man connected to it had to have been just over six feet tall. "Hi there. What can I do for you?"

"We called earlier today. I'm Paige and—"

The guy stepped out and raced forward so fast that Paige's hand twitched toward the baton holstered in her boot. He wore khaki shorts and a gray T-shirt stenciled with the MEG logo. "Paige and Cole! Am I right?"

Recognizing the eager expression of a fan, Cole stepped up and held out his hand. "You're right. I'm Cole Warnecki."

"ID number?"

Somehow, that question drained the fun out of being treated like a celebrity. Cole rattled off his number and Paige did the same. By the time she was finished, the guy in shorts looked about ready to jump out of them.

"You're Skinners. You're really Skinners," he said. "Should I not have said that?"

"Only if you think someone has bugged your office and knows what you're talking about," Paige replied.

The guy in shorts laughed and nodded. "Yeah, I guess you're right. We were told not to talk about you guys in the open. To be honest, I've never personally taken any Skinner calls."

"Skinners?" someone in one of the back offices asked. "Are the Skinners here?"

Now Paige glanced around nervously. "All right," she said. "Maybe you should stop using the S word. We're just Paige and Cole."

"Sorry about that," the guy in the shorts said. "I'm Mick. Lead investigator for Branch 18, and that," he added, pointing toward the woman who'd emerged from the other office, "is Stone."

The woman who walked down the hall and stepped into the front room was nearly a foot shorter than Mick. She had long black hair pulled into a single braid, which she swatted over her shoulder. Her smooth, dark face was accentuated by high cheekbones and full lips. When she smiled at Paige and Cole, she shook their hands in a grip that was both strong and friendly. "Stone's not my real name," she said. "It's Rosetta."

"Ah," Cole chuckled. "Rosetta Stone. I get it."

She nodded and shrugged. Although she did seem to be impressed with him, she was just as impressed with Paige.

"You're not what I expected for . . . you know . . . people who go after those . . . ?"

"We get that a lot," Paige said. "Right now we're working on what's happening in Kansas City. Do you know about that?"

Now, Rosetta seemed more impressed with Paige than Cole. "Do we know about that? We've all been working late nights sifting through the pics and videos that are being posted to the site. I've never seen anything like it! So are those things the same as what you're looking for in Valparaiso?"

"Not exactly."

"Thank God," Rosetta sighed. "I mean, we want to help, but not with . . . I mean . . . "

"I know just what you mean," Cole said. "Those things in Valparaiso aren't the same as what's in KC, but they might be able to help us deal with that situation." As he spoke, he felt Paige getting ready to silence him with a quick backhand. They'd spent a good deal of the ride to Omaha discussing just how much the MEG guys needed to be told, and the consensus was to let them know what they were getting into without saying anything that might get them too worked up. Paige seemed happy with his choice of words. Mick, on the other hand, was happier.

"I've heard some stuff about what's been going on in Valparaiso," the lead investigator said. "When I called some of the people out there, they say they still hear various noises. Knocking, some disembodied voices, rattling, the usual stuff."

"Wait. You contacted someone?" Paige asked. "Someone other than one of us or another MEG office?"

"Well, yeah."

Rosetta jumped in and said, "When I spoke to you on the phone a few hours ago, you said you wanted to check out the locations where that Rico friend of yours was doing his tracking. Those places are mostly private homes. *Occupied* private homes. You're on a tight schedule, so we did a little digging and made a few calls before you arrived."

"We didn't tell them much of anything, though," Mick added.

Rosetta nodded eagerly. "Right. Of course. I made the calls myself and didn't mention anything about you guys or anything that might scare them."

"All right, then," Cole said. "What did you tell them?"

Rosetta shrugged and replied, "That their houses may be haunted."

"And that's not supposed to scare them?" Paige asked.

Mick smiled reassuringly and waved his hands as if smoothing off a pile of shaved ice. "We didn't use the word 'haunted.' We never use that term unless we've been there and gotten sufficient proof. We told them there were reports of suspected supernatural activity in their area and that we'd like to investigate. Remember the knocking and voices I was telling you about?"

Both Cole and Paige nodded.

Although Mick had been the one to ask the question, Rosetta picked it up and ran with it. "Turns out we've been getting reports from there since your other friend was tracking whatever he was tracking. We haven't followed up on it yet because of a string of disturbances here in town. We never got around to those Valparaiso calls and they stopped coming. Also, we've been busy with other stuff."

"Like what other stuff?" Cole asked.

Rosetta held up her hand and ticked her fingers down one at a time. "Kids, family, real jobs, school, you name it. MEG's a great time, but she doesn't pay the bills."

"So when can we get to Valparaiso?" Paige asked. "It's about an hour from here, right?"

"Yes, but we need to set up an investigation," Rosetta said. "The lady I talked to earlier sounded pretty nice, so I should be able to set something up within the next week or so."

Rosetta and Mick seemed enthusiastic, but Paige and Cole weren't smiling. Since he could feel Paige getting a little too impatient, Cole told the other two, "This is kind of an emergency. Well, not kind of. It *is* an emergency. How much have you been told about shapeshifters?"

Both of them looked at him without blinking. "We've heard some of it. Like there's some way for people to really be turned into werewolves and that you guys hunt them."

"And the vampires," Mick said. "We know about them. Nymar, right?"

Paige pressed her hands against her eyes and turned toward the door. "This was a really bad idea," she moaned.

But Cole wasn't about to give up so easily. "You've seen what's going on in KC with the murders and everything."

Nodding, Mick said, "Those aren't rottweilers, are they?"

"Not even close. We took out a bunch of them the other night—"

"At that nature preserve outside of Kansas City!" Rosetta said as she snapped her fingers and hopped excitedly.

"You know about that too?" Cole asked.

"There was stuff on the news about a bunch of animals that escaped from a private collection or wandered in from the woods. Apparently some security and stoplight cameras caught some things running by, but they were just a bunch of blurs. You should see some of the wild stuff being posted onto our website about that. It's just . . . wow."

"That about sums it up," Cole said. "More people will get hurt, and we want to put an end to it as soon as we can. So if you need to cut a few corners or bend a few rules to get us into those homes, it'd be for a good cause."

"We know you guys do good work," Mick said earnestly. "That's why MEG agreed to help you in the first place. But in this field, reputation means everything. If we lose ours by harassing clients, we won't be able to help you guys at all."

"But don't worry about all of that," Rosetta said. "I just need to call that lady back, set something up, and get the team together so we can all get on the same page. Should only take like two hours or so. Okay?"

"We are overdue for lunch," Paige said. "How about we come back after we get something to eat?"

Rosetta smiled and clasped her hands together. "Perfect. That'll give us some time to make the arrangements."

"And no matter what the home owners say," Mick added, "we'll be glad to take you out there and show you where your other friend was hunting."

"Sounds great," Cole said. "Now, what's the word on that hot dog place next door?"

* * *

The Chicago Dawg House was one long room, half of which was filled with an order counter and kitchen. At the other half, a row of stools was lined up beneath another counter that was just wide enough for people to share some table space with napkin dispensers and plastic condiment bottles.

Paige squawked the entire way into the restaurant, but quieted down when she saw the Vienna Beef sign. Her mood improved even more when she saw that the menu describing the ingredients in a classic Chicago dog was practically a transcript from when she'd described it in Kansas City. She was about to order that when her eye caught something a little farther down the menu.

"Oh my God," she sighed. "Look at that. Right beneath the 'Butkus.' "

Cole had been eyeing the Butkus anyway, which was a sausage covered with what seemed to be anything the cook could find that would singe the hairs on the back of his arm. "You mean the Fridge?"

"Yesssss."

"Looks like it may even take up some space in that bottomless pit you call a stomach. Go for it."

Their order was taken by a balding guy who stood a few inches shorter than Cole. The subtle squawk in his voice and the thick mustache on his face made it seem equally plausible that he was either a Chicago native or an off-duty cop. "You want that Fridge hot and wet?" he asked.

Cole reflexively flinched, but Paige wore a smile that lit up her entire face. "Real hot and a little wet," she said.

The guy behind the counter winked at her and nodded once. "Lady after my own heart. It'll be right up."

They moved down to sit at the counter on the opposite wall and waited for their food.

"Do you really think it was a mistake coming here?" Cole asked.

Paige craned her neck to look around at the autographed pictures of Cubs players that were hanging around the occasional framed jersey. "I don't know. We'll see what happens with those phone calls. To be honest, though, sometimes you've just got to gamble. If we were in KC, we'd just be checking in on more empty Half Breed dens or guessing where to find new ones. Not that that matters anyway because any Full Blood can just replace the Half Breeds we killed."

"That means we've only got another few days before the new Half Breeds become a real problem."

"Maybe not even that long," Paige said. "The Full Blood looked like he was whipping the surviving Half Breeds in line somehow. If it wasn't for that bait you threw at him, he might have steered those things right back at us."

"Have you ever seen anything like that before?"

Reluctantly, she cast her eyes down and shook her head. "Never. I only hope the Mongrels we find are willing to fight, because we may need their kind of backup more than a few extra sets of noses."

"What if they don't agree to come back with us at all?" Cole asked.

Paige pulled in a deep breath and let it out with an unconvincing smile. "Then we'll throw everything we've got at them one more time. It's not like we have much choice. Every new Half Breed means someone else was killed, and it's not like when a Nymar attaches its spore to someone's heart. That whole process is an easy morning of slow lovin' compared to how someone is made into a Half Breed. First they've got to be attacked and torn up almost to the point of dying. If they survive that, they get to feel all their bones snap as they take their new form. I don't even want to know what it feels like to have all their muscles unstrung and knotted around the bones that are left. Werewolves are more than supernatural. They're some kind of horrible miracle."

Thanks to the loud music blaring through the speakers inside the place, Paige's words didn't carry much farther than a few feet. Apart from the guy who'd taken their order and the tall woman refilling supplies behind the counter, there were only two other people eating at the far end of the room beneath a flat screen TV suspended from the ceiling. Nobody seemed to have heard anything worthy of their attention. Cole envied them.

Both of their faces brightened when the guy behind the counter called Paige's name. Cole's sausage was served on a huge roll, covered with peppers. Paige's Fridge overshadowed his meal in every way.

"Good Lord," he gasped when he got a look at the monstrosity she was about to consume.

The Fridge needed to be served on a larger roll, since the Italian sausage was covered by a thick layer of shaved Italian beef. On top of that was a mess of peppers that practically sent a wave of heat through the air. The whole thing had been dipped into an au jus sauce that dribbled from the soaked-through bread when she picked it up.

"Good Lord is right," Paige said. She turned her head sideways, opened wide, and bit off a good chunk of the upper layer of shaved beef and peppers. She said something after that, but only a few sloppy syllables made it through her food. Having barely swallowed that, she took a bite of the lower sausage portion. If she'd looked happy before, the sip of strawberry pop she took to wash it all down nearly pushed her straight into the orgasmic range.

"You like that Fridge?" the guy behind the counter asked.

Paige turned and threw a few unintelligible words his way before she swallowed and wiped her mouth. "You're an artist! I've never had one of these outside of Chicago."

"Neither have I. That's why I opened this place. What about you, guy? How's that Butkus treatin' ya?"

Cole took a bite that was equal parts fire and flavor. "Damn! That's . . . " His hands worked on their own to snag a few fries and stuff them into his mouth. They were just the right kind of greasy without being obnoxiously so. "These are . . . *damn!*"

The guy behind the counter nodded and gave them a thumbs-up. "Glad to hear it." Then he turned and started cleaning off his grill.

For the next few minutes Cole and Paige just sat and ate. He made it halfway through his meal before his stomach burned with a heat that felt warm and friendly without showing any signs of letting up. It was perfect.

"Youff neffer had one of deés before?" Paige asked through enough food to stop a weaker heart.

"No, but I'll be getting one before we leave town. Now I see why you get so pissed off when people screw up Chicago hot dogs."

"It's messing wiff pure beauty," she said, accenting those last three words with a beefy spray.

They finished their meal a bit too quickly and headed for the door.

"I want to get a few more dogs for the road," Cole said, "but we probably won't be on the road for a while."

"We're leaving right now, but we're not getting any more to eat. You need to be able to move."

"What's that mean?"

"It means you ate enough already," she said while cheerily patting Cole's gut. "Any more and I'll be able to rub your belly to make a wish."

"No, I mean about being on the road. Rosetta still needs to make her calls."

"So we'll leave them alone for a few hours," Paige said. "They need to gather the rest of their team, which gives us enough time to zip out to Valparaiso and have a look around."

Cole knew better than to argue with her, so he piled into the car and hung on as she drove for the interstate like a winged rodent fleeing the proverbial home of the damned.

"If we can do this on our own, why did we even bother those MEG guys?" he asked.

Paige grabbed the directions he had written down when he looked up Omaha and Valparaiso on the Internet during the drive from KC. Steering onto the ramp for southbound I-680, she replied, "We'll see if we can speed things up a bit for our new friends. That's all."

Cole had a few other questions, but they wound up lodged in the back of his throat after Paige slammed her foot against the gas pedal. Thanks to her maniacal disregard for road safety and the general flatness of Nebraska, she was able to spot speed traps from miles away and rip across the distances in between them. They made the trip in less time than the website had estimated, which put them in Valparaiso at about four-thirty.

Once there, she slowed down and asked, "You feel that? Mongrels are tricky little buggers. They're shapeshifters, but not like Full Bloods or Half Breeds, so we can't sense them like we can a real werewolf. What we can feel doesn't change much if a Mongrel is a block away or right in front of you. It's kind of like the heat you get from a Half Breed, but deeper down." Flexing her hands, she added, "Sort of . . . arthritis with a purpose."

That analogy didn't make a whole lot of sense, but thinking about it that way, Cole could feel something flowing from his shoulders down to his elbows that was more focused than the ache he always got after sitting too long at his keyboard. "The houses are supposed to be down this street a little further."

Paige found a place to park along the street and killed the engine. Reaching down to grab one of the levers near her left leg, she popped the trunk and said, "Get that trash bag from the Blood Parlor."

"That's still in there?"

"Yeah. Turns out the greasy invisible stuff lasts longer than I thought. It's not as strong as it used to be, but it should be enough to do the trick."

Rather than ask her what she had in mind, he did as he was told and waited to be surprised. Paige took the bag, pulled out the crumpled hooded sweatshirt and slipped it on. The garment smelled like sweaty glue, but the sun was just low enough in the sky to work in her favor. When bright rays hit the greasy fabric, they were bent enough to make her shimmer in a few spots.

"How do I look?" she asked.

"Like a crazy lady in an old sweatshirt."

Pulling the hood down and stretching it to cover her face, Paige vigorously rubbed and pushed the hood back into its spot on the top of her head. "What about now?

There must have been more of the greasy stuff in the fleece lining, because Paige's features were all but erased. "Not invisible, but kind of like those drunks who get their faces blurred out on cop shows."

"Good enough. Get in the car and drive down to the corner. I'll be there in a few."

Cole watched her dash down the sidewalk toward a nearby row of houses. The street was mostly empty, with the exception of a few kids playing in a yard and a couple of cars rounding the opposite corner. Spotting Paige from a distance, he could see a few more spots where the Mongrel grease was kicking in again. She was a long way from invisible, but the sunlight curled around her just enough to make a few sections of her back and side fade away.

A lot more cars were at the next intersection, probably because of the bank and Dairy Queen located there. Braking at a stop sign, Cole idled for a full minute without anyone else pulling up behind him. When he got a curious look from a kid on a bike, he waved.

Then something tapped against the window behind him and he turned to find a blurry sweatshirt racing around the back of the car. By the time he shifted toward the passenger side, that door was pulled open and a mass of stinking cotton slapped against the side of his face.

"Keep going," Paige said after she'd tossed the sweatshirt toward the backseat. "Don't speed, but just get moving."

"What happened? Is anyone chasing you?"

"Nobody's chasing me, but I did get a look at those houses from Rico's report. Even better, people in those houses got a look at me."

Chapter 24

When Cole and Paige drove back into Omaha, they were just in time for rush hour. Compared to the snarled tangle of metal and pissed-off commuters they would have found in Chicago or Kansas City, it was nothing more than a time for drivers to slow down and listen to the radio. The heat had eased off and lunch was still a very fond, very spicy memory, so they took their time and moseyed back to MEG Branch 18. Their easygoing mood lasted until they walked through the doors of the ghost chasers' office.

"There you are!" Rosetta said from behind the front desk. "You'll never believe this! We caught a break and we can head out to those homes in Valparaiso *tonight!*"

Cole blinked and reflexively looked over to Paige. "Really? What happened?"

Mick strode down the short hallway with a spiral note-book in one hand and the nub of a pencil in the other. "I don't know if it's what you're after, but there's been activity reported. One lady called less than an hour ago and told us she saw some sort of faceless figure in her backyard."

Still watching Paige, Cole said, "That's interesting."

Her poker face held up well enough.

"This isn't just one isolated instance!" Mick continued. "There really may be something out there. A kid next door to this woman saw a similar figure run down her driveway.

She said it had holes in her back and no face. I've never even heard of anything like this."

"Don't get all worked up," Paige said. "If we find it, we'll deal with it."

"I know, but if there is a presence or some sort of entity there, that falls under our jurisdiction, right?"

Cole saw a flicker of conscience pass across Paige's face. "Yeah," she said. "If you find anything in the ghost family, it's all yours."

Mick and Rosetta turned to each other, grinned, and went through a few other congratulatory motions. "The lady who called back was freaked out enough to give us free access to her home," Rosetta said. "I asked about her neighbors and she told me she'd have a word with them. Even if we don't hear back, once the neighbors see us parked in someone's driveway, they'll start asking questions. At the very least, I think we should be able to get in and have a quick look around one or two more houses."

"Perfect," Paige said. "When do we leave?"

"I've already called Quentin and Val. We'll have a briefing, I'll introduce you, we'll get the equipment together . . . what's that smell?"

Cole averted his eyes, but Paige shrugged as if she truly didn't have remnants of the acrid scent of invisibility oil drifting from her clothes.

Cutting the awkward moment short, Mick said, "We should be on the road by seven-thirty or eight. You guys want to hang out here until then?"

Just as Cole was about to cover for whatever excuse Paige came up with for them to leave, he heard her say, "Sure. I'd like to see what you guys do here."

Mick and Rosetta were almost as surprised as Cole. Once they got over that, the grand tour began.

"This," Rosetta said proudly as she waved toward her desk, "is my phone."

It was just past seven-thirty, and the sun stubbornly refused to drop. In fact, it seemed intent on hanging at just the right angle to blaze directly into Cole's eyes as he drove toward

Valparaiso for the second time that day. It was too low for the car's visor to do any good and still too high for him to look away. Due to the fact that the driver of the MEG van actually obeyed the speed limit, it took them just over an hour to reach the light blue house Paige had terrorized earlier. The van Cole followed was dark red and had MEG BRANCH 18 stenciled on one side. After pulling into the driveway, Mick hopped out from behind the wheel, waved, pointed toward the front door, and held up five fingers.

Cole parked the Cav and stepped out as the side door of the MEG van noisily rolled open.

The guy who emerged from the van had about a hundred clones wandering the halls of Digital Dreamers, Inc. He was in his mid- to late twenties, a little taller than Cole, but several pounds lighter. Thick, brushy hair looked like an abandoned project residing on his head, and the glasses he wore seemed thick enough to act as windows on a space station.

"Real great to meet you, Cole," the younger guy said as he approached the Cav. "Is that Paige there with ya?"

Paige got out and shook his hand. "That's me."

"I'm Quentin. Historian and director of Special Projects for Branch 18. If you've got stories you wouldn't mind telling or just want to fill me in on what you guys have been up to, I'm ready to listen."

"He's not a stalker, by the way," added a skinny blond girl who looked just old enough to be somewhere in the first couple years of college. "Special Projects is pretty much anything regarding people like you two."

Quentin nodded. "I probably connected a few phone calls for you both at one time or another."

Flipping her short hair behind an ear, the blonde stepped past Quentin to say, "And he never lets us hear the end of it. I'm Val. Just an investigator around here, which adds up to a whole lot of walking around in dark rooms and sifting through hours upon hours of video."

"That cool video they show on TV?" Cole asked.

"Mostly it's just video of us walking through dark rooms. The audiotapes of that are riveting, by the way."

Paige grinned and followed Val around to the back of the

van. "I like her. Let's make ourselves useful and unload this stuff."

While Cole, Paige, and Val unloaded the van, Quentin tried to look busy at a tricked-out laptop. After a few minutes of that, Mick opened the front door of the house and waved at them again.

"Time for us to get set up inside," Val said.

Paige hefted a large plastic case from the van and set it down on the driveway. "Are all those waves some sort of code?"

"Nah. He waves at us and we do things how we always do them."

There were a lot fewer wires and cords than Cole had been expecting. Val handed out flashlights, cameras, and digital audio recorders, while Quentin set up his own equipment at the back of the van and Mick escorted the home owner to the next door neighbor's place. By the time they were ready to head inside, the last remaining traces of sunlight were orange smears across a prairie sky.

"Is there a reason why you always do this in the dark?" Cole asked. "Or is that just to make it all seem scarier?"

"We're not trying to make anything look scary," Mick replied. "We need to worry about reflections showing up in pictures or windows, stray light hitting dust particles, not to mention keeping on the lookout for anything giving off its own light. That's the good stuff, and we can miss it if it's being washed out by too much sunlight."

"The short answer for that," Val said as she walked by, "is yes. There are reasons for doing this in the dark."

Paige chuckled mostly to herself as she followed along behind Val. "I really do like her."

They filed into the house, which was an odd mix of decorating styles, including several layers of afghans draped over the sofas and a few pieces of modern art hanging on the walls. The living room was small and led into a smaller dining area, but none of that caught Cole's attention as much as what was in the back corner near a closet.

"Is that a stripper pole?" he whispered.

Mick leaned over and hissed, "Just keep checking your equipment."

"If the lady who owns this place has a stripper pole, maybe I should check her equipment."

"She's sixty if she's a day. Besides, we're not here to make fun of her home. Are you going to do your job or should you wait outside?"

Cole let Val and Paige walk ahead and down a hall that led past a fairly nice kitchen. The light from their flashlights was just enough to cast a dull glow throughout the space.

Mick stood beside him, rummaging through the various pieces of electronics clipped to D-rings on his shirt and belt. "This," he said while tapping a black box he handed over to Cole, "is a K2 meter. It's basically a simpler version of our EMF detectors. See those lights?"

The box Cole had been given was bigger than a cigarette lighter but slightly smaller than a glasses case. An arc of little lightbulbs crossing along the top of the box went from green to red as they progressed from left to right. At the moment the first two green lights were flickering.

"Those register fluctuations in the electromagnetic field," Mick explained. "The field should be pretty stable under normal conditions, but can be affected by other energies. When you see those lights jump into the red, there's a fluctuation."

"What about your meter?" Cole asked.

The one Mick held was larger and looked like any number of items pulled from a shelf at Radio Shack. It was larger than a digital camera and about twice as thick. The front was mostly taken up by a gauge with a needle waggling around various numbered scales printed on the face. Mick kept the box cupped in one hand and said, "This is a Tri-Field meter. It measures both AC and DC electrical current along with EMF."

"How does that help?"

"Spiritual energy is still energy. AC current is man-made, but DC can come from natural sources. One time, I picked up a cat running through some bushes with this thing."

"That's pretty cool."

"Yeah, it really is. But to get truly accurate readings, this meter needs to stand still. Otherwise, you might just be picking up natural fluctuations of energy coming from the earth's normal field."

"Seriously?"

"There's more to it than that, but basically yes."

Cole followed Mick around the living room and into the dining room. In the time it took for the equipment to be handed out and the investigation to start, the sunlight had dwindled down to nothing. All that filtered in from outside was the dull glow of streetlights.

"We don't have enough time to thoroughly check this place from top to bottom," Mick whispered. "The owner wants us out of here before ten. Do you need any longer than that?"

"I honestly don't even know what I'm looking for on this meter."

"You're after living creatures, right?" Mick asked.

"Yes."

"Then let me know when you pick up spikes. I'll let you know what you might have found. We may also catch something from that faceless apparition, so stay alert."

"Is there a basement?"

Mick nodded. "Yes, but there's not supposed to be any activity there."

"The things we're after are burrowers, so there may be more activity than this lady knows about. Let's have a look."

"Hold up." Mick grabbed his cell phone from his shirt pocket and tapped a button. The phone chirped and established a quick two-way connection that must have cost a bit extra on the service plan. "Quentin, bring the thermal in here."

After another chirp, Quentin replied, "Be right there."

Mick continued shuffling through the kitchen. "We've had this camera on layaway for months but haven't had the money to snag it."

"A thermal camera must be a tax write-off for MEG," Cole pointed out.

"Yes, but each branch pays its own expenses. Don't get me wrong," he quickly added. "You guys make lots of generous donations, but it's all gotta be spread around. I went and picked it up as soon as I heard why you two were coming, but it'll have to go back tomorrow before the check is cashed, so don't scratch it. Just don't even touch it. Tell me where to point it and I'll do the rest."

"That should pick up any living things in here?" Cole asked.

"In here or under here within a reasonable distance." Mick appeared somewhat menacing with just the faint glow of his little flashlight reflecting up onto his features. "This baby detects heat, so it'll also pick up changes in temperature due to hollow spaces stuck in the middle of a wall or under the floor. If there are tunnels or even secret compartments where this lady keeps her porn, we should be able to scope them out."

Cole whistled softly. "That's really cool."

"Tell me about it."

Mick left the kitchen, walked down the short hall, and headed for the room currently filled with an eerie, bobbing white light. Tensing as he tried to get ahead of Mick, Cole almost reached for the spot where his weapon was normally kept. The weapon wasn't there, but it turned out he didn't need it. Paige and Val were in the bedroom, checking the floor and walls with penlights that cast the weird shadows.

"You two find anything in here?" Mick asked.

Val nodded enthusiastically. "Paige picked up a hot spot with the K2."

Walking into the little bedroom, Mick expertly side-stepped piles of dirty clothes and a few shoe boxes to get over to where Paige was standing. "Really? Let's see."

Paige crouched down under a window built high up on the wall that looked out to the narrow space between the house and its neighbor. Every time she waved the meter over a spot on the floor, the lights jumped from the first two greens all the way up to the last two reds.

"See if you can confirm that one, Cole," Mick said.

Stretching out with his right hand, Cole waved his own K2 over the same patch of floor. The spike he got wasn't quite as drastic, but he also wasn't able to get the meter as close to the floorboards. Nodding slowly, Mick hunkered down and placed his Tri-Field meter near that spot. Almost instantly, it made a screeching noise, and kept it up even after he and Val pulled Cole and Paige away from it.

After a bit more screeching, Mick nodded and took his meter back. "Could be wires under the floor," he said. "Could be a naturally occurring magnetic field. It could also be something giving off its own energy. Do you know if these burrowers manipulate magnetic fields at all?"

With a genuinely perplexed look on her face, Paige replied, "That might explain a few things, but I'm not sure. We should definitely take a look under here when we get to the basement."

Placing his foot on the edge of the bed frame, Cole hoisted himself up to the rectangular window and took a look outside. He then lifted his left hand to wave. "Is the owner a rat-faced lady with her hair in a bun?"

"You could call her that," Mick replied.

"She's watching from the next house over."

"She'll probably be checking in on us throughout the night."

Just then the front door opened and thumped shut. Mick's phone chirped and Quentin said, "I've got the thermal. Where are you guys?"

"Bedroom at the end of the hall," Mick replied.

A few seconds later Quentin stomped into the room carrying a camera in one hand and what looked like a small laptop computer in the other. He handed the camera to Val and then flipped open the laptop to show what the camera was seeing.

The new equipment smelled like an expensive trip to the electronics store. Cole watched intently as it was all switched on. Once it warmed up, Mick aimed the camera at the floor and asked, "See anything, Val?"

"I think we've all been spending too much time in this spot. Either that, or there's too much going on with the wires or insulation or whatever."

"How about we take this all down to the basement?" Cole asked. "Whatever we're looking for would most likely be down there anyway."

Before anyone could say anything, a muted thump echoed through the room.

Val, Mick, and Quentin all looked at each other and then swung their flashlights toward the hall.

"What was that?" Cole asked.

There was another thump, followed by a scratching that seemed to come as much from the floor as it did from the walls.

Val handed the monitor back to Quentin so she could dig a small digital audio recorder from her pocket. She flipped it on and asked, "Is there anyone in here with us?"

When Paige started to say something, she was quickly silenced by the entire MEG team. Walking over to Cole, she whispered, "You brought your spear, right?"

"It's in the car."

"Go get it."

He headed out of the room as they heard more scratches from the vicinity of the closet and under the floor. Instead of the quick, skittering sounds of a critter trapped in a crawl space, the noises were more like thick claws scraping against the underside of the wood beneath Cole's feet.

Once he was outside, Cole could barely hear anything coming from inside or under the house. A short lady with her hair tied into a bun raced from the neighboring house to meet him at the Cav.

"Did you hear any noises?" she asked. "It's not rats! I keep a clean house and my son is an exterminator. There's no rats!"

"I'm just getting some more equipment, ma'am," Cole said as calmly as he could.

"You're not making a mess, are you? Maybe I should come over there."

"We've got some expensive stuff set up," Cole said as he rooted around in the car and took what he needed from under the front seat. "I'll send Mick out here to answer any questions you may have." He shut the car door and headed back to the house. "We just don't want you to trip on anything, that's all."

"Expensive equipment, huh?" the lady asked. "Is that a stick you're carrying?"

Cole pretended not to hear that as he went inside and locked the door behind him. The moment he crossed the threshold, he was surrounded by the scraping sounds, which were now accompanied by the rattle of pots within the lower kitchen cabinets. The lights coming from that area let him know that someone was already investigating the disturbance.

Quentin and Val were in the kitchen, sweeping their meters along the floor and cabinets. "The lady who owns the house was outside and she seemed pretty upset," he told them.

Turning to look at Cole, Quentin nearly blinded him thanks to the penlight gripped between his teeth. "She's not gonna come in, is she?" he asked.

"She might. I told her Mick would go out to explain what's happening."

"Good. We're busy in here."

The two of them switched their lights off so they could use the thermal camera. Val dropped to all fours to get to one of the lower cabinets and pointed the camera in there while Quentin watched the portable monitor.

Although Cole knew the basics of how the camera worked, all he could see on the foldable screen was a mix of bright reds and darker blues. "Find anything?" he asked.

"We're picking up traces of a heat signature moving around under the floor," Val said. "There's a spike in the EMF just before it comes along. It's really cool!"

Cole hurried to the bedroom, where Paige and Mick were crawling around knocking on the floor. "You might want to go smooth out the lady who owns this place," he said.

"Why?" Mick asked as he pressed his ear to the floor.

"Because she's about to come in here, that's why." When that didn't get the other man moving, Cole added, "She seemed to think you guys were breaking stuff in here."

Mick jumped to his feet and grumbled, "I knew we shouldn't have asked her to leave. Go against standard practices once and all you get is grief." He continued grumbling, but couldn't be heard once he left the room.

"What's going on in here?" Cole asked.

Paige stood up and waved the K2 meter over the floor. "There's something under the floor, and I think it knows we're looking for it. Either that or it's just getting restless. Did you hear all that scratching a few minutes ago?"

"How could I miss it?"

"Something moved right below the foundation of this house."

"Hasn't anyone checked the basement?"

"That's the thing," Paige replied. "Val went down there and came right back up again. There's just a single room big enough for the water heater and some storage located below the living room, but no basement under this half of the house."

"Then maybe—"

As soon as Cole started to talk, the scratching noises became loud enough to make him hop away from where he'd been standing.

"Are you recording this?" Val shouted.

Heavy steps thumped down some stairs and up again before Quentin replied, "Yeah, but it's not as loud downstairs. I can hear it, but just a little."

"Hey!" Paige shouted. "Get that thermal camera in here!"

More heavy steps along with some labored breathing announced Quentin's arrival.

"Point it right here at the floor," Paige said.

Quentin nodded and rushed over to her. Aiming the camera at the spot where she'd been pointing, he held the monitor for about two seconds before he nearly dropped it. "Whoa! Did you see that?"

"Sweep that spot again," Paige said as she took the monitor from him.

The scratching sounded like nails raking against concrete. As it flowed up through the floor, it was distorted by all the layers of wood, insulation, wiring, dirt, and whatever else was between the MEG team and the source of the noise.

Then the scratching stopped.

"Have you heard anything like this before?" Cole asked.

Quentin continued to move the camera back and forth while shaking his head. "A few times, I've heard banging and whispers, but nothing this bad."

"Did the home owner mention anything like this when you talked to her?"

Although he didn't look away from the floor, Quentin shook his head. "Not that I remember." He used his free hand to grab his phone and then keyed it to send a few chirps through instead of one.

After a few seconds Mick whispered, "Yeah?"

"Did the home owner ever mention scratching sounds?"

"Yeah. Those and some knocking."

"I mean loud scratching like what we heard."

There wasn't a reply through the phone's speaker, but Cole could hear muted voices coming from outside. After they died down, the phone chirped and Mick said, "She says there was scratching, but not from rats."

"There!" Paige said. "Did you see that?"

Cole had been watching the monitor while also glancing down to see where Quentin was aiming the camera. "I saw something flash by on the screen, but don't know what it was."

"Here," Quentin grunted as he got up from where he'd been kneeling. "Rewind the feed. Right here." He pointed to a button and then tapped it. When he saw the movement in reverse, he backed up another few seconds and played it frame by frame.

Most of the screen was a mess of dark blues and greens. Brighter lines crossed the screen in bundles, which had to be wires or possibly narrow pipes under the floor. The thing that slowly moved from one side of the screen to the other wasn't a bundle of wires, however, and it sure as hell wasn't a pipe. It was, however, very hot.

"What the hell?" Quentin gasped.

Val raced into the room and pressed between Cole's and Paige's shoulders so she could get a look. "What? What is it? What did you find?"

"Is that . . . some sort of beak?" Quentin asked as he used his finger to trace a long hooked shape at the bottom of the glowing red and orange blob. "There's another one. And another! It's all connected."

"Maybe it's some sort of snake," Val offered. "Looks like those beaks or whatever connect down at a neck and . . . move it ahead a bit."

Quentin sped the video up a notch so he could watch the hooked shapes slide along until the bottom of the screen was covered by the larger body. He stopped the video, rolled it back, and played it at regular speed. Although Cole knew what to look for this time around, he still couldn't see much before the entire shape wriggled past.

"That looks like a big snake to me," Quentin said. "What do you guys think?"

Paige didn't say anything, but glanced around as if waiting for the scratching to return. When nothing happened, she looked down and asked, "Where's that big meter Mick set down?"

"You mean the Tri-Field?" Val asked.

"Yeah. Where is it?"

"I've got it," Quentin replied. "Picked it up so it wouldn't interfere with the thermal."

"Let's get another look downstairs."

The entire group rushed to the basement. Cole's first observation was just how small it was. The steps were narrow, and the stairway felt more like a tunnel as it led down to a pair of brick walls and single door to the right. The small storage room was almost directly below the living room, just as the others had mentioned.

"Point that camera there," Paige said as she slapped the wall to her left.

Quentin did, but the only thing that showed on the monitor was a mix of black and dark blue.

"Give me that Tri-Field thingy," Paige said.

"Actually, it won't do much good down here with all the wires and—" Quentin stopped short when he saw the glare on Paige's face. Knowing that glare all too well, Cole wasn't surprised when Quentin dug out the meter and handed it over right away.

Paige held the meter in her hand and flipped it on. Almost immediately the needle on its face waggled back and forth.

It jumped in one direction, fell back, and then jumped again. All the while, it made the staticky high-pitched wailing that they'd heard before.

"It's the current down here," Val said from where she stood halfway up the stairs. "There's just too many wires and stuff in this cramped space."

Moving the meter up and down along the wall, Paige looked as if she truly knew what she was doing with it. Within seconds more noise emanated from deep behind the brick wall. It rumbled and scraped until the source got close enough to the back side of the bricks for the screech of nails against rock to be added to the delightful audio mix.

Paige smirked, turned the meter off and waited. When the scratching faded, she smirked again. "There's something behind this wall, and this meter is driving it nuts."

"Are you sure about that?" Val asked as she hunkered down to crouch on the stairs.

"Yep. All that scratching started when the meters were on, and it got worse when all of them were gathered in that same spot. Do these things give off any noise besides what we can hear?"

Val shrugged. "Just the normal hum most electronics give off." Looking to Quentin, she added, "Unless there's some sort of interaction with the electromagnetic field that the detectors have picked up. We've never heard of anything that could hear that sort of thing so well before. Not through a brick wall anyway."

"There are bats and other rodents that hear plenty we don't," Quentin offered, "but nothing that burrows like this. I mean . . . there can't really be something under here like what we saw on the thermal. Someone would have seen it, right?"

"That's what we're here to find out," Paige said. "Cole, go outside and look at the ground around the house. Whatever it is must come up for air. If it's as big as it seems, you might be able to see something squirming around beneath the grass."

Val's eyes widened. "Oh, is that what the stick's for? I want to go with you!"

"No!" Cole snapped. "Stay here and take some more readings." As he stormed up the stairs, he almost ran into Mick. Paige came up right behind him and pointed back down to the basement.

"They caught something on the thermal," she said to Mick. "Go take a look."

The haggard expression on his face brightened and he ran toward the basement door.

Once they were alone, Cole asked, "You think some sort of snake is down there?"

"The thing in that video wasn't a snake," Paige told him. "It was a bunch of fingers connected to a hand connected to an arm. It was just a lot closer to the bottom of the floor than anyone thought."

"Ohhhh, yeahh. Good call."

"Whatever is underground is moving back and forth from the wall. It's gotta come up for air, and when it does, try to stick it."

"We're not here to kill it," Cole reminded her. "We need its help, remember?"

Gritting her teeth, Paige said, "Then get its attention or try to draw it out. Do you have your earpiece radio?"

"No. I lost that in Indiana."

She sighed "What about an earpiece for your phone?"

"It's one of the smallest models made and I had to import it from a special store in Tokyo that only gets—"

"Great," Paige snapped. "Put it in and keep in contact with me. I'll go back to the bedroom and try to stir it up. When you see anything, let me know. Mongrels are hit and miss as far as temperament goes. They're not all exotic naked cat ladies, so don't do anything stupid."

Giving her a quick, halfhearted salute, Cole headed out the front door. There were just enough clouds in the sky to keep the moonlight down to a minimum. It didn't take long to circle around the little house and get to the side with the bedroom where everyone had been gathered.

A small patch of flowers ran along the front, sectioned off from the lawn by inch-high wooden beams set into the ground. The flowers grew in thick patches, clustered together as if competing to live there. He didn't hear anything, but he could see lights moving behind the little window a foot or so over his head. Before he could get to his phone's earpiece, something shifted beneath the ground as though a patch of grass had decided to shrug. Cole held his weapon in both hands and cautiously approached the moving earth. When the hands reached up from the ground to grab his ankles, he was barely able to gulp in some air before being pulled under.

Chapter 25

The first thing Cole thought about when he felt the sharp jabs at his ankles were the bear traps that Paige had used to trip up those Half Breeds. In the fraction of a second following that thought, he wondered if he'd stumbled into a hole. Half a second later he kicked around the possibility of quicksand being a hazard native to central Nebraska. By then the dirt had gotten into his mouth and up into his nose.

The sharp jabs worked up along his legs and were now scraping against his chest. When the hard, gouging talons found his shoulder, they were replaced by the touch of long, bony fingers. The claws Paige had spotted on the thermal camera wrapped around his chin and shoved his face upward.

"How many did you bring, Skinner?" The voice was like a wire brush that had been forced into his ear by a set of rough, sandpapery lips.

When Cole tried to speak, more soil filled his mouth. Wet granules hit the back of his throat, speeding up his pulse and commanding the rest of his body to crawl up and out of the ground. His legs were wrapped up tightly, however, and couldn't even bend. His arms were stretched over his head and barely flexed in response to the frantic pleas coming from his mind. His palms ached with a familiar pain that told him he was still gripping his weapon, the only part of him still above ground.

"Relax," the hissing voice commanded. "The dirt's freshly turned, so there's just enough air to keep you alive for a while. Answer my question, Skinner, or I can drag you a whole lot deeper. How many others did you bring?"

Feeling more dirt trickle in, Cole closed his mouth until there was only the slightest break between his lips. When he spoke again, he did so more from his throat. Those ventriloquist lessons he'd taken as a kid had finally paid off. "Partner nearby."

"I know you've got partners. I can smell the Nymar drug coursing through your veins." Whatever pressed against Cole's face was twice as coarse as the earth that surrounded them. When it moved, muscles tensed and joints shifted all along the length of his body. Not only was he surrounded by dirt, but he was also wrapped in the embrace of whatever the hell had dragged him down. When he started to panic and felt his heart crash desperately against his ribs, the hand under his chin forced his face up until the slightest trickle of air arrived from between the chunks of dirt overhead. Pulling himself up with his arms increased the flow a little, but not nearly enough to take a real breath.

"You're not the one that came here before," the rough voice said.

Cole was so intent on breathing that he didn't even try to respond. After a few agonizingly long seconds of silence, he felt the strong, clawed hands grip his shoulders and force him down another inch or two. His arms stretched to the point of dislocating at the wrists and shoulders. The thorns in his weapon tore his palms apart. Every gulping breath was accompanied by a rush of dirt.

"I can sit down here all night, Skinner," the voice whispered almost directly into his ear. "We spared the one that came before you, but we won't allow our home to be destroyed. Speak to me or I'll bury you deep enough for the worms to steal your last breath."

As it became impossible for Cole to breathe, an eerie calmness settled upon him. He felt the rest of the world turn while he remained perfectly suspended in the middle of it. Not only did his heartbeat thump through his ears, but the pattering of the heart within the other creature could be heard as well. Thickly muscled limbs clutched his torso and sharp talons dug into his legs. Even if he could crawl up, he'd have to pull through those claws to get there.

Muffled yet familiar voices drifted overhead. Footsteps thumped against the ground and the MEG team's equipment gave off its high-pitched shriek. All of those things had to be relatively close, but might as well have come from another planet.

Suddenly, the thing wrapped around Cole started to shake him. "Don't drift off, Skinner," the voice rasped. "You probably won't wake up."

If he kept perfectly still and focused on what little air he could get, he was able to push the panic down a few levels. "Came to . . . talk."

"So talk."

"We need help."

The voice became quicker and more excited as the muscled limbs cinched around him like a tightening fist. "That why you came poking around? That why you brought your weapons and your traps? To draw us here?"

"Just wanna talk." Cole was fading. His lungs were so emptied that the little gulps of gritty air just weren't cutting it anymore. "Have . . . deal . . . "

Talons clamped down upon his shoulders.

Voices around and above drew closer.

Something coiled around his body and tugged until his hands felt ready to snap off.

"Let go of your weapon," the voice insisted, "or you'll suffocate."

Cole tried to pull his weapon in but couldn't get it to budge. He didn't have the strength to pull himself up, and when he tried to get a better grip, he was torn away and dragged farther underground.

Dirt, rocks, and pockets of dampness slid past his face or scraped against his arms. The body coiled around him was in constant motion, and the talons gripping his shoulders dug into his clothes to drag him deeper through what felt like a vat full of sludge. He couldn't see anything but a field of glowing dots that pulsed in time to his frantic heartbeat. His lungs burned with the effort of trying breathe and his throat ached as more grit was pulled in.

He couldn't last much longer.

Hopefully, Paige would find his body.

Air hit Cole's face like a bucket of cold water. He reflexively tried to suck in a breath, but his mouth was filled with soil and small rocks. His stomach heaved and he hacked up a good portion of the filth he'd taken in. Although he still couldn't move anything from his neck down, he at least caught a hint of light when he opened his eyes. As his body worked to pull in as much air as it could, he realized he was being held a foot or two over a bare, water-stained floor. Then he realized only his face was sticking out from a spot on the wall about that high up.

Something rustled directly beside him and a trickle of dirt hit the floor. When the voice came again, he could feel the leathery face moving against his cheek. "Say your piece, Skinner."

Cole's eyes rattled in their sockets, but apart from a cracked cement floor illuminated by a distant light, there wasn't much to see. "Where am I?"

"Not far from where you started."

The walls were broken and unfinished. There were no furnishings or shelves in the little room, but the rust stains and squared-off shapes in the dust told him that hadn't always been the case. He heard footsteps above him. "We're not here to hurt anyone," he said. "We need your help. You're a Mongrel, right?"

The rustling against Cole's cheek grew louder and something appeared in the corner of his eye. He could turn just enough to see part of a black eye covered in a leathery flap that opened into a narrow slit.

"Don't worry about me," the dirt encrusted thing told him. "Just take the air I give you and convince me not to plant you half a mile beneath the foundation of this house."

Having had enough time to figure out where he was, Cole pulled in a breath and shouted, *"Help me! I'm in the basement!"*

That didn't go over well.

The thing let out an angry hiss and tightened its grip around Cole's torso. In a series of wriggling motions, it pulled itself and him back into the wall. Before his head was enveloped again, he heard the familiar voice of the lady who owned the house where MEG was conducting their investigation. She'd been waiting at the neighbor's place, which meant he had only been dragged one basement over from where he'd started.

With most of his senses either shut down or overloaded, Cole could only tell he was moving through the dirt a hell of a lot faster than before. The earth sped past him on all sides, and he held his breath to keep from being filled up by it. Just when he felt his lights start to dim again, the movement stopped.

The Mongrel's limbs tightened around him like a colony of thick snakes. The clawed hand eased past his head, brushed against his chin and shoved his face to one side. When the dirt parted in front of his eyes, Cole was shoved into an open space like a giant rock being squeezed from a dirty tube. He emerged from the soil, fell onto an earthen floor and was held in place by clawed hands that reached out from the wall to wrap around his neck and chest. Despite the circumstances, being able to draw a full breath was better than any sex he'd ever had.

"Feel better?" the kidnapper asked from over his shoulder.

Cole nodded and replied, "Yeah. Much better."

"You want to talk? Talk."

After wiping some more crap from his eyes, Cole saw he was in a space about the size of a walk-in closet. The walls, floor, and ceiling were dirt and stone supported by a few wooden beams. A single electric lantern was the room's only illumination, but that was enough for him to spot another Mongrel, a female sitting directly in front of him. Tight, sinewy legs were folded under a lithe frame, and her hands were placed daintily upon her knees. Firm, rounded breasts swelled beneath a layer of fur that covered her entire body.

Using the only card in his deck, Cole sputtered, "I know a Mongrel named Jackie. She was in Canada a few months ago and followed me to Chicago. She . . . looks like a cat and could become invisible. Do you know who I'm talking about?"

The card was far from an ace, but it caused the figure in front of him to tilt her head to one side. "No," she said, "but this person sounds very interesting. I suppose you killed her for the fading properties of her fur?"

"Killed her? No!"

Leaning forward, the figure stretched out her arms and slipped her legs back so she could crawl toward him. Her face had the narrow bone structure of a bird, but the rounded brow and jawline of a cat. Her short nose tapered to a point and turned upward at the tip. When she spoke, she displayed a set of short, spiky teeth that retracted into her gums so only a few rows of white nubs could be seen. "Why do you sound so surprised?" she asked in a smoothly textured voice. "Isn't that what Skinners do? Kill people like us so you can tear what you want from our corpses?"

"Uhhhh . . . technically yes," Cole sighed. "But only with werewolves."

"What of this Jackie? If I ask my scouts to find her, will they only find a grave?"

"No!"

"No grave?" snarled the harsh voice of the thing that had him in its grasp. "Just a pile of discarded bones and pulp?" The limbs wrapped around Cole's body tightened and the claws sunk a little deeper into his shoulder.

"The last time I saw her, she was alive," he insisted. "She ran away and we wiped up some of the invisible stuff. That's all. We found a way to make our own!"

When the thing behind him moved its eye, it sounded like a rusty ball bearing scraping against sandstone.

The figure in front of Cole shifted into a more human form. She still had a thin layer of fur, but the soft flesh and rounded curves of a human woman. Talonlike claws sprouted from the fingertips she placed beneath his chin. "What of the ones in the house nearby? You're telling me they're not here to hunt us?"

"We came to find you. I already told snake boy here that we wanted to talk."

The head next to Cole's face moved up and down. "He did."

"Let him go."

The limbs and claws that had kept Cole's back against the wall now pushed him forward. As soon as he landed, he reached for his only hope for salvation. After a quick search, he realized the pocket where he'd kept his phone had been completely ripped away. "Who are you?" he asked in the toughest voice he could manage.

"I'm Kayla," the woman said. "And that is Ben."

Feeling movement behind his back, Cole scooted away to see a long, scaly body wriggle through the wall before slipping farther into it like a crocodile swimming through a tank of dirty water. Some dirt came loose as an elongated head poked out, but it was tough for Cole to say if the beak capping Ben's mouth was smiling or frowning. Once he locked eyes with Cole, Ben nodded once and blinked with eyelids that flipped open sideways instead of up and down.

"What's your name, Skinner?" Kayla asked.

"Cole. My name's Cole. Where the hell am I?"

Kayla settled back into her cross-legged sitting position. "You'd be surprised how many little spaces there are underground. Forgotten cellars, old septic tanks, sometimes a bomb shelter or an actual cave. And before you ask, no. We're not in a septic tank."

"All right. That's good, I guess."

"What did you want to talk about?"

Cole had spent plenty of time during his last few car rides thinking about that. Of course, planning a speech while listening to the radio was a lot different than forming a complete sentence after being dragged through an agoraphobic's personal hell. "There's a big problem just a few hours from here."

"You mean the werewolves attacking Kansas City?" Ben asked from his spot halfway wedged in the wall, showing an elbow and part of a shoulder just below his face.

"Yeah," Cole said as he turned to get a look at him. "How do you know about that?"

Appearing at another spot in a different wall, Ben snapped, "Oh, just because we live in a hole under someone's lawn, you don't think we can keep up on current affairs?"

Chuckling at the look of supreme confusion etched upon Cole's face, Kayla said, "Our scouts are very effective. If we are to survive, we must keep track of the Full Bloods. We also spend more time up top than you probably know."

"My partner and I . . . we've killed a bunch of Half Breeds," Cole explained.

Kayla shrugged. "Half Breeds are often left in the Full Bloods' wake."

"It's more than that. The Half Breeds are being made on purpose. A Full Blood is planting them."

"Planting them?" Ben asked.

Cole turned to look Ben in the eye, but didn't find the Mongrel where he'd last left him. Instead, Ben had moved to a spot somewhere between the wall and the ceiling, like a gravity-challenged house cat getting comfortable in the wrong corner. "That's right."

"So they've heard the voice of the Mind Singer."

"You mean Henry?" Cole asked.

Kayla nodded. "Visions of blood-spattered walls and cells with holes looking up to the heavens have been drifting through every shapeshifter's head. Before that there were rantings about the Nymar being scattered and disorganized. I believe Jackie already told you about this."

"So you do know Jackie," Cole said. "Is she here?"

"Here and gone," Ben replied from yet another spot over Cole's head. "Some time ago."

Excited that he was actually gaining ground, Cole said, "If you saw her, she must have told you about the Blood Blade. She brought it to me and my partner in Chicago!"

Ben's eyes scraped within their sockets. Kayla looked up at him and said, "She did mention something about that."

"Then you must know we didn't try to kill her." Cole prayed Mongrels weren't psychic, because he and Jackie had one hell of a wrestling match when she first tracked him down, and it wasn't the social kind. Judging by the look on Kayla's face, the report hadn't been too bad.

"So the Full Bloods are attacking Kansas City," she said. "Something like this was bound to happen. Maybe now the humans will join us in putting those monsters out of everyone's misery."

"So far, the cops are blaming the deaths on dog attacks or gang fights," Cole said. "By the time they realize what they're up against, a lot more people are going to die."

"That's what Full Bloods do," Kayla said, with disgust tainting every syllable. "They kill. Perhaps it is good for the humans' blissful ignorance to come to an end."

"Sounds to me like you're not a fan." Raising his eyebrows, Cole asked, "How'd you like to help us take this Full Blood down?"

"Our kind have been fighting them for centuries," Ben said.

Cole stretched his neck to look up, but only found a few grooves in the dirt where the Mongrel had been. Looking around until he spotted one side of Ben's face emerging from the soil behind Kayla's shoulder, he asked, "But have you ever had help from Skinners? We've got a few aces up our sleeves, you know."

Kayla smirked. Even though her face was a bit too round, small, and furry to be human, the gesture was still attractive. "If you had any aces, you wouldn't have come here looking for us. Or was I correct the first time in thinking you came to strip us for parts?"

"We can take the Half Breeds," Cole said with a confidence that he didn't have to fake. "We can hold our own against a Full Blood now that we have the Blood Blade." That wasn't quite a lie, but drifted into that territory. "We need you guys to help us find all the dens that are hidden throughout KC. Until we find them all, we can't put an end to what's going on there."

Studying Cole through beautiful, unnatural eyes, Kayla asked, "That's all you need?"

"We know you guys have a problem with Full Bloods, so—"

"A 'problem'?" Kayla sneered. "Is that what you heard?"

Cole quickly added, "And you may just have a problem with the Skinners if I'm not returned. If I'd wanted to start any trouble, I would have done more than allow myself to be sucked down here for this little chat."

Despite the fact that neither of the Mongrels were buying into his act completely, his words did make a dent. "What can you offer us?" Kayla asked.

"We're giving you the chance to attack your enemies when they won't be expecting you," Cole replied. "Do you need more than that?"

Speaking from a spot in the floor beside Cole's foot, Ben replied, "Yes."

"Then I'll need to talk to my partner."

The face in the floor disappeared, and Ben's beak emerged from the wall behind Cole's shoulder to look at Kayla. "Should we let him make a call?"

Kayla nodded.

Ben stuck out his hand, which was comprised of the bony fingers and curved claws that had showed up on the thermal camera's monitor. He opened his fist and dropped Cole's phone along with the ripped square of denim that had once been his pocket.

"Thanks," Cole said. "I'll let you slide on tearing up my jeans."

"Gee," Ben said as he lifted his chin so Cole couldn't miss the sharp point of his beak. "Thanks."

They must not have been too far underground because Cole actually had a bar's worth of signal strength. He dialed Paige's number and got an answer in less than half a ring.

"Cole, where the hell are you?" she asked.

"I found some Mongrels."

"Are you okay? Did they hurt you? Tell me where you are!"

"I'm underground somewhere. They didn't hurt me. Actually," Cole added, "I've already mentioned the deal we came to make."

Paige was silent for a few seconds. When she spoke again, he could easily picture the dazed expression that must have been on her face when she asked, "Seriously? If you're tied up or a hostage, just say yes."

"I'm serious."

"Are they there with you?"

Cole replied, "They're here."

"Put me on speaker."

Cole pressed the speaker button, held the phone out toward the middle of the room, and then instantly regretted it.

"All right," Paige snapped. "Anyone who hears this is dead if my partner isn't released pretty damn quick!"

"Who might you be?" Kayla asked.

"I'm the one who can see to it that a whole lot of other Skinners will come back here and turn this town into mulch just to get at you. But," Paige added in a calmer voice, "I can also be the one that makes sure nobody comes around to bother you again. It all depends on how quickly I can see my partner and what condition he's in."

"We'll set him free and then find you again. It's probably best if none of us are too excited when we try to discuss any propositions." With that, Kayla reached out and snatched the phone away from Cole. After cutting off the call, she tossed the phone toward the wall. Ben had to extend his arm out a little farther, but he caught it.

"When we get up top," she said to Cole, "don't step out of line. And in case you're going through the math right now, just know that you and your partners do not outnumber us."

To prove her point, Ben stuck his face up from over half a dozen spots around the earthen chamber. Cole looked around to find each of those sets of slitted eyes staring back at him. Now that they weren't peeking out from odd angles or slithering from one spot to another, he could see subtle differences in facial structure and skin tone that made it clear he'd been surrounded by several of the burrowing Mongrels the entire time.

"Any chance there's some stairs behind you?" Cole asked the one figure in the room that wasn't embedded in the wall.

Kayla nodded and got to her feet. The ceiling directly above her cracked and began to crumble. As bigger chunks dropped away, Cole could see a flurry of leathery arms and curved claws reaching from the upper portions of the walls to push even more of the ceiling down.

Blind, instinctive panic flooded through Cole's mind as the entire room caved in on top of him. The certainty of being buried alive would have made him cry out if he wasn't already so familiar with how unpleasant it was to get his mouth stuffed full of dirt. Just as Kayla's lantern was buried and he was forced to shut his eyes, the dirt stopped falling and a glorious rush of fresh air flowed down to fill the hole. He looked up to find Ben sticking halfway out of the side of the hole, offering a hand down to him. Seeing the uncertainty in Cole's eyes, Ben said, "You can climb, but it'll take longer."

Just to prove he wasn't afraid, Cole took the hand Ben offered and was hefted up to a damp patch of grass. After he had cleared the dirt from his eyes, he saw Paige crouching down behind Kayla. One of her sickles was held so its blade was tight under Kayla's chin and the tip of the other sickle pressed against the feline Mongrel's belly.

"Anyone makes a move I don't like," Paige snarled, "and I'll open her up in two very undesirable places."

Kayla didn't move. Her eyes darted back and forth, which seemed to be enough to keep the remaining burrowers from emerging. Cole could see several sets of limbs, shoulders, and eyes pushing up from the ground within a radius of about ten yards. One by one the burrowers sank beneath the freshly turned soil.

"I'm all right, Paige," Cole insisted as he got up and dusted himself off. "See?"

She looked him up and down but didn't relax her weapons. "I know there's at least ten of you around here," she said to Kayla. "Where are the others?"

"Ten?" Cole asked. "How do you know that?"

Jogging to catch up to Paige, Quentin held up his expensive toy and said, "This thermal camera rules! I just had to fiddle with the settings and point it in the right spot to—"

"Get back and keep everyone else away from here," Paige snapped.

Quentin and the rest of the MEG team headed back to the nearby houses. Now that he was in the open again, Cole could see he'd emerged in someone's backyard surrounded only by the skeletal remains of a chain-link fence. The house appeared to be either half finished or partially demolished. Either way, there wasn't anyone home. Less than fifty yards behind Paige were the houses under investigation.

"Typical Skinner treachery," Kayla spat. "Your partner is unharmed and you still intend on killing me."

Retracting her arms to ease the weapons away from her captive, Paige said, "Lady, I don't think you have the slightest idea of what I intend. How about we meet somewhere a bit more private so we can discuss it?"

"I won't meet you anywhere you've probably rigged with traps."

"And I won't meet you somewhere just to be surrounded and ripped to shreds."

"Okay, so we've got trust issues," Cole said. "We came to make our proposition, and I already filled her in on the basics. Paige can tell you whatever else you need to know."

Reaching up to make sure there wasn't a blade at her throat, Kayla positioned herself so she could see both of the Skinners. Her body was athletic and slender in a way that would have made any human seem frail. The Mongrel was anything but frail, and her fur was about halfway sprouted. Depending on the way the pale light from the moon and surrounding neighborhood hit her, she either looked naked or wrapped in a form-fitting jumpsuit. Her features had flattened out as if her entire face was wrapped a bit too tightly around her skull. "He says you want us to track werewolves for you."

"That's right," Paige replied. "Half Breeds and a Full Blood. As far as I know, Mongrels have always been into that sort of thing."

As Kayla spoke, the earth around her rippled with the movement of all those burrowers. "Even if we do show up to surprise them, many of us will be killed."

"Welcome to our world," Paige replied as she tossed Cole his spear.

Kayla raised her chin and straightened up to her full height. A long, curved tail retracted into the small of her back until it was just a nub. Her coat slipped beneath her skin in spots, leaving only a trail of fur that wrapped around her hips, upper thighs, belly, and breasts. "We have our own concerns," she said carefully. "Whether humans thrive or die doesn't really affect us."

"There are wild packs of Mongrels, but you're not one of them," Paige pointed out. "If you were, you wouldn't care about speaking our language, or making yourself presentable when in plain sight. You'd also be living in a forest or swamp or a field instead of right here where you're close enough to hear people's voices and buy your supplies."

Shifting on her feet, Kayla made no attempt to dispute Paige's claims. "Why should we risk our lives fighting a Full Blood that hasn't even threatened us?"

"If you help us find the werewolves we're after, we'll see to it that no Skinner comes to this town unless you force us to. On the other hand," Paige said, obviously weighing every word, "if you step up and fight those things with us, the Skinners will let you and your pack settle in Kansas City. You can do whatever you want so long as it doesn't involve eating people."

"We don't eat people," one of the burrowers said.

Turning to what sounded like Ben's voice, Cole said, "Then I recommend the barbecue. It's superb."

"What do you say?" Paige asked. "Willing to shed a little blood to live in a real city or would you prefer to keep tilling lawns?"

After glancing at the multiple sets of eyes peeking up from beneath the grass, Kayla nodded. "Our scouts will meet you in Kansas City and we'll take it from there."

Cole distinctly heard muffled voices coming from belowground as Ben and the other burrowers slithered away. "Meet us where?" he asked.

Kayla walked past him and turned around just in time to catch him scoping out her twitching tail. "Don't worry," she told him. "A Skinner's scent is hard to miss. We'll find you." She dropped to all fours while transforming into a sleek mix of human and leopard. Keeping low to the ground, she bolted away with speed that neither animal could hope to attain.

Chapter 26

Mick, Val, and Quentin stayed behind to continue their investigation. Since Paige was convinced the Mongrels weren't about to come back after being discovered, she left them to it.

As much as he wanted to hose himself off and change his clothes, Cole was only allowed a few extra minutes in the bathroom of the first gas station Paige could find on her way back to the interstate. She volunteered to drive all the way to Kansas City, which would only be a slightly longer trip thanks to the extra miles they'd gone past Omaha. Cole figured they'd get back around midnight, and he wanted to spend those hours resting. After some restless shifting in his seat, it became clear he wouldn't be able to get to sleep.

"What's wrong with you?" Paige asked.

He glanced over to find her face illuminated by light from the dashboard as well as the glow of the semi she was passing. "I can't sleep. I think I'm hurt. You got any of that serum?"

"You're not hurt," she replied with a little shake of her head.

"Excuse me? Were you the one dragged underground and nearly suffocated?"

"No, but you're flopping around like a fish, which means you didn't break anything. You're not bleeding and I didn't see any wounds. Anything smaller than that should be cleared up by the serum that's already in your system. Just shut up and close your eyes."

"I guess you know best, huh?"

She looked at him again, furrowed her brow, and sighed. "How were you hurt?"

Cole reached for the lever on the side of his seat and shoved the backrest down. "Forget it," he grunted as he stretched out and crossed his arms.

"Mind if I turn the radio on?"

"Yes."

She gave him a few minutes to pout and then found some classic rock.

"Filling up on gas again?" Cole grumbled as he rubbed his eyes. "I must've been out longer than I thought."

"Even longer than that," Paige said. "We're here."

"Back at KC? No way."

"Not KC. The hotel. If that ink isn't ready to be used, I'll beat Daniels until that squid attached to his heart crawls out through his ears."

The hotel's parking lot was more than half full of SUVs and cars with out of state plates. Paige used her room key to unlock a side door so she could walk inside without having to go past the front desk. Even though he'd just woken from at least a four-hour nap, Cole nearly collapsed onto the bed the moment he saw it.

Paige went to a phone situated on a table that had a TV remote bolted to it and poked out Daniels's room number. After a few seconds she said, "We're back . . . It doesn't matter where we went. Are you done with your homework?" Somehow, Paige's eyes had yet to droop after all the driving she'd done. Suddenly they grew a little wider. "That sounds good enough. We'll be right over." When she hung up, she froze with her hand still on the receiver. "You feel that?"

Cole shook his head.

"Your scars," Paige said. "Aren't they burning?"

"That's kind of the problem with KC right now, isn't it? Daniels is right down the hall and we don't even know how many Half Breeds are around."

Reluctantly, Paige said, "Yeah, I guess."

"Could the Mongrels have made it here already?"

"They could have beat us here, actually. What are you doing?"

Freezing with one foot in the bathroom, Cole said, "I'm still filthy from—"

"You can shower later," she said curtly. "If we don't get that ink ready to use, dragging Daniels along this far would have been a huge waste."

"But, if it's not ready . . . "

Paige already had the door open. "He's always like this toward the end of a project. He wants to work it all out before someone tests it, but you've gotta have someone test it before you know what needs to be worked out. He's a smart guy and has come a long way, so we'll just test it for ourselves. Besides, didn't Prophet tell you I needed to yell at someone to finish?"

"Yeah, but—"

"Then that's what I'm gonna do." Pulling open the door, she stepped into the hallway and waited for him. "Come on. You're the new guy, so you get the first needle."

"Wow. I'm honored." At that moment he couldn't tell for certain whether or not Paige was kidding. Since it was too late to run away now, he just followed her to Daniels's room. Along the way, he felt heat run up from his scars all the way to his elbows. It wasn't as bad as when the Half Breeds were within eyeshot, but enough to make him feel as though he'd been injected with cayenne peppers.

After knocking a few times, Paige positioned her face directly in front of the peephole and waved. On the other side of the door, latches were flipped and knobs were turned to unlock everything. "Sorry we took so long, Daniels. You'll never believe what we've been doing."

When the door opened, Cole could only see Daniels's bald, blackened dome over Paige's head. Another wave of heat slithered beneath the bones of Cole's shoulders. He turned to look for its source but could only see a man at the far end of the hall whose hair looked more like soot growing from his scalp. The man leaned forward and raced down the hall in a flurry of powerful strides.

Before Cole could react, the skinny man was upon him. He slapped a hand against the small of Cole's back and shoved him into Daniels's room and against another door frame, where Cole landed on the bathroom floor. When Paige spun around to face the man, he knocked her into a luggage rack. She scrambled to her feet but wasn't quick enough to avoid being grabbed by the neck.

"All in one spot," Liam said in his guttural brogue. "How convenient." Holding Paige at arm's length, he glared at Cole with the crystalline eyes of a Full Blood.

Although Cole realized what he was dealing with fairly quickly, Daniels was even quicker. The Nymar flew through the air with all three sets of fangs bared in a show of ferocity that made him seem an entirely different creature from the guy he and Paige had been dealing with so far. His jump wasn't exactly graceful, but Daniels managed to scrape his curved venomous fangs into Liam's upper arm before he caught a blindingly fast backhand that sent him bouncing off the top of a dresser.

Paige bared her teeth and brought her knees up close to her chest. Frustration showed in her eyes the moment she grabbed for her weapon, only to realize that she'd kicked her boots off in the other room. Grabbing onto the man's wrists with both hands, she kicked and flailed in a continuous flow of punishing attacks. Her heels smashed against Liam's knees and shins. She pulled her legs up to kick at his groin and landed at least a few blows that should have gotten the job done. As it was, the skinny man hardly flinched.

"She's a real pistol," Liam said as both of Paige's heels landed simultaneously below his waist. "I like that."

Having brought the .44 up from the car, Cole snatched the revolver from under his belt and pointed it at Liam. "Here's another pistol. Let her go before I unload it in your goddamn face."

The skinny man flicked his eyebrows up and moved Paige aside to show Cole part of the crooked smile he wore. His free arm swiped out and just managed to clip the end of the gun's barrel to send it flying from Cole's hand.

"I'm appearing in this form to show you that I am a man of reason," Liam said. "I was going to offer to let her go in exchange for the location of every Skinner you know, but since it was this easy to find you two, I don't believe I need to deal."

Until now he had seemed amused. He examined Paige as if she was a Thanksgiving turkey while she balled up her fists and punched him as if tenderizing a slab of frozen beef. Even as she dug her nails into his wrists, Liam simply peeled his lips back to show a set of human teeth widening out and stretching down to form sharpened stakes in his mouth.

"Or maybe I won't kill you, luv," he said in a cockney accent that grew along with his hair and teeth. "I could turn you into one of those poor wretches. Wouldn't that be perfect? After every brittle bone in your human body snaps, you can run with the rest of the wild dogs that are so eager to rip this city to shreds." His lips tightened against his teeth as his hand tightened around Paige's throat. The fight drained from her in less than a second. One second after that, Liam's eyes snapped wide open and he let out a stifled growl.

Not only had Daniels made it back to the Full Blood, but he'd sunk his fangs deep into the meaty part of his right shoulder. Liam tossed Paige into the television just to free up that hand. She hit the TV on one side, but also twisted her body around so she slid along the edge of the bulky set rather than bounce off it. "Go get our weapons!" she shouted to Cole the instant she landed.

Cole had already been thinking along those lines, but hadn't seen a way to run around Liam without getting knocked through a piece of furniture. Now that Daniels had made his move, Cole was able to slip past both creatures and make a break for the door.

Liam was shifting into his upright wolf form very quickly. Every movement he made was more powerful than the last as one layer of muscle piled on top of another, but no matter how much Liam struggled or swung his arm, Daniels would not come loose. In the few seconds it took for Cole to get by them, the black tendrils along Daniels's neck and scalp had swollen into thick ridges. The Nymar's fangs broke Liam's skin, and the thicker bottom set were dug in deep enough to keep him in place. If Liam intended on ripping Daniels away, he stood to lose a sizable chunk of his arm in the process.

The commotion had already drawn some attention. As Cole raced to his and Paige's room, he saw a few other doors opening just enough for some nervous guests to peek out-side. Not worrying about them, he rushed into the room, took Paige's batons from the boots she'd kicked into a corner, and then grabbed his spear. On his way back to Daniels's room, he could only see the rush of hallway flowing around him and felt nothing but his feet pounding against the floor.

Cole wrapped one hand tightly around the grip of his weapon so the thorns could dig into his palms. Unfortu-nately, the door to Daniels's room had closed and locked behind him when he left. "Someone open this door!" he shouted as he pounded on the painted metal surface. A few more doors along the hallway opened and someone asked what was going on, but Cole didn't even acknowledge them. He kept pounding and was about to try kicking the door down, when it came open.

Cole could only get the door open an inch or two because something was blocking it. Leaning his shoulder into it, he looked down to find Daniels slumped against the other side. The Nymar looked up at him and then scooted forward so Cole could step inside. "I . . . set him up . . . for you," Daniels groaned as venom dripped from one of his curved upper fangs. The rest of his teeth were either cracked or covered in blood.

Just as Cole stepped into the room, his vision was blocked by a massive wall of black fur. Thanks to the venom in his system, Liam was unsteady upon his feet. He'd also trans-formed to roughly double his original size. For the moment, he didn't seem at all interested in Cole. Instead, he swatted at Daniels and snarled, "God damned leech!"

Taking the opportunity he'd been given, Cole hurried toward the back of the room where Paige was leaning over a small round table situated beneath a lamp that hung from a painted chain. "Here," he said as he handed over the batons. "That thing's about to kill Daniels."

But Paige didn't take the batons. She didn't even turn around to look at Cole. "Our weapons aren't enough. We need more."

"This is all we've got. Just take them!"

The high-pitched grinding sound that followed was a cross between a wasp's buzz and a dentist's drill. Paige hunched forward with her right arm resting upon the table so she could use her left to work the tattooing machine Daniels had modified.

"What the hell are you doing?" Cole demanded as he tried to grab Paige's wrist. "Stop that!"

She knocked him back with her shoulder, clenched her right fist, and said, "It's either this or we all die here."

"No! We fought it before, we can—"

The rest of his plea was drowned out by the grating whine of the machine as its needles were dragged through her right forearm. Cole wanted to pull the machine away, but it was too late. The ink was already being inserted under her skin through hundreds of motorized punctures. Moving her now would only cause more damage.

"Don't stand there watching," Paige snapped through gritted teeth. "Cover me until I get this done."

Daniels struggled with Liam in the other part of the room. One quick glance over his shoulder was enough to show Cole that the Full Blood had indeed been slowed by the venom he'd absorbed. Liam was far from unconscious, but his head waggled slightly and Daniels had managed to get close enough to sink his fangs into his left wrist.

"You don't know what you're doing, Paige!" Cole said. "This shit needs to be tested."

"I *am* testing it! Just go help Daniels."

Knowing better than to argue with her, he leapt onto the bed with the intention of hitting Liam anywhere he could. If his only target was the Full Blood's back, he wasn't too proud to take it. By the time Cole's foot sunk into the mattress, Liam ripped his arm from Daniels's fangs. The creature's other hand elongated and snapped forward to grip the Nymar just below the chin.

Cole pushed himself forward with both legs and extended his weapon out to try and get one solid hit. The tooth attached to the spearhead sank into the meat above Liam's waist as easily as a knife would cut through mortal flesh. The original spearhead snagged upon the wound, but there was enough momentum behind the strike to drive it farther into Liam's side.

Liam opened his mouth and let out a furious, pained roar. His eyes glittered with an ancient fire while Daniels hung from his fist like a broken plaything. When he clenched his fist and ripped out the Nymar's throat, Liam did so with as much effort as he might expend to shred a wet napkin.

Oily blood sprayed across Cole's face and spattered against the wall, but he couldn't allow himself to be distracted. His spear wasn't more than an inch or so within Liam's side, and he knew he wouldn't land such a clean blow again.

After tossing Daniels to the floor, Liam grabbed the spear and lashed out with his other paw. Cole ducked under the incoming claws while swinging his lower body around to plant one foot on the floor and the other on the edge of the bed. If not for the thorns in the spear's handle, the weapon would have easily been shaken from his grip. The more Liam struggled, however, the more the weapon twisted within the wound it had created.

"You're fucking dead!" Liam bellowed. "When the rest of this city is covered in blood, I'll hunt your mothers down and wear *their* skins!" As he spoke, Liam completed the change into his upright wolf form. His head trembled with agony and fury. His hands stretched into even more horrifying weapons, but the transformation stopped at the muscles around the spot where he'd been impaled. He reared back and howled. His long arms and extended fingers scraped against the ceiling and one leg buckled under his weight.

Seeing how much pain Liam was in, Cole planted both feet on the floor and twisted his spear. Even though the weapon was tightly wedged between layers of steely muscle, he got it to move ever so slightly. That little bit was enough to cause Liam's eyes to glaze over and his jaw to open so wide that it looked as if it might have come unhinged.

"Don't like that, do ya?" Cole asked. "How about this?" When he tried to twist the spear some more, he could barely get it to move. Pulling it out would have been easy, since all the muscles in the Full Blood's body were rejecting the weapon in the same way they might push a splinter from his finger. Cole leaned forward but simply couldn't get the weapon to budge.

Liam drew in a low, rumbling breath, embracing the pain that wracked his body so he could turn it into fuel. Looking down at Cole, he gripped the weapon protruding from his side and started to pull it out. "You'd better pray . . . that you die tonight . . . along with the rest of this fucking city."

All of Cole's strength wasn't anywhere close to what was needed to finish the job he'd started. Even with his legs braced and hands clenched tight enough for blood to trickle from his palms, he couldn't prevent Liam from tearing the weapon out from where it had been lodged. The backs of Cole's legs hit the bed and he toppled onto the mattress, bringing his spear along with him. The Full Blood leaned forward to bite off his face, but was stopped by the jarring impact of a stout wooden baton against his chin.

Paige gripped her weapons and willed the one in her left hand to shift into the sickle-bladed form she normally used. The one clutched in her right fist was barely able to form a cutting edge and looked more like a small, poorly crafted machete. When Liam swung a paw at her, Paige blocked with her left and was instantly driven to her knees under the force of the blow. The Full Blood lunged at her, but was stopped cold when Paige drove her right weapon straight up into his side. The tattooing machine had dug several crooked trenches through her skin, leaving messy black lines in their wake. Where Nymar tendrils appeared as smooth, flowing markings, these looked harsh and rigid. Even so, that arm was now strong enough to bury almost half of her weapon into Liam's torso.

Liam's eyes had regained the keenness they'd had before Daniels poisoned him, and he looked at her with renewed interest. Using more speed than strength, he jumped away from Paige. While he might have intended to disarm her in the same way that Burkis had taken the Blood Blade fragment away from Daniels back at the apartment, the thorns in the weapon's handle allowed Paige to take it back. Sweat glistened on her face as she rushed at Liam to hit him again. Cole joined her, and both Skinners were nearly decapitated by a vicious slash from Liam's paw.

Paige turned and pushed Cole out of the way, using her

right arm. When she hit him, the impact took Cole off his feet and knocked all the air from his lungs. Even as the Full Blood's claws sliced through the air dangerously close to them both, Cole was more concerned with the widening black tracks surrounded by gray skin on her arm. Before he could get a closer look, Paige sprang up to block another attack.

After wildly knocking Paige aside, Liam snapped his head forward to take a quick bite at Cole. Thanks to a lot of adrenaline backed up by even more training, Cole brought his spear around so the Full Blood bit down on that instead. Like a dog unwilling to part with its favorite chew toy, Liam locked eyes with him and bared thick, twisted fangs. It was nothing but reflex that got Cole to whip his hand away before it was bitten off as the Full Blood gnawed the middle of the spear. Liam growled even louder as the thorns in the handle dug into his gums. Perhaps frustrated by his inability to break the weapon, Liam spat it out and climbed to his feet. By then Paige was back to deliver another punishing right-handed blow.

She let out a cry as she drove her partially formed machete into the same spot Cole had stabbed before. Her weapon didn't look like much, but she had the strength to open a deep gash in the Full Blood's torso. The moment she was shoved away, Cole stepped up to drive his spear into the wound before it closed up. As soon as the modified spearhead sank into the werewolf, he leaned back, pulled with every bit of muscle in his arms, and snapped the tooth off between his ribs.

Rather than continue the fight, Liam dropped to all fours and made a shaky transformation into something that looked like a barrel-chested coyote. The tooth was still lodged in him, and he twisted his head toward that spot as if he wanted to dig it out with his teeth. All of that effort caused the Full Blood to clench its eyes shut and yelp in pain.

Both Skinners prepared for another attack. Instead, Liam ran toward the window and exploded through the glass.

Chapter 27

Cole raced to the window but stopped short of jumping out. The Full Blood landed awkwardly and crumpled on the side where the spearhead had been broken off. He regained his footing, then ran a few paces and leapt high enough to disappear into the shadows of the western horizon. Lowering his weapon, Cole said, "He's gone. Is Daniels all right?"

Paige started to respond but stopped when they heard frantic knocking on the door.

"Shit," Cole growled as he forced himself to look at what Liam had left behind. Daniels was a bloody mess and Paige hovered over him. "Is he gonna make it?"

Daniels's eyes were wide open. His mouth moved as if he was forming words, but he couldn't put any breath behind them. When he tried to inhale, a soft yet horrible sucking sound came from the flaps of shredded skin under the Nymar's chin. As he slowly turned to look at him, the tattered remains of his throat and windpipe pulled apart even farther.

At more knocking from the front door, Paige snarled, "Get rid of whoever's out there!"

Cole went to the door and opened it to find two of his neighbors peeking in from the hallway. One of them, a man with gray hair that looked as if it had been blown onto his scalp by a cotton candy machine, asked, "What on earth happened in there? Where's the man who ran down the hall?"

The other person at the door was an old lady with a towel

wrapped around her head and moisturizing cream on her face. "I think we scared him away, Kenneth," she said. "I'll call the police."

"Don't bother," said someone else in the hallway, whom Cole couldn't see. "I already called them."

"Kenneth, call an ambulance, I think these kids are hurt really bad."

Cole nearly jumped when Daniels crawled over and grabbed his leg. He saw Paige clutching her arm, but she turned her back to him before he could see much else. "Just give us some room," he said to the people in the hallway. "Everybody stay back."

Just as he got the door shut, the spark in Daniels's eyes returned and the Nymar wedged the back of his head against the floor. Propping his lower body up while arching his spine caused the gaping wound to yawn open. For lack of anything better to do, Cole placed his hand on Daniels's stomach and forced him back down again.

"We've got to get out of here," Paige said in a harsh whisper. "I'll get our stuff."

"We're just gonna leave him here?" Cole asked.

"Just give him a minute." When Paige tried to leave, she was blocked by the people who had gathered in the hall.

"You need any help in there?" Kenneth asked. "The manager called for an ambulance."

"We're taking him to the hospital," Paige replied.

"What about you?" the old woman asked. "You don't look so good. What happened to your arm?"

Cole wanted to know the answer to that as well, but couldn't get it before Paige forced her way out of the room. "Damn it," he grumbled as the faint echo of sirens reached his ears.

Daniels's eyes were open and frantically darting back and forth. He reached up to touch his throat, but Cole stopped him. Before he could offer any comforting words, he flinched at the sight of black, oily filaments reaching out through the hole in Daniels's neck to pull the gaping wound shut. When the loose flaps of torn skin were more or less together, the filaments knitted a glistening web to close the gap. Within a second or two Daniels was able to pull in a few haggard breaths.

Cole slipped his arms under the Nymar and helped him sit up. "You still with us?"

"Y-Yes."

"Can you stand?" Turning to see a gaggle of strangers slowly pushing through the doorway, Cole quickly added, "Doesn't matter. We gotta go."

Daniels not only made it to his feet, but draped an arm over Cole's shoulder and shuffled along beside him.

"We're going to the hospital," Cole announced to the group. "He won't make it unless we go right now."

The people who'd wandered into the room looked as if they were going to protest, but changed their minds when they got a look at the black mess holding Daniels's throat together. As the crowd parted to let them pass, someone asked, "Should he be moved? The ambulance will be right here."

All Cole could think to say was, "I'm a paramedic! I know what I'm doing, so just get the hell out of my way!"

Fortunately, nobody asked for ID. A few people asked if they could help, but Cole pushed past them and dragged Daniels toward a stairway that led down to the parking lot.

Once they were in the stairwell, he asked, "Do you need anything?"

"Just give me a minute," Daniels replied.

After making it halfway to the ground floor, the doorway behind them flew open and slammed shut as quick steps rattled down the stairs. Cole turned and saw Paige racing to catch up to them with cases and bags hanging from both shoulders and gripped in both hands. "I've got everything but the test tubes and lab crap."

"I need . . ." Daniels gulped and sucked in a breath. When he spoke again, his voice was clearer than it had been even a few seconds ago. "I need to—"

"Save your breath, buddy," Cole said. "He probably needs to feed."

But Daniels shook his head and growled, "I need my burner and that equipment! It's expensive!"

"Oh for crap's sake, I'll get you more equipment," Paige

said. "It sounded like that Full Blood was going to get the Half Breeds moving again. He mentioned tearing down a city, so he must be headed back to KC, and if we don't get out of here, we'll be stuck talking to cops."

Daniels was so pale that even his markings had turned gray. He was still covered in blood, but his neck looked less like it had been ripped apart than smeared with motor oil and tomato sauce. "Fine," he said meekly. "Let's go."

Cole played the part of getaway driver. He got the Cav started and backed out of his space as Daniels settled into the backseat. Paige slumped into the passenger seat, cradled her right arm, and stifled a gasp.

"Let's see your arm," Cole demanded. "And don't tell me it's fine. I know better."

Paige cleared her throat and placed her left hand over her new markings. She must not have liked what she felt there, because she pulled her hand back and shook it as if she'd accidentally touched the belly of an eel. "That ink worked, but something's wrong," she muttered.

"I know. Let me see."

Daniels lunged forward as if he'd stopped just short of launching himself through the windshield. "You *used* the ink?

"Let me see it!" The tone in Cole's voice left little room for back talk. Also, he'd slammed his foot on the brake and made it clear he wasn't about to drive another inch before he got what he'd asked for.

Angry at first, Paige raised her right arm and then turned her head away as if she didn't even want to look at it.

Having braced himself for the worst, Cole was somewhat relieved at what he saw. The lines on Paige's forearm were just deep scratches highlighted by black lines and dried blood. The skin around those scratches was a strange shade of gray, but was already a better color than it had been a few minutes ago. He took hold of her wrist in one hand and used the other to delicately wipe some of the blood away. "Does that hurt?"

"No," she said with a wince.

"Yes it does. How bad is it?"

Daniels leaned forward again so he could squint down at her arm. "Do you feel the substance interacting with your muscle tissue?"

Paige yanked her arm away then and glared at each of them in turn. "Yes, Daniels, I can feel it interacting with the muscle, and *yes,* Cole, it hurts! I fucked up, all right? What else do you want me to tell you?"

Cole realized there wasn't a lot he could do for either of them, and could do a whole lot less if the sirens he heard got any closer. When he saw the hotel manger jog out the front door toward the parking lot, he drove for the highway. If he'd steered in the other direction, he would have rammed into the emergency vehicles screaming toward the hotel.

For a moment it looked as if a cop car might try to follow him. Instead, it stayed put to block the entrance to the hotel parking lot so the ambulance had easier access. Shifting all the way around so he could look into the backseat again, Cole said, "Someone's going to tell those cops about us. They may even post someone further along the highway."

"I didn't leave enough real info at the front desk for anyone to find us," Paige pointed out. "Besides, anyone in the hotel will tell them we're just wounded victims."

"Some more wounded than others," Cole grumbled.

Paige stared at him with enough intensity to burn through the car's engine block. "I heard that."

"Interesting," Daniels said. "Did the ink improve your hearing?"

"Sit back and conserve your strength," she said. "Don't you need to feed?"

Daniels shrugged. "I can wait. The Nymar spore expended some extra energy, but that doesn't translate directly into blood usage any more than running excessively hard would force you to eat a meal immediately afterward. It's a somewhat independent entity that will improve with some rest, which is—"

"Great," Paige cut in. "Then just sit back before I open up another wound for that thing to sew back up."

"Hey!" Cole barked. "If you hadn't jumped the gun back there—"

"If I hadn't jumped the gun, that Full Blood would have stuck around to kill everyone in that hotel!" Paige said. "In case you hadn't noticed, this ink actually worked!"

For the next few seconds the only sound in the car was the rumble of the engine and the movement of the tires rolling over I-29. Paige had reflexively used her right hand to grab the dashboard during a swerve to avoid a motorcycle, which gave Cole a good look at the rock-hard muscles of her forearm. They weren't much bigger, but appeared to be more solid and defined. As if to prove that beyond a doubt, the dashboard had cracked in several places under her hand. The blackness of the ink was no longer in the bloody lines where the tattooing machine had made its mark, but had soaked down to further darken the fibers below.

"Holy shit," he breathed as he tried to watch the road while also looking at her. "That stuff really did work. Did you actually punch that Full Blood?"

"I think so," Paige said. "I sure couldn't put much of a dent into Burkis."

"You said it hurt," Daniels pointed out. "How bad is it?"

Never one to admit she was wounded, Paige pulled her arm back and turned toward her passenger-side window. When her fist slid off the dashboard, it dropped into her lap like a dead weight. "Feels like it was dipped in acid."

"On the surface? Where you used the machine to administer the substance?"

"No. More on the inside."

Daniels leaned forward again, and this time reached for her with both hands. "May I?"

Paige glared at him, then her expression softened and she nodded. That's when Cole noticed that she was either unwilling or unable to lift her arm toward Daniels's hands.

The Nymar slid his fingers along her forearm before pressing it harder with his thumbs. Paige pulled in a few sharp breaths, and Cole knew it took a lot to get that much of a reaction from her. "The muscle is shifting, but slowly," Daniels said. "Very slowly."

"Then it's probably wearing off," Paige said.

Daniels leaned back among all the stuff piled in the backseat. When Cole looked at him in the mirror, he saw the Nymar nervously shake his head.

"What about your weapon?" Cole asked Paige.

"I grabbed them both, and yours is here too," she replied.

"No, I mean the weapon you held in your right hand was different. Did you do that on purpose?"

She looked down at the crude weapon lying across her knees. Wincing when she closed her fist around the handle, she quickly switched it to her left hand. Only then did the weapon creak and flow into a finely etched sickle that matched her other one. "It's fine," she grunted. "I can hurt a Full Blood, so that's what we're gonna do. Just drive."

Cole knew better than to try to argue. The fire in her eyes wasn't quite the same as usual, but the idea behind it was the same: fight now, talk later.

It was a relatively short drive to Kansas City and traffic was at a minimum. Once they got close enough to see downtown silhouetted against the night sky, Paige glanced at Daniels and asked, "Which of your cases has the Blood Blade?"

"You gave that to me for use in creating the ink," Daniels replied uneasily. "I needed to melt pieces of it down to create the compound. Each dose requires a piece of the blade to provide the ingredient I couldn't replicate."

"Right, so give me what's left."

"It's right here," Daniels replied as he patted one of the satchels containing their essential belongings.

"Give it here. We're gonna need it."

The Nymar grumbled and fussed for a few seconds, before extending his arm to hand her a plastic Baggie with a zip seal across the top. Inside the bag was what appeared to be large flakes of silver confetti.

"What the hell is this?" Paige asked.

Daniels immediately retreated as far back into his seat as he could. "You told me to prepare the ink, so I prepared it. You told me to get everything ready so you could mix up as much of it as you could whenever you wanted, so I did!"

"And you said you weren't even ready to test it yet!" she

shot back. "What if it didn't work and we're stuck with some black crap and a bag full of shavings?"

"That wasn't enough to stop you from using it!" The moment those words came out of his mouth, Daniels clamped it shut. Cole didn't see the look Paige was shooting at the Nymar, but he could imagine it. Daniels tapped him on the shoulder. "Could you help me out here?" he asked.

Cole turned toward Paige to keep her from pulling Daniels's head off, but was cut short when she flipped the plastic bag out in front of him. Not one of the silver pieces in it was bigger than a penny. "*Seriously,* Daniels?" he roared. "What the hell!"

Flattening himself against the backseat, Daniels gripped the cushion as though he feared he'd be ejected from the car at any moment. "You left me in that room all day and all night! I wanted to feel useful, so I prepared as many doses as I could."

Cole snatched the bag from her and swung his hand back as if he didn't only want to show the metal chips to Daniels, but force him to eat them. "*This* is what you consider useful?"

"Also . . . maybe . . . I got bored."

After handing the bag to Paige, Cole nodded and gripped the steering wheel. "That's it. I don't care whose life he saved. Baldy dies tonight."

For the first time since they'd left the hotel, Cole saw a glimpse of the Paige he truly knew. She tucked the bag into a pocket and sighed. "If you boys keep fighting, I won't take you to see the big scary animals."

"That's another thing," Cole grunted. "How are we supposed to find those things anyway?"

"Something tells me finding them won't exactly be the hard part."

Chapter 28

Liam covered the first few miles in a loping run. Every time a front paw touched down, the corner of his mouth curled into a pained grimace. His chest remained low while his thick rear legs pushed him forward and his front paws swatted at the ground to keep him going. Whenever he collected enough strength, he launched into a jump that allowed him to move at twice the speed.

By the time he reached Kansas City, his wound had stopped bleeding. Scampering into an alley, he shifted into human form just long enough for his body to shed most of its wounds the way it would expel any other waste. The broken tooth remained wedged between his ribs, even after changing back into his four-legged frame. The pain that accompanied every wheezing breath wasn't enough to mar the night ahead.

The moon hanging above him was slightly more than halfway full, a natural beacon drawing his eye straight through the garish glow of electric illumination surrounding the city. He ran from the alley and tore straight down the middle of a street, snapping at cars as they honked and swerved out of his way. Henry would have enjoyed himself on this night, but that one was nowhere to be found. The other Full Blood's trail seemed to lead everywhere at once. Liam hadn't smelled anything like the traces that mingled with Henry's scent and he wasn't going to waste time trying to figure them out now.

Randolph's scent was stronger, which meant his old friend was nearby. Bounding off the street to land on the hood of a pickup truck, Liam barked gleefully as the truck's windshield shattered and its driver fought to regain control before swerving into a streetlight. If Randolph was watching, Liam knew he would be throwing a fit.

Running from the street to the sidewalk, he sped up when he caught sight of a group of humans gathered around the front of a building that thumped with an obnoxious, pounding rhythm. When he clambered over a cluster of cars, he made sure to scrape his claws against the painted metal and shatter as much glass as possible along the way. All those people looked at him. Some screamed. Some fled. Some poked at their little phones and called for help. Some even pointed their devices at him and took his picture.

So many years of so-called progress, and the humans could only come up with more machines to play with. Liam scattered them like pheasants being flushed from a bush. He nipped at some of their legs, ripping a few tendons and sending weaker members of the herd to the pavement. Unfortunately, he couldn't indulge in any more than that. He ran down the next street that caught his eye and trampled anything or anyone in his path. Sometimes he chose a new path just so he could trample some more.

Running free through a place that his kind had avoided for so long was akin to walking straight up to someone else's woman, lifting her skirts, and bending her over the closest piece of furniture. It didn't matter what that woman looked like, if she was kind, sweet, or even tolerable. She, like this city, was not to be touched. Liam spread his paws out wide, touching the city as much as possible with every single step. He wanted to get to higher ground. There were plenty of fire escapes to climb and ledges to grip, but those were the proper ways. For he and every shapeshifter within the sound of his voice, this was not a night for propriety.

The building he chose was in a part of the city all but deserted after business hours. Weathered stone cracked beneath his claws and thick glass cracked too as he scraped and tore at the side of the structure to create his own footholds. While he climbed, Liam shifted into his upright form. His limbs stretched out and the mass that clumped around his chest and shoulders flowed down to more evenly cover his growing torso. Every time he passed a window, his reflection was different. He completed his change a quarter of the way up, so he was able to cover more distance with higher jumps.

Once he was atop the building, Liam paced between the ventilation and air-conditioning units, savoring the cool touch of night air upon his face. He turned toward the ledge and raced to the brink of a long drop to the pavement, but stopped himself by digging his claws into the roof. Gripping the ledge with both hands, he gazed down upon the city. His tongue lolled out the side of his mouth as he watched the growing number of flashing lights and cars racing below like fireflies trapped beneath a glass table.

He could smell the Skinners drawing closer.

Some of the Half Breeds were strong enough to poke their noses from their dens, but most were probably content to sleep. Randolph might have found some of the wretches, but he couldn't have found them all.

Liam's heartbeat quickened and his breath poured from his mouth like steam from an engine. Leveling his gaze to a point in the distance had something of a calming effect. Things were clearer when he only looked straight ahead. The Full Blood closed his eyes, pulled in one more breath, and sifted through the thousands of scents every passing breeze carried upon its wide back.

There were dozens of reasons to hate humans and plenty of lessons his own kind needed to be taught. At that moment, however, Liam felt no need to justify his actions other than it was a hell of a night for a siege.

He held on to the breath he'd taken, raised his nose to the heavens and howled.

Where any other sound would have died off or been carried away, this one continued on. Where any other creature would have run out of breath, Liam pushed his howl out further and further until it reached every last ear for which it was intended.

The howl was a great and terrible thing.

In comparison, the other howls that rose up in response to it were frayed and ragged. When the creatures answering the Full Blood's call could howl no more, they scampered from their dens in savage, barking stampedes.

Liam allowed his voice to taper off so he could listen to the Half Breeds' desperate replies. They were hungry, eager, and still in pain from their first transformation.

They were perfect.

Now that the wretches had been coaxed from their pits, the dead would pile up and the wounded would replenish the Half Breeds that had fallen, until every street became a butcher's killing floor. Perhaps some of them would run to another town or tear through another city. Skinners would fall until the most powerful among them would finally be flushed out of hiding.

Liam could barely contain himself.

The blood in Cole's arms hadn't stopped burning since Liam left the hotel. It took less than an hour to reach downtown Kansas City, where his early warning pains flared up all over again. Looking over to Paige, he asked, "Do you feel that?"

They'd stopped along a quiet street with an all-night diner on the corner. Paige had allowed Daniels to examine her arm during most of the drive, but pulled away from him now. "Yep," she replied. "Daniels, you stay put. Have some coffee or something and we'll call you when we're ready to get you."

"Mind if I track down something a bit more to my tastes?" the Nymar asked as he reflexively curled his lips back to show the set of feeding fangs that drooped lazily from his gums.

"You know the rules."

"Sure I do," Daniels assured her. "The maid at the hotel even came back a few times while you were gone because she—"

"Don't need the details," Paige cut in. "Just get what you need and don't be messy about it. If you don't hear back from us, find your way back to Chicago and call that number I gave you to tell them we're gone."

"Miss Sunshine means we'll pick you up when we're through cleanin' up this town," Cole said in a drawl that would have offended any true cowboy. "I'll leave you with something you can use in case you get in trouble. That shotgun's still in the trunk, right, Paige?"

She nodded, told him to hurry, and got out so she could circle around to take her seat behind the steering wheel.

Once Cole had dragged Daniels around to the back of the car and opened the trunk, he asked, "Is Paige really all right?"

"That ink didn't work like she thought it would, but I *told* her we needed more tests. It's not my fault!"

"I just wanna know if she's all right."

Although Daniels was clearly rattled, he forced himself to reply, "She's in pain, but seems to be handling it. The muscles in that arm are thicker, but appear to be hardening as well. While the shapeshifting properties are present, the ink has also bonded the metallic elements to her living tissue more than I thought it would."

"So . . . her arm's turning into metal?"

"No, nothing so dramatic. I need to test some tissue samples, but I know she's losing feeling in that arm and is having trouble moving it. There may be other effects, but I can't just guess as to what they may be."

Having seen Paige's trouble in getting her weapon to change shape, Cole already knew of one more effect. That didn't need to be spread around, though. "Is she in any immediate danger?"

"She didn't use that much ink, and while the effects don't seem to be going away, they're not spreading either."

"I don't have a lot of time here," Cole pressed. "She won't tell me anything until this is over except that she's fine. Is she or isn't she?"

"There could be prolonged, possibly permanent damage to those muscle groups, but there really isn't anything I can do for her at the moment."

"And if she was poisoned, she would have died already," Cole said. "Right?"

Daniels winced and started to shrug. "Not . . . necessarily."

Slamming the trunk shut, Cole walked around the back of the car toward the passenger side. "Thanks. Big help. Go get somebody to drink."

"Hey! What about my shotgun? I still need to protect myself, you know."

"You think I'm really giving you my shotgun? Are you nuts? You're a vampire. If something comes close, flash them the fangs."

Daniels had a few choice words for that, but Cole didn't listen. The Nymar was still gesturing after Cole was in the car and being driven away.

"What's that about?" she asked.

Cole looked in the side mirror and waved at Daniels. "Looks like he's wishing us luck. He wouldn't take the shotgun. Real noble guy."

"Sure. Whatever." She drove slowly for a few seconds, which was all the time she needed to spot the cop cars racing down an adjacent street.

Cole watched carefully as she gripped the wheel in her left hand and allowed her right to lie across her lap. She seemed able to move a little better than a few minutes ago, but continued to flex her fingers as if they'd been asleep. The tattooed lines had faded to a few traces, and the muscles beneath the incisions were losing the gray hue they'd had earlier that night. "So," he said, "was all that worth losing the Blood Blade?"

Paige ground her teeth and snarled, "Ask me later."

"What's the plan now? Just follow the cops?"

She sucked in a breath and seemed ready to clam up for good. When she exhaled, it was more of a reluctant sigh. Judging by the look on her face, the pain she felt cut deeper than any set of claws. "We took a gamble on a lot of things lately. I should have known better about this one."

"We were caught by surprise, Paige. There's no shame in admitting it. We're doing all we can. It's not like there are policies for werewolves tearing through an entire city." He paused and then asked, "Skinners *don't* have a policy for this, do they?"

"No," she said with a tired laugh. "But if we get ripped

apart on some video that winds up on the Internet, at least other Skinners will know what not to do."

Cole shifted in his seat and looked out his window. The squat buildings on the outer edges of the city had given way to the thicker and taller ones of the downtown area. Depending on where he looked at any given moment, Kansas City either seemed alive and kicking or dead and buried. Streetlights were on, but most businesses were closed. Offices were empty, while bars and clubs were still attracting crowds. Cops swarmed in packs, leaving empty pavement in their wake. People gathered on some corners, leaving others alone. Sometimes there was a giant rat running alongside the car and sometimes there wasn't.

"Wait, whoa!" he yelped as he grabbed onto the door frame with both hands.

"What is it?"

Of course, now that he was looking for it, the creature he'd spotted wasn't there. "I saw something, but I'm not sure what." Cole kept his eyes on the pavement flowing past his side of the car until the creature came into view again. Its body might have had the mass of a Half Breed, but was stretched out to something much longer and lankier. It ran like a ferret, with its body rippling from front to back in a constant wave. When it looked up at his passenger-side window, the creature knocked the side of its head against the door to make a sound that he realized he'd been hearing in the background for the last few blocks.

"Pull over, Paige." As soon as those words were out of his mouth, Cole quickly added, "But not to the right!"

"I'm not pulling over. We're too close and I don't wanna lose sight of these cops."

The burning under Cole's skin grew with every second. Rather than argue with her, he rolled his window down and stuck his head out. The creature outside kept up with the car as if it had barely found its stride. Its beak was even with the front tire of the Cav, and its thick, segmented tail stuck out straight behind its body to a spot well past the rear bumper. The last time Cole had seen the face that now looked up at him, it was poking halfway out from a dirt wall.

"What took you guys so long?" Ben asked. When he glanced back and forth between Cole and the road ahead of him, flaps on either side of the Mongrel's neck became visible. Every breath he took caused the flaps to open and shut like a set of gills.

"You guys beat us here?" Cole asked.

"By quite a while, unless you've been laying low!"

"Who the hell are you talking to?" Paige asked.

"One of the diggers from MEG's backyard." It wasn't exactly an accurate description, but was enough to get his point across.

Paige nodded and asked, "Is he alone?"

"I hope not." Leaning outside, Cole asked, "You bring anyone else with you?"

Ben spoke as if he was walking briskly next to Cole instead of keeping pace with a speeding car. "We're all here. Kayla wanted to hang back and make sure you two were going to get your hands dirty. Seeing you charge into the thick of it like this is enough for me."

"Do you know what we're charging into?"

Ben hopped over a pothole and then darted to one side while lowering his head to scramble beneath the car Paige was passing. He emerged from under the other vehicle's front bumper and fell into step where he'd been before. "You mean you don't know what's up there? I hate to admit it, but I admire you Skinners. Just crazy enough to get the job done."

"Thanks. I think."

"There's a Full Blood perched on a building a few blocks ahead," Ben reported. "He started howling, and Half Breeds sprouted up all over town. From what we could see, they all seem to be heading in this direction."

"Then we might as well meet them there!" Paige shouted.

"We'll do our part, Skinner," Ben said in a surprisingly calm tone. "When this is over, be sure to hold up your end. This city is ours."

"I remember the deal!" she shouted. "But if we don't stop chatting, we'll both lose a whole lot more than this city!"

Ben nodded, lowered his head, and ran in earnest. Seeing

him pull in front of the Cav and tear down the street, Cole didn't have any trouble believing the Mongrels had gotten all the way to Kansas City from Omaha in record time.

Paige sped down East Eleventh Street but was forced to slow down due to the growing amount of police traffic clogging the road. Some uniforms were posted to divert the night owl civilians, and others jumped out of their cars to get a look at a tall building a bit farther down the block. Cole's window was still open, so he could hear the deep, rumbling howl that shook the particles in the air. Until now he'd thought that sound was just a mix of sirens, engines, and music blasting from a club somewhere. As more howls joined in, he reflexively reached for the glove compartment.

Several police cars were parked around a single fire engine that had pulled up to a spot where two civilian cars had crashed into each other. Although he couldn't see details amid the flashing lights and four-legged creatures darting from one live body to another, Cole spotted plenty of figures sprawled in pools of gore. At least a few of those figures were still in one piece.

"What do we do about all these cops?" he asked as he checked the .44.

"I don't think they'll object to a little help with these things. They may have enough guns to take down a few of the Half Breeds, but we'll have to take the rest."

"And what about the Full Blood?"

Paige slammed her foot against the brake hard enough to make Cole kiss the dashboard. A couple police officers held their ground in the street and waved at her to turn around and clear the area. They walked toward the Cav but didn't even make it to Paige's window before being taken down by a pair of Half Breeds. Bones snapped loudly enough for Cole to hear them as one of the cops was knocked off his feet. The other officer near the Cav was bitten at waist level and pulled down like an unsuspecting gazelle in a nature documentary. She pulled her gun but was overpowered by the gangly werewolf.

Cole kicked open his door and jumped outside as his hands tightened around the thorns set into his weapon's handle.

The pain barely registered, and the blood trickling from his palms felt warm and comforting. When he jabbed the end of his spear into the closest Half Breed's side, it nearly tore straight through the creature. He attempted to lift the thing up and off the female cop but wasn't able to divert it from its meal. The attempt did cause the werewolf to lift its head and twist it 180 degrees around, to urgently gnaw upon the spear.

Cole pushed the Half Breed down against the pavement so the cop could drag herself away. The creature flopped and contorted to try and get at him. Its teeth were bared in a gruesome display, and bony claws tore at the pavement until a gunshot cracked through the air. The Half Breed's head snapped to one side and then twisted back around to face the cop. Cole twisted his spear within it, holding it down just long enough for the cop to empty the rest of her rounds into its body. The creature let out one last grunt before dying. Before the cop could say a word, she and Cole spotted more werewolves attacking another group of officers.

Paige had freed the female cop's partner by sticking a curved sickle blade behind the creature's shoulders like a meat hook. As she pulled it closer, she drove her other weapon down through its back. Her right arm wasn't moving quickly, but she was able to drop that weapon straight down and impale the Half Breed through its spine with enough force for the end of the machete to crack against pavement. Just to be sure, she pulled her sickle blade free and drove it an inch or two through the top of the creature's skull.

The cop watched Paige with wide, disbelieving eyes. Suddenly, he pulled his trigger again and again. Paige jumped, but quickly realized he was firing at a Half Breed running toward them. Unfortunately, the creature didn't seem too distracted by the bullets chipping away at its chest and body. The moment it got close enough, Paige swung her right weapon straight across, connecting with the creature's jaw and lifting the front half of its body off the ground.

Trembling as he reloaded, the cop asked, "What the fuck are these things? Who the fuck are you?"

All Paige said to that was, "Behind you."

The cop was reluctant to take his eyes off her, but turned around when he heard the sound of claws raking against the cement. Then he added to a chorus of gunfire that dropped one of the smaller creatures charging a police cruiser. When the cop turned around again, Paige had moved on to fight somewhere else.

A few yards down the street, Cole pinned another Half Breed to the pavement. The wretch clawed at the cement, tearing up chunks of concrete while snapping at both him and the female officer he'd already saved. She'd taken a bad bite to the hip but was able to stay upright thanks to another policeman who'd come to lend her some support. The creature's head twisted around to angles that should have killed any living creature. Since the Half Breed didn't have a bone that wasn't already broken, it frantically knotted itself up until enough of the cops' bullets hit something vital.

But even after it stopped moving, Cole was reluctant to pull the spear loose. When he noticed that there were only three gaping wounds, despite all the shots that had hit, he braced his foot on the creature and freed his weapon. "Nice grouping," he said to the closest officer.

The policeman, sweaty, scraped up, and shell-shocked, muttered, "Wh-What the hell?"

Cole looked over to Paige just as she swatted at one creature with her left hand and then knocked it into oblivion with her right. When he looked back again, the flummoxed cop had disappeared in a blood-soaked flurry of teeth and claws. From then on, none of the remaining cops were about to stop shooting long enough to ask the Skinners another question.

More Half Breeds raced in from all angles. They knocked over mailboxes and scrambled over patrol cars in their haste to get to the buffet of fresh meat. Some were sent tumbling due to gunfire from the officers on the scene, while others darted around to flank the shooters from a different angle. Every last one of the creatures howled and barked with enough unfocused energy to rend their throats in the same way their claws tore up their prey.

Cole waded through the Half Breeds to help as many cops as he could. One creature dragged a screaming man toward a police cruiser, so he aimed his .44 in that direction. Before he could fire a shot, however, another pair of creatures reached out from beneath the car to grab the Half Breed's legs. Even with that quick glance, Cole recognized the curved claws and shorter legs of burrowing Mongrels.

At first the Half Breed twisted around to snarl at whatever was interrupting its feast. The surprise it felt when it saw what had snagged it by the hindquarters was enough to show up on even its mangled face. The werewolf barked frantically before yelping in pain as the Mongrels dragged it under the car.

"Can you walk?" Cole asked as he helped the surprised cop back up.

The officer winced, but nodded. "It pulled me a ways, but I can keep going."

Suddenly, the gunfire rose to a frantic level. Cops screamed at each other and through their radios as stray rounds shattered glass and tore into one of the nearby buildings. More specifically, they fired at the hulking Full Blood that had sunk its claws into the building and was climbing down. Once the coal-black monster made it to the twelfth floor, he pushed away from the structure and dropped into the chaos he'd started.

Chapter 29

Liam's feet slammed against the pavement with enough force for Cole to feel it through the bottom of his hiking boots. The Full Blood flattened for a moment and then arose in his full upright form. Unlike the twitching attempt in the hotel room, this transformation was a nightmare firing on all cylinders. It stood just over seven feet tall, was covered in pure black fur, and had muscles that looked twice as solid and unforgiving as the steel of the cars surrounding it. A patch of gray fur marked the spot where Cole's spear had wounded Liam earlier that night.

Gunfire continued to go off, but Liam barely reacted to the constant pecking of bullets against his coat. The werewolf sucked in a lungful of air, shifted his gaze toward Cole and Paige, and then let out another howl that was raw fury given a body of sound. It directly challenged Cole in a language that predated words, reaching down to the core of every living thing to spark the simplest, most primitive of all choices: kill, run, or die.

Cole was snapped out of his paralysis by the thunder of shotgun blasts. Some police officers were still firing their pistols at Liam, but others had ditched the handguns in favor of something bigger. Liam vaulted over the nearest car, tearing the sirens from its roof with the ease of a bad magician sending a few place settings to the floor. Before his paws touched cement again, he was swiping at one of the cops holding a shotgun. He clipped the man with his claws, which was enough to send the guy twisting through the air amid a bloody spray.

The shotgunner's partner still had a pistol in hand, which he'd already emptied. The instant Liam's eyes found him, the cop raced for another one of the cruisers. He dove head-first into the car to grab the shotgun, which was still in its rack. As Liam approached, the cop pulled the door shut and wrestled the shotgun free of its housing.

Meanwhile, the remaining cops were firing or calling for backup. Mongrels picked off several Half Breeds by snatching the wretches from alleys, under cars, or any other cover they could find. Paige and Cole had been singled out by another small pack of Half Breeds, but those creatures were already nursing multiple gunshot wounds. Although they'd absorbed enough lead to put down a pack of any other animal, the werewolves were slowed down just enough for the Skinners to finish them off before moving on to bigger game.

One policeman stood frozen with gun in hand, apparently unable to decide whether he wanted to fire at Liam, one of the hidden Mongrels, or one of the circling Half Breeds. Before the cop could make up his mind, a Half Breed raced forward to sink its teeth into his hip. The werewolf's fangs snagged on the officer's gun belt, and then Cole's spear snagged the creature's ribs. Cole pulled the impaled were-wolf to one side so the cop could use his pistol to put it out of its misery.

A few more Half Breeds stalked toward the cops who were firing at Liam. Their eyes were fixed upon the of-ficers' backs, so they didn't see Paige coming until she was wading through them. Her first attack wasn't half its normal speed, but she swung her crudely shaped machete with enough power to decapitate one of the Half Breeds in a single swipe. She snapped the sickle in her left hand down to bury its curved blade into the neck of the next creature. Paige wanted to answer a third creature's growl with another swing, but her right arm wasn't up to the task. The weapon in that hand moved like it was being pushed through water, giving the Half Breed more than enough time to duck beneath it and sink its teeth into her.

Screams erupted from Liam's direction. There was a crunching impact as the Full Blood tossed three men in full riot gear into the air, sending one of them through the fourth floor window of a nearby building.

Cole barely had time to register what he'd seen before reflexively twisting his spear to block a Half Breed's attack. Since the werewolf stopped just outside of the spear's range, Cole adjusted his grip on the weapon to hold it more like a long bat. He waited for the Half Breed to charge at him again, then swung at just the right moment to bury the thorns of the spear's handle into the creature's face. It let out a shrieking cry and scampered away.

Rushing toward Paige, Cole found her on the ground, using her feet to push herself away from the Half Breed latched onto her right arm. The creature snarled and snapped its head from side to side like a dog that wasn't about to let go of its favorite old sock. She took a few swings at it with her sickle, but its frenzy was too far along for it to feel any pain.

It took several attempts, but after Cole stabbed the creature's chest several times, it finally noticed and opened its jaws. Paige jerked her arm away and then sent it straight back to pound the creature's temple. The werewolf staggered sideways, only to be impaled by Cole's spear as well as Paige's machete.

When it stopped moving, Cole placed a bloody hand on Paige's shoulder and asked, "How's your arm?"

"Fine," she snapped as she pulled away and looked at her arm. The skin had been stripped away along several tracks where the Half Breed's teeth had dug in, revealing what looked more like a broken sculpture of human anatomy than something that was actually alive. Some of the tissue beneath her skin was scraped, but not nearly as bad as it should have been. "It's . . . fine," she repeated.

They were distracted then by the groan of twisting metal.

Liam had grabbed onto the top of a police cruiser with one hand as round after round of pistol and shotgun bullets thumped against his back, ribs, and head. The cop who dove inside for his shotgun was still there, and fired a powerful blast up through the roof. Liam pulled in a breath that swelled his entire body. The streetlights shining on his coat glinted off the spent bullets trapped in his fur like lead ticks. Squatting down to look through the cruiser's windshield, he saw the single petrified officer who'd sought refuge there. He then brought his fists down on the top of the car, crushing that section of the roof.

Paige got to Liam first and used her sickle to slash at the base of his spine. Her curved blade didn't even penetrate the outer crust of bullets acting as makeshift armor within Liam's fur. Cole arrived then and announced his presence by driving his spear into the Full Blood's chest. The bone and muscle in that section of torso might as well have been an iron plate.

Whatever pain Liam felt was channeled into his fists, which continued to hammer the top of the car. Inside the vehicle, the policeman shouted and kicked at the other door. The frame was so bent by now that the man's only avenue of escape was through one of the shattered windows. Before he could take his chances at crawling between shards of broken glass, however, he was knocked down by a section of roof that buckled under Liam's fist. Snarling and panting more from excitement than effort, Liam climbed onto the roof to flatten it under his weight.

Cole hopped onto the hood of the car, where he was immediately grabbed and taken down by several policemen.

"Clear our line of fire, damn it!" one of the cops bellowed.

"Let go of me!" Cole shot back. "Can't you see we're the only ones scratching that thing?"

By now Liam was pounding both fists onto the roof to silence the man inside. Squatting down on the ruined vehicle, he looked around at the officers and issued a challenging roar. His jaw hung open, exposing dozens of daggerlike teeth that filled a mouth large enough to clamp down around a telephone pole.

"Brave Skinner," Liam snarled as more gunshots blazed through the air and bullets thumped harmlessly into the thick tangle of black fur. He didn't look at the cops or even at Cole. Instead, he glared down at Paige. The Full Blood took one step off the roof and reached out for her, but was forced to pull his hand back before Paige's sickle chopped it off. "Strong Skinner," he mused.

Liam's attention was drawn skyward, where Cole thought he could hear the distant chop of helicopter blades approaching. As much as he would have liked to see an Army gunship swooping in to save the day, he had a much easier time imagining live video of him getting his head knocked off, filmed by the traffic copter of a local news station.

Pushing that out of his mind, Cole yelled, "Hey, you skinny little fuck!"

The Full Blood turned away from Paige to look at him.

Cole stood in the street a few paces from the police cruiser with his staff held in both hands across his body. "Yeah, I just said that. I've seen what you look like when you're not covered in all that hair. You're a little prick who was probably a smart-mouthed, sickly little runt his whole life. I bet you got your ass kicked a lot in school too."

As Liam listened, the cops around him let up on their firing. Cole assumed they had either taken a moment to reload or finally realized their bullets weren't even making a dent. The Full Blood narrowed his eyes and crawled down to the street. From between rows of saliva-drenched fangs, he growled, "Dead Skinner."

As the Full Blood's steps thumped on the concrete, Cole worked to keep his cocky smile in place. He backed up at the werewolf's approach, however, and nodded to Paige, who looked at him as if to ask just what the hell he was doing.

Liam had just taken his third step forward when a flurry of arms, legs, and narrow bodies exploded from under the police cruiser. There were only two of them, but their elongated torsos and slender limbs wrapped around Liam's legs like an army of serpents, to claw at him anywhere they could reach.

Another wave of gunfire erupted from nearby, but none of it was directed at Liam. The next batch of Half Breeds answering Liam's howl were tearing down Eleventh Street like a whirlwind of sharp teeth and scraping paws. The cops managed to slow a few of the creatures down before the Half Breeds got to the main group of humans, but the remainder split up to charge the police from other angles. In another few seconds they would be inside of shotgun range.

Cole and Paige didn't have time to worry about them. Liam might have been brought down to one knee by the Mongrels, but he was quickly regaining his composure and furiously digging his claws into the creatures attached to him. He grabbed one Mongrel by the head to pull it off of him, but the burrowing shapeshifter had sunk all of its claws in, and it came away like a barbed arrowhead carelessly pulled from a deep wound. Flaps of skin tore loose from Liam's thigh and a spray of blood trickled from the wound, all of which only served to further enrage him.

The sickle in Paige's left hand moved through the air in a blur, while the one in her right stayed close to her body, to repel anything that might attack. Cole prodded the Full Blood again and again but was at a bad angle and risked hitting one of the Mongrels instead. It wasn't until he buried the spear into the patch of gray fur where the broken tooth was embedded that he knew he'd struck pay dirt.

After hitting the chink in Liam's armor, Cole wished his spear was sharper or even hooked at the end to do more damage. It creaked in his hands, and the Full Blood twitched as if something had scraped against a raw nerve. Judging by the howl that ripped through the air, the spearhead might have even made contact with the tooth still lodged in the werewolf's flesh. Liam grabbed the spear and pulled it out, but howled as it snagged on a piece of flesh before finally coming loose. Sure enough, the end of the spear had sharpened to a finer edge and curled into a hook.

Liam howled and grabbed a Mongrel that had clamped onto his arm. Tightening his fist around its chest, he squeezed until the burrower's spine and several ribs cracked. For good measure, he pounded his other fist into the limp Mongrel's skull and then gnawed off a large portion of its body.

Ben crawled up along Liam's back and bit his neck with a set of short, thin teeth. Liam pulled him off, but the burrower wriggled out of his grip and scurried onto the street. From there, Ben let out a series of high-pitched chirps that sounded like a mix of lizard and bird cries.

Within seconds more of the burrowers came to Ben's side. Some of the Mongrels were wounded and a few were still wrestling with Half Breeds, but no fewer than eight of them answered the call. Cole had expected Paige to join the battle as well, then saw that a Half Breed had blindsided her. He ran past Liam, impaled the Half Breed on his spear, and pulled it away so Paige could drop her right-handed weapon down like a sledgehammer.

"Thanks," she breathed.

By now some more policemen had arrived, and they opened fire on Liam. One of them screamed into a radio while huddling behind a car, "Any press I see around here will be brought up on obstruction charges. Keep this area *clear*, damn it! We got enough civilians to worry about!"

Liam was still hurting from Cole's attack, so Paige jumped onto the police cruiser and launched herself at his back. When her body hit the Full Blood's shoulder blades, she drove her machete in like she was planting a flag.

Liam reared up to his full height, but since he didn't have the unnatural flexibility of a Half Breed, he was unable to turn his head around and bite Paige. After missing her with a few wild swipes of his claws, he dropped to all fours and took off like a shot.

Cole stood with weapon in hand, feeling like a useless bump on that particular stretch of road as he viewed the scene. Gunshots crackled around him, mixed with the occasional shotgun blast. More people ran farther down the street as he stood there, and he saw others leaning out of open windows in buildings down the block. The helicopters had drifted away, but he could still hear the flutter of blades in the distance. An ambulance was parked near several cops dressed in riot gear, but the EMTs had been taken out by the Half Breeds. Werewolves snarled and attacked the police. Seeing one of those creatures pounce on an officer in riot gear got Cole moving again.

He reached the officer just as the man had emptied his weapon into the Half Breed's face. Slug after slug punched into the werewolf, but it still wasn't enough to put it down. The creature was about to clamp its jaws around the officer's leg when Cole drove his spear through its upper body. It occurred to him that he might have been overcompensating for allowing Paige to get away, after he brought his spear down so many times that he could have turned the thing into paste.

"Cole?"

He turned at the sound of his name and spotted a familiar face among the frazzled cops. "Officer Stanze!"

Stanze jogged toward Cole with his gun drawn. "Is Paige around here?" the officer asked. "These things look just like the one I sold her."

"She's with the big one that got away."

"Huh?"

"When did you get here?" Cole asked.

"Just now. Damn near every unit in the city will be here in another minute or two."

Stanze suddenly straightened his arms and legs into the classic firing stance. He pulled his trigger once before Cole got a look at what he was shooting at.

The Mongrel darted from one shadow to another like a six-foot eel slithering through shallow water. Cole slapped his hand beneath Stanze's arms so his next bullet tunneled into a wall across the street.

"Hey!" Stanze said. "I just saw another one of those things!"

A low growl rolled through the air, followed by the scrape of claws against pavement. A Half Breed jumped over an empty police car, its eyes wide and glassy, front legs outstretched and teeth bared. Just as it cleared the top of its arc, the Half Breed was intercepted by the Mongrel that had just crossed the street. Both furry bodies met with a thud and slammed to the ground.

"There's some of them!" another cop shouted. "Fire!"

Bullets filled the air, chipping the street and punching into their targets. Cole tried to think of a way to save the Mongrel, but wasn't about to dive into the middle of all that lead. Fortunately, it seemed that none of the bullets were doing much damage. Ben came along to sink his teeth into the Half Breed's thigh, and then both burrowers dragged the wretch into the nearest alley.

"What the hell is going on here?" Stanze asked him. "Damn near the whole force is here instead of on patrol. Shit's getting busted up. Wild animals are all over the place. Now I heard there's another riot down on the other side of the highway."

"More animals?" Cole asked.

Stanze shook his head. "Just a bunch of assholes who see this kind of general craziness as a license to steal," he said with an exasperated sigh. "Wait! Where do you think you're going?"

Cole had turned away and taken several steps toward the Cavalier. "I need to get to Paige," he said.

"Get in my cruiser," Stanze said. "If you know where to look for her, I'll get you there a hell of a lot quicker than you could on yer own." Cole hesitated, and Stanze grabbed his arm. "Seems like you both know what these things are, so don't try to tell me any different. I wanna help, so let me help."

"You want to help? Fine." Raising his voice and looking toward something creeping through a shadow, he said, "Those weasel things are running straight for her! Maybe you should follow them."

One of the Mongrels within earshot got the hint and scampered into the open just long enough to be spotted.

Cole pointed and said, "Right there!"

"Aren't you coming with me?" Stanze asked.

Cole held up his hands and replied, "Hey, you're the guys with the guns. All I got is this stick."

Stanze slapped him on the shoulder. "Smart man. If you get ahold of her, find out where she is and tell any of these cops to radio me." With that, Stanze jogged to his car, and he and another officer piled in to pursue the Mongrels.

Even though the cops would just be led somewhere out of harm's way, Cole had to admire their willingness to charge after them. He got to the Cav and was about to turn the key in the ignition when he realized someone was there with him. Kayla had taken a form that was almost human, but was wiry enough to be nearly absorbed by all the crap piled in the backseat. A portion of her body was camouflaged by the same type of substance that had been soaked into Paige's hooded sweatshirt, and the smell had given her away.

"Ben and the others must really trust you," she said. "We've already lost three of our number clearing most of the Half Breeds from this area."

"Yeah? Paige just got carried off to Lord knows where. Think you can track her down?"

"The stench of Full Bloods is so powerful that they might as well have spotlights strapped to their backs."

"More than one?" Seeing Kayla nod into the rearview mirror, Cole grunted, "Shit! Right now I need the one that's got Paige."

"Ben and I can take you to her."

"Perfect," Cole said, starting the car. His hand was poised over the gear shift when he stopped before taking the Cav out of Park.

Kayla leaned forward and placed a hand on his headrest. "What's the matter? I said I'll take you to her. After all we've done, you don't trust us?"

"No, it's not that. I can't leave yet."

"Why?"

"How many of these cops have been hurt?"

She looked through the windows on either side and said, "Several, but at least they're still alive."

"And what about guys like that one?" Cole asked, pointing to a group of officers clustered around a large man lying on the sidewalk. "How long before they start to change?"

Kayla drew in a quick hissing breath. "You're right. We must end the lives of the badly wounded before they can continue the cycle."

"Or, you can hand me that tackle box on the floor back there and I can end it another way." When Kayla handed over the medical kit, Cole told her, "You go find Paige. Take as many of the others as you can and try to help her. Ben can lead me to you."

"If even one Full Blood is to be killed, we'll need all the fighters we can get."

"Do you know how to help these wounded cops without killing them?" he asked.

After a slight pause, Kayla replied, "No."

"Then let me do it. In case you haven't noticed, they took out a few Half Breeds on their own. I won't just drive away and let them die for it."

"Do what you must here, but be quick. Ben will stay behind and take you to the fight." With that, Kayla left the car. She'd shifted into an agile, vaguely feline form before all four of her paws touched the street, then she faded away.

Cole rummaged through the medical kit until he found the bundle of turkey basters and some eye drop bottles marked HB.

The street looked like a war zone, but was quieter than it had been a few minutes ago. Cars were parked at odd angles, some of them on the sidewalk, while others were badly damaged or completely destroyed. Shots crackled from random spots in the distance. Men and women in uniform scrambled to find each other and talk on radios while dealing with civilians or wounded who lay stretched out on the ground.

As far as Cole could tell, there were only a few Half Breeds in the vicinity. He couldn't see any of them, but heard barks and snarls nearby. One wild howl was ended by a chorus of shotgun blasts. He hurried to the fallen cop he'd spotted from his car and was stopped by a burly man in a black jumpsuit and a heavy bulletproof vest with a badge sewn into the spot where a breast pocket should be.

"Whoa, back up," the big guy warned.

Despite the rifle in the cop's hands, Cole kept moving. "That man's hurt," he said. "I can help him before he gets worse."

The guy with the rifle shook his head. "More paramedics are on the way. Go back to your home and let us do our job."

"I just need to get a look at the wound," he insisted. "I'm a doctor, and having him lying flat or on his side or with his head elevated could make the difference between whether or not he lives long enough for the paramedics to help."

The words had flown out of him in a way that reminded him of a religious zealot speaking in tongues. They were a mix of some things he'd heard on TV and in a couple classes he'd gotten at Red Cross class, tied together with a dash of bullshit. The recipe was just good enough for the heavily armed man to let him get a little closer.

The wounded cop was hurt badly, but he was strong enough to hang on. His uniform was ripped open at the waist and shredded all the way down to the knee. When the man saw his fellow officer escort Cole to him, he opened his eyes wider and said, "I think it's got rabies or something. My leg feels li—like it's burning."

Making a loose fist around an eyedropper, Cole leaned forward until his hand was over the wound, then tightened his fist to spray some liquid from the dropper onto the wound. "Keep his head up," he said. "It'll help him stay awake."

The man on the sidewalk made a sound as if someone had tightened a belt around his injury. He held onto his breath for a moment and then let it out as if the invisible belt had been loosened. "Burning stopped," he sighed. Cole bent down to hear him better.

"I don't know what you did, but thanks, man," the cop said. The frantic edge to his expression had been dulled and his muscles no longer looked as if every last one of them was pulled taut.

From there, Cole made the rounds to anyone else he could find who looked wounded badly enough to be in danger of becoming a Half Breed. According to Paige, little nips or cuts didn't matter, but if a wound looked just shy of fatal, the Half Breed infection would take root.

Somewhere along the line he was joined by the woman he'd helped when he and Paige first arrived in Kansas City. The female officer had received some treatment for the minor wounds she'd gotten, and now insisted on escorting him to all the other wounded she could find. When he'd treated the worst cases, he handed her one of the larger turkey basters and said, "Squirt this stuff onto as many more wounds as you can find. It'll keep them sterile until they can be stitched up."

"Where are you going?" she asked.

Another ambulance had wailed down the street and was rolling into the middle of the commotion. "The pros are here, so I'll give you room to work."

"You did some great work yourself. Got a name?"

Fortunately, he was spared the task of deciding if he should give his real name or come up with a fake one. As the paramedics spread out to help the wounded, the freshest batch of cops barked for all civilians to clear the scene. Cole followed the order, wondering if it had been a mistake to distribute the solution. It had only taken a few minutes, but his gut told him he'd wasted too much time.

Paige was still out there with that Full Blood.

She could be lying wounded somewhere waiting for him.

Maybe she was already dead.

As soon as he got to the Cav and pulled open the driver's door, a Mongrel poked his head out from under the vehicle's battered back end.

"You've got a fan club," Ben said.

"Any more Half Breeds around here?"

"Not for a mile or so."

"Can you find Paige and that Full Blood?"

"Most of us went to lend your partner a hand. I can take you to her."

Cole turned his key in the ignition. "Then let's go."

The Mongrel skittered ahead like a shadowy mirage.

Chapter 30

Paige hung onto her weapons with a grip that was nearly tight enough to drive the thorns in the handles all the way through the tops of her hands. Liam's back was wide as a bull's, and it took nearly everything she had to keep from being thrown.

The city rushed by on all sides. Pavement flowed under her like a whitewater current. Buildings, cars, people, street-lights, glowing neon, brake lights, more buildings, more cars, all of it flew past in a stream that overloaded her senses and caused her stomach to clench. When Liam leapt over something in his path, she flopped onto her side and cried out as the tendons in her shoulders and wrists threatened to snap. She tried to flatten herself against Liam's back but was almost thrown off again as the Full Blood dug its claws into the pavement and came to a stop.

Paige slid along Liam's back, hit his shoulders and felt her body swing into the air. Her left hand came away from her weapon, but her right remained locked. In fact, even when she dropped back down to bump against Liam's side, her wounded arm held fast. The savage bite from the Half Breed had already healed to a set of jagged scratches. But while she didn't feel any pain in that limb, she couldn't feel much of anything else either.

They were on an interstate.

She didn't know which interstate, but the road was wider, el-evated, and filled with a steady stream of cars. Liam wanted to pick the sickle from his back with his teeth, but Paige plucked the weapon free and drove it back into a thick section of meat at the base of his neck. He tried to shake her off, forcing her to push the weapon in as far as it could go and hang on.

The Full Blood reared up then and made a sound like a train being derailed. His front paws flailed in the air as Paige fought to stay in place. Her feet dangled more than a yard off the pavement as she used every muscle she could to jerk the machete downward like a giant lever embedded behind his shoulder. The crude blade tore through the meat in his back, causing the massive werewolf to drop back to all fours, angle his head to one side, and sink his front claws into the pavement. A honking car sped by to clip Liam's leg just as he turned to nip at her. Paige swung around and out of his reach, and was just quick enough to avoid a second snapping attempt.

Liam roared and ran straight down one lane of the interstate. Several cars skidded to avoid him, but the Full Blood leaned into them and used his shoulder to knock them aside. Then, like a bear using the trunk of a tree to scratch an itch, he angled his back toward the cars to try and rid himself of his unwanted rider.

Paige kept her hands wrapped around the weapon grips but couldn't use them as anything but handles to keep from dropping onto the road. When Liam lowered his shoulder to slam that half of his body into a bus, she barely managed to pull her lower body up and tuck it in so her legs wouldn't be mashed against steel. Once she'd adjusted her weight on that side, Liam lowered his head and kicked his back legs up in an attempt to fling her toward an oncoming truck. Her left hand slipped from the handle of her sickle, but her right fist remained locked so tightly that she wondered if she would ever be able to open her fist again.

Then Liam did the one thing she'd been praying he wouldn't do. He stopped in the middle of the road and rolled onto his back.

Paige reacted without thinking, bringing her knees up to her chest, placing her feet against the Full Blood and pushing herself away. Liam hit the cement and rolled back and forth as if putting out a fire. Headlights from cars that had stopped or were wrecked around and behind them bathed the two combatants in illumination from several angles. The moment Paige whipped around to get a look at the Full Blood, she was forced to dodge a set of claws that were longer than short swords. She raised her right arm, but her weapon only blocked a fraction of the blow. Claws raked through her hardened flesh as though scraping against brick, the impact of the swing knocking her flat against the pavement.

More cars honked and crashed into each other, but Paige couldn't see any of it. Her face rested against the concrete and she was too tired to lift it. The Full Blood snapped at a pair of cars that honked wildly as they drove by, straightening his upper body and shifting effortlessly to stand upon two legs.

Reaching over his shoulder, Liam grabbed at what seemed a large thorn protruding from his back. His thick fingers brushed against the sickle, which brought something resembling a smile to his face. When he got ahold of the weapon and pulled it out, he released a breath that might have been lodged in his throat since the blade first hit home. He was about to toss it away when Paige threw the machete in her right hand with enough inhuman force to plant it solidly within the gray spot on Liam's side.

He reacted to the blow as if she'd stabbed a raw nerve. Craning his head all the way back, he roared and allowed the sickle to slip from his hand. Paige, certain that he was about to flee, scooped up the weapon and got to Liam before the pained howl had completely left his throat. When he lowered his head to run along the shoulder of the interstate, she'd already grabbed a handful of fur in her powerful right fist and used the machete to pull herself up and back onto him. The Full Blood was no longer interested in flipping cars. He ran along the highway for the quickest couple of miles Paige had ever experienced before launching himself up and over the guardrail.

They sailed over a canopy of branches and leaves, but Paige could tell they weren't anywhere near a park. The air smelled of smoke and rusted steel. The ground beneath Liam's feet crunched with loose gravel or broken cement as he brushed against a few large things to try and knock her off. Failing that, he came to a stop. His chest heaved like a powerful engine on the verge of overheating. Just as Paige recognized one of the nearby things as a boxcar, Liam threw himself against it. She was barely able to dismount with her weapons in hand before being squashed.

"You're accomplishing nothing, Skinner," Liam said while shifting into his upright form. "If I don't kill you now, I'll only kill you later."

They were in a train yard. Several darkened warehouses were lined up just beyond a couple sets of tracks. Behind them Paige saw smaller sheds and rows of empty boxcars, all a stone's throw from the Missouri River. She didn't know exactly how far Liam had taken her, but could no longer hear police sirens.

Liam squatted down with his knees bent and his elbows resting on them. He eyed her with a little bit of everything showing upon his face: exhilaration, lust, hunger, even a good deal of curiosity. "If the Mongrels are here, that means this city is way out of your control. Or did you have something to do with that?"

She didn't answer his question. Instead, she tried not to think about the pain flooding her body while she opened and closed her right fist to get some blood pumping through it.

Liam wrinkled his nose and said, "I already know you deal with the leeches, so I'm surprised you didn't recruit them to help you. But the Nymar don't fight for their territory any longer, do they? They hide inside their noisy taverns and frilly clothes, whining endlessly about how hard they've got it. Maybe I'll show them what to do with their power. Wouldn't that be funny?"

"You know what I think is funny?" Paige sneered. "A big bad wolf like you doing so much talking when there's a fight to finish."

"Just picking your brain," Liam mused as he casually waggled his long, clawed fingers. "I suppose I can do that just as well when the wretches tear your head open."

Before Paige could charge the Full Blood head-on, Liam leapt up and back. His hands touched the side of a crane used for loading oversized cargo containers, then he grabbed onto the steel beams and climbed toward the top of the crane. It began to groan and shift under his weight, so he stopped halfway up and raised his face to the black sky.

Paige recognized the howl from when she and Cole had been driving downtown. Being so close to its source was another experience altogether. The sound shook her on a primordial level. Instincts came to the surface that made her want to run until her legs would no longer carry her.

But she wasn't the only one to feel that urge. Half Breeds emerged from the nearby warehouses and from beneath the dirty sheds bordering some of the older sets of tracks. There were at least ten of them scraping up from their pits, hungry and eager to stretch their newly formed muscles. Just when things looked like they couldn't get any worse, stragglers from downtown howled from other parts of the city. The first of those creatures to arrive showed plenty of wear and tear from tangling with cops, Mongrels, and Skinners, but didn't show any signs of slowing down.

Not only could Paige feel those demonic snarls grating inside her ears, but she felt a rumble beneath her feet. She tried to loosen up her right arm in preparation for a fight, but the limb felt too thick and heavy to be of much use. Standing alone in that train yard, she swallowed the regrets that rose to the back of her throat and got comfortable with what remained.

She'd had a good run.

As the Half Breeds circled, their crazed, once-human eyes focused upon her. Then every set of thin, pointed ears perked up as another voice demanded to be heard.

It was a howl, but compared to those she'd heard earlier, this was musical. The new voice didn't need to compete with Liam's. It was a pure, single note that wove through everything else in the simple, unstoppable way a river might cut through a mountain. Liam took notice and shifted on his perch to look toward the row of low buildings along the river to the north.

A second Full Blood stood on top of a warehouse at the far edge of the train yard. Its head was pointed straight up and both of its massive arms were stretched out, with fingers splayed as if it was preparing to battle anything the gods dared to send his way.

For a few moments the Half Breeds seemed confused. Then one of them started running toward the other Full Blood. Before it had gone more than twenty yards, the rest of the wretches followed suit. They bolted straight past the crane where Liam snarled down at them and raced for the opposite end of the yard. Once all of the Half Breeds had gathered at the foot of their new master, that Full Blood unleashed the full fury of its teeth and claws upon them.

What followed was an ugly display of nature's most unsympathetic rule. The newly arrived Full Blood ripped the first Half Breed apart and sent both pieces flying against the side of the building behind him. The rest of the leaner werewolves attacked in a frenzied battle for survival, simply because they knew it was too late to try and escape.

"To hell with you, Randolph!" Liam shouted from on high. "I don't need them!" Shifting his eyes to Paige, he dropped from the crane and scrambled toward her. His eyes were unnaturally clear. Every one of his features had become angular and rougher around the edges, as if the last drop of humanity inside of him had dried up.

The rumbling beneath Paige's feet grew stronger, but she was too tired to run from it. Instead, she tightened her fists around her weapons and waited for Liam to come to her. As the rumbling passed directly under her and moved on ahead, she realized that something else was going to get to the Full Blood first.

Four lanky arms exploded from the dirt to grab Liam's feet, the earth rising in large chunks that sent Paige tumbling to one side. The Full Blood shook one leg free, but lost his momentum and came tumbling down. Another pair of burrowers grabbed Liam's hands and yanked them down, and when he pulled them from the dirt, they sank their short, wide teeth into him.

In the distance, Half Breeds yelped and snarled, ripping at Randolph's hide before he tore them to shreds.

Directly in front of Paige, Liam struggled to climb to his

feet as Mongrels swarmed at him from the ground. Most of the burrowers attempted to pull him down just to keep him from moving, but one had climbed up and onto the Full Blood's powerful frame to gnaw on the side of his neck.

Wincing as dozens of teeth and claws tried to get through his thick layers of fur, Liam looked at Paige and growled, "Do your new allies know you'll be hunting them next?"

Paige got to her feet and searched the writhing contingent of Mongrels for an opening to strike.

"Humans who survive a wound from our kind become wretches," Liam said as he grabbed one of the burrowers by the neck. "Mongrels surviving the same wound become Full Blood. Did you think about that when you sought their help?"

The moment Liam tossed the Mongrel he'd grabbed, Paige ran toward him. She used every bit of anger, frustration, even desperation she felt to try and regain a connection that she seemed to have lost. The thorns in the handle of her right-handed weapon had practically been swallowed up when the thing shifted into its crude, vaguely machetelike shape. The remaining nubs were sharp, but barely sharp enough to puncture the hardening skin of her damaged hand. Once her grip tightened enough to do the job, all the emotional fire she'd ignited allowed her to will the handle of her machete to peel back and expose the tooth she'd attached to it when it had been her more familiar sickle. The tooth emerged like a Nymar's fang, and carried the same message: blood was going to be spilled.

The sickle blade snagged in Liam's fur, where it became tangled amid a thick layer of spent bullets. Paige pulled herself forward to add even more power when she drove the modified end of her other weapon straight into the tuft of gray fur on Liam's side. As soon as the blow landed, she could feel the tooth on her weapon scrape against the one that had snapped off of Cole's spear. Liam batted one Mongrel away as if flicking an insect, bellowing a roar that quickly deteriorated to a pained wheeze. When he tried to jump away, he was held in place by the Mongrels that had remained in the dirt.

He bent down to swipe at the Mongrels holding his feet, but was dropped to his knees when Paige pushed her weapon in even farther. The more she strained her right arm, the more the dark shading beneath her skin faded away. Before the ink could fully burn off, she twisted and pulled to do as much damage as possible.

The Full Blood lashed out with one hand, but Paige tucked her head down as the set of deadly claws sliced over her. His follow-up strike was a wild slap, but it connected and sent her straight to the ground. She tightened her fists and was relieved to find both weapons still in her possession.

Liam pulled loose, climbed back to his feet, and raised both fists over his head. Before he could drop those fists onto Paige, Kayla flew at him like a battering ram. The feline Mongrel didn't have the strength of the Half Breeds or the coiling serpentine bodies of the burrowers, but her claws raked at Liam's chest and face in a flurry that was impossible for human eyes to follow. While the werewolf's fur absorbed most of the strikes, Liam's blood soon sprayed through the air. He wrapped both hands around Kayla's torso and slammed her to the ground. When Liam hunched over to finish her off, he saw Paige trying to approach him from another angle and knocked her aside.

Paige landed flat upon her back and curled up to keep her head from knocking against the packed dirt. Her right arm, once the best weapon in her arsenal, flopped uselessly, like a log that had been stitched to her sleeve.

Suddenly, Liam realized he was being pulled deeper into the ground. His claws turned one burrower into mulch, but he was too focused on the next figure writhing in the dirt to spot a third Mongrel scampering across the open train yard. It was Ben, and the Mongrel's momentum allowed him to knock Liam off balance so only one hastily placed leg kept the Full Blood from falling over. Liam recovered from the impact and viciously slashed at Ben's face, but was then knocked flat by the Cavalier, with Cole behind the wheel.

Liam rolled for a few yards, and when he came to a stop, three sets of clawed hands reached up to hold him there. The Full Blood struggled and nearly broke free until Kayla leapt onto his chest and sank her teeth into his neck. The pain from that lit a fire under Liam, allowing him to pull one hand free from the burrower that had been holding it in place. Ben flattened himself against the ground and was scrambling away when Liam's jaws snapped shut around his leg. Letting out a high-pitched screech, Ben rolled onto his back and thrashed against the ground. Blood sprayed from his left leg in a torrent, but everything below his knee remained in Liam's mouth. The Full Blood would have been able to finish his meal if Paige hadn't rushed over to stop him. Her right arm still dangled uselessly, but her left was strong enough to drive the sharpened handle of her sickle down into Liam's right eye.

The only sound Liam could make was a strained wheeze. Kayla lay across his arm to prevent him from decapitating Paige. Just as he was about to pry his other arm free from several sets of hands emerging from the ground, Liam's wrist was pinned down by the forked end of a battered spear.

Cole's face was now illuminated by the headlights of the nearby Cav. Leaning down to keep the Full Blood's arm trapped beneath his weapon, he grunted, "What does it take to kill this thing?"

"It takes a Blood Blade," Paige snarled while rolling onto her back. She grasped her tattooed arm, only to feel it tightening up like a husk under a desert sun. "Be sure to thank Daniels for all that extra work he did!"

The Full Blood's muscles twitched and writhed as he arched his back and attempted to change shape. Every little move he made only intensified the agony in his voice, anchoring him to his current form.

Ben lay on his side after shifting into a form that was somewhat smaller but still nowhere near human. Since the remains of his leg had closed to a gnarled stump, the change had apparently served its purpose.

Kayla had enlisted the help of the remaining burrowers to hold Liam down. He twisted his entire body around to shake the Mongrels loose, but the attempt to transform had sapped his strength. The Full Blood opened his eyes and looked toward the buildings along the water's edge.

Randolph sat atop a pile of Half Breed carcasses and stared back at him before launching himself toward the horizon with a powerful leap.

Forsaking whatever healing he could get from climbing into his human skin, Liam fought to climb back to his feet. When another set of burrower's arms emerged to wrap around him, the Full Blood was unable to keep himself from being dragged underground.

Paige struggled to her feet and stood near the freshly turned soil. "Where is he?" Looking at Kayla, she demanded, "Bring him back! We need to finish this."

Kayla and a few of the other burrowers gathered around the spot where Liam had just been. A few Mongrels tended to Ben. Another peeked up from the ground.

"Well?" Kayla asked.

The partially submerged burrower said, "Max took him deep. I can't even hear them anymore."

"That doesn't mean much," Cole said. "I was carried underground so deep I couldn't even see, but I could still get enough air to stay alive."

Ben pulled in a breath and raised his narrow head. "I kept you within a foot of the surface. When you got too fidgety, I dragged you beneath a few flower gardens where the ground was loose enough to let some air through."

"Full Bloods aren't built the same as Cole," Paige said impatiently.

Kayla was studying the way she cradled her right arm tightly against her chest. "They still need to breathe," she told Paige. "We all heard as much."

"So what do we do now?" Cole asked.

"You go home and we take care of this," Kayla announced. "This is our city now. Or are you planning on going back on our deal?"

Paige held her bloody face up to glare directly into Kayla's eyes. Although she couldn't see all the Mongrels, she could feel them sizing her up as she spoke. "I'm not going back on any deal, but I'm not going anywhere until that Full Blood is dead."

"Max is taking him as far down as he can go," Ben said. "If

that Full Blood could survive in the ground indefinitely, he'd be one of us. Even if he can hold his breath, he won't be able to do any damage stuck a hundred feet below ground level. There are measures we can take to be sure he stays put."

"What measures?" Paige asked.

Kayla reached out and placed a thinner, clawless version of her hand upon Paige's shoulder. "That Full Blood killed more Mongrels than it did Skinners tonight. If we are to live here, we have more reason than you to put an end to the beast. Wouldn't you have felt it if he was still close enough to be a threat?"

Both of the Skinners knew better than to discus the limits of their senses with the Mongrels. Paige looked over to Cole, who rubbed his fingertips against his palms the way he always did when trying to hone his skill at detection. Reluctantly, Paige nodded. "They're both gone," she sighed. "I can feel it."

Cole led her away from the dirt pile and didn't say anything until they were at the base of the crane that Liam had climbed earlier. The Mongrels had plenty of wounded to tend and didn't bother following them. "You're really just gonna let them stay here?" he asked. "They were a big help, but doesn't that kind of defeat the purpose?"

"You're toughening up, Cole," she said affectionately. "I like it. What does your gut tell you? Can you trust them or not?"

He thought for a second before a wave of relief, quickly followed by surprise, washed over him. "I guess I do. But this city isn't just going to forget what happened. Not with all the people who saw these things. There are still bodies lying around!"

Paige shook her head and clutched her arm as she made her way back toward the Mongrels. "You'd be amazed at how much people are willing to forget. I've got some lighter fluid in the car. We'll torch the bodies so there's not quite so much evidence in one place." Looking toward Kayla, she raised her voice and added, "You guys might as well leave."

"Leave to where?" the feline Mongrel asked cautiously.

Paige shrugged. "Wherever you want. Enjoy your new city. I'd suggest making sure all the Half Breeds are gone, though."

"It's already being seen to."

"Good. One of us will stop by every now and then to make sure things are running smoothly."

Kayla smiled and nodded. "It was easier than I expected to work with you two. Thanks for not disappointing us." She offered her hand and each Skinner shook it. Once they'd collected their dead and wounded, Kayla and the other Mongrels left to stake their claims.

"Let's set this fire and get back to Chicago," Paige said.

Cole followed her across the empty train yard. He didn't bother looking for any trace of the Mongrels and barely paid any attention to the distant sirens. "We're really going to leave?"

After unlocking the trunk, Paige opened it and stuck her hand under a few duffel bags to retrieve a half-empty bottle of lighter fluid. "Do you feel any shapeshifters around?"

"No," Cole replied. "But that doesn't mean the whole city is clear."

"If these Mongrels were making friends with Full Bloods, they did a real shitty job of it. And if that particular Full Blood isn't dead after all we did tonight, I'll settle for it being buried under this place. We will come back to check on everything some other time, but right now . . . I need to rest."

"I just didn't think you'd really make a deal for them to claim a whole city."

"Relax," Paige said. "How do you think the Nymar got their hooks so deep into Chicago?"

The Half Breeds in the train yard burned like a stack of old tires and smelled twice as bad. Cole set a new speed record crossing the city to get back to where Daniels was hiding. Along the way, police cars sped in small packs to respond to any number of calls that flooded the emergency lines. Even though Kansas City looked like a disaster area, the Skinners knew things were a hell of a lot better than they appeared to be.

Chapter 31

Chicago
Four days later

Cole's spear hit Paige's upraised baton with a crack that filled the cellar beneath Raza Hill. Throughout the entire practice session, he couldn't help staring down at the arm that was held against her side by a sling.

"Stop worrying about it," she said.

"I can't help it. Are you sure you're feeling well enough to spar? Maybe you should rest some more."

Paige twirled the baton in her left hand like a drummer showing off between solos and replied, "If you don't start swinging that weapon like a man, you're the one that's gonna need some rest."

"Come on, now." Pausing just long enough to swat away a fairly strong swing, Cole lowered his spear to block the lower shot that followed. "You can't even use your right arm."

"It's a lot better." When he scowled at her, she added, "Well, better than it was."

"Can you move it?"

"A little. Daniels took some samples and already knows what went wrong with the ink. The next batch should work just fine."

"*Next* batch?" Cole said as he sent a few quick attacks her way.

Paige stepped into a sideways stance that allowed her to bat away the spear while keeping her right side out of its range. "Trial and error. You should read the journals of the guy who put the finishing touches on the varnish we use for our weapons. There's one old picture of the first set of hands to get stuck by those thorns, and it ain't pretty. Now, we don't even think about it."

"Maybe you don't," Cole grumbled. "So losing your arm just gets chalked up to the greater good?"

Sighing, she waited for him to swing at her again and shifted her stance to deflect the spear with her right forearm. Despite an impact that Cole could feel all the way up to his shoulders, she didn't even flinch. "I didn't lose my arm," she said. "Yes, it's messed up. No, I can't move my hand. Yes, it hurts. Daniels is working on the problem, so I'd rather not dwell on it. Okay?"

He actually felt relieved to hear her say that. Since leaving Kansas City, Paige had been quietly allowing Daniels to slice her up for tissue samples while stubbornly refusing to acknowledge the pasty appendage that dangled from her shoulder like a rock. Now that she'd taken to wearing the sling so she could practice, the more familiar Paige was making a comeback. "What about you?" she asked. "How are you holding up?"

Looking around at the gray walls of their basement practice space, Cole forced a nervous smile. "I could do without being underground for the next year or two."

"Sounds good to me," she said as she headed for the stairs and motioned for him to follow.

"Every part of my body hurts in one way or another, but the serum cleared it up pretty well."

Paige stopped at the bottom of the stairs, turned around and asked, "Nothing broken? No bruises that won't go away? Dizziness?"

Cole shook his head.

"How are you sleeping?"

"With my eyes closed. Heh." Since she didn't respond to the lame joke, Cole added, "Pretty good."

"Then you're done with the serum until you get hurt again,"

she announced. "Since you didn't need to go to the hospital after everything you went through, it's in your system and doing its thing."

"Maybe it'd help your arm," Cole offered.

She started climbing again. "Already tried and it burned like hell. I think it's got something to do with the charmed metal of the Blood Blade mixing directly with the Nymar juice in the serum. That stuff isn't just some magic *Hammer Strike* health pack, you know."

It made him warm in all the good places to hear her throw around some geek talk while also climbing stairs in her tight sweatpants directly in front of him. "Health pack, huh? If I got you into some more *Sniper Deathmatches*, you'd be pretty damn irresistible."

She glanced over her shoulder and cocked her hip in a way that made it obvious she knew she was being watched. "And if you stopped talking about video games so much, you might gain a few hot points yourself."

Cole knew better than to chase after that line of conversation. While some parts of him were more than willing to see it through, the other ninety-five percent was just too damn tired. He climbed up the stairs and then heard something that made him rethink those statistics.

"Come with me, Cole," Paige said as she headed to her bedroom. "I need you for something."

Letting his spear drop from his hand, he maneuvered through the spotless kitchen and to the rooms in the back of the old restaurant. Paige's had once been the manager's office, but had plenty of space since the wall between the original office and adjoining storage area had been knocked down. As she walked past a few mismatched dressers and a full-sized bed on a cheap wooden frame, she peeled off her sweatpants and tossed them onto a pile of clothes that had been festering there since before they left for KC. She wore her tight runner's shorts under the sweats, which hugged her backside quite nicely.

Following her to a small desk at the back corner of the room, Cole deduced that the computer set up there was probably good enough to play a few games, but not at the proper graphical resolution needed to get the full effect. When Paige sat down at the desk, he groaned, "Seriously? Do you really need to strip just to get help with your computer?"

"Who says I need help with a computer?" she asked.

"So . . . you want to . . . ?"

"No. I need your e-mail password. MEG forwarded some stuff, but sent it to you."

"So you're just trying to torture me?"

She crinkled her nose and shrugged. "Maybe just a little."

"It's not funny."

"Yes it is. You should see the look on your face."

Cole let out a sigh and walked over to see what was on the monitor.

"Oh come on," Paige said. "My sweats smell like I stole them from a wino. They're gross and sticking to me."

Since he was trying not to look at her, Paige leaned closer so he could see the puppy dog eyes she was flashing him. Unlike the ones that had gotten him bruised up in practice a while back, these were genuine. "Sorry. After seeing you in your carrot patch boxers, I thought we could relax a little more around each other."

"Relax, yes. Torture, no." He tapped in another password and went to the most recent arrivals to his in box. "Here it is. It's from Branch 18. They say thanks for the thermal. What's that mean?"

"That fancy camera they were using was on layaway, so I paid it off for them. After all they did for us, I figure they earned it."

Cole scrolled down. "Here's one from Branch 40. It's a bunch of links to . . . ohhhh . . . yeah. Have you seen these?"

Staring at the e-mail, Paige glanced down a long line of links to other websites, most of which steered them back to HomeBrewTV.com. Although the site's bread and butter were videos of teens slamming each other in the groin or trying to sing, there were also plenty of clips from real television shows posted under various categories. All of the links in Stu's e-mail fell under the same category: Kansas City Riots.

"Isn't this the same site with the series about what can fit into a blender and the webcam journal from that whiny little college girl?" Paige asked.

"Just watch."

The first video Cole opened was of a blond woman standing about forty yards away from the police car that Liam had smashed. Judging by the washed-out quality of the sunlight, it looked as if the report had been filmed not long after dawn. "Local authorities are still cleaning up the mess from Wednesday's riot," she said. "Although believed to have started during the most recent attack by a pack of rottweilers suspected of being set loose from an illegal fighting ring, the incidents quickly elevated to alarming proportions. Nearly all of Kansas City's police responded to calls ranging from wild animal sightings to random assaults."

The scene cut to another location, and had been recorded at another time, because the dazed old woman in a housedress was cast in the warmer light of early evening. "I don't know what the police say they was, but they weren't any dawgs. I had plenty of dawgs and I ain't never seen dawgs like these."

"What did they look like?" the blond reporter asked from off-camera.

"They was big and scary and . . . *big*. Fast too!"

The scene cut to a newsroom, where an older woman with graying hair sat beside a guy who looked like he'd been sucked out of an ad for cologne. The blonde from the previous scene was on a smaller screen behind cologne guy, and she said, "Many other witnesses claim to have seen what they describe as wolves running through the downtown area. While several cameras posted throughout the city were able to catch glimpses of large animals, this station was able to catch the following footage."

Her image was replaced on the screen by a two-second clip of three animals racing across the frame so quickly that they weren't much more than shaggy blurs. When the clip was slowed down and looped, the animals became even blurrier. The blonde reappeared just long enough to say, "Back to you, Madelyn and Jeremy."

"Weren't there wolves sighted in Chicago a few months ago?" the older woman asked.

Cologne guy nodded just like the prompter told him to and said, "Chicago police did report being attacked by a large animal at the scene of a domestic disturbance in Schaumburg, but refused to elaborate." The monitor behind him flickered to show people of all shapes and shades running down the streets in a panic while throwing heavy things at each other or into nearby windows. "As for the riots, Kansas City authorities have issued a statement saying they were sparked by an unfortunate chain of events that led to nearly disastrous results. Since Wednesday, no more wolves, rottweilers, *or* pit bulls have been sighted. But that doesn't go for cats and dogs, which brings us to Dennis Martins and our weather report . . ."

The next link in the e-mail was to another news video. The channel identification was different from the first, and the reporter was a rugged man who stood in a train yard with several fire trucks behind him. "Responding to a call that was placed toward the end of tonight's riots," he said, "the fire department found a grisly sight here at the Pyat Train Yards." The reporter turned to reveal a blackened pile in the distance that had a thick plume of black smoke rolling off it. The camera then panned to show a slender man in his late forties dressed in full firefighter gear. A label at the bottom of the screen identified him as Lieutenant Bradley Speck.

"Tell us, Lieutenant Speck, what happened here?"

"Near as we can tell, someone killed a bunch of the dogs or whatever that were running loose and burnt them here."

"So these are the dogs that were attacking people?"

"I don't know about that," Lieutenant Speck replied, "but they were a bunch of animals with some big teeth. They were burnt up pretty bad, so it's hard to tell what breed they were."

"There have been witnesses saying these were wolves or possibly something else. What can you say about that?"

"I just put out the fires. After a night like this, we're lucky there weren't more to put out. That's all I've got to say."

A third link was to a report from one of the national news

stations. It was a short piece about the riots, which focused mostly on how many were killed and injured. Cole was about to skip right over it when he spotted a familiar face. He rewound the video and played it from there.

"I'm standing here with Kansas City local Alvin Monroe," stated a stern but vaguely attractive woman wearing a sharp blue suit. Next to her was the skinny Nymar who'd approached Cole in North Terrace Park.

Alvin gazed into the camera as if staring into an alien probe, and then smiled just wide enough to show the chipped tips of his lower fangs. When he waved to his viewing public, his tattered sleeve fell down to show the thick black markings along his wrist.

"Mr. Monroe is being honored by local residents for saving a group of professors who were nearly attacked outside of the medical university."

"Tha's right," Alvin slurred.

"Tell us what happened, Mr. Monroe."

"Buncha big dogs came runnin' along. Looked like they were gon' hurt those teachers and so I jumped on 'em."

"You jumped on them?"

"Yes'm," Alvin said with a nod. "I jumped an' scared 'em away. I bit one of 'em too. They din' taste too good."

The reporter chuckled nervously and asked, "Were they the same rottweilers or pit bulls connected to tonight's events?"

"Are rottweilers big 'n' mean?"

"Generally, yes."

"They got big teef?"

"Yes."

"Then these were them," Alvin declared. "Dat's dat."

The report shifted back to the studios, where the regular anchor said, "There's been plenty of speculation about what sort of dogs these were. Preliminary testing on several sets of remains have led examiners to conclude they were canines affected by a disease that may have also led to their feral behavior." After that, he briefly acknowledged the efforts of a pair of "martial arts enthusiasts" who came to the aid of police during the riots by fending off several of the wild dogs. He then apologized for the correspondent's comments regarding rottweilers and assured dog owners that the network had no intention of offending them.

"There's a lot more like that," Cole said, "but that's pretty much the gist of it. Check this out, though."

The next link went to a website that looked as if it had been put together by someone with some tech know-how and a rig in their basement, as opposed to a media conglomerate. After one click of Cole's finger against the mouse, Paige's screen was covered with still pictures of Half Breeds running through different sections of Kansas City and the surrounding areas.

"Haven't we seen enough of these?" she asked.

"These are pics taken by people on their phones or cameras who sent them in to MEG's site. These," he said while using the cursor to circle the pictures in the left column of the screen, "are the originals, and these," he said while circling the right column, "are the ones I touched up."

The left column was labeled, GOOD TRY. The right was labeled, BUT NOT GOOD ENOUGH.

"Let's just try an experiment," Cole said as he clicked to an online search and typed in the words, *Kansas City riot monsters.*

Within .28 seconds, several pages of results came up. Some were in the vein of, "Hundreds claim to see monsters in streets of KC" and "rottweilers or werewolves?" while others had labels such as, "Monster pictures proven to be fake" and "Werewolf hoax turns into riot."

When Paige looked over at him, Cole was beaming and nodding as if he'd just cured a disease. "Nice job," she said.

"Nice? Just *nice*?"

"KC has been quiet and the press won't stop talking about sick dogs, but you did a very nice job with adding to the confusion." She got up and patted him on the head. "Now if you'll get out of my room, I need to pack."

"Pack for what?"

"A trip to Kansas City. I want to check in on those Mongrels."

Cole logged out of his e-mail account and walked toward

her door. "You're going to see Officer Stanze, aren't you?"

"He was a big help," she said with a shrug. "And a pretty nice guy."

"Staying in the good graces of the authorities for a change, huh?"

Flicking her eyebrows up and putting on a dirty little smile, she said, "I guess you could call it that."

"Wait. What?"

She had more than enough strength in her left hand to shove him out of her room and shut the door behind him. "You stood toe-to-toe with a Full Blood, so you can handle Chicago for a few days," she shouted through the door. "Check on Stephanie tomorrow. I don't like the . . . "

Although Paige continued to issue orders, Cole turned away from her room and walked back through the kitchen. After having been gone for a while, the door to his freezer took some coaxing before it swung open. Once he was inside his metallic, somewhat cool living space, he sat on the edge of his cot and sighed, "Just because I sleep in a freezer doesn't mean I'm stuck here like some piece of meat."

He picked up his phone from a stack of plastic crates that served as a table and pressed one of the speed dial buttons.

After two rings the connection was made and a voice said, "MEG Branch 40, what can I do for y— Cole! Sorry about that. Just looked at the caller ID. What's up?"

"Hey, Stu. Is Abby around?"

"She's listening to some EVPs."

"Can I talk to her?"

"Sure. Hold on."

A few minutes of static was finally interrupted by a click and a tired, vaguely interested, "Hello?"

"Hi, Abby. This is Cole Warnecki. Remember me?"

"Yes."

"I was wondering if you were free some night. Maybe for dinner or something? I'd like to hear some of your ghost stories. Heh."

"Like . . . a date?" Abby asked in a more interested voice.

"Sure. Yeah. That's what I had in mind. How about it?"

"Welllll . . . "

Cole pulled in a breath, during which he reminded himself that he wasn't some nervous kid wringing his hands. All right, so maybe he was a little nervous, but his hands were steady. "Look, I'm not a stalker or anything but you sound really nice and I'd like to treat you to a meal. We can swap weird work anecdotes. It'll be fun."

After a pause that stopped just short of unbearable, Abby said, "I'd like to hear more about Digital Dreamers."

Cole smiled in a way that used muscles he'd all but forgotten about.

"There's just one thing," she added.

Bracing for the worst, he asked, "Yeah?"

"Do you even know where Branch 40 is?"

"If you'd like to meet, just tell me when and where. I'll be there."

"Really? Wow. How about the diner across the street from me in fifteen minutes?"

"You might have to work with me a bit more than that," Cole said.

"I know. I'm just messin' with ya. Got a pen?"

Cole wrote down the where and discussed the when. They talked for about two more hours and then met online in one of the roughest games of *Sniper Ranger 3* he'd ever played. After signing off, he downloaded a few maps and plotted a course that allowed him to sample some of Abby's favorite chop suey on his way to the Digital Dreamers offices in Seattle. It had the makings of a very interesting road trip.

Epilogue

The chamber was so hot and cramped that it might as well have been carved from a living thing. Mud was caked onto the rounded cement walls over layers of mold and multicolored, multilingual profanities. Daylight poured into one end of the tunnel, along with sounds of passing cars and the rumble of planes from the nearby Kansas City International Airport.

A few people in dirty clothes kept even dirtier faces turned away from the trio huddled just beyond the reach of the sun. Every so often the vagrants would sneak a quick glance into the tunnel to find lean figures in the darkness looking back at them with wide, inhuman eyes. When the things in the tunnel spoke, the vagrants hurried off to find their shade elsewhere.

"Do you think Ben will be all right?"

Kayla glared toward the tunnel's opening for a few more seconds until it became clear the human inhabitants wouldn't be coming back. She and her companion remained in their true shapes so their senses would be at their peak. Her squat, oval head turned toward the shadows and she narrowed her round, multilayered eyes to study a figure that lay on its side. Her small, triangle-shaped ears perked at the sound of the figure's shallow yet persistent breaths. "He should be fine, Max," Kayla whispered. "Ben could burrow faster than any of you with one arm tied behind his back. He will become even better when he learns to compensate for his loss."

"But he doesn't belong at the front of the tunnels any longer. I do!"

Kayla's lips curled as a hiss passed between her rounded, knitting needle teeth. "This is not the time for campaigning. You did well and the others will take that into consideration. If Ben hears you saying these things while his wounds are still fresh, you'll have to do a lot more than talk to prove your worth."

Like the other burrowers, Max had a long, lean body, short arms, and stout legs. His narrow head seemed to be whittled down to a curved beak. Fidgeting nervously, his leathery eyelids flicked open and shut like vertical flaps over solid black orbs. When his brow furrowed, he narrowed his eyes down to a pair of dark creases. It was tough even for other Mongrels to tell if the expression was of shame, deference, or frustration.

Claws scraped against concrete as the wounded shape-shifter stirred on the floor. He curled his damaged body in the muck and then fell back into a pattern of shallow panting, accented by the occasional grunt.

In a low whisper, Max asked, "Do you think it's true?"

Kayla continued to watch the prone shape.

"What the Full Blood said," Max pressed. "About humans beings turned into Half Breeds, while we can become like them. Stronger. Immortal. Do you think it's true?"

"I honestly don't know," Kayla replied. "We can ask this one when he wakes up."

Max stretched his neck toward the prone figure and slunk forward until he could see Liam's partially changed form. The chunks of fur that still sprouted from his chest were graying and crusted with blood. An ugly puncture wound marred his ribs, and the right side of his face was all but obliterated. "It was my idea to take him. I want to be the one to—"

Snapping her head to stare directly into Max's eyes, Kayla hissed, "You'll be the one to take him somewhere he can't do any more damage. Dig down as far as you can go, make a chamber and plant him there. If there was truth in his words, we'll find it before the Full Blood regains his strength. If not, we drink the marrow in his bones and bury the remaining pieces in a hundred different holes across ten different states." She slowly turned to study Liam's twitching body some more. "Now take this murderer away from our city. If you are to have a place at the front of our tunnels, you'll find a spot that Ben cannot reach."

Although he seemed reluctant at first, Max opened his beak and twisted it into the closest semblance of a smile he could manage. "I know just the place."

A special sneak peek at
Book Three in the Skinners series,

TEETH OF BEASTS

Available soon!

Cole parked in the alley next to Raza Hill. He popped the trunk, dug out a smelly plastic bundle, hefted it over one shoulder, and carried his spear in his free hand. Standing in front of a metal door that had recently been reinforced, he kicked it and listened to the echo roll through the building. Since he didn't get an answer, he used one arm to steady the bundle so he could dig out his keys and unlock the door. Before he could take a full step inside, the metallic clack of a shotgun slide filled his ears.

"My day was great," Cole said cheerfully as he stepped in. "How was yours?"

Even after she saw who was coming inside, Paige didn't lower her shotgun. "What are you bringing in here?"

"A Chupacabra."

"What do you want me to do with it?"

"I heard they were good eatin'."

Cole leaned against the door to make sure it was closed all the way and walked through a large storeroom toward the kitchen. Stopping well before the inner door, he dropped the bundle and began working the kinks out of his arms and legs. "I tried calling you a few times to see if you could use any parts from this guy, but you never answered so I just brought the whole thing home."

The storeroom was illuminated by a single bare bulb hanging from the ceiling, making Paige's hair look more like an inky mess while giving her sweatshirt and jeans a dingy quality. Studying her carefully, Cole reached out for the other two light switches on the wall next to the door. When the rest of the bulbs came on, he said, "You look like hell."

Paige not only kept her shotgun raised, but seemed ready to use it. "And you're home a day early. Your date must have gone *real* well."

Nodding at what seemed like a fair jab in response to his own comment, Cole said, "OK, OK. Sorry I said you look like hell. We're even."

Paige shifted the shotgun to her left hand and let it hang at her side. Now that the bulky weapon was out of the way, Cole could see the paleness of her skin and the sunken qualities that had appeared on her face. Her hair didn't just look like a greasy mess. It was a greasy mess. Normally, she tied it back or wore a cap to keep it in check, but now it hung as if it was just as worn out as the rest of her. Cole's eyes were then drawn to her right arm, which was wrapped up in bandages and kept tight against her torso by a sling. Although she'd been able to grip the shotgun and put her finger on the trigger, her hand remained in that position like a claw that slowly curled into a fist.

"How's your arm?" he asked.

"Fucked up. Next question."

Paige stormed into the kitchen and Cole followed. "Did Daniels take a look at it?" he asked.

"Yes, Cole."

"Let me see it."

"No."

She'd led him through the kitchen and was on her way to her room. Before she could get there, Cole ran ahead of her. "Let me see it," he demanded.

Paige was easily more than a foot shorter than him, but glared at Cole as if she was about to squash him under her sneakered foot. Eventually, she let out a terse breath and shifted so her right side was a little closer to him. Cole was genuinely surprised she'd caved in so quickly.

Reaching out tentatively, he placed one hand on the sling

and slipped the other inside of it. On the surface, Paige's arm was smooth and finely toned. Her skin was on the cool side, but wasn't as clammy as the rest of her body. Considering the heat of any given night in Chicago during the summer, clamminess wasn't much of a shock. Since Paige hadn't budged, Cole pressed his hand down a bit more.

"Does that hurt?"

"No," she replied evenly.

Just beneath the skin, her arm felt more than just stiff. It was unmoving. Petrified. Cole couldn't help but be reminded of the process that had turned a sapling into the lightweight, almost unbreakable spear that was his first line of defense against anything supernatural. He gently ran his fingers along her arm, watching her face for any reaction. The source of her injury was a smeared, jagged line that looked as if it had been left by a felt-tip pen. A mass beneath the skin felt like a thick piece of wire that had been embedded in her flesh.

"Can you move it?" he asked.

"You had your look, Cole. Just give it a rest."

"You need to move it. And don't look at me like that!" His fingers probed away from the line that had been tattooed into her skin and quickly found scars that were grisly reminders of their time in Kansas City. The Full Blood's claws and teeth had marred her flesh about as much as a key marred the paint upon a car door.

"All right," she said. "That's enough."

"Does it hurt?"

"No. I can barely feel anything."

"Then move it." When she tried to pull away, Cole tightened his grip on her wrist and said, "Can you just move your hand?"

Paige set her jaw into a firm line, pulled in a deep breath and let it out in a hiss. He could see the pain in her eyes, but didn't bother asking her about it. Thanks to the healing serums she'd already mixed and administered, Paige could have recovered from wounds bad enough to make the toughest soldier scream in agony. But healing wasn't enough. Skinners had to chew through regular pain and go in for seconds.

And thirds.

And possibly tenths.

The sheen on Paige's brow grew into several trickles of sweat as she forced her arm to rise up from where it rested within its sling. Her shirt was already soaked, which told Cole she'd probably been working at this for some time before he'd arrived. When her arm was about an inch and a half above the bottom of the sling, she bared her teeth and extended her hand another inch or so. Paige's arm moved like a ponderous mechanism that had been forged from rusted steel and held together with joints that had been dipped in cold glue. While letting out her breath, Paige lifted her arm just a bit more and uncurled her middle finger.

"You flipped me off a little quicker this time," Cole said.

After allowing her arm to drop back into its sling, Paige swatted his hands away impatiently and headed for the fridge. "So you finally met up with your MEG girl, huh?"

Cole sat on one of the two stools in the large room and placed his hands on the stainless steel countertop. "Abby's great, but the whole Chupacabra thing made for a strange date."

"The package in the storeroom says that you handled it, though. Good job."

Catching the can of pop she tossed to him, Cole said, "Thanks. It really tore after me, too! Remember how long we had to shake the grass in Indiana before that little one came sniffing?"

"Chupes grow differently wherever they live. All it takes is one generation for them to sprout another ear to hear through too much farm equipment or longer toes to grab onto a certain kind of tree. Did you know I saw one that literally had an eye in the back of its head? That's what makes them so tough to track." Opening her can of fully caffeinated soda, Paige took a sip and sat down on the stool directly across the counter from Cole.

He couldn't help noticing that they were in the same spots they'd been during his very first visit to Raza Hill. It was less than a year ago, but was farther away than his desk job and his old apartment.

"I didn't need to do much of any tracking with this one," he told her.

"Chupes aren't usually so aggressive. At least, not with humans. They tend to go more for smaller game like dogs or maybe a deer."

"Or goats," Cole pointed out. "Chupacabra means goat sucker, you know."

That got a smile from Paige that wasn't tired or forced. It went a long way in making her beautiful despite the run-down state she was in. "You're right," she conceded. "Or goats."

"You did great. It turned out to be a perfect training run. Speaking of training, when are we going to spar again?"

She shifted her right arm within its sling and said, "I'm not in any condition to spar. I don't even know when this will heal."

"And what if something happens and we're not ready for it?"

"Nothing's going to happen. The Mongrels are so entrenched in KC that they'll chase away any shapeshifter within four hundred miles to either bring them in or tear them up. On top of that, the cops are on the lookout for anything suspicious on four legs. Did you hear about all the dog-fighting rings that have been broken up recently?"

"No. Does that have anything to do with werewolves?"

"Not at all. It just shows that we're not the only ones cracking down. If another Half Breed shows itself anywhere near Kansas City, it'll get blasted to pieces by a freaking SWAT team."

"So what happened to all those Half Breeds, anyway?" Cole asked. "They were running wild through the streets and now they're all gone. I know we had some help from the Mongrels, but we couldn't have gotten all of them."

"Officer Stanze had some things to say about that."

Cole waggled his eyebrows and asked, "So you did spend some time with him, huh?"

"He said there's been a lot of dead Half Breeds turning up all over the place," she replied while completely ignoring the suggestive tone in Cole's voice. "KC seems pretty clear, but after all the stuff that's been on the news or plastered all over HomeBrewTV.com, most of the country considers the KCPD to be the authorities on freaky-looking dogs."

"And a lot of them are turning up in places other than KC?"

"Yeah. Turning up dead. Even if half of the reports are just misidentified roadkill, Stanze says there are still plenty of reports that are similar to the Half Breeds he saw in KC. That doesn't cover all the stuff on the Internet or TV. Stanze's been pretty helpful, but I doubt even he knows how much footage the cops are sitting on and trying to figure out. There was a Full Blood jumping on their cruisers. Somebody had to have gotten evidence of that. Have you seen any pictures of a Full Blood online?"

"Not yet."

"Then we either got real lucky or someone is real busy gathering all the pics and video for themselves." After considering that for a few more seconds, Paige rubbed her sore arm and finished her drink. Finally, she crumpled the can in her good hand, missed a three-point shot at the trash can and stood up. "Plus everyone's all worked up about this Mud Flu thing, so that makes for a good distraction."

"I heard that's actually kind of bad," Cole said. "You throw up, get this gunk in your stomach, and there are even these weird open wounds."

"Has anyone died from it?"

"I don't think so."

"Then it's just another kind of sick," she said. "The press always has to get worked up about something. At least they've moved on from Kansas City. Right now, I just want to go to bed."

"Are we sparring tomorrow?"

"Spar on your own."

"You can tighten that sling and go a few rounds. Come on!"

"You heard me," she shouted from the door to her room.

Cole stood up and threw his pop can across the kitchen. Storming over to her, he asked, "I thought you were recovering. What happened to that?"

She marched out of the kitchen and Cole followed her.

Paige's bedroom was messier than usual and, despite the soap she'd made to mask her scent, still carried the fragrance of her skin and the shampoo she treated herself to when she didn't expect to go out hunting.

"I think you're forgetting something pretty important here," he told her.

Paige stopped and squared her shoulders in a way that told Cole he was very close to regretting having stepped foot in her room. "What did I forget?"

"Your experiment worked. Sure, it may have backfired a bit, but you threw down with a Full Blood. That thing should have torn your arm off, but it didn't. It couldn't even bite down to the bone! That stuff can work. You just need to keep working on it."

"I've got one more trial left in me, Cole. What happens after that? Should I start experimenting on you or just random people we pull off the street?"

"You can still fight."

"Apart from allowing myself to become a chew toy, what the hell am I supposed to do against anything anymore?"

"So that's it, huh?" he asked. "You're pissed because you realized you can't walk through fire after all."

Paige lunged forward and grabbed hold of Cole's shirt. Having already been grabbed, hit, punched, swept, and generally knocked around during countless sparring matches, he knew what to expect. What he didn't expect was the impact of her fist against his chest, which hit him like an aluminum baseball bat.

"I know all too well that I'm human," she snarled. "That's been made perfectly clear to me in more ways than you can imagine. How about you shove your analysis up your ass right along with your goddamn pity!"

"Hey, Paige. Look down."

Her scowl deepened as if her opponent had just tried to tell her that a shoelace was untied. When Cole nodded and looked down first, she followed suit.

The hand she'd used to grab his shirt was her right one and she'd gotten it to move faster than she'd been able to in days. Her fingers were locked around a clump of his shirt and the sling dangled from her arm as if it was being supported by her rather than the other way around.

"Oh my God," she breathed.

Cole placed his hand on hers and held it even though her fist felt more like dead weight. "You're shaken up, out of your element, and not feeling too good right now. Believe me, I know all about that sort of thing."

No longer trying to get away from him, she slowly flexed her arm as if the muscles had been packed in ice. Finally, she opened her fist and lowered it into the sling.

"You could always just twist that arm around and slap it where it needs to go," Cole offered. "You know, like that constable in *Young Frankenstein* with the wooden hand?"

Paige tried desperately to keep a straight face. When she surrendered that battle, it was one of the prettiest things Cole had seen in a long time. She let her head droop and took one step forward which was enough to push up against his chest. "Goddamn it," she groaned. "I've messed up before, but why did I have to mess up like *this*?"

Cole wrapped her up in his arms. Her hair was a tangled, unkempt mess but still felt good as he ran his fingers through it. "Look at the bright side," he told her. "If we ever need a light, we can set the tip of your finger on fire."

She chuckled and leaned against him.

"Or if there's a door we can't open, we can use you as a battering ram."

"I get it. You can stop now."

A heavy knock thumped through the room.

"That's enough, Cole. No need for sound effects."

"I didn't do that," he said. "Someone's knocking on our door."

Another couple of thumps rolled through the restaurant. Paige stepped away and looked down at his feet. "You weren't stomping on the floor?" she asked.

"No."

She whipped around so quickly that she almost knocked Cole onto his butt in her haste to get to a panel on the wall closest to her door. Once there, she poked at the panel's buttons with her left hand. "Someone's at the front door," she

said as she reached around to take a little .38 caliber revolver from where it had been tucked at the small of her
back. "Take this."

"You really don't like salesmen, do you?"

Scowling in a familiar, "do what I say and be quick about
it" sort of way, she hurried into the kitchen where her shotgun
was propped against a wall. Cole got a feel for the weight of
the pistol and then flipped the cylinder open to double-check
that the gun was loaded. He didn't have time to check what
sort of rounds they were, but they all came out of the barrel
fast enough to do some damage.

The windows at the front of the restaurant were boarded
up. The main door was latched, bolted, and held shut with
steel posts. Cole stepped up to a slit in one of the windows
that allowed him to get a look at the solitary figure standing
just outside the front entrance and a cab that tore out of the
parking lot as if the driver had just been tipped off about a
shipment of drunk tourists arriving at O'Hare.

Cole stood to one side of the door and said, "We're
closed."

The voice that came from outside was strained to the point
of cracking. "I need to talk to you."

Cole's scars itched due to a reaction with the ingredients
that were used to treat his weapon and bond it to him on a
blood level. They burned when shapeshifters were close and
itched in the presence of Nymar. Even if the man outside
was the only Nymar in the vicinity, the scars should have
alerted him sooner. Since Paige hadn't said anything about
the Nymar before, she must not have felt much of anything
either. Cole found her in the shadows on the other side of the
door with her shotgun aimed at the entrance.

"What do you want?" he asked the visitor outside.

"I have to talk to the Skinners," the man replied. "If you're
one, then you've got to open this door!"

Cole glanced at Paige again and got a single nod from her.
Whatever was on the other side of that door, she was ready
for it.

After removing the iron bar from its bracket in the floor
and pulling back the bolts, Cole twisted the knob to unlock

one of the more traditional mechanisms. When he finally pulled the door open a few inches, he held it there with the side of his foot as if that could keep out a rowdy drunk, not to mention anything much farther away from the human side of the spectrum.

The man outside was dressed in dark cargo pants and boots that could have come off the shelf of any army surplus store. His denim shirt was open to reveal a bare chest covered in black markings that looked like a massive tribal tattoo. Unlike a tattoo, however, the Nymar's markings trembled beneath the flesh as the spore attached to the vampire's heart shifted within its shell. He had a young, slender face with a minimum of whiskers protruding from his chin, and greasy hair that hung down to his shoulders. His cheeks were shallow, but not sunken, and his eyes were wide with barely-contained panic.

Cole held the .38 down low where it could be seen before being shoved into the other man's face. "What do you want?"

"Are you Cole?" the man asked. "I need to talk to Cole or Paige. I was told they're here. I need to talk to them."

"Who are you?"

Although the man appeared to be looking around while self-consciously pulling his shirt closed, it quickly became obvious that his eyes were twitching as much as the tendrils under his skin. "I need to speak to Skinners and this is where I was told to go."

"I'm Cole. How did you know to find us here?"

"Stephanie told me you were here."

"Damn it."

Even when she wasn't anywhere in sight, the redhead who ran Chicago's Nymar skin trade still found ways to make things difficult. If the shaky man was sent by Stephanie, he could be anything from an annoying junkie to a suicide bomber.

When the Nymar reached out for him, Cole brought the .38 up and tightened his finger around the trigger almost enough to drop the hammer. "Stay where you are!"

The man pressed one hand against the door and the other

against the frame. Leaning forward, his shirt fell open and his long hair dropped like a set of light brown curtains on either side of his face.

"I said stay put," Cole warned as he extended an arm to keep the man from crossing the threshold.

The man outside gripped the door and frame with enough strength to break them both. His entire body convulsed and pink foam spilled from his mouth. He sucked in a breath, which sounded like air being pulled through a tube, and his exhale was nothing but a gurgling heave.

When the black tendrils pressed out to become swollen ridges upon the Nymar's torso, Cole fired instinctively. Although the impact of the shots held the Nymar back for a second, he quickly stumbled forward again.

When the flailing black tendrils tore completely through the Nymar's skin, Cole jumped backward to give Paige a clear shot. Even as the shotgun roared, he doubted it would be enough to do the job.